SMALL TOWN
GIRL

Also by Patricia Rice

GARDEN OF DREAMS
BLUE CLOUDS
VOLCANO
IMPOSSIBLE DREAMS
NOBODY'S ANGEL
ALMOST PERFECT
McCLOUD'S WOMAN
CAROLINA GIRL
CALIFORNIA GIRL

SMALL TOWN GIRL

A NOVEL

PATRICIA RICE

DOUBLEDAY LARGE PRINT
HOME LIBRARY EDITION

IVY BOOKS • NEW YORK

This Large Print Edition, prepared especially for Doubleday Large Print Home Library, contains the complete, unabridged text of the original Publisher's Edition.

Small Town Girl is a work of fiction. Names, characters, places, and incidents are the products of the author's imagination or are used fictitiously. Any resemblance to actual events, locales, or persons, living or dead, is entirely coincidental.

An Ivy Books Mass Market Original

Published in the United States by Ballantine Books, an imprint of The Random House Publishing Group, a division of Random House, Inc., New York.

IVY BOOKS and colophon are trademarks of Random House, Inc.

ISBN-13: 978-0-7394-6542-4
ISBN-10: 0-7394-6542-2

Cover illustration: Ben Perini

Printed in the United States of America

This Large Print Book carries the
Seal of Approval of N.A.V.H.

To Robin and Linda, who gave me a chance
to write this book, sight unseen. To say
I'm thrilled with your trust would be
an understatement of cataclysmic
proportions.

And to Charlotte! Your patience in the face
of authorial nervous breakdowns
is deeply appreciated.

❧ONE❧

His badass days were over. Flynn Clinton rubbed his whisker stubble with his damaged left hand and gazed over the dance floor of lithe, gyrating bodies. He might be bad, but he sure the hell wasn't young enough to make an ass of himself anymore.

The thick smoke of the bar seared his eyes and throat. He'd forgotten that North Carolina was tobacco country. Smoke never used to bother him. Hell, he wouldn't have noticed a bomb exploding when he had music pounding through him. Like a narcotic, music had blinded him. Withdrawal hurt, but he could see clearly now. Music was as addictive as cigarettes, more lethal than narcotics.

He was here because he didn't know a better place to start searching for the writer who'd scribbled that unforgettable rhyme on the envelope he carried in his back pocket. He was just about positive the scrawl didn't belong to his two-timing partner. He had to know the depth of the crook's dishonesty, even if it set his gut on fire thinking about it.

But he didn't know how to be a detective, which was why he was fretting over losing his *sexy* instead of taking care of business.

Surreptitiously, Flint brushed his hand over his hair to reassure himself that it hadn't receded farther. He even had friggin' gray threading through the chocolate brown the ladies had once run their hands through.

At least months of working out his frustration in a gym had kept him wiry, even if he hadn't been able to punch bags while wearing the cast. Maybe he'd grow a paunch to prove he was a staid old man. Then his kids would really laugh at him.

He winced, remembering the painful scene at his parents' house earlier today. He supposed he deserved every bit of their castigation. His sons had totally ignored him while his parents had laid out the ground rules for getting the boys back into his life.

Basically, if he wanted his sons to come home, he had to change his ways.

He definitely wanted his sons back. He remembered each of their births with shocking exactitude, the awe and responsibility and love that had welled up in him the first time he'd held those tiny lives in his wicked hands. He'd made promises then that he hadn't kept too well.

Looked like fate had caught up with him, and he had no choice except to grow up and start keeping those promises. Flint turned his back on the stage and the bright lights and signaled the bartender.

Once upon a time he would have been in the center of that crowd of hot bodies performing mating rituals to the music of a rocking band. He would have had a beer bottle in hand and been howling along with the songs as he two-stepped with the best-looking lady in the bar.

He took a long pull on the cold beer the bartender set in front of him. Dirk was an old friend who'd known him back in the days, but like any good friend, Dirk had the good sense to keep his tongue in his head.

"How's Betty Sue?" Flint asked to open the conversation. It wasn't as if he were here to have fun. Dirk's bar was a place to start searching for answers. Flint fully expected the answers to be painful, but shouldering responsibility was part of his new maturity.

He had a feeling he wasn't going to like adulthood.

"Betty went back to school and sells real estate now. Hardly ever see her." Dirk dried a wineglass and set it on the rack. "What are you doing back in these parts?"

Flint wasn't much inclined to share his troubles, so he shrugged and took another swig. Tomorrow, he was moving to a dry town to become the staid owner of a coffee shop, if he could pry the hooks of his old life out of his hide. "Got tired of the city lights, I guess. I've got two boys to raise, and I want them to grow up with a simpler life."

Dirk snorted. "I think they're building snowmen in hell these days. Tell me another one. Did the rebel finally find a cause?"

Flint contemplated the possibility for all of a second before shaking his head. "It's complicated. Melinda dying sudden like that tore the kids to pieces. Even at their age, they understand alcohol and driving don't mix. The counselor says they're feeling rejected as well as grieving."

Another reason why they thought he was a major asshole. He didn't blame them.

He'd never had a problem with alcohol until the divorce. According to his mother, his drunken accident on top of Melinda's had robbed the boys of all security.

Currently, the kids liked it right where they were—with their yuppie grandparents who provided a fancy house with a big rec room, video games, and soccer. In addition, his parents provided a stable home that didn't include two screaming semi-adults who used to spend most of their time anywhere but with their offspring.

That was going to change. He couldn't bring back Melinda, may she rest in peace, if peace was what she wanted. And he wasn't about to bring back the open lifestyle they'd shared. This time, he was taking a different route. Somewhere in this wide world had to be the maternal sort of woman who would provide the nurturing his kids needed. He'd woke up and smelled the coffee, so to speak.

While Dirk made sympathetic noises about Melinda's death, Flint turned to gaze over the tables of couples laughing and talking while he looked for a way to broach the subject fretting at his mind. "You've got a good crowd."

It wasn't the kind of crowd that would include the kind of woman he was looking for as a wife, but it was just the kind of crowd that would attract RJ and his friends. He had a bone to pick with his *best old ex-friend,* as Croce phrased it, but he had no desire to be sued again, so he was moving cautiously.

"Asheville is booming," Dirk agreed. "We do pretty well on weekends with the tourists. It's a little slower the rest of the week."

Flint nodded as if he understood. He'd learn soon enough. Even a bonehead like him could figure out why business was better on weekends. Maybe he could figure out how to do something about it. He'd need more cash than weekends could bring in if he meant to give his kids the same lifestyle that his parents provided.

"I remember playing here back when. Betty Sue used to wait tables then, didn't she?"

"Yup, but she had highfalutin ideas of how a bar should be run, and I wasn't adding no ferns to keep her happy. It's been easier since she quit to have the kids."

"Amen to that, brother. Women don't understand that a man needs a place where everything stays the same so he feels comfortable. You can't fill a bar with frilly girl things." Flint sure intended to keep his shop just the way it was, a place a man could read a newspaper and drink his coffee in peace. He had fond memories of his dad taking him and his brothers there for fat muffins on Sunday mornings. That's what he wanted for his boys.

Flint stopped from reaching for his beer as a frilly girl thing caught his eye. "Although I sure don't mind admiring the women ornamenting a place."

Dirk chuckled. "You haven't changed all that much after all. I swear, I never saw a woman in here besides Betty Sue until you started playing."

"I was never much of a player," Flint protested, but he was talking guitar, and he knew Dirk was talking women. He'd learned a lot since those days. Women messed with his head. He didn't particularly like them anymore except in his bed, and it had been a scary long time since he'd seen one there. But for his boys, he was willing to look around again for someone a little more suitable than their mother, some quiet, mousy woman who would love them and leave his head alone. Melinda had taught him that wild women don't make good parents.

That didn't mean he couldn't howl a little tonight, especially if he could howl with that blond number flirting those long, fake lashes at him. He leaned his elbows back on the bar and enjoyed the view. "You got a film crew in town that's bringing in starlets?" he inquired, winking at the blonde but not making his move yet.

"Not hardly. It's the usual lot out there far as I can see, mostly locals at this hour. It'll pick up later. Who you eyeballing?"

"The blond, bronze bombshell with the big gold earrings."

"Ah, you've got good taste," Dirk responded with an inflection that passed right over Flint's head and out the door.

He was too busy studying the scenery. His engines were revved and roaring as she leaned forward to say something to one of her girlfriends—giving him a full view of her most excellent cleavage. She wore a big gold heart that dangled right between her breasts. Over this past grim year, he'd forgotten how much he enjoyed this part of the game, the teasing and being teased.

He ought to be too old for this. With his hand aching like it was decrepit, he'd been feeling too old for it just five minutes ago. Irritating how one flirtatious look from a pretty young thing and an instant hard-on could turn him into a randy chowderhead.

He turned back to the bar. "Bring me another, and hit me if I look again."

"He's checking you out, girl. Quit pretending you don't notice."

Joella Sanderson sipped her daiquiri and pretended not to notice. "I'm not doing men anymore, remember?"

"Even tall, dark, and yummy? Give me a break. If you don't want him, can I have him? I swear, I need ice just looking at him. That man is *hot.*" Dot fanned herself with her hand and continued to stare in the direction of the bar.

"You can still *do* men and not get involved," Rita said seriously. "You can't give up sex entirely."

Rita had a point there. Joella stole a surreptitious glance at the bar. Tall, dark, and dangerous had turned his back on her. That got under her skin a little. He'd got her all hot and bothered for nothing? If he thought she would come on to him, he needed to find another girl to play games with.

"He's not my kind," she said decisively. "I want an accountant this time around. A steady man with a steady job."

Both Dot and Rita laughed until they nearly fell off their chairs. Jo figured it was high time to cut off their alcohol intake if one lousy daiquiri had them this giddy.

"Not her kind," Dot spluttered, drawing letters in the air. "He's got *Jo's Kind* spelled out right across his forehead."

"Arial, all caps, and bold," Rita agreed with secretarial humor. Rita had moved down the mountain to find office work and wore her newfound sophistication in blond highlights and bright blue contacts.

Jo kind of liked the image of branding the cowboy, but she bit back a grin rather than let her friends know it. "I mean it," she asserted. "He's too good-looking to be anything but married." That was as good an excuse as any for his turning his back on her. "I'm not messing with any more lying, cheating lowlifes. I'm buying my own ticket out of town this time around. Men are off my radar."

"They're not all Randy," Dot objected.

"You've had a long dry spell since he left. It's time to jump back in the ring."

"Jump back in bed, you mean," Joella corrected. "Didn't your mama warn you about sex with men you don't know?"

But warnings and common sense didn't apply when her hormones were humming, and just looking at broad shoulders in a sexy cowboy shirt and a tight ass in designer jeans had her squirming in her seat. Her friends were right. Upright businessmen were not her style.

But she'd sworn off lying, cheating men who promised fame and fortune. As her mama always said, she had ambition far beyond her means. That didn't mean she was giving up making something of herself. She was just wise enough now not to expect a man to get her where she wanted to go.

"Anyway, I have to get up early tomorrow. The Stardust's new owner is coming, and I want to impress him with my promptness."

"He'll probably have a family to run the place, and you'll be out on your rear," Rita said with a pessimistic wave of her hand. "Go for the joy now."

Joella set her mouth in a firm line. "I can't get fired. Mama's unemployment runs out next month. I want to try that singing-server idea out on him." Her gnawing ambition again, but she had so many *ideas.* "Charlie wouldn't let me change anything, but a new owner might listen. The place is a dump. A few ferns, some pretty paint, and an espresso machine could turn the café right around."

"We live in Hicksville, Joella," Dot reminded her. The purple stripe in her long, black braid showed her opinion of their rural home's values. "No one drinks espresso, and they've all heard you sing at church. Forget it. Go after the gold." She sighed and admired the same sight Jo had been studying.

"I'm not doing sex without commitment these days," Jo said airily.

Rita hooted. "You're scared, admit it. He's out of your league."

"Is not. I may not have your brains or Dot's artistic talent, but I know men. I just don't want one," Jo added hastily when Rita opened her mouth to argue.

Dot gave a disparaging *pffttt.* "Chicken, squawk, squawk. You gonna let wimpy Randy burn you?"

Hell, no. In the immortal expression of

Granny Clampett: Thems was fightin' words. With a glare, Jo scraped her chair back and stood up.

Rita and Dot cheered. "You go, girl! Strike a blow for jilted women everywhere."

Jo tugged her spandex shirt into place and plastered on her whitened-teeth smile. So, maybe she needed to test her skills again. One itty-bitty dance couldn't hurt.

Dirk laughed and slid Flint another cold one. "Melinda soured you, did she? A man can't go forever without getting some. You'll fester up and bust."

"That might be preferable to living in hell," Flint growled, taking a swig of beer and resisting checking the table of young things again.

A powdery scent that raised images of bubble baths and candlelight enveloped him, and a soft drawl purred near his ear. "I hear tell hell is a tropical paradise compared to one of our winters."

Leaning over the bar, Flint nearly choked on his drink. He could feel her all over his skin without a touch. The stacked height of her hair brushed his cheek, and he had an insane urge to turn and bury his nose in all that glorious softness. He bet it would drift to her shoulders in a single tug.

"Way-ellll," he drawled right back, not looking at her, "you can fry on a beach in paradise as well as anywhere, I suppose."

She chuckled and reached past him for the daiquiri Dirk had prepared for her without asking. "Who's your surly friend, Dead-eye? You don't need air-conditioning if you stock the place with icebergs."

"Joella, meet Flint. Maybe the two of you could compare notes on absent partners."

"You're *so* funny, Dirk," she said without rancor.

Flint was concentrating hard on ignoring all those flirty curves and nearly jumped at the brush of slender fingers wrapping around his biceps.

"Come along, Mr. Flint. They're playing my song."

Actually, the band was playing one of *his* songs, but he wasn't the type to show off. Mostly. The *Mr.* hurt though. He didn't want to be old enough to be a mister.

Deciding it wouldn't hurt to let off a little steam with a bar babe who knew the score, Flint obligingly applied his hand to the small of her back and urged her toward the dance floor. It wasn't as if she would report him to his kids in the morning, or to the good citizens of Northfork. Knowing RJ's taste in women, she might be the one who could provide the answers he was seeking. "Happy to oblige, Miss Joella," he said, bending close to her ear so she could hear over the music.

She shot him a laughing glance that buoyed his spirits to record highs. He liked being reminded that he wasn't entirely over the hill yet.

He let her weave the way through the tables so he could admire the sway of her nicely rounded rear in her skin-tight jeans. It had been too damned long since he'd allowed himself the pleasure of looking at another woman. Life owed him this dance.

Slipping into the mass of bodies, she raised her arms above her head and started swaying her hips before he'd caught up with her. Her gold earrings and necklace sparkled against the tanned column of her throat. She wore some kind of shimmery red top that clung to high, full curves and revealed a line of trim brown waist above her low riders.

It was a damned wonder he could move at all after that.

⪻TWO⪼

Joella grinned as the stranger's gaze dropped to the glittery new shirt she'd picked up at a bargain price at Belks earlier today. She'd been kicking herself for pretending she'd ever need sequins again, but the hours the shirt cost were worth every penny if it held the admiration of the sexy cowboy.

She gyrated her hips so he could get a good look, then dropped her hands on his shoulders. The two of them were a perfect fit, just like her and Randy, but she wasn't going there tonight. Flint's closed expression and character-lined face made Randy look like a young punk in comparison.

And when Flint finally moved into the music, he didn't look so much older after all— just experienced.

Joella whistled and grinned as he

stepped into the dance, swinging his narrow hips as smoothly as a professional dancer. Once he had her attention, he shot her a wicked look that smoldered with suppressed laughter and sex. He knew he was good.

She knew she was in over her head.

He caught her hips in his big hands and drew her into him without losing the beat, timing his swaying moves to hers. It was like having sex upright and in public, except he didn't use any of those crass pumping rotations that Randy had. Flint just moved that way naturally, as if they were really bed partners.

Or maybe she was just in lust.

"I *love* this song," she shouted in his ear, hoping to remind herself as well as him that this was a public place. "It's wry and sexy and tells a story. That's my kind of music."

In reply, Flint slid his hands to her bare waist and all bad thoughts vanished into smoke. Just one dance, she promised herself. Enjoying his expertise, she fell into his rhythm as he twisted her back and forth while stepping sideways with the coordination of an athlete. She nearly melted at his firm lead. Her lower parts tingled when his gaze dropped admiringly to her flat midriff. It was times like this that made her glad she had chosen the single life.

"It's a damned stupid song," she thought he said, but the chorus was reaching a crescendo, and she couldn't be certain she heard right.

Randy had preferred screeching guitar to words, but she'd taught him better. Surely a smart-looking man like Flint . . .

Uh-uh. She wasn't going down that road again. She was just having a little fun, not training another puppy. Although Flint was more like a full-grown hound dog than a puppy, only prettier.

He spun her around on the last refrain and dipped her nearly off her feet with the final note. She came up breathing so hard she couldn't speak. Or maybe that had something to do with the smoldering depths of gray eyes studying her from behind thick, dark lashes.

"Are you a professional dancer, Miss Joella?" he inquired politely as the lights flashed and the band announced an intermission.

Now was the time to make or break it, she knew. Her mama hadn't raised a coward, but she wasn't about to tell him she was only a waitress in a two-bit coffee shop. She was doing her best to accept that she didn't have what it took to be anything more, but tonight she wanted to shine as if she'd finally bought that ticket to fame and fortune she craved.

She laughed to put off his question and headed for a table in a dark corner. Her friends would get the signal and leave them alone. "Hardly," she replied, thinking fast. "Dancing wouldn't be fun if I had to do it for a living." Amen to that, she added fervently and silently. Been there, done that, wrote the song.

He had a gentlemanly way of escorting her with a touch at her waist, blocking the drunks stumbling into their path. He even pulled out a chair for her. Maybe she should have looked at older men a lot sooner—although he lost a lot of years when he danced. Or smiled. He didn't smile enough. From the creases beside his eyes, she gathered he must have laughed a lot once.

"That's a wise observation." He gestured at the waitress and ordered two beers. "I suppose we lose the fun in anything we have to do for a living."

"It's that 'have to do' part that sucks the fun out of it." She propped her chin on her hand and tried to act casual as he took a seat and all that formfitting cotton rippled right before her eyes. She admired a man who could wear a checked shirt and still look as if he belonged in a Marlboro ad instead of on a pig farm. She checked out his ring finger—not even a pale circle where a ring might have been. "When I reach the point in a job when I figure I *have* to do it instead of wanting to do it, I quit."

"That's a rather irresponsible policy, Miss Jo," he said, but his eyes twinkled as he said it. "I take it that means you aren't married because if you had to do your husband, you'd quit?"

She laughed. "You're right! I never thought of it that way. When sex becomes a requirement, it isn't fun anymore."

"A woman who thinks like a man! I wouldn't have thought it of you."

His gaze slid over her like molten silver, saying he liked her looks, and Jo shivered at the sexiness of it. They were both practically humming with impatience while they danced around the polite chatter required of first encounters. At least Dirk knew him. He'd warn her if Flint was a stinker.

"Men don't usually want women to think like them." She wriggled slightly to hold his attention while she reached for the glass the waitress set in front of her. "They want us to coo and pretend they know everything so they can feel superior."

He grinned. "I *am* superior. You don't have to coo to prove it."

"Ooo, a masterful man, I like that," she cooed sweetly.

He chuckled and lifted his bottle in salute. "To a masterful woman."

Damn, he was good. Randy had always looked at her as if she'd lost her mind when she tried to apply irony to an argument. And she was going to quit thinking about that unfaithful pissant right now.

"So what brings you to the foothills of North Carolina, Mr. Flint? The little lady need a spa? Or the kids into white-water rafting?"

The way he quit grinning, she may as well have kicked his shins. Maybe she would if he planned to pull some sorry-ass tale of the bitch who got away. She'd hung around enough bars to have heard them all.

"My kids are with my parents. They're not speaking to me these days. Guess it serves me right. I didn't speak to my old man much when I was their age."

Wow. Her eyes widened. "That's probably the most honest thing a man's ever said to me. Did you take responsibility class along with the honesty ones?"

A deliberately slow and sexy grin riveted her gaze, and she watched in awe as the smile rose to light his eyes and crinkled the laugh lines above his sharp cheekbones. He probably wasn't movie-star handsome, but he exuded sexy masculinity as if he had a corner on the market. Oh, man, she'd really done it now. She couldn't resist sexy *and* responsible.

"I learned in the school of hard knocks, as my pappy used to say," he drawled mockingly. "How about you? Did you go to sexy school?"

"I'm from the mountains. We come by *sexy* naturally." She was used to men looking at her as if she were a ripe peach ready for tasting, but admiration from a man with his kind of raw power injected hormones straight to her bloodstream. "I like dancing," she warned him before he started getting any ideas about where they were going with this.

"So do I," he agreed. "But there's dancing, and then there's dancing. I'm good at it all."

Like the dance of flirtation he was doing right now. Damn straight he was good at it. If she'd ever been the sensible sort, she'd run. But her sister, Amy, was the sensible one, thank goodness.

Fireworks were popping between them, and she didn't notice Dot's approach until her friend touched her shoulder. Joella didn't look away from the man across the table as Dot leaned down to tell her that she and Rita were leaving.

"That's fine." Jo waved her off. "I've got my car. I'll talk at you later."

Flint seemed as focused on her as she was on him. He smiled a triumphant masculine smile when she sent her friends away.

"You're an excellent dancer, too, Miss Joella," he mocked.

"It's not often I find a good partner," she retaliated.

They both knew they weren't talking about the two-step.

She didn't do casual sex, but she could

see making an exception for this man. How often did a Hugh Jackman look-alike walk into a girl's life? Besides, since she was giving up on men and relationships, she might have to rethink her position on casual sex.

The band began tuning their instruments, and she didn't have to beg Flint to stand up with her. He pushed back his chair and offered his hand before she could ask.

"You got any more favorite songs you want to hear?" he inquired, steering her toward the dance floor.

"None of that crying-in-your-beer stuff," she warned. "I'm not crying anymore."

He touched her cheek and looked serious for a second. "Any man who would leave a woman like you hasn't got the sense to recognize pure gold when he sees it."

She'd heard all the lines before. It would be nice to believe he meant it, but he didn't know her any better than she did him. They were faking it, but they both knew it, so that worked. "Or the sense to keep his pants on when he sees anything in skirts," she retorted, to keep her achy-breaky heart from leaping in expectation.

His smile was better than a margarita.

"Darlin', no man has that kind of sense. C'mon, let's shake away the blues."

Tomorrow, she could go back to scrubbing floors. Tonight, she'd enjoy her handsome prince.

Life was good.

He'd paid his penance, resolved to change his ways, and Miss Joella was his reward.

"Want to step outside for some fresh air, Miss Jo?" Flint murmured through the final bars of a slow song. She moved so close to him that it was nearly like dancing with himself—if his hand weren't cupping one sweet handful of ass and her breasts weren't imprinted on his chest for life. She had to feel what she was doing to him.

She tilted her head back to study him, and a loosened blond curl fell along her cheek. Maybe those long lashes were all hers, but she'd darkened them so her eyes looked as big as twin full moons. Or emeralds.

"If you'll just steer me toward that booth over there, we can slip behind the curtains to the side door," she agreed.

With an alacrity that said he hadn't completely lost his touch, he had her at the curtains before the last note rang out.

He was familiar with the back exit of this place and a lot of other bars just like this one. Bands used the exits to slip out for a quick smoke, a toke, or a make-out session. There were some things he'd miss about that life—maybe a *lot* of things—but the sleaziness wasn't one of them.

But it didn't feel sleazy when Joella took his hand and stepped outside under a bowlful of stars in the clear mountain air. He didn't know which way was up. She sparkled like the night sky. Lights glittered along her long gold earrings and sequins.

"I'd forgotten how the stars look up here." Drawing her into him, Flint gazed above Asheville's limited excuse for a skyline. "If you wore midnight blue, you'd blend right in with the night."

She laughed softly and melted into his arms as if she belonged there. "I'd have to wear silver with blue, and I was in a gold mood tonight."

That didn't make a lick of sense to him, but he wasn't out there to talk. Any thought of his reason for being in the bar had fled several songs ago.

Flint leaned over and nuzzled Joella's ear. When she lifted her head to him, he accepted the invitation and claimed her mouth.

Had it been so long since he'd had sex that he couldn't remember any woman's kiss being as delicious as hers? Her lips softened invitingly, and his tongue accepted the invitation. He tasted the strawberry sweetness of her daiquiri and drank deeply.

Her long fingers stroked his nape, and he nearly shook his leg like a horny dog. Her kiss was liquid fire that swept down inside his soul and incinerated all the bad times and lit the empty hollows with promises. Her lips didn't cause just a physical ache, but the kind of longing the poets wrote about, of moments missed and ships passing in the night.

For his own mental health, he needed to stick with the physical. He slid his hand down her slender back, finding that thin line of nakedness at her waist and glorying in the warmth of sun-browned flesh.

She practically purred into his mouth. Hope flourishing, Flint slipped his fingers beneath her sequined shirt and along the supple muscles of her back. She returned the favor, unbuttoning his shirt and branding his skin with the heat of her palms.

"I've got my truck right over there," he managed to say against her kiss-softened mouth. "Want to take this somewhere a little more private?"

She hesitated, and time froze as he waited. He wanted her so bad he would have cracked molars chewing nails if she asked it of him. He needed this one last night of irresponsible freedom before conforming to small-town ways. He needed *her,* an angel sent straight from heaven to tell him he was on the right path.

"You're not from these parts, are you?" she whispered, not opening any distance between their sandwiched bodies, much to his intense relief. "I've got you pegged as a traveling man."

"You've got me pegged well," he admitted. He would be hobbling like a pegged horse if he didn't get her into that truck and back to the motel.

"You don't look like a salesman," she said with soft inquiry, running a finger beneath his shirt and shooting electric shocks to his groin.

Ah, he'd forgotten that part of the game.

Women liked sexy jobs and bad boys, not respectable businessmen. Without lying, he whispered in her ear, "I play a little guitar." Very little, now that his fingers were out of commission.

He slid his hand up to her breast, expecting the instant gratification he'd always received after recognition of his name or talent or career. Lots of people associated the music business with fame and fortune. He wasn't one to discourage their foolish fancies.

Instead of the excited reaction he'd expected, the beautiful Miss Joella shoved away and glared at him with wintry eyes. "A musician?" she asked scathingly, as if it were a filthy word. "And a lousy guitar player at that. Hell, I'll never learn."

Without further explanation, she stalked off to a rusty pumpkin-orange Ford Fiesta, leaving him rock hard and in shocked misery.

❊ THREE ❊

The Stardust Café was even seedier than Flint remembered, the perfect joint for a man suffering blue balls and a hangover. With luck, a few cups of hot java would ease his headache. Unrequited lust was a little more difficult. But he'd promised Charlie that he would open on the first of June, and he wasn't copping out because he'd gotten wasted the night before.

He shoved the key into his back pocket and opened a front door flaking with ancient red paint.

Faded gray café curtains on the big front window hid the June dawn. Flint flipped a switch by the door, electrifying the bulbs hanging in tin cans over the tables, creating more shadow than illumination. Good. It felt like a dark bar where he could snarl all he liked, not that there was anyone here at this ungodly hour to notice.

The old wooden floors and dark paneling stank of must and mold and old cigarette smoke. Kicking aside a chrome dinette chair with a cracked pink vinyl seat, he stalked between the gray Formica tables, trying to recall what had inspired the pleasure of his childhood memories.

Instead, last night's debacle seared his brain cells, stealing all the satisfaction he'd anticipated of owning this piece of his past.

The worst part was that he didn't even know what he'd done wrong. Since when had *guitar player* become bad words?

He refused to dwell on it. The lovely Miss Joella had ruined his last night of freedom. He had a pounding hangover from taking a six-pack to his room and drinking himself to sleep.

He sure the hell wouldn't let a woman ruin his first day back in Northfork.

He had fond memories of this tiny mountain town where his daddy had once run the textile mill. He and his brothers had run wild through field and stream. It was the ideal place to bring up boys. His counselor had agreed he might figure out where he'd taken the wrong turn if he returned to his roots, whatever in hell that meant.

He switched on the light over the grill. Charlie had sure been one hell of a lousy housekeeper. There was grease on here that was probably personally acquainted with the original Cherokees who'd discovered these mountains. And Noah had probably dropped off the rest of the equipment on his watery sojourn. Judging from the water stains on the paneling, it looked as if the river, if not Noah, had visited a time or two.

He grimaced at the aging Bunn burners that constituted his coffeemakers. He knew he'd purchased the place cheap. It wasn't as if he could afford a lot. At the time, he'd hoped Charlie had a good pension fund because what Flint had paid for the shop wouldn't finance a trip to Florida for a month much less Charlie's retirement. Now he was thinking Charlie had milked the place for all it was worth and left him the hollow shell.

He had a head for business that could pull this together, if he'd just apply it instead of wasting it on wine, women, and song. He wouldn't be in these straits if he had paid attention to his accounting statements instead of listening to the siren call of his muse. Guess he'd have to learn on his own, the hard way, because he wasn't trusting anyone else these days.

So, he was still paying penance. And instead of being an angel of deliverance, the woman last night had been an imp sent straight from hell to remind him of his sins. Wasn't there some saint who'd suffered all the torments of the damned before being blessed? He sure the hell wasn't any saint, which made any blessings unlikely.

Wondering if he had to start attending church now that he was a reformed, respectable citizen, Flint dug around in the cabinets until he found a bottle of ammonia and some rags. One thing about growing up middle-class, he had learned how to clean. He hadn't done it in twenty years, maybe, but some things were ingrained.

He had the antiquated coffeemaker scrubbed to a stainless steel shine when the front door creaked on its rusty hinges. "Not open yet," he called over his shoulder, trying to read the frosted print on the coffee bean package he'd found in the freezer. For the life of him, he couldn't figure out how to measure a pot of coffee. He wanted real caffeine smelling up the place, not that sissy stuff they served in hotel rooms.

"I wouldn't recommend opening until you de-crudify the grill," a cheerful voice sang out. "I came in early to help out."

Even without the raucous noise of a bar band as backdrop, Flint recognized the angel's heavenly soprano. Surely even God wouldn't be cruel enough to punish him in such a humiliating fashion?

Turning slowly, searching the gray shadows of the sad café, he met the wide-eyed shock of last night's blond goddess. Lowering his gaze, he could just make out her shapely silhouette wearing a midnight blue bib apron with *Stardust Café* embroidered across it in flowery pink.

"Well, hell, if it isn't little Miss Starshine come to add twinkle to my day. Do you do dishes like you do men?"

Joella debated the relative merits of sinking through Charlie's filthy wood floor, ripping off her apron, and fleeing, or brazening it out in the face of Flint's temper and her own shock. Since she possessed no magic traits for liquefying, and she needed a job to eat, brazening it out was her only option.

"A guitar player?" she asked, ignoring his insolence and forcing a chuckle as she swayed her hips and crossed the floor. Damn, but he was even hotter looking than she remembered, although slightly green around the gills once she got close enough to see. "Do you also play the coffeepot?"

She rounded the corner and removed the bag of coffee beans from his hand. Without asking permission, she measured a full load into the grinder, ignoring the intimidating height and breadth of pure furious male hovering over her shoulder.

"Just the guitar," he growled with a note of threat in his throat. "I'm Flynn Clinton, lately of the Barn Boys, fresh out of Nashville."

"No wonder you can't make coffee." She tried to sound perky, but he'd pretty much ruined her day. She was going to have to quit this job now. She couldn't work here and suffer the daily electric zing of attraction to another lying, cowardly guitar picker who would be gone as soon as he found the next gig.

"Since when do guitar pickers play cafés?" was all she asked.

"I can make coffee," *Mr. Clinton* growled, completely unlike the sweet-talking hunk of last night. "And it's a coffee shop, not a café. We won't do music."

"Well, so much for my singing-waitress routine," she answered saucily, tapping his blue work shirt with a cup to get him out of her personal space.

He backed off, but Jo noticed he watched her intently as she set the grinder.

"Got any other ideas how you'll rebuild business? Maybe a little soft-shoe, hmm?" She danced a step or two to her own music.

"Why, you got something to sell?" he taunted.

She accidentally on purpose stomped his boot toe while reaching for the chicory. "Unless you're planning on charging ten bucks a cup, you'd better sell something besides coffee, and your good looks don't count."

She ought to block what she was doing so he had to rely on her if he wanted to keep his customers, but she'd never been the spiteful sort. Besides, she didn't want to be responsible for the repercussions if people didn't get their caffeine fix.

"Good looks?" He snorted. "Is that the best you can do to keep from getting fired?"

Since she figured he was getting a good look at her ass, Jo ignored the frisson of fear at the possibility of losing her job. She reached for the filters in the cabinet and poured in the ground beans as she'd done every morning for the last year.

With the heady aroma of brewed coffee sweetening the stale air, she took a deep breath and turned to face her surly boss, hands on hips. "I'm Joella Sanderson, café manager, hostess, short-order cook, and waitress. I have a résumé as long as your arm. You can keep me on, or I can go down the street and become your competition."

She had brazen down real well. Her honesty lacked a little polish.

Flint scowled at her from his greater height. His muscled physique in a formfitting shirt and jeans was silhouetted against the gray dawn of the picture window. He ought to have red neon across his forehead flashing *DANGER!* instead of that intriguing lock of too long hair that any woman in her right faculties would love to push out of his eyes.

She didn't shy away while he studied her, from the flyaway wisps of yellow grazing her forehead, to the long ponytail that kept her mass of hair out of the food, down to the tips of her practical Nikes. She had been in a hurry to arrive early and hadn't bothered with any more makeup than mascara and lipstick this morning. The air-conditioning in the Stardust left something to be desired so she wore her sensible *Frog Prince* T-shirt and red shorts under the apron.

He didn't offer a single smile or look of approval. Admittedly, she didn't look as good as she had last night, but she didn't think she was Godzilla either.

"These are the mountains," he said, seemingly irrelevantly. "I thought women only got a tan like yours at the beach."

Well, if that's the way he wanted it, she could give as good as she got. "Never heard of tanning beds?" she mocked, crossing her brown arms over the apron.

"Never heard of skin cancer?" With a grim look on his lined face, he walked off, grabbing a bottle of ammonia from the counter as he headed for the back.

Ammonia? Jo lifted her eyebrows and looked around. He'd cleaned the machine!

Flynn Clinton, lately of the Barn Boys— and despite her blasé reaction she knew damned well who the hottest country band in a decade was—sweet-talking, sexy dancer and kisser par none, had cleaned the ancient, filthy Bunn burners that should have been tossed in the trash during the last world war.

He was human after all. Maybe she could tolerate the intolerable hunk until she found the road out of here.

Hearing him slam the door of Charlie's office, Joella examined the greasy assortment of antique equipment and pondered where to start. Heaving it all in the trash was her preference, but the place wasn't hers. The griddle then. After that, the refrigerator. The oven had died many moons ago and deserved a decent burial.

She had been just a little less than honest earlier. Charlie had never let her back here except to fix the coffee. He liked her out in front of the counter, entertaining the customers. She'd had no problem with that since talking to people was her preference, and Charlie wouldn't have let her clean up anyway. He thought grease added flavor.

But Flynn Clinton obviously thought otherwise. Hopes soaring despite their first minor setback, she grinned and set to work. Surely *working* for a musician wouldn't be as hazardous as dating one. And his occupation could be good news for the band.

Her spirits took a decided rise at that thought.

Despite her lifelong desire for fame and fortune, Jo enjoyed the café. It was like an empty canvas waiting for an artist's stroke. It had so much *potential.*

And with the accomplishment of that potential, she could hope for more tips and maybe more tourists feeling expansive and buying things, which would ultimately lead to more tips because people around here might have a little extra spending money then. She knew how economics worked without the professor at the college telling her. She'd bought her Fiesta with tips. Well, tips and a hefty loan.

The bank wouldn't give her a loan to save her mother.

It was almost seven before Dave from the hardware store noticed the OPEN sign and wandered in. "Hey, Joella! Back in business I see."

She slid a cup of leaded across the counter at him and a Krispy Kreme from the boxes she'd had her sister, Amy, pick up at the grocery when she'd found the cabinets bare. Mr. Guitar Player had come out of his office long enough to ask where they bought their muffins and to put some cash in the register. She'd showed him the doughnut receipt, and he'd reimbursed her without arguing, so he was still on her good books, although just barely.

"Yup." She placed a cheap metal spoon on a paper napkin and slid it down the counter to him. "Mr. Clinton is in the office if you want to introduce yourself."

That was evil, but it had to be done. Dave sat on the Chamber of Commerce board and was president of the Rotary. Her new boss would have to learn to deal with the community, not lurk in his office, if he wanted to build a business. And what was good for his business was good for hers.

"I'll do that, thanks, Jo." Dave slipped a five on the counter and moseyed over to the side door into the storage room where Charlie kept his desk and files.

Business picked up after that, and she didn't notice when Flint finally emerged from his cave.

"The pig is almost done," Sally was saying excitedly as Jo poured coffee into a Styrofoam take-out cup for her. "Do you think Mr. Clinton will take her? The kids had so much fun putting red ribbons on her tail!"

Jo knew the instant Flint came up behind her. The hair on the back of her neck stood up and her insides did an excited shimmy. Coffee sloshed over the side of the cup before she caught herself. Sally's look of shock said it all.

"You put ribbons on a pig's tail?" he growled in disbelief. "Doesn't the Humane Society have something to say about that?"

Well, he wouldn't attract a lot of customers with that attitude. Jo flashed him a ruby smile over her shoulder and decided to yank his chains about Sally's art project to see if he had a sense of humor at all. "Why, sho 'nuff, Mr. Big Stuff. We're proud of our pigs around here. Sally, meet Mr. Flynn Clinton, our new proprietor. Flint, Sally Benton, the art teacher at the elementary."

To her total astonishment, the lummox turned on his charm and practically kissed Sally's hand, giving her that sexy half-smile guaranteed to have a girl swooning. Sally blushed bright red and giggled like a teenager. Sally was height-challenged—from childhood, she'd always been a half foot shorter than the weight chart suggested. Men didn't often melt her with their best smiles.

"My sons should love your class if it involves putting ribbons on pigs," Flint declared in that same sweet-talking voice he'd used with Jo last night.

"You have children?" Sally asked brightly, although her face fell a good country mile in disappointment.

"They're with their grandparents," Jo said helpfully. Sally was a wonderful person. She deserved better than a two-timing, high-living guitar picker. But Sally was an intelligent adult who could make her own bad decisions. Who was Jo to stand in the way?

"I'm planning on bringing the boys up here once I get settled in."

Jo noticed a stubborn set to his mouth when he said that. She had customers waiting for her and didn't have time to wrestle it out. "So you'll take Sally's pig?"

"I don't think so," he said with all the appearance of regret and none of the sincerity. "It's good meeting you, Miss Benton. Maybe we can talk later." He walked off to speak with one of the lawyers who liked his cup kept filled.

Sally looked crestfallen. "I know she isn't the prettiest of the pigs, but you'd think someone would take her."

Jo patted her shoulder. "He will. He just doesn't know it yet."

"Hey, Jo, what's your sister saying about the mill closing?"

Silence descended as everyone waited to hear her answer to George Bob's accusatory question.

One good thing about being off work these past weeks had been avoiding spiked questions like that. Negative rumors got the town nowhere. "Same as she's telling you, I reckon," she called, filling all the cups on the counter. "Been to church lately to ask her?"

With that explosive topic closed, she laughed and joked her way through the morning rush hour. Her new boss seemed to favor his left hand and was a bit slow on the uptake, but Charlie had been slower, so Jo wasn't complaining.

She had a hard time putting the sexy swinger from last night into the shoes of crummy-café owner today, but by the time Flint had wiped a few spills and dished a few doughnuts, she was mentally adjusting. Physically, she was a hive of buzzing hormones every time she had to brush by all that virility in the tight space behind the counter. He even *smelled* better than a Krispy Kreme. She detected a distinct note of vanilla in his aftershave that made her want to rub her nose against his chest.

Business slacked off after the doughnuts ran out. People hardly ever came to the Stardust for Charlie's cooking. The lawyers were still in the corner, reading their newspapers and mooching pots of coffee for the price of a cup, but they weren't occupying valuable real estate at this hour.

"I'll call the bakery and order the deliveries resumed tomorrow," Flint said, coming up behind her.

His customary growl sounded almost apologetic, so Jo forgave him. "Didya think the food was delivered by magic fairies overnight?" she teased.

"It's not? And here I thought I'd discovered the magic genie who's going to make my life all better if she wants to keep her job." He gave her nonsexy Stardust apron bib a wicked once-over, but she heard the sarcasm just fine.

"Oh, right, I forgot genie duty." She untied the apron and flung it aside, leaning her elbows back on the counter so he could get a good look. It seemed they needed to clear the air after last night's little fiasco. "Any other magic acts you want me to perform?"

He inspected the goods she blatantly revealed. "Do you make magic by jiggling those instead of your nose?" He held up his palm to halt her scathing reply. "Don't answer that. I was over the line. Pax."

She ought to slap him silly, but she'd stuck her breasts in his face first to get the obvious out of the way. "Guess that makes us even, then." She tapped his hard chest in retaliation, and electricity crackled and zapped. She hid her grin as he tensed all over. At least she wasn't the only one suffering. "Down, boy."

He growled and spun around to clean the coffeepot. "Charlie told me this was an open operation," he said, as if she hadn't just scorched them both with that tap, "and all I had to do was show up and pay the bills. How long have you been closed?"

"Two weeks." Well, so much for making nice. "Charlie had a heart attack. He meant to keep things up until you arrived, but he couldn't." She grabbed a dishcloth and started wiping down the faded Formica.

"And I'm guessing I have to do a little more than pay the bills?" he asked wryly, dodging the dishwasher door when it dropped to the floor, just missing his boot toe.

"You could hire another waitress." She shrugged as he knelt to examine the heavy panel. "But you only need help in the rush hours and weekends. Cheaper to do it yourself." Be still her heart, what was she saying? Work here every day with *the hunk*?

"Guess I can get the hang of it. I didn't catch that about the mill." He tinkered with the door hinges. "My daddy used to work out there. Is it closing?"

Sighing, Jo poured a cup of coffee and took her morning break to watch the guitar player fix a dishwasher door that had been broken for a decade. Flint added a certain savoir faire that Charlie never possessed, she acknowledged, and she wasn't just talking about the muscular back beneath that tailored Ralph Lauren work shirt. Even after he gave up on the door and started emptying the load of clean dishes, Flint added his own touch by drying off the wet bottoms of the mugs before stacking them. And when he bent to empty the bottom rack, his jeans fit a sight better than Charlie's.

"I prefer to play Pollyanna and believe the mill will survive."

Flint polished a glass and actually glanced her way with approval, as if maybe she had a few brains instead of cooties. She let the look slide rather than resume their flirtation. She was writing off men, and especially male bosses. Naked cowboys, on the other hand . . . Wow! So not going there.

"But people around here think it will close," he continued for her, his gaze momentarily igniting from the impact of hers before he returned to putting dishes away.

Jo fanned herself with a towel. Maybe she'd be better off fired. "It's that kind of negative thinking that will close down the whole town," she groused. "A lot of people got laid off when the economy went south of the border. Tobacco doesn't make money anymore. Tourism dropped. A few stores closed. And everyone sees disaster where it isn't. If we'd just work harder to turn things around, we'd be fine."

"Uh-huh." He looked at her as if she'd just sprouted wings. "You running for office?"

"Put Sally's pig in the doorway," she said angrily. She hated being dismissed as if she were a dumb blonde. Maybe she wasn't highly educated, but she wasn't *dumb.* "Take down those moldering curtains. Buy an espresso machine to bring in tourists. Things will turn around if you give them a reason to do so."

"Will that stop the mill from closing?" he asked. "And if it doesn't, how will I pay for that espresso machine if my customers are broke?"

The question was obviously rhetorical. He put the last mug on the shelf and returned to his office.

Not for the first time, Joella wondered if she could afford an apartment down in Asheville. Maybe Rita would share. She heard Hooters paid well. If she wasn't going to get any respect, she ought to at least get paid.

≪FOUR≫

Trying to drive the encounter with Joella and his own personal demons out of his mind, Flint called his sons the instant he returned to the house he'd rented.

The call thus far hadn't been very successful.

"Mom, I have a great place out in the woods," Flint tried to say convincingly to the protective gargoyle keeping him from his kids. "The boys will love it."

He didn't tell his mother that the log house he described with such enthusiasm had been built in the fifties and not updated since—no dishwasher, one and a half baths, and pink tile. At least he had a microwave. The boys could survive without a swimming pool for a weekend.

He worked the spongy ball with his left hand, feeling the pain from the mending bones and unused tendons shooting straight up his arm.

"If you're working, what will they do with themselves all day?" his mother asked with arctic frost. "Have you given that any thought?"

"They can work with me. It's not as if I'm hauling coal. It will be good for them to get out from in front of the idiot box." He sank deeper into the leather recliner he'd saved from the auction that had divided all his worldly goods between Melinda and the IRS. "I'll take off work for the weekend if that's your concern."

Working the ball in his left hand, he crossed the fingers of his right. He'd have to hire another waitress to perform that magic act. *Magic.* Right. Joella the Jiggling Genie had scarfed up his brain. He couldn't help grinning, recalling her brash act. If he could afford to fire her, he would, just for the sake of his own mental health. But he needed experienced help, and she sure had a way of brightening the day.

He'd hire the devil if it would get his boys back here with him. Maybe he hadn't been the greatest father in the world, but now that he was home and could be there for them, he needed to start learning what a father was supposed to do.

"Maybe when you're better settled in, as we discussed," his mother said. "Your father and I can bring them up, and you can show us around."

Flint ground his teeth. She'd been there when the kids needed her, latching onto his sons like a mother hen with her chicks. He didn't want to fight her now. "Sure, Mom, that would be good. The town hasn't changed though. I survived it."

She didn't like being reminded of her country origins, he remembered too late.

"Just barely." The frost in her voice grew icicles. "If you'd had a better education, you might have made something of yourself. You could have been a banker like your brother."

"Or sell insurance like Jim, right. Four gold records don't mean a thing. Tell the kids I called. I'll try again tomorrow night." Hurt in more ways than he cared to count, Flint flung the ball at the shelf where the stereo should have been.

"They have a game tomorrow night," she reminded him. "If you can stagger out of bed before nine on Saturday morning, you might catch them then."

Okay, he deserved that. He clicked off the phone, dropped his head back against the leather cushion, and stared at the arched rafters of his ceiling. He'd never been around when the boys needed him. Why shouldn't they return the favor? His mother aiding and abetting them didn't help though.

If he hadn't been such a horny bastard, he would probably never have married at all. His uptight mother was enough to permanently put a man off women. But he'd been just twenty-three when he'd knocked up Melinda, and even though he'd known marriage would be a disaster, he'd done the honorable thing and ruined both their lives for the sake of the baby. Schools needed to teach common sense instead of math.

The phone rang, and he contemplated flinging it across the cavernous room, but he was used to company, and loneliness didn't suit him. He punched the button. "Last Chance Ranch, Flynn the Barbarian speaking." He waited for the pleasure of shocked silence.

"Not Flynn the Kung Fu Fighter or Clint the Crooner?" a sultry soprano sang in his ear without hesitation.

Sopranos weren't supposed to be sultry. Blondes weren't supposed to be quick on the uptake either. "I never crooned," he growled. "I'm just a picker." And a song-writer, but no one cared about that. Besides, he wasn't either anymore. "What did you want, Miss Joella?"

He wished she had a name like Miss Prune or a voice like rusty hinges so he could keep the employer/employee thing at an icy distance. Just one more example of his rotten luck that he'd inherited a blond sex goddess for a waitress instead of a shriveled-up battle-ax.

"Your night shift didn't show up, and the boys want to know if it's still okay to play in your back room."

He thought the café closed at three. He had every intention of being home for his sons when they got out of school. "Want to run that by me again?" he asked, just in case something had been lost between his hearing and his imagining of Jo nibbling on his ear.

"Charlie always let Slim and the boys play the back room if Mary Jean kept the café open. But Mary Jean had a baby last week. I've got the lot of them at my place pacing the floor. I can open up the café tonight, but I can't do it every night. Amy is taking classes, and I keep the kids on Tuesdays and Thursdays since her lout of a husband is always at the office and too busy to look after them."

Information overload. Bells rang, whistles wailed, and his brain refused to get beyond *boys* and *play.* "What boys?" he asked, trying to sort through the info dump.

A sigh of impatience emanated from the receiver, and his overstimulated brain translated it to the heave of Joella's amazing breasts.

"Didn't Charlie tell you anything? Local groups use that stage in the back room. They charge admission on weekends and use it for practice during the week. The acoustics are better than a garage, and it's warmer in winter."

"Joella, would you mind answering just the question I ask and not half a dozen I don't care about?" He'd been thinking about turning that back room into a real office. He should have asked about the drums he'd seen in there. "Charlie was supposed to call and fill me in before he left for

Florida. What hospital is he in? Maybe I can go visit him."

"We don't have a hospital," she answered. "He's recuperating with his daughter in Charlotte. I'll give you his number. Got paper?"

Once he'd scribbled the number, his brain had processed her problem and developed a few of his own.

"Do I have liability insurance to cover bands and audiences?" He hadn't been oblivious to the business around him, just the people.

That shut her up for all of five seconds, a new record, he calculated.

"I'll talk to George Bob. He carries Charlie's insurance. But there's no audience tonight. I've got a key. You don't need to come in."

He didn't want to go in. He didn't want to get near music ever again. It was a temptation he could do without, kind of like a drunk and alcohol. "All right," he agreed. "Just tonight. I gotta find out how much this is gonna cost."

"It'll cost you more if you kick out some of your best customers. See ya in the mornin'."

She hung up, and the big cabin echoed

with emptiness again. Flint gazed at his bare shelves. His state-of-the-art stereo equipment hadn't brought half what it was worth at auction, but he'd seen a certain justice in Melinda getting half of his soul as well as most of his money.

At the time, he'd been too livid to realize how fleeting life was.

Slim and the boys watched Joella anxiously as she hung up the phone. She flashed them a bright smile and a thumbs-up, even though she'd heard the negativity in her boss's voice. It looked mighty like Flynn Clinton would be even more mule-headed than Charlie.

The guys cheered and began packing up their gear to carry it down the fire escape to the café's back room.

She unlocked the back door, turned on the overheads, and held the sagging door while Turbo entered with his keyboard, and Slim and Eddie carried in their guitar cases and amps. Bo's drums were already there. She didn't want to think where in town he could leave them and the bass amps if they had to move out.

"Hey, Jo, you got any new material for

us?" Slim asked. "Now Randy's using the old stuff, we need something of our own."

"Why, so you can all make it big and leave me behind, too?" she half-joked. It still hurt real bad when she thought about Randy's desertion just as he was hitting the big time. He'd promised to take her with him on his path to fame and fortune.

She was a little slow to make the same mistake twice, but she'd finally learned her lesson.

"You know us better than that, Jo-Jo," Slim said. "We think you're the best thing to come along since Jack met Daniel."

She'd feel a little better about that if Slim were looking at her and not his guitar while he said it. People around here pretty much took her for granted. She was about the only person who thought she had what it took for a bigger and better life than being a small-town waitress. Maybe she was wrong, and it was time to admit it, but Stubborn was her middle name. Or Stupid, if she believed the men in her life.

"I've got a few rhymes you can play with, if you want." Jo pulled a crumpled paper out of her pocket. "But the words aren't all there yet. They need some work." The lines needed a *lot* of work. Kind of hard to do upbeat with a broken heart. Or even a numb one.

Eddie took the paper from her and scanned her nearly illegible handwriting. "Kinky. You've got a way with words, girl." He passed the paper on to Slim and strummed a few chords. "Same key?"

"Y'all know I can't compose worth diddly. You work it out. I gotta make a few calls." She left them with her foolish verses and ran back upstairs. She'd taught herself basic piano and guitar, but mostly she hung around the band because they were willing to play her ditties. She'd given up hope of singing her way out of here after the Atlanta humiliation. Then Randy had come along and played on her hunger for respect by claiming her songs and his singing could make them rich.

Well, he'd taken himself to fame and fortune, although that probably had more to do with his good looks, charm, and sexy tenor than it did with her rhymes. If she scratched both singing and songwriting, she didn't have too many escape hatches left.

Nights like this, she was so lonesome, she could cry, just like the song said.

≪FIVE≫

"George Bob, so help me, if you don't give Flint a good deal on that insurance, I'll tell your mama about the time you took me behind the shed and talked me out of my panties." Jo slid a doughnut and a coffee mug to her childhood nemesis.

George was three years older than her twenty-eight, and he looked every year of it. Tall and thin, he'd never been bad looking, but his nondescript brown hair had grown thinner, and now that she looked close, so had his mouth. He looked like a priggish stickler who sold insurance. When had they become their parents?

He shot her an annoyed look. "You were five and I was eight. This is business, Joella. A man has to make a living. Keep your nose out of it."

"When pigs fly, Georgie-boy," she sang,

unfazed by his refusal. He'd remember her threat when the time came.

"Which reminds me, that blasted flying pig you talked me into is blocking the sign on my door. Why don't you sweet-talk your new employer into taking it?"

"Flying pig?"

Jo rolled her eyes as Flint used his amazing timing to walk up at the wrong moment. Familiarity hadn't bred enough contempt yet, she reflected, nor driven out the memory of his mind-melting kisses. She'd woken up in the middle of the night sweating over a tasty dream of his buff chest all naked and propped above her.

She tried not to admire the way his short-sleeved shirt clung to his muscular biceps and his too long hair brushed the collar, but every damned woman in here had taken notice. Even the blue-haired ladies had flirted when Flint had walked by. And he smiled at all of them—just as he had at Jo that first night. And hadn't done since.

"The flying pig is the very best one," she told George, ignoring her boss. "It's bound to win the prize. Move the pedestal."

Jo sauntered on to the next customer. Both men watched in appreciation. She was wearing a narrow, black miniskirt and hot pink golf shirt under her apron today, color-coordinating with the café's fifties colors. The apron hid nothing from the rear.

"She's a bossy brat," George Bob opined. "I don't know how you put up with her."

Flint gazed around at the customers occupying his tables. The ones remaining after rush hour were all men. "It helps to pay her," he said noncommittally, sliding into the booth seat across from George. "I tried calling Charlie last night, but his wife wouldn't let him come to the phone. Says he needs his rest, and worrying about this place won't help him. So I'm out on this limb alone." He produced a sheet of paper from his pocket. "I picked up a few estimates before I called you."

George held out his hand. "Mind if I see them?"

Flint stuffed the folded paper back in his shirt pocket. "Give me your best offer, and we'll work from there. I'm on a tight budget and have to work out the cost differentials."

"Charlie never had enough coverage," George asserted.

"I have no assets," Flint countered. "Going broke paying too much insurance is a certainty. Getting sued isn't."

Well, actually, given past experience, getting sued almost was a certainty, but he wasn't inclined to mention that. He'd decided to make one last call this morning before he started digging his own grave.

As George talked liabilities and assets, Flint watched his waitress greet a shorter, sensible version of herself entering the shop. The brunette in a blue suit held a kid in each manicured hand, and Joella crouched down in that breath-stealing skirt to hug them.

He almost missed his insurance agent's quote when Jo stood with a sexy swirl, the little boy's hand gripped in hers. Returning his wandering attention to business, Flint put on his good-ol'-boy grin and took the paper George pushed at him. "I'll crunch the numbers and let you know."

"You sure you don't want a flying pig to go with that?" George asked in disgruntlement, sliding out of the booth. "I might even give you a discount to take it."

"A purple cow, if you have one," Flint replied agreeably, clueless about the joke but willing to pass it on.

"Damn good thing Jo didn't think of cows." Grumbling, George walked off, greeting the newcomer with a nod before departing.

"Hey, Flint, come meet my sister." Jo poured coffee for her customers at the counter and nodded toward the newcomer.

Warily, Flint left the booth and held out his hand. "Just call me, Flint, ma'am. Howd'ya do?"

"Amy Warren. This is Louisa, and that's Josh." She indicated the kids with a harried nod. "Pleased to meet you, Flint. And bless you for letting Jo have Josh for a while. I knew Charlie would find a good man to take over. I have to run. I'll bake you some muffins this afternoon."

Flint blinked and wanted a televised re-play of what had just happened here as Amy Warren picked up her daughter and rushed out. He'd bask in the woman's ap-proval, except he didn't know what the heck he'd done to gain it.

"Here, take the kid while I get some more beans out of the back." Jo shoved the boy's hand into his.

Flint was left staring into solemn blue eyes with ridiculously long lashes. A grimy thumb popped into the kid's mouth. He remembered his kids at that age. He'd give half his life to have that time back.

"You're too old to suck your thumb," he admonished, sounding like his mother.

The kid sucked harder.

"Does it taste good?" Flint deposited the boy on the counter with the full intention of leaving him there and getting back to work.

The kid offered his wet thumb for tasting.

"No, thanks, I'm on a diet and had to give up thumbs. How about a doughnut instead?" He opened the case and selected a chocolate one.

The kid reached in and helped himself to a sticky one.

"Josh doesn't like chocolate." Jo closed the case as she passed by with the bag of coffee beans. "And now he'll have sugar all over everything and be hyper for hours. Better get a paper towel."

"Tell me again why I'm babysitting?" Flint reached for the towels. Sugary fingerprints already adorned his shirtfront.

"Because Mary Jean just had a baby, and Peggy goes to bed if she sneezes, and Louisa has a doctor appointment."

"Okay, that's one inanity too many. I've

got to work on the books." Not even admiring the way Jo's feathery earrings accentuated her pouty lips was sufficient to cope with her diarrhea of the mouth.

Hauling the chubby cherub out of the way of his breakfast crowd before the kid ate up the profits, he escaped to get the phone call off his agenda.

The office wasn't bigger than a storage closet. He dropped Josh on a cracked overstuffed chair, handed him pencil and paper, and took a seat at his desk. Vowing to buy a cordless speakerphone to bring some piece of the twenty-first century in here, Flint dialed the number for his ex-manager's office and set his feet up on the battered oak desk. Putting his big clodhoppers anywhere else involved endangering overflowing wastebaskets or kicking file drawers spilling yellowed invoices.

"Darla, put me through to Ned right now, or I'll sue his pants off, and you'll be out of a job," he told the gum-smacking secretary who answered.

As soon as he heard Ned pick up the receiver, Flint launched into his tirade. "You lied to me again, Slick. The album is slated to hit the stores *in August,* and I have yet to see RJ's approval for a correction on that cover."

He tried not to sound as desperate as he felt. He'd worked his heart out on the tunes for the record company's latest greatest star. He'd thought RJ was a *friend*. He'd given the lying, thieving bastard some of the best work he'd ever done. Maybe the last work he'd ever do. He had wanted to go out in a blaze of glory, not in a sleazy river of lawsuits and name-calling between ex-friends and ex-managers.

"Flint, you're bulldozin' mountains out of cesspools, son. The cover is fine."

"He left my name off! It's damn well not fine, and you know it!" Flint roared.

Startled by Flint's shout, the kid looked up so fast that he dropped his pencil. He puckered up, whether at the shout or the fact that the pencil had rolled under the desk, Flint couldn't determine. Grimacing, he tried to maneuver the long, curly cord of the phone around the tarnished brass accountant's lamp to reach under the desk.

In a lower voice, Flint continued his rant. "Tell RJ if I don't get credit on that album, I'm coming up there to cut him a new asshole."

Ned started more of his backpedaling bullshit. Fed up, Flint let the receiver dangle and crawled beneath the desk to retrieve the pencil from the dust bunnies.

He had a real bad feeling about lying scum like RJ. He had an ulcer shouting *lawsuit* every time he thought about the lyrics on that scrap of envelope RJ had passed off as his. In his experience, any man who could rip off a friend would cheat his own mother. That writing wasn't RJ's.

Grabbing the pencil, he started backing out from under the desk.

"Hide-and-seek, now why didn't I think of that?" called a melodious voice over his head. "The café has emptied out and I've come to retrieve Josh, but if you're having fun—"

"What's an *asshole,* Aunt Jo?" Josh asked.

Flint whacked his head against the desk coming up too fast.

All five feet six inches of blond bombshell beamed at him as he staggered up and fell into his desk chair, nursing his bruised head.

"Teaching the boy a new vocabulary, are we? How thoughtful." Without missing a beat, she scooped up the dangling receiver and hung up on Ned, abruptly cutting off the whining—whether intentionally or not, Flint wasn't about to guess. Joella looked like the kind who didn't get mad, but got even.

"C'mon, Josh, let's draw on the counter where Aunt Jo can help you with your letters."

"He's fine in here," Flint protested, annoyed at being caught in fatherly incompetence with a kid who wasn't even his own. His language skills had deteriorated from years of hanging out in bars.

Jo grabbed a new pencil from the desk and helped Josh out of the chair, ignoring Flint's protest. "Did George Bob give you the go-ahead for the back room?"

"I'm not sure it's a wise idea to open up when I'm not—"

"Mary Jean is great with the customers, and she needs the tips. You're not even paying her," she pointed out. "She's doing it for Eddie and the guys. If we had an espresso machine, you could make a fortune in the evenings."

"I'm not paying her?" Shocked, Flint got up and followed Jo to the front. "I could have the Feds down my throat for that. That's all I need, one more fight with the fu—" He cut himself off before he completed that word.

"Nobody cares what we do up here," she said with a dismissive wave. "As long as Mary Jean doesn't complain, who's to know? You're not running Starbucks."

"You have no *idea* how . . . frigging . . . wrong that is," he yelled. "It's that kind of lame-assed thinking that gets everybody concerned in deep shit."

"Mommy says *shit* is a bad word," Josh said, climbing up to reach the doughnut case. "Daddy says *damn* and he's going to hell," he continued in the ensuing silence.

Jo giggled and dried off a butt-ugly green dish from a stack she'd been hand washing. Flint rubbed his face. He wanted to back out of here as fast as his boots would carry him, but he had nowhere to run these days. Besides, she ought to be the one to go, not him. Knowing this was *his* place made him feel better.

"I'm already in hell, so I don't reckon you ought to try out any bad words in front of your mama," he advised, lifting the boy off the counter and back to a seat. "If you're hungry, we have bananas."

"Yeah, I wanna banana." He looked up at Flint expectantly. "You got any little boys I can play with?"

"I have two boys. Adam is twelve and Johnnie is eleven. Maybe you'll meet them when they come to visit." He'd missed most of their childhoods, and at this rate, he'd miss their adolescence, too.

"You got any big boys *I* can play with?" Jo murmured, brushing past him to hand Josh an apple instead of a banana.

Her aphrodisiac cologne filled his head with images of rose petals, bubble baths, and tan lines. "Am I big enough?" He lifted one eyebrow suggestively. Out of self-defense, he was already reverting to his old ways.

She slanted him a wicked look from beneath long, dark lashes. "Oh, you're big enough, all right. The question is, are you *good* enough?" she purred, running a finger down his chest and setting it on fire.

"*Good* ain't hardly the word for it," he promised.

Cursing inwardly that he'd let her push his buttons, Flint leaned against the counter at a safer distance, only to be distracted by the lift of Joella's breasts as she reached for more dishes in the cabinet over the stove. He'd been within inches of having all that in his palms. . . . He breathed a sigh of relief when the front door creaked open to let in a customer.

He had to be out of his mind to even consider discussing his ugly quest with Joella, but she was just the sort of person who would know RJ. He had to find out if his partner had plagiarized those lyrics they'd sold to the record company *before* he got his kids home and raised their hopes.

Flint waited until Jo finished pouring coffee for their customer. When she reached to take down a purple platter, he asked casually, "You know a guy called RJ Peters used to play around here?"

The platter dropped from Jo's hand to hit the stove with a splintering crash. She stood there wide-eyed, not bothering to glance at the destruction. "Why d'ya ask?"

Wondering what the hell that was about, Flint checked to make certain Josh was still safely in his seat. Then he knelt down to pick up the pieces. He had about ten seconds to figure out if she liked the lying cheat or wanted RJ's head smashed like the platter.

"I'm trying to make RJ live up to his obligations," he explained, figuring he was already in deep shit and might as well dig deeper.

"Well, you find a shotgun and a lawyer, and I'll do that for you." Without another word of explanation, she left him picking up china while she grabbed Josh and headed for the door. "We're going for a walk," she called as she departed.

Well, hell, Flint thought as he cut his finger on a porcelain splinter. Looked like ol' RJ had left an entire trail of shattered lives behind him. And at least one heart.

⫷SIX⫸

"Swing low, sweet chariot, comin' for to carry me home...," Joella sang as she pushed the porch swing with her toe, peeled potatoes, and admired the purple rhododendron blooms spilling over the rail. Her mother's house was way out in the woods where no one would hear or care if she sang her heart out or cried a river.

"You ought to sing in church more often." Marie wandered out to the rough-planked porch with a glass in her hand. Once as tall as Jo, she'd shrunk some with time and ill health, but she still stood straight and feisty, cigarette in hand despite doctor's orders.

Her hard-living mother hadn't touched alcohol in years, but Jo automatically eyed the glass with suspicion before deciding it looked like lemonade. Her mother's current situation was enough to cause anyone to pick up a bottle and start drowning. She admired Marie's strength in avoiding temptation. She should take lessons.

Jo shrugged. "They sing boring old songs here. I'm thinking of going down to Asheville and looking for a church that does contemporary music."

"Don't be silly." Marie sat on the swing and picked up a potato and peeler. "You don't belong down there. You belong here where people know you. I thought you'd learned that by now. You're all the time trying to be bigger than you are."

"I'm a pretty big girl, Mama. I couldn't afford new clothes if I get much bigger." Jo shoved aside the slight with twisted humor. It was the only way to take her mother when she went down this path, which was at least once a visit. Her mother spoke from experience, after all. "That reminds me, the kids need summer clothes, and Evan's hoarding money again. Maybe I could buy some material with my next check and you could make it up into some little shorts and things."

Her mother had worked as a sewing machine operator in the samples department at the mill for years, despite the crippling pain and fatigue of hepatitis. It had taken the layoff of half the workforce last year to end her decades of hard work.

Social Security had turned down her disability request, and the unemployment benefits expired next month. Jo had hoped maybe her mother could take up making clothes for others—just enough to cover her COBRA insurance until they could hire a lawyer to help with the disability application. The house was paid for, and she and Amy could provide groceries for a while.

Once COBRA ran out, however, no other insurance company would take her on. Without continued treatment, the doctor said Marie would die.

There had to be a way—Jo just hadn't found it yet. Her mama was only fifty-five.

"Evan is being smart about their money." Marie brushed off Jo's implied criticism. "Things are bad out there, and he's trying not to go into debt."

Jo cooled her anger at her brother-in-law by envisioning dumping the pot of potato peelings on Evan's shiny blond head. The man was a control freak who would stab his own mother-in-law in the back, but Marie had old-fashioned *values* and would never find fault with a man who provided for his family.

"Evan laid you off, even knowing you need insurance," Jo protested. "He won't pay for day care so Amy can take a job and use her education. It's all about *him.*"

"That's you talking, not Amy. You just don't understand men. You should have known that fast-talking Randy was just using you."

Like Jo's first boyfriend and so-called business manager, He-Who-Should-Rot-in-Hell. Any reference to that dangerous episode went unspoken, but the fear was there in her mother's eyes.

"Tell me something I don't know." Cutting the potato into quarters and nearly taking off her finger with the viciousness of her slice, Jo decided they had enough potatoes. She picked up the pot and carried it into the house.

Her mother had good reason to question Jo's poor choices. She was not only a bad judge of men, but it seemed she'd recently turned coward. She'd waited until the lunch rush had started before taking Josh back to the café. That wasn't like her. She should have waited to see what that no-good, cheating, rotten . . .

Which was why she hadn't hung around. She couldn't think of Randy—RJ!—Peters without looking for a rope and a gun. *RJ!* For heaven's sake alive, who did the miserable, rotten cur think he was? *Randolph John* wasn't good enough?

He'd been good old *Randy* while he was playing with the Buzzards. He'd left for Nashville and the music circuit a couple of years ago, but until she'd heard through the grapevine in January that he'd finally sold an album, she hadn't fully comprehended she'd been dumped along with the band. Stupidly, she'd had high hopes that his visits and sweet promises meant his heart was growing fonder with his absence. She'd just been waiting for him to keep his word to take her with him.

She didn't know who was stupider, her for believing him, or Randy for turning his back on the people who'd got him where he was today.

The phone rang at the same time that Amy's SUV chugged up the gravel drive. Balancing the potato pot on her hip, Jo picked up the cordless on the way through the shabby living room to the even shabbier kitchen. "Jo here."

"Has Amy arrived yet? I have some new clients in my office, and I've promised we'd feed them. I need to talk to her when she gets there."

"Hello, Evan, good to hear from you, Evan. How's life treating you these days, Evan?" Jo slammed the pot on the stove, added more water and some salt, and turned on the burner. Evan's pomposity was another of the traits that made her skin crawl. "Have you moved all the mill jobs to Mexico yet, Evan?"

She heard the kids shouting to their grandmother and waited to hear if Amy would come in. She glanced at the old Seth Thomas wall clock. Her sister was running late. She'd probably go on down the road. Amy hated to be late for anything. That was just fine, because Jo had no intention of handing dickhead over to Amy to ruin her evening out. He was perfectly capable of feeding clients in Asheville. He did it all the time. He just hated that Amy was taking classes instead of waiting on him.

"Just let me talk to my wife, dammit,

Joella. This doesn't have to be the Spanish Inquisition."

"Inquisition! Big word. I'll have to go look that up. I'll be right back." She set the phone on the counter and went out to greet the kids.

"Who was that on the phone, dear?" Marie tickled Louisa's belly beneath her too small shirt. Josh had already taken off for the apple tree.

"Just an encyclopedia salesman. I left him dangling."

So, she had a little problem with the truth. The problem with truth was that it sometimes got in the way of justice and hurt people who didn't deserve to be hurt. Every once in a while, she'd like the good people to win.

And she figured whatever Flint had intended to say about Randy John Peters wouldn't have much to do with good people winning. Not unless he handed her a gun and told her it was okay to use it.

On light feet, Joella raced down the fireescape steps of her apartment over the café on Friday morning. She didn't think Flint had figured out yet that she was his tenant. Some surprises were better left to time.

Humidity met the night breeze in a fine mist that blended with the gray light of dawn here in the alley between the café and the hardware store. She liked the isolated feeling of having the town to herself for these few minutes before she went to work.

A new day gave her a chance to start over. She'd kicked herself all night. She hadn't given Flint a chance to explain. Maybe he wanted to take Randy down, too. She ought to at least give him the benefit of the doubt.

She was just a little sensitive on the subject of the man she'd invested the best three years of her life in. She thought the one damned thing she did right was to know people, and Randy had shattered her illusions. She'd believed him when he'd said he was building a career on the road. She'd even believed him when he'd said he was too busy or too tired or traveling too late to call her often. She'd let him into her house and into her bed whenever his circuit had come back through here.

He'd told her he *lived* for the days and nights with her. Just last Christmas he'd been telling her how he *loved* her. He must have known then that he'd sold the album. Jeez, you'd think she was eighteen all over again. She must have beans for brains to believe Randy actually liked her rhymes as much as her bed.

Great track record, Jo. He-Who-Should-Rot-in-Hell had taught her stage fright and Randy RJ Ratfink had taught her not to trust a lying, conniving music man. And now she had to work for one. Well, at least she knew better than to trust Flint. She just needed to think with her head instead of her hormones for a change. Easier said than done.

She stepped out of the alley into the early morning of Main Street, Northfork, North Carolina. She loved the picturesque brick storefronts with their sagging signs and wood benches strategically located under awnings. The side of a mountain didn't leave a lot of flat land for building, so the highway between the shops was narrow and the sidewalks tight. Tourists had to park in the lots on either side of town, or on the residential streets that wound up into the hollows. Foot traffic, the big-city planners had called it. Good for business.

But tourists came up only on weekends.

To survive, businesses needed a thriving local population. Since the mill had started laying off, the local economy had flattened. She could see evidence of it already in the *For Sale* signs on houses, the closed gift shop, and the empty pharmacy that used to always be there on the corner. Asheville was less than an hour away, and people went down there on the weekends to do their shopping now, to the big box stores that could offer cheaper goods—made in China.

She couldn't do anything about the mill, but she had lots of ideas about other ways to boost business. The big MusicFest the first week of August was one of them. And if Flynn Clinton really was an ex-member of the Barn Boys, then he might be just the man they needed on the committee.

Speak of the devil . . . There he stood, contemplating the flying fuchsia pig in front of George Bob's insurance office. He had his fingers stashed in his front jeans pockets and his head tilted as if in conversation with the pig on its pedestal. Jo admired his long legs in boot-cut jeans and smiled in memory of his dancing. Her boss was one hell of a sexy man. It was a pity she wasn't trusting men these days.

She'd have to pry his story out of him sometime. His story, and nothing more, she reminded herself. And she'd take any tale he told with a grain of salt. She planned on learning cynicism before her thirtieth birthday.

She sauntered across the street to stand beside him. "Impressive, isn't she? That's Dot's creation. She sells ceramic artwork, so she's a professional at this kind of thing. The purple pig the kids painted isn't quite so neat, but it's cute."

"What the hell is it?" he asked in obvious confusion. "An ashtray?"

"It isn't *anything*. It's art. Knock knock." She tapped his temple with her knuckles. She liked that she had to reach a bit to do so. She liked the heated look he shot her as well. She needed to be reminded she still had what it takes, even if she didn't plan to use it. "Where have you been? Everybody's doing them. I think Chicago started it with the cows. We can't do anything quite so fancy, but if it makes money for the festival, who cares?"

"How do they make money?" He leaned

his head back to look the fuchsia pig in its checkerboarded eye. "It's the ugliest damned thing I've ever seen."

"Folk art. People like whimsical. We take bids on the pigs all summer and start the auction where the bids leave off at the festival in August. Cute, huh?"

"People are going to put these things in their houses?" He shook his head in disbelief and started across the street to the café.

Jo stayed in stride with him. "Or their gardens. Whatever. Will you take Sally's pig? It will look adorable by the front door."

He shoved the key in the lock. "If everyone else is doing it and I don't have to keep it forever, reckon I can give it a try. It won't trip any customers, will it?"

"That's why George Bob asked for the one on the pedestal, but you'd have to be blind to trip over one. I'll call Sally. She'll be delighted."

"Has she got anyone special?" Flint asked, not looking at Jo as he flipped on the lights.

Jo tried not to reel in shock. This handsome cowboy who could have any woman he wanted was interested in little Sally? Boy, she really was losing her judgment about people. "No one special. She sings in the choir at First Baptist. You might go up there on Sunday if you're out to make an impression."

"Better class of people in church than in bars," he agreed, apparently forgetting where he'd met Jo.

She contemplated socking him over the back of his oblivious head with a coffee mug, but he was a man and clueless. "You'll see some of the same people in both places," she said with what she considered great restraint.

He regarded her tight expression with suspicion. "Right. If you'll start the coffee, I'll go back and unlock for the delivery truck."

They were stepping around each other as if his mention of RJ yesterday had planted a mine field. Maybe it had. Figuring she'd better wait until they both had some caffeine before approaching him about Randy, Jo tightened her apron bow and sauntered back to the counter.

She had coffee brewing and Charlie's newly washed Fiestaware collection stacked all over the counter by the time Flint returned. He carried boxes heavy enough for two forklifts and efficiently stacked them in the pantry without dropping one. Jo sighed in regret over all those rippling muscles she shouldn't touch.

After storing the delivery and breaking out the Krispy Kremes to stack in the counter case, Flint gazed over the array of plates she'd set out. "Having a party?"

"They're Fiestaware," she said proudly. "They're real popular now, and I bet these are the genuine things, not the cheap ones from the discount store. I looked them up at the library when I was in Asheville, and we have some of the old colors. I had this idea—we could paint the café in tangerine and persimmon and juniper and line shelves with the plates. Sit some in the front window. Tourists would come in and want to buy them. We could serve them coffee in the cups."

"Tangerine?" He looked as if he'd swallowed the persimmon. "I don't think so. You think these things are worth money?"

"Maybe turquoise and cobalt then?" she asked hopefully. "The place is so gloomy and dull. Bright colors would attract kids, but I guess blues . . ."

He shook his head. "I like the place like it

is. Just because I agreed to a purple pig doesn't mean you can change everything. But if those plates are worth something, I could fix up a shelf in the window maybe."

That was a start, she supposed. She traced the tip of her finger lovingly over one of the colorful coffee cups. "And serve coffee in them maybe?"

"They need saucers. Twice the washing." He poured coffee into the plain white restaurant mug and leaned back against the counter to sip it.

Jo could feel the heat of his gaze burn straight through her clothes, but she was practicing *focus* this morning. Men seldom turned down her ideas, but Flint probably had lots of women throwing themselves at his feet. She apparently had to appeal to his pockets if she wanted to win this one. She kinda liked the idea that he couldn't be swayed by sex.

Before he asked about the cost of the platter she'd broken, Jo switched the subject. "Why did you ask about Randy yesterday?"

"Randy?" He had to change mental gears for that one. "RJ? I'd forgotten we used to call him Randy when we were kids."

She poured herself some coffee and leaned her hip against the stove, far enough away from him that she could keep her mind on the subject and not how it had felt to be held in Flint's big brown arms. If she wanted to learn more, she had to keep this low-key even if she had the urge to fling a plate every time she heard RJ Ratfink's name. "You knew him when he was a kid?"

Flint set down his cup and headed toward the door to switch the *Closed* sign to *Open*. "He was a few years younger than me, but he lived next door until my family moved away when I was ten. We bumped into each other regularly on the circuit."

That meant he could probably tell her all about the two-timin' bastard's escapades. As if he heard her thought, Flint avoided her proximity by straightening chairs. In those cowboy boots, he looked almost too tall for the room.

"How do you know him?" he asked with an edge in his voice.

"He used to play with the Buzzards," she replied, keeping it casual. She could see George Bob opening his office across the street. She'd have to be quick.

"Yeah? I didn't know that. When he came

up to Nashville, I helped him get a few jobs." He stacked a few misplaced chairs and held them over his head to carry them to the back where they belonged.

Jo sighed in regret again. He looked good in jeans. "I heard about his recording contract." She moved the ugly white mugs to the closed cabinet to make room for the pretty cups in the glass display cabinet and tried to look disinterested. She didn't know why she ought to be interested in RJ's doings, except he seemed to make Flint real uneasy.

When she didn't throw a tantrum or drop anything, Flint returned to top off his cup. "Yeah. That's why I asked about him. Is he a real good friend of yours?"

"When Nashville called, he walked out on the Buzzards and left them stranded. I don't reckon he has a lot of friends here right now."

His hard expression eased a little. "Well, that's the music business. His manager and the record company probably made that decision."

She nodded knowledgeably. "The Buzzards weren't pretty enough."

"Right." Flint straightened his shoulders

as if to steel himself and produced a multi-folded scrap of paper from his wallet. "You wouldn't happen to know if any of the band wrote this, do you?"

That caught her by surprise. Jo stopped stacking plates to stare at the scrap. It looked like one of the invoice envelopes she usually scribbled on. She was afraid if she took it, it might self-destruct. Or she might.

A sunbeam through the newly cleaned plate-glass window struck Flint square on his bronzed cheekbone, and she had to admit he had the deepest, most honest eyes she'd ever seen on a lying, conniving music man. That high brow of his gave him an earnest, intellectual look that appealed to her, and the jut of his square chin begged for her to lean over and suck his sculpted lips.

And she knew better than to believe the image or give in to the urge.

"Why do you want to know?" she asked, without taking the scrap. Her hands were sweaty with anticipation. Despite the peculiarity of the conversation, Jo thought that had more to do with kissing than any expectation of what Flint was about to say.

"I composed the tunes for the lyrics RJ

gave me, but later, I found that rhyme from one of his songs in his car. It's not his handwriting." He hesitated, then plunged on. "I have some reason not to trust him, so when he sold his album based on the songs we wrote together, that scrap made me nervous."

"*We* wrote?" She was trying hard to follow this while watching a kaleidoscope of pain, confusion, and anger in Flint's flashing eyes. He looked as volatile as she felt. "Randy's been using some of the band's material on the circuit," she said carefully.

Which was why he was such a sneaking low-down thief, using their songs to make his career and not paying the band—or her—a dime, and then forgetting their existence when he cut a deal. Just thinking about it made her want to reach for a shotgun—and then Jo's brain did a quick backtrack. "Wait a minute. *You* composed the music?"

Taking a seat on the far side of the counter, Flint visibly braced himself. "The tunes he was playing sucked, but the audience loved the lyrics. I was staying home at the time, so I put the words to better music."

"The words? To *Randy's* songs?" She couldn't really believe where he was going with this. *She'd* written the only original lyrics Randy ever sang. As Randy said, it was all crapola, but it was good for a laugh to warm up the audience, right?

She must have been playing cool real well because Flint relaxed.

"Yeah, some of them were kind of cute. 'Let's all join together, and summon stormy weather, and when the skies fall, we'll bring them to their knees, and make the rat finks crawl.' Silly, but he could change the subject from politics to business, if he liked. Audiences love thinking they can bring the fat cats to their knees and make them crawl."

Sipping his coffee, Flint was getting into his subject. Jo was a damned good listener. He hadn't had an opportunity to talk music in a while, and he was feeling deprived. He'd had a roaring good time creating the upbeat on those verses. It had matched his vengeful mood at the time and washed away some of the bitterness of his divorce.

"Silly?" Joella asked silkily, taking the scrap from his hand.

Still sailing on one of his favorite topics, Flint didn't hear the torpedo coming. "Yeah, some of them. Once I added the bass to the chorus of that one, the audience really got into it, pounding their bottles on the table and singing along when we tried them out in a few bars. The lyrics have the kind of passion that sells. The album's bound to go gold." He might hate the man behind it, but he was damned proud of the music.

"How nice for Randy." Glaring at the envelope as if it had turned into a spider, Joella dropped it on the counter and started polishing one of the hideous rainbow dishes she'd been raving about earlier.

Since she was being more rational than yesterday, Flint got a little bolder. Maybe he ought to talk to the Buzzards first, but he'd been a little startled to discover the potential source of the rhyme so easily. That chorus was the cornerstone on which the first release was laid. Maybe Joella really was an angel in disguise and could break it to the guys in a manner that wouldn't get his pants sued off. He prayed they'd only written the one line.

"Yeah, well, the thing is," Flint said slowly, looking for a cautious way to word his problem, "RJ told me he wrote *all* the lyrics. He's been singing them around the country for years, so I didn't doubt him. I'd helped him out when he needed it, so he helped me out by letting me compose. I'd been doing it for the Barn Boys, but I quit the group when I quit traveling." Flint heard the front door open and knew the morning rush was about to start, so he hurried. "But right after RJ and I copyrighted the songs and our manager sold them, I found that scrap and asked him about it. He swore it was just a line a friend back home had jotted down. I kinda wanted to make sure everything was on the level."

"He said that? A *friend*?"

Joella sounded so perfectly calm that the red plate flying past Flint's ear caught him off guard. Stunned, he watched as her tanned arm reached across a stack of plates for a green saucer. "If the line isn't his, I'm trying to find that friend and make it right!" he yelled, ducking as the saucer blew over his head and ricocheted off a tin lamp with noisy accuracy.

"*I* wrote *all* Randy's songs, damn the lazy, lying, lowdown, conniving— My mama *needs* that money."

A yellow cup whizzed straight at him and Flint dropped just in time to save his scalp.

More cups, saucers, and plates flew in accompaniment to each pejorative and with
increasing strength as she built up steam.
Hunkered down behind the counter, Flint
caught a glimpse of George Bob fleeing out
the front door, and his rage boiled up and
threatened to spill over. This was his *career*
on the line.

"*All* RJ's songs?" he yelled. A growing
terror built behind the dam of rage.

Jo broke into a wild, high-pitched chorus
of "He's my man, and I'm proud to know it.
He's my man, so I knew he'd blow it . . ."

Except RJ had changed the personal pro-
noun and said *woman* instead of *man*. The
line came from the first song they'd done,
and she was singing it to the tune RJ had
used before Flint had fixed it. No wonder it
had sounded rotten. The meter was all off
for a man.

Flint listened in horror as Jo switched into
a medley of every song on the recording,
punctuating each change of verse with another plate. She was winging them like Fris-
bees now, keeping time to the beat with the
crash of crockery. And his terror swelled his
rage right to the brink and over.

"If you break any more of those damned

plates, I'll fire you!" he yelled, rising from behind the counter with his fingers gripping
the Formica so hard they ought to leave
dents. Pain shot through his crippled left
hand, but it aided and abetted the rage.

"You can't fire me," she shouted back,
flinging an orange teapot into the coffee
machine. "I'll *own* this place before I'm
through with you and Randy RJ Ratfink
Peters!"

≪SEVEN≫

Joella wrote RJ's lyrics? The blond bomb-shell? *His waitress?* Did hell have an open-ing right here on earth just for him? *All* the lyrics?

A plate bigger than Flint's head flew past his nose and bounced off a photograph of the town from the early 1900s. The frame crashed to the floor, cracking the glass, re-minding him that they were wrecking his current source of income. His fury reached explosive proportions.

Flint shoved so hard on the counter that he lifted it straight off the rotten floor. Foam-ing at the lousiness of the construction as well as every other damned faulty thing in his life, he slammed the counter back down with a force so strong that it rattled the re-maining dishes in the cabinet just as Joella reached for a second load of ammunition.

She jumped and stared at him in shock. Now that she was disarmed, Flint vaulted over the now-loose counter, trapped her arms at her sides, and lifted her off her feet. She wore a midriff-revealing cutoff shirt beneath her apron this morning, and his hands hit warm flesh—kicking-and-screaming and not melting-with-lust flesh.

"I don't owe you a damned thing," he roared, dragging her from the plates.

She was all ripe curves and smooth skin in his arms, but she didn't give him time to appreciate what he held. She aimed a kick at his shin. He couldn't dodge that, and he staggered as he carried her to his office and flung her down in his tattered office chair.

"Sit!" he commanded.

To his amazement, she did. Except within seconds, she'd crumpled into a ball and started sobbing as if her heart would break.

Every sniffle became a wail of anguish in Flint's ears. His own wounds over RJ's treachery were too raw to tolerate her pain easily. Everything he'd worked for these last years, his reputation and his talent and his career and the future he'd hoped to own for his sons—all were in imminent danger of disintegrating before his eyes.

He wanted to collapse and cry with her, but men weren't supposed to cry. Instead, he stalked the tiny strip of open floor, holding the raw wound in his gut closed, praying Jo pulled herself together before he went berserk.

She had come entirely too close to being right. Stealing original music was a hanging offense in the industry. If she'd really written that material, she could sue everyone from God on down. He'd have to mortgage the equity in the coffee shop just to pay the lawyers. He'd made the down payment with the advance from that album. *Shit.*

Action, any action, was preferable to hearing her cry. Flint crouched down in front of Jo and offered all he could. "If you can prove you wrote those songs, I'll help you find a good lawyer."

She nearly bowled him over with a wallop upside the head. He was a big man and had been in bar fights before and never been knocked down, but she'd turned him into a feather. Or fear had. He'd need *two* good lawyers—one to sue RJ and one to protect him from Joella. He couldn't afford even a chickenshit lawyer these days.

Deciding there was only one way of dealing with hysteria—his or hers—Flint lifted Joella from the chair and sat down, carrying her with him. Trapping her treacherous arms, he held her in his lap and hugged her against his chest so she couldn't go anywhere. Apparently giving up the fight again after that slap, she broke into renewed sobs, and he rocked her like a baby.

Somehow, holding a handful of sweet-smelling woman comforted his raging temper. Her soft hair brushed his jaw, and soft curves eased the tension in his chest. He unwound as her sobs diminished into hiccups, and he prayed rationality was returning.

He just had to get past the smoothness of her bare waist beneath his hand. And her rounded bottom in a place that didn't need any further stimulation.

"Put me down, you big oaf." Apparently recognizing what she was doing to him and deciding to quit crying, Jo attempted to elbow him, but Flint held her too close.

"I've got a big deductible on my medical insurance. You're paying the bills if you gut me," he warned, trying not to give in to the instinct to protect the vulnerable.

"I damned well am not!" She squirmed

and kicked, nearly maiming him in a sensitive area, reminding him that Joella was the last thing past vulnerable. "I'm hiring the nastiest lawyer in this entire country, and I'm cutting that rat fink's throat, and you'd better let me out of here right now to do it."

Flint didn't bother to mention that if the law went after one copyright holder, it went after both, and he was the other. He didn't figure she was thinking business at the moment. If he could put aside his own rage for a second, he could understand hers. RJ had only ripped off Flint's livelihood, but if he knew anything at all about music and life, RJ had gouged out Joella's heart and soul.

"Hey, can we get a little coffee out here?" someone yelled from the shop.

"You damned well know where the pot is, Georgie," she yelled back. Her elbow glanced off Flint's ribs, but it wasn't as hard a blow as earlier.

"Joella, honey, are you all right?" inquired a woman's soft voice.

Flint groaned and shoved Jo off his lap.

She landed feetfirst, hands on hips. "I'm purely fine, Sally. Me and Flint here just had a little disagreement."

"That involved half the crockery in here?"

George Bob came up behind Sally to look in. "It's a good thing Charlie only stocks that cheap cutlery or it looks like she'd have carved you into beefsteak. Insurance won't cover it."

"Go to hell, George. Sally, we'll take the kids' pig," she informed her. "And if there are any others left over, we'll find a place for them, too."

Flint watched as Jo stalked out of the office as if she owned the world. Or at least, his shop. She behaved as if she hadn't been a mewling ball of tears just minutes ago. She still had tearstains on her cheeks, but he could hear her out there pouring coffee for all the usual customers, telling jokes and kicking broken plates around with a forced laugh.

While he stood here with a hard-on that wouldn't go away and a terror bigger than his heart could hold. *He could lose his coffee shop.*

He could lose everything.

Well, hell, he'd already lost just about everything, so what difference did the damned shop make anyway? His parents would never agree to let his sons live up here in rural poverty, so who cared? He'd go back to cheap hotel rooms and . . .

Nope, he couldn't do music either. No fingers to play chords.

All right, then, he'd be a homeless bum. That took the stiffness right out of his groin and put it in his spine where it belonged.

Grabbing a push broom from the closet with his good right hand, Flint joined Joella behind the counter. "This comes out of your pay," he warned, not because he meant it but because he had to say something in front of a shopful of staring customers.

"Fine, I won't pay the rent," she agreed with false cheer.

He didn't know what one had to do with the other, but he started sweeping anyway. "There's no telling how much money you just threw away. I ought to hire an appraiser."

"It's not as if you knew they were worth anything until I told you anyway. So call those the price of my commission when you sell the rest."

He squelched the urge to throw one of the damned plates. He'd been rolling in dough not two years ago, and now he was reduced to sweeping up after a temperamental waitress in a two-bit . . .

Work with it. Flint's fingers itched for his guitar to translate the anger into music as he'd always done. Like he didn't dare do anymore. Instead, he swept the broom rhythmically, getting into the swing of it. *I'm cleaning up the pieces after the Queen of Mean . . .*

"Thank you for taking the pig," Sally murmured, startling him from his reverie.

He'd forgotten all about her. She was a foot too short but a cute little thing, just the kind of mother the boys needed. He glanced up from his grim contemplation of the floor with a polite smile. He'd need a wife just to support him after Jo got through with him. Life being what it was, maybe he ought to look for a rich woman instead of a maternal one. "No problem, ma'am, now that I know what it's for. Do I need to pick it up?"

She brightened. "Could you? That would be wonderful. It's out at the school. It's the last day of classes so it will be a little hectic out there, but the kids will be thrilled! They'll all be by to check on Myrtle."

"Myrtle?" he asked, fearful he would be saddled with more than a purple pig.

"That's what they call her. They had a turtle named Myrtle but it died this winter, so they named their artwork after her."

A turtle named Myrtle. That was kind of cute. He could get something . . . Been there, done that, not going down the music road again. He didn't know why the hell the muse that had deserted him this past year had suddenly decided to show her shriveled ass today. Guess it was just one of those days.

"Things slow down here about ten. I'll be out then," he assured her, and was rewarded with a sweet smile. A powder puff like Sally was far better than dealing with a blond temptress who threw hissy fits and broke crockery. He'd had enough of that for five lifetimes.

He wasn't in the least surprised a few minutes later when Joella's sister appeared bearing a tray full of muffins—iced and decorated with pig snouts. His life had now officially fallen from the sublime to the ridiculous.

Jo waited until Flint had backed his pickup onto the sidewalk, partially obstructing highway traffic, before deciding to talk to him again.

She tried to block out the memory of the night she'd almost ended up in that pickup with him, but it was hard to forget while watching her employer's muscled arms wrestling the heavy purple pig out of the truck bed. Those arms had snuggled her close as if she were no more than a little bitty baby. This morning he'd held her for comfort, not sex—until she'd wiggled once too often anyway. When was the last time a man had done that for her?

She was *so* not going there, especially with a man who could rip counters right out of the floor. She hadn't been appropriately appreciative of that act until she'd tried to shove the counter later. It hadn't budged. Flynn Clinton was one scary man—and he held a painful piece of her hopes. She clutched her fingers into her palms in a form of prayer.

She was still so furious she couldn't think straight, but she'd recovered enough sense to understand that maybe Flint wasn't to blame except as the messenger. Had he really meant that he'd written music for *her* words? Real music, with melodies and not just hot guitar riffs like the band played?

"Dot said she could use the plate pieces in birdbaths and mosaic tables and give you a percentage on every one sold," she called when he was close enough. She hoped it sounded like a peace offering.

Holding the hefty pig with its red-ribboned tail curling near his ear, Flint scanned the sidewalk for the best location. "Do I have to put the birdbaths with the pig?" he asked in a note of disgust.

Catching his arm, Jo led him to the dwarf juniper she'd planted at the corner of the alley. The pavement was broken there, and she'd dug it up to make a little in-ground planter. "If you don't want her blocking the door, Myrtle should be fine with her tail tucked around the corner of the alley. Maybe we could put a red bow on top of the tree for her to admire. We could dress her up so she'll bring a higher price."

He willingly lowered the painted statue to the spot indicated. "Myrtle is even uglier than George Bob's flying hog. Nobody's going to buy her."

They both stepped back to study the pig, who did seem to be tilting her polka-dotted snout upward to admire the tree. The purple paint had been inexpertly applied by childish hands and had already cracked over the pig's ample hips. Its eyes had been painted a particularly virulent pink to match the polka-dots. Some wit had given Myrtle's fat jowls grassy green whiskers. Bright yellow flowers adorned her porcine back like a pig saddle.

"The flowers are kind of pretty." She defended the kids' creation.

"Cracked ham hocks," he asserted. "Anyone who buys this can use it to frighten coyotes."

"I think she needs a hat. Pigs sunburn."

Jo could feel him glaring at her inanity, but she didn't try to interpret the emotion behind it. She just wished she were wearing heels instead of Nikes. Flynn Clinton was a big man, in more ways than height. She'd slapped him, and he'd just turned the other cheek. She didn't know how to take that, but it made her sick inside that she'd done it, and warm to know that he hadn't taken it too personally.

"I apologize," she said bravely, for the second time in their rocky acquaintance.

"Yeah. You're still fired. And I'm still docking your wages. Did you fix the bank deposit yet? It's Friday and I have to pay the bills." He headed back to the truck.

"The deposit is ready, and I talked Dave into fixing a shelf in the window. Did you see it?" Jo chose to ignore the *fired* part. She didn't have another job lined up, and if he docked her wages, she couldn't pay his rent. It evened out.

"You really thought my songs were good?" she asked while she was being brave. That had been the only momentum keeping her going all morning. She knew people laughed at her ditties. She liked making people happy. But if a professional Nashville musician like Flint had thought they were worth composing real music for . . . She was afraid to let the possibility go to her head. She'd been cut down before when she'd dared to believe she was more than a hick waitress—as her mother could attest.

"The lyrics had flair," Flint asserted noncommittally, peering under the torn blue awning to check the window with *Stardust Café* written across it in hot pink. "People will come in here to buy that stuff?" he asked incredulously at the display of purple, orange, and green. "It's even uglier than Myrtle."

So much for discussing her music. "Maybe we have a theme going. We could change the name to Ugly Café." She wanted him to tell her about her words having *flair*. Irritated that he wouldn't talk about her poems, equally annoyed that her brilliant Fiestaware idea was so easily dismissed, she resisted slugging him. If she hadn't knocked any sense into his head earlier, she might loosen what few brains he possessed if she did it again.

"Ugly Pig Café," he countered, sauntering back to the truck with a lean-hipped swing. "The kids could paint pigs on all the plates."

Jo tried not to laugh as he drove the truck away. If she looked beneath his cynical attitude, her boss just might have a sense of humor.

He'd need it if he meant to date Sally. Sally thought a good time was taking the church school class down to the park and feeding them homemade ice cream until they turned into hyperactive monsters. Jo shuddered at the memory.

She vowed to pry more out of him about the songs. All she needed was a little hope to cling to, and she'd dare mountains. She tried to check the excitement fizzing inside her like bottle rockets at the possibility of *her* words being heard by millions of people.

She had the dishwasher emptied and hamburgers frying for the early lunch crowd when Flint returned. She handed him the bank bag. He took it and walked out without comment. If she was fired, he hadn't thrown her out on her ear yet, at least.

She couldn't get fired. This was Friday. The Buzzards had a gig here tonight. Her rent was due, and she needed her paycheck.

Lunch was too busy for asking questions. Jo flipped burgers and poured coffee and iced tea while Flint took orders and stacked them on the spindle. She was more than a little surprised that in a few days the big-time guitar player—and composer, she had to remember—had learned the names of his regulars. He chatted like a native, which she supposed he was. She'd done the math. If she'd guessed his age correctly, he'd left Northfork before her mama had moved back up here. He might not know everyone, but they knew him.

Around two, after the lunch crowd trickled out, Flint returned to his office while Jo unloaded the dishwasher. She was just wishing she'd thrown the ugly restaurant mugs instead of the pretty dishes when he returned and shoved a piece of paper under her nose.

"Here. I can't figure out Charlie's bookkeeping, but this looks right."

She stared in wonder at the amount on the paycheck before accepting it. "I take my tips in cash out of the register. You only owe me hours."

"I've watched them tip here. You deserve more." He looked around with a puzzled frown. "Where did all the muffins go? I didn't get one."

He'd noticed how the customers tipped? A man who noticed something beyond the needs of his own . . . *Bad, Joella.* Play nice.

"Word got around and they sold out before noon. I'll snag you one next time." If there was a next time. She'd like to do cartwheels over the size of the check, and the fact that Flint had actually given her one. Once upon a time she would have been seriously impressed and overwhelmed that he'd noticed she wasn't getting paid what she was worth, but she was learning to do suspicion well. She folded the paper and stuck it in her apron. "You can't buy me off," she warned.

"Wasn't planning to." He looked uncomfortable. He stuck his fingers in his back pockets and rocked on his heels. "We have to talk sometime."

"Maybe we'd better do it with a lawyer present." Not that she'd trust Fritz and Freddy from down the street. All they were good for was filing documents at the courthouse. But talking with Flint alone involved sizzling in her own juices. She got all hungry just watching him lean his hips on the counter and remembering how he swung them when he danced. She was a basket case without his telling her he'd *sold her songs.*

She had so many hopes and questions whirling around inside her that she could hardly stand still. Her hands had been shaking all morning. Randy had been paid a lot of money for that album. If she could have some small fraction of it . . .

"I have a lawyer." Flint crossed his arms defensively.

Joella figured a man that sexy was better

behind a guitar than a counter, but she was determined to listen and not talk right now.

"My lawyer drew up the publishing contract for the songs on RJ's album. If we tell him RJ stole the lyrics, he'll have to call the record label, and the album will get yanked."

Jo imitated his stance, crossing her arms and leaning her hip against the stove to hide her shakes. "And this is a problem, how?"

Flint turned a gray glare on her. "Because you can get a whole lot more money suing a rich man than a poor one. RJ will have spent his cash advance by now. The record label is a better target."

Jo narrowed her eyes. "I'm no CPA, but if RJ got an advance, then I figure you got one, too. Sounds to me like you're protecting your own hide."

"Of course I am," he said impatiently. "But I'm small potatoes. My stake is big to me, but pretty small next to RJ's since he's the performer. It won't do you any good raising a ruckus before you've documented your case. The record company has a raft of lawyers that will keep you at sea until they drown you in legal mumbo jumbo. You want to win this, you have to sink the raft before

they see you coming, then mow them down
with AK-47s."

"That's just crazy enough to make
sense," she admitted. "I don't care about
lawyers and record companies or even you.
I just want RJ taken down." Which was another lie, but she'd rather get mad than
sound needy.

She studied the tall cowboy grabbing a
dish towel now that he'd said his piece. He
was sexy even when he was domestic.
She'd love to trust him enough to confide in
him, but she'd done that before and look
where it had got her. "Although why you told
me any of this is a mystery. What did RJ do
to you?"

"Besides leaving me liable for a lawsuit
that can ruin me?" He dried a mug and
slammed it into a cabinet as if it were
Randy's head.

"If you hadn't told me, I wouldn't have
known," she pointed out.

"You would as soon as you heard the
songs on the radio. I didn't have to doctor
the words much to make them fit my music.
You have a naturally comedic rhythm."

She'd like to preen at that grudging compliment, except she wasn't believing a word

he said yet. "But I wouldn't have known it was you that composed the music. I would have gone after RJ with a butcher knife and got myself arrested. What did he do to you, run off with your wife?" She knew she'd hit the bull's-eye when Flint flinched.

"Melinda died in a senseless car crash." He slammed another mug on the shelf hard enough to crack it, but he didn't walk away for a change.

Jo grimaced. She hadn't meant to rile bad memories.

For the first time since they'd met, Jo let herself see past Flint's good looks and smooth charm to the pain eroding his in- sides. She hadn't wanted to see inside him. It was a lot easier despising him for his out- side. "I'm sorry. I didn't mean to take my meanness out on you."

He shot her a glare. "It was over a year ago. She'd been out drinking with RJ, and they had a lovers' spat right before she crashed."

Jo sighed. She had never been good at hating people. She put down her towel and held out her hand. "Well, Mr. Flint, it looks like you and me are about to go into part- nership to carve Randy down to his knees. I reckon I know what part of him I want to cut off first."

He winced, hesitated, then held out his hand and shook on it. "You'll listen to my advice on how to go about it?"

"About as often as you listen to my advice on how to run the café," she agreed with a smile that grew from ear to ear at his scowling reaction.

"Can you prove you wrote the lyrics?" he asked in retaliation.

Shot down in one. She didn't let her smile falter. "Are pigs pink?"

She hoped he didn't understand the ambiguity of that reply while she scrambled to figure out how to accomplish the impossible.

≪EIGHT≫

"Look, just have them cut the lights, okay?" Jo paced her room over the café nervously, trying to ignore the voice inside her head screaming, *Run now, while you can.* "I think I can do it if I just pretend I'm sitting in church."

Slim snorted. "You don't write hymns, Jo. Just get up there and sing. You'll bring down the house."

She caught her elbows and hung on. The guys thought she was good ol' Jo who could do anything she put her mind to, and she'd really like to protect the image. She'd had a lifetime to learn how to disguise anxiety, but this particular anxiety was a purple monster.

After the Atlanta debacle, she'd lost interest in performing onstage. She could do it, if only to prove to Flint that those were *her* songs. But after Atlanta, spotlights made her downright nauseous, and claiming her songs was too important to look like a fool. She'd had to quit singing in church after the choir director had added spotlights. "I'm not singing a birthday ditty, Slim. People expect a performance if I get up on that stage, and I'm no performer." As she'd proved once already.

"Just sing the song, Jo," Eddie said impatiently. "We've got to get down there."

"Promise you'll cut the lights or I'll never give you another verse again."

"Tell the kid to cut the lights when I give him a high sign," Slim said in disgust, carrying his guitar toward her door as the other band members gathered up their gear and prepared to follow. "There won't be anyone out there that'll care one way or another."

"Except me," Jo whispered to herself as the guys trudged out. She didn't mind making a fool of herself in front of them. She simply couldn't handle an entire audience waiting expectantly. She'd freeze and squeak like a mouse—or hurl all over someone's wing tips like last time—and she'd never be able to face the town again.

But Slim didn't know her new material, so she had to sing it herself. Her mother's life might depend upon her ability to convince Flint and a courtroom that she was more than a cleavage-blessed waitress.

For a little past eight in the evening, the back room of the coffee shop was amazingly full. Flint reckoned there weren't too many other places to go in Northfork on a Friday night. He hid his grimace in a sip of bad coffee as the bass player hit a flat note. No one else seemed to notice or care that the Buzzards were the next best thing to mediocre.

With the racket from the audience, the music didn't stand a chance anyway. The band was loud, enthusiastic, and could set feet stomping, which was all the crowd needed.

Since this was a dry town, coffee, soft drinks, and tea were the only beverages available. Jo's espresso suggestion might have its place, but he'd checked the prices of machines. New, one could set him back nearly three grand. And he'd need new cups. He couldn't see the locals paying more money for smaller cups of caffeine. Scratch that idea and get back to the real problem that had him sitting here listening to bad music on a Friday night.

Joella had promised to meet him tonight to prove she'd written RJ's songs and that her earlier inspired medley wasn't just a repetition of the songs he'd sung with the band. But like all women, she was running late.

"Hey, Flint, did you like my muffins?" With a shy smile, Amy Warren stopped beside his table.

"Your sister fed them to the hogs before I got one," he admitted. He had some difficulty seeing the resemblance between Joella, with her flashy good looks, and this slender woman in her taupe pants suit, sensible heels, and short, salon-styled brown hair, but there was a similarity in the big green eyes, he guessed. "The pigs on top were cute," he lied.

She beamed as if he'd handed her a gold watch. "You liked the pigs? Evan said icing on muffins is silly, but Charlie said cupcakes don't sell." She settled on the edge of the chair as if prepared to take flight if he said boo. She leaned forward so he could hear over the noise of the band and audience. "I *love* to decorate cakes."

Flint would like to say that he wasn't a dessert man, but he didn't want to hurt the sparrow's feelings. Besides, the stage had just darkened, and the band broke into a rollicking number that brought the audience to an expectant silence. Even the little bird turned to watch.

"Muffin man," a clear soprano rang out from the darkness over the sound of an off-key fiddle, "muffin man, you listen. You don't know what you're missin'."

Flint nearly choked on his coffee as he located Joella perched on the edge of the stage, not feet from where he sat. The vixen obviously knew she was borrowing words and music from another song. Even in this dim light, he could see her point straight at him and flash a sexy, naughty smile that revved all his engines.

When she caught his eye, her hundred-watt grin of mischief exploded from the stage. She didn't need bright lights. The raucous guitar that erupted behind her was irrelevant. Flint could hear only Joella as the lyrics changed to a laughing paean to life behind a counter.

She not only filled the room with her voice, but her presence. She had donned some outrageous attire of buff leather with fringe that struck her midthigh, drawing the unwavering attention of every male member of the audience even in the dim houselights. Beneath her short jacket she wore a glittery red shirt he thought he recognized from the night they'd met. Red, beaded earrings swung near her long throat, and Flint almost vowed to become an ear man instead of a breast man.

She had the same effect as a lightning bolt zigzagging across the room. She had a voice that crept down inside him and threatened to turn him inside out. She poured her soul into the music, and if he wasn't so wise to the ways of the world, he'd already be head over heels for her.

And she was mocking him and the Stardust with her words. *Her* words. She may as well have autographed them. There was no mistaking the subject and the sly wit, even though he'd never heard the lyrics in his life, and she was borrowing music from an old Beatles song. The whole audience recognized her satire and sang along with the chorus.

He was so totally knocked out that she caught him off guard when she jumped down from the stage and wriggled into his lap to the accompaniment of loud whistles.

"Muffin man," she crooned more softly,

wrapping her arm around his neck and branding his chest for life with the heat of her breasts, "are you listenin' now?"

Hell, no, not if she meant with his ears. But the rest of him was wide-awake and hearing every vibration where her body met his. He was one giant tuning fork. He wanted to bury his face in the thick hair she'd loosely pinned up, inhale her powdery scent, and kiss her nape—just for starters.

But she was so far off his road map for the future that she might as well be from another planet, so Flint fought his natural instincts. As the fiddle died out, he caught her waist, stood up, and reluctantly deposited Joella back onstage. "Not bad," he murmured for her ears only.

Then he returned to his table and the quiet woman watching in wide-eyed awe.

"Wow" was all Amy managed to say.

Well, he'd wanted a quiet woman. Pity this one was taken.

Unfazed by his reaction, Jo waved at her wildly clapping audience, then ignoring the crowd's shout for more, she handed the mike back and slipped from the stage to join Flint and Amy. The spotlight returned, and the band struck up a tune Flint recognized from RJ's repertoire, a disrespectful salute to school rules and young love—a song Joella must have written. He recognized the style.

"Hey, Ames. Where are the kids?" Jo stole a sip of her sister's cold drink.

"Evan had to go to Charlotte for a meeting this weekend, so I left them with Sally for a little bit. I've forgotten what it is to hear adult conversation."

Flint signaled the teenager serving drinks. She produced a cola and set it down in front of Jo, who flashed him a smile more challenging than grateful.

"Well, boss man, how'd I do?"

Was that nervousness he heard in his brash waitress's voice? He couldn't imagine it. She had to know she'd just knocked him out with the power of her voice and talent. She ought to be rubbing his nose in it.

"You need a tune with an extra meter in the chorus, and a faster beat." He tried to play it cool, when his mind was a riot of lyrics, music, and sex. The damned woman had turned him on as if she'd flipped a magic switch. It was frigging unsettling that she had that kind of power over him. "Humor has a rhythm all its own."

"Uh-huh." Her smile lost its high voltage as she sipped her drink. "It's just a few re-arranged words that I put together today. It's not as if I was taking them anywhere."

Today? She'd put all that together in one day? That she took so little pride in her tremendous talent rocked him, but Flint figured it was just a shield of self-depreca-tion. Women had odd habits like that. He stuck to the topic. "I can hear the same style in the material RJ brought me, but a lawyer isn't likely to notice the similarity. What other proof do you have?"

"Everybody knows Jo's songs," Amy protested in puzzlement. "She writes rhymes for our birthdays. That's part of the fun, to see who she'll skewer next." She turned to Jo. "I think the 'Muffin Man' was one of the best things you've ever done."

Jo patted her sister's hand. "I don't need a peacemaker, Mama Warren, but thank you."

"Well, then, I'll let the two of you slug it out. Don't think I haven't heard about the plate fight." Amy waved at someone com-ing in and hurried away.

Joella leaned over the table to sip through the straw, flashing her cleavage under his nose. When she saw the direction of his gaze, she offered a sultry smile. "Want to slug it out or go over in that corner and shimmy?"

Flint crossed his arms on the table and leaned forward so he could growl into her ear. "If we go over in that corner and I shimmy, you'll have to beat off every woman in this room. We wouldn't want that now, would we?"

She laughed. "Okay, you want to slug it out, I got it."

Her laughter stimulated parts that needed no encouragement. "You got it in one," he agreed. Most women wouldn't have understood the reasoning behind his aggressive suggestion. This one had his number without even trying—if they didn't fight, months of abstinence would overrule sanity, and testosterone would do the talking. He was already prepared to write an ode to that skimpy red top she was wearing.

To his relief, she shoved her drink aside and sat up straight so he could fall into the green pools of her eyes instead of her chest. Except those dangly red earrings held him fixated.

"Every person here could sign an affidavit

acknowledging I wrote ditties for the band,"
she announced in her most businesslike
voice. "Slim probably has the original copies
of my scribbling in that trash bin he calls an
apartment. We made a demo a few years
back in Charlotte. How much proof do you
need?"

While he was still pondering kissing her
splendid long throat, she hit him with icy
pragmatism. Flint had the urge to grab his
ears and jerk his head back on straight, but
he attempted to sound functional. "That's a
good start, but a lawyer will ask for proof
that RJ wasn't the author."

Instead of taking him up on the challenge,
she raised a quizzical eyebrow. "How do
you know so much about lawyers?"

That cleared the cloud of lust from his
head. Flint drained his coffee cup and set it
down with a thud that the drum player
drowned out. "Because I've spent these last
few years in more law offices than I ever want
to see in a lifetime, and I'm in no hurry to re-
visit one again. Lawyers have nasty minds."

She raised her color-tinted eyebrows expectantly. When he hesitated over spilling,
she reminded him, "We're partners in this,

remember? If I'm dealing with a crook about to go to jail, I'd like to know it now."

"You don't read the trade papers, do you?" he said with a disgust directed at himself and not her. She backed off warily, but he gestured to erase what he'd said. "Sorry. I thought the entire galaxy knew my story."

She relaxed a fraction. "Maybe the Planet Earth, but you've come to Planet Northfork. We don't even have cable, remember."

"How could I forget? Listen, we can't talk here. How about some other time?" Anything to avoid the issue. Damn, he didn't know if it was cowardice or polite reluctance to spread shit.

"Now's good. Here's not." She stood, and for a moment the spotlight created a white-gold halo of her hair. She gestured at him to follow, then started winding between the tables.

Flint had already deduced that all the movable tables from the shop had been hauled in here in his absence. He wasn't certain where the rest of them had come from. The chairs were mostly the uncomfortable metal, folding kind that the church probably rented out. He hoped he didn't have to clean this up in the morning.

Those thoughts carried him safely through the room so he didn't focus too hard on the rhythmic swing of Joella's fringe over the sway of her hips. She laughed and touched people on the shoulder as she passed by. Flint suffered a mild resentment at watching male faces brighten everywhere her hand lit. With his newfound maturity, he squashed the negativity. No more bad-boy fistfights, he reminded himself. He had to get up in the morning and call the kids, and he didn't want to do it from jail. Joella was her own woman, not his, and he had no reason for jealousy.

To his surprise, she led him out the back door and up the fire escape. Summer thunder rolled in the distance, and the air was thick with humidity as she took a seat on the plank landing and doffed her fringed coat. The clingy red shirt blatantly emphasized her curves, and standing on the stair below her, Flint could see straight down her cleavage.

He eyed the narrow space beside her with misgiving. Sit and avoid staring at her breasts? Or fry in hell smelling her mouthwatering scent without nibbling her nape?

"Did my tenant move out or don't they

mind people using their stairs?" he asked in self-defense. The rent wasn't a lot, but it covered some of his mortgage.

She flashed that taunting smile again, and he had to sit down or fall down.

He'd climbed his way to the top of the musical heap by using all the resources available to him and hanging on by his fingernails when necessary. Miss Joella's smile was a challenge to match any competition he'd faced. He took the seat offered.

"I'll give you my rent check in the morning. Charlie didn't mind waiting until the first weekend of the month after I got paid."

Flint gazed out at the heat lightning playing across the mountain until he fully comprehended this new slap in the face. "*You're* my tenant. If I fire you, you can't pay the rent, and I don't get paid."

Her voice filled with mock admiration. "You are quick, Mr. Clinton. On the other hand, you could also appreciate the convenience in the winter. Charlie stayed home snug and warm while I opened up for the macho men showing off their four-wheel drives."

Flint leaned forward with his forearms on his knees, trying not to get too close to the source of that sultry voice. He wanted to kiss the mockery away and make her purr, but that was one of those wrong turns he'd made the first time around, thinking he could control life with sex, as his counselor had so thoughtfully pointed out. He didn't think Joella was the type who could be controlled. Besides, he had other priorities these days.

"Business is bad in winter?" he asked nonchalantly.

"Once there's a snowpack down, we get the skiers on their way up the mountain, but, yeah, people don't have much reason to vacation here in winter. That's why we've got to find ways to bring in more jobs."

Flint nodded knowledgeably, fighting the growing fear in his gut. He'd known the opportunity had been too good to be true. "I looked at Charlie's books. He seemed to be doing okay." He'd hoped to do better.

"That was last year. The mill laid off half its workforce last Christmas. People living on nothing can't pay a dollar and a half for a cup of coffee. But that's another topic from the one we're out here to discuss. How much trouble are you in, Mr. Big Shot?"

He refused to let her scorn get under his

collar. "None now. The law is done with me, and I'm setting out on a clean slate."

Joella caught a firefly and peered into her fist to admire its flash. Her casual acceptance of his statement reduced the last frustrating, humiliating years to an old song, encouraging him to continue. After today's tirade, he'd feared she would push him down the steps, but she apparently didn't believe in grudges.

"Melinda and I parted a few years back because I gave up trying to make her happy. I'd quit playing on the road when she complained about my traveling, but then she bitched about my songwriting income not being enough to buy the pretty things she liked."

"You don't have to tell me this part, if you don't want." She opened her fist and let the firefly go. "There's a reason I don't sing love songs."

Maybe someday, in his old age, he'd ask her about those reasons. She was a woman meant to be loved—by someone more stable than him.

"Smart girl, but I'm telling you this to explain what happened. We married young and in lust. The music business is lousy for relationships. My divorce lawyer talked her lawyer into taking a lump-sum settlement instead of draining me dry for the rest of my life. I figured I needed to be home for my sons. If I didn't tour, my income would decline. Paying her off from the big money I'd earned touring seemed a fair move to all concerned."

Jo was sorry she'd asked. Flint sounded casual enough, but she heard pain bleeding from every word. She'd known heartache. She could relate. She just didn't want to. But she'd started this, and he seemed to need to talk.

Besides, she was enjoying having the big hunk beside her. If Flint shifted half an inch, their hips would rub. His broad shoulders filled all the space, and she had to turn slightly to avoid bumping elbows. That position gave her a better picture of the way his muscles worked over his taut jaw. Despite his sexy charm, he was one unhappy man.

"You gave up a group like the Barn Boys for your kids?" she asked, pretty much in awe of such a sacrifice. She could see him up on that stage. He *belonged* there. No wonder he was unhappy.

"The money from the albums and touring was real nice, but I was just a backup guitarist. They're a dime a dozen. It's my composing talents that they appreciated."

She was starting to like sharing space with this complex cowboy who was all toughness and pain, even if she had vowed not to have any truck with men these days.

Besides, to prevent upchucking onstage, she hadn't eaten any supper, and the fight had gone out of her. "You figured you could stay home and write songs. That makes sense. So what went wrong?"

Given their closeness, it was kind of hard to miss his shrug. "Turns out I know the music business fine, but I don't understand diddly about people. I'd made a bundle over the years, socked away what Melinda didn't spend, but when I tried to raise the cash, I didn't have any. I had a music manager, a business manager, and a lawyer to keep up with investments and accounting statements. All I ever saw were the big dollars under assets. Turned out there were even bigger dollars called things like 'FICA Payable.' My business manager hadn't paid the Feds in years, and the cash didn't exist.

"I hired auditors and lawyers and sued,

but there's no sucking blood out of turnips. And of course, the IRS came along with their hands out. By the time the Feds were done socking on penalties and interest and whatnot, they wanted triple what I was worth. And I still had to pay off Melinda."

"Wow." Jo tried to imagine the mansions and cars he must have owned, but she couldn't, not any more than she could calculate the sum he'd had to pay. "That doesn't seem fair. If your manager stole the money, they should have got it from him."

"I owed it. I didn't pay it. I neglected my fiscal responsibility. That's how the law works. I had lots of lawyers explain it to me."

"Divorce lawyers, lawsuit lawyers, IRS lawyers." She counted up the woe and hit staggering sums. Just asking Fritz to send a letter to the IRS explaining her tips really were less than 10 percent had kept her in fear of jail for a year.

"And insurance lawyers," he added. "After the divorce, I had to go back on the road to pay my bills. I was getting by on no sleep some nights, operating on empty the rest, and drinking too much. About a year ago, I stupidly borrowed a friend's Harley after a few drinks and crashed it into an ice cream stand. Lucky for everyone concerned, it was closed, but people crawled out of the woodwork to sue me."

Oh, dang, and here she was thinking she'd found a man with a head on his shoulders. That's what happened when she fell into sexy eyes. "With all that going on, when did you have time to write RJ's music?" she asked with just a hint of scorn. She had no sympathies for drunks. She understood the hell they wreaked real well.

"We finished the song collection a couple of years ago, before I hit the road again." He didn't seem to mind her derision, as if he'd already dumped enough of it on his own head and was immune to more. "That collection was the one good thing to come out of that time." He settled into bitter silence.

"What happened to your wife and kids?" she asked, thinking of roaming daddies and abandoned kids. She knew how that felt.

He stared at the heat lightning in the distance without replying immediately. When he finally spoke, his voice was strained. "The night I got drunk? That was the night the cops called to tell me Melinda had died in a car crash. So like an idiot, I went out and did the same. Counselor said it was a form of self-destruction."

Shaken, Jo couldn't think of a thing to say. He'd just admitted to a selfish stupidity worse than anything her father had ever done. Or her mother. Instead of thinking of his kids' devastation, he'd thought only of his own.

A loud crack of thunder accented the pain in Flint's admission as he continued, "I was messed up pretty bad, in the hospital for weeks, in physical therapy for months. My parents had to hire estate lawyers to settle the mess Melinda left with her death. They came up and got the kids and took them home with them while I was in the hospital. I wasn't working, didn't have a home. They've been with my parents ever since. I've given up music and moved here so I can have them back."

I'm not feeling sorry for him, she swore. She'd been hearing some version of this story her entire life. He'd effectively abandoned his kids, just as her father had abandoned her and Amy. Just as He-Who-Should-Rot-in-Hell had deserted her in Atlanta ten years ago and Ratfink Randy had skipped out. One day, Flint would hear

the siren call of music and forget what he'd
said here tonight. She was slowly accepting
these things.

The thunder rolled louder, and Flint
glanced up at a jagged streak of lightning
on the mountain peak.

Jo let the thunder be her reply. The band
down below struck up a slow tune, and the
audience was singing along, probably to
drown out Slim's nasal notes.

"Still trust me to find a lawyer for you?"
Flint asked. His voice was so distant that he
might as well have been standing at the foot
of the mountain.

That he accepted his responsibility in his
fate and hadn't hid his faults were strong
points in his favor. He'd been square with
her. Jo wanted everything in the open between them, so she returned the favor.

"My mama started binge drinking when I
was little. At least she had the sense to
never drive drunk." If he winced over that
acid comment, she couldn't tell.

"My dad abandoned us to tour with some
oldies group that's working Europe these
days," she continued. "My first love was a
lying talent scout who took me to Atlanta
with promises of fame and fortune. I was

eighteen. When we got there, he signed me up at a strip bar. I learned waitressing to earn the bus fare home."

She didn't bother repeating the whole humiliating scene that still had the power to wake her up, shrieking, in the middle of the night. She had pinned all her teenage hopes on becoming a singer like her father, of earning the fortune that would make her mother happy again. She'd won a regional beauty contest with one of her songs. He-Who had promised her a recording contract. She'd had huge stars in her eyes when he'd bought her a glitzy costume and taken her to a nightclub for her first paid performance.

And then she had stepped onto a real stage, in front of an all-male audience so shit-faced at that hour they'd instantly started screaming at her to take it all off. They'd been too busy crawling up onstage to grab her breasts and crotch to hear a note she sang—not that she'd managed more than a whimper before trying to run. He-Who had blocked the exit. After the crowd had torn off her meager costume, she'd really believed they would strip off a piece of her hide next. Eighteen and ignorant, nearly naked, she'd collapsed in hysterics right there in the spotlight and spewed out her guts on the club manager, who'd hauled her to her feet. The audience had roared with laughter and rage.

She'd been thrown out on the street, broke and friendless, to make her own way home.

Everyone in town knew the story, so she didn't have much to hide. She just figured she owed Flint after he'd bared his soul to her.

"Jeez," he muttered. Leaning his hands on the landing behind them, he stared out at the light display. "No wonder you told me to go to hell."

"I was politer than that," she reminded him.

"The first time. Today, you tried to kill me."

She laughed a little. "Yeah, maybe I did at that."

He chuckled, a pleasant sound from deep in his chest. "I think we may have the first partnership based on complete and total distrust."

She laughed out loud as she realized he probably was right.

❈NINE❈

"How'd the game go last night? . . . You won? That's great."

Jo tried not to listen in on Flint's strained conversation with his sons on Saturday morning, but he was pacing behind the counter with his cell phone, talking loudly in nervousness. He seemed to have a strange notion that he was being helpful through the morning rush hour by staying out here instead of holing up in his office.

She needed to summon more antipathy for a man who'd deserted his kids when they'd needed him, but he was trying so determinedly to win them back that he was breaking her feeble heart.

"Who's he talking to?" Sally asked as Jo poured her a second cup of decaf. Her soft cow eyes were pools of sympathy. "He looks miserable."

"Apparently that's what kids do to you." Jo poured another cup for Amy at the same table. "Did Josh and Louisa get to see their dad this morning or did Evan have to go in to work?" Jo had always thought her sister had a real marriage, but lately, her new-found cynicism had been kicking in where her brother-in-law was concerned.

Amy poured sugar into her coffee and shrugged. "They're trying to get the samples out before the show. You know how it is."

"You know I'll babysit anytime you want to go in and help him out." Jo did her best not to show her skeptical side to Amy. She'd just remove Evan's balls if he hurt her sister. Despite her petite size, Amy had been the bulwark who had shielded Jo throughout their dysfunctional childhood. Amy deserved fairy-tale happiness.

"Next week?" Flint shouted, unaware of all ears in the place turned in his direction. "Yeah, sure, that's fine."

"He doesn't look fine," Jo observed, watching her macho boss run his hand over his thick hair, tousling it nicely. "You'd better run to his rescue, Sally. Something tells me

he's gonna need help with a couple of hel-
lions."

"Oh, no, I couldn't do that," Sally whispered. "That would be too forward. Maybe
he could bring them to Sunday school."

Jo snorted. "Want to bet they're chips off
the old block? I don't think Sunday school
will hold them."

"Hey, Jo, where's my doughnut?" a customer at the counter called.

"I keep it right next to my heart, Hoss."
She sashayed over to the big man and
leaned over his shoulder to fill his cup. "You
really want me to go back there to get stam-
peded for a doughnut?" She shot a look at
Flint, who had thrown his cell phone on the
stove but still stalked back and forth looking
like last night's storm.

She'd invited him into her apartment last
night when the clouds had opened. Instead
of coming in, Flint had sat there with the rain
pelting his broad shoulders, staring at the
thunderbolts crossing the sky. "What's that
old church song?" he'd asked as she'd
taken refuge behind the screen door. " 'I got
to walk that lonesome valley all by myself'?"

She'd almost wept as he'd walked down
the stairs in the pouring rain looking as mis-

erable as a man could be. If she wasn't so immune to men these days, she'd have run after him, thrown her arms around him, and dragged him back to her bed.

That would have been disaster for both of them.

She knew the solution to misery, though. Unable to tolerate his restless pacing a second longer, Jo walked around the counter and shoved a spatula at him. "Number one wants scrambled eggs. Henry will want more toast in a minute. I'm taking a girl break."

She left him standing there with his hands full and his mouth open as she ran back to the restroom. Flint wasn't the only one who couldn't sit still. She'd scarcely slept a wink last night. She was just about to bust out of her skin in anticipation and anxiety thinking of Randy and her stolen songs. It was time to apply both their excess energies to something useful. Pity it was Saturday and they couldn't call lawyers.

Behind closed doors, she pulled her cell phone out of her pocket and punched up a number. "Hey, Dave? This is Jo. You still have that paint on sale?"

At his affirmative, she took a deep breath. "How much longer?"

"Until you talk your boss into remodeling?" he guessed.

Dave's recognition of her ability to talk anyone into anything lifted her spirits. She did have a knack for doing what was best for people, if they'd just let her meddle a little. Flint might be a bit more difficult than most, but she needed a challenge.

With something more productive to do than worry about lying, cheating scoundrels and sexy, hurting hunks, Jo returned to the café with a big grin.

"What?" Flint asked with suspicion at seeing her expression. He handed the spatula back to her and reached for the coffee beans.

"What what?" She flapped her lashes and scooped eggs on a plate. "I didn't say anything."

"Watch it when she gets that shit-eater grin on her face," George Bob warned from the counter. "We got stuck with the pigs last time she looked like that."

"Do I need to tie her down and stuff her in a closet until she gets over it?" Flint asked in a surly tone, although the corner of his mouth curled in a hint of a grin.

"The women would go looking for her," Hoss said. "The trouble with this town is that the women run it. I don't know when we let them get so out of hand."

"When you started keeping your brains in your jeans," Jo retorted. "Those pigs are *good* for the town. We've already had a re- porter up here from Charlotte to see them. Once that story gets out, we'll have lots of people up here, spending money."

With a fresh batch of coffee cooking, Flint slid a plate of toast to Hoss, glanced around to see that all his other customers had been served, then leaned his hip against the counter and crossed his arms. "People will come up here just to see purple pigs?"

Jo hurriedly refilled more cups rather than admire her boss's muscled biceps in his short-sleeved shirt. Even when he was look- ing at her with suspicion, her heart per- formed a drum solo. She needed to get laid real bad if she was contemplating, even for a moment, a volatile man like Flynn Clinton. He was way over her simple head.

"Some of those pigs were painted by fa- mous artists. We have more talent up here in these hills than just country bumpkins, you realize. Present company excluded of course. George Bob and Hoss are bump-kins." She slid them each a doughnut as she said it. She'd traded insults with these guys since grade school.

"Yeah, well, I don't see any pigs in an art gallery, and I don't see rich tourists coming up here to admire any," Flint challenged her with logic instead of insults.

"Negativity," she admonished, flashing him a high-voltage smile that knocked some of his attitude askew. She liked how all his muscles tightened when he was forced to look her way. "With that mind-set, it's a wonder you ever get a girl."

"It doesn't take a mind to get a girl," he growled.

She had his number now. He put on the grouchy bear act to make her back off. She winked, and he had to wipe his grin away with the back of his hand.

"Maybe not," she countered, "but it takes a mind to get a woman." Now that the sub-ject was safely off her, Joella redirected it. "Are your kids coming up to visit?" She re-turned to buttering toast.

"Yeah, only because my parents promised to take them rock climbing. Know any good rocks?"

"If they ain't ever been climbing, better take them down to Chimney Rock," Hoss advised, standing up with his doughnut-to-go and leaving his money on the counter. "If they want white-water rafting, I'm your boy. Just give me a call."

"I'll do that, thanks." Flint put the bills in the register and Jo's tip in her jar. "Chimney Rock will be busy on a weekend, won't it?"

"Yup, but Hoss is right. Unless they know what they're doing, rock climbing is hazardous, and the rescue squad has started charging to save idiots." Seizing her opportunity, Jo offered him a seductive smile. "What will you trade me if I find your kids a bona fide rock-climbing expert to show them the ropes?"

"Trade?" he asked with a lift of his eyebrows that did wonders for her pulse rate.

"Yeah. What are your kids worth to you? A new paint job in here, maybe?"

Flint studied Jo's saucy grin and wished he were a mind reader. He was damn glad she covered her front with that ugly apron because just watching her from behind all morning had burned out his last brain cell.

She had on a little blue, knit halter top and white short shorts beneath that thing, and even with his eyes closed, all he could see were long, shapely brown legs.

How much were his kids worth? He'd trade the whole café for them, but he didn't need to give Joella that bargaining chip. "I reckon I can find a rock climber on my own," he said confidently.

He'd learned enough about his waitress this past week to figure she could find the best climber in the mountains faster than he could drum up a rank amateur, but he didn't want to make this too easy. She already had him over a barrel, and he wasn't liking the position.

"Reckon you might," she agreed. "But he's likely to be busy on weekends unless you ask him right."

"And you know the right way to ask?" Flint was aware that half the coffee shop was listening, and he was wondering why in hell he'd thought it would be a good idea to operate gossip central.

"Just give her the paint job," George Bob urged, pulling out his billfold. "Jo knows every man on this mountain and each of their weak spots. Everyone knows if you want something done, Jo knows how to do it."

She blinked demurely, but watching her out of the corner of his eye, Flint could see that big grin she'd worn earlier. He hadn't just bought gossip central. He'd acquired the local database, troublemaker, and sex goddess along with it.

And he couldn't fire her. He'd have to learn to work with temptation so she wouldn't sue him. He'd remembered that saint's name last night. Job. Except Job wasn't a saint either, just a poor beleaguered businessman that God decided to pick on. Like him.

"What color and how much?" he asked grumpily, to keep her from being too sure of herself.

"Yellow and purple and all of it," she said so promptly that he knew she'd been planning this for a long time.

"Tan and brown and only the two walls by the booths," he countered. He couldn't remember why he'd thought mud ugly was so wonderful as a kid, but he'd be damned if he'd paint his shop *yellow.*

"Oh, ugh, why don't you just paint it with sludge? How about the color of the pretty persimmon and sunflower plates?" She pulled the dishes out to show him.

"You want to turn this into a tea shop?" Flint shouted. Since the whole place was listening by now, he might as well get his point across. He wasn't turning into his daddy and becoming a rug under any woman's feet.

"How about a creamy white for the wainscoting, and Jo could put up rose curtains?" one of the women suggested.

Wainscoting? What in hell was that? Sounded like something that went in castles.

"How about we leave it just the way it is?" a disgruntled male customer asked. "If this was good enough for our daddies, it's good enough for us."

Flint almost agreed to yellow and purple after that. He had the sudden urge to offer his kids something *better* than his daddy had.

He studied the battered brown paneling—wainscoting?—and beige walls with faded sepia photographs from the 1950s that had rested so fondly in his memory. His tastes must have matured a lot since childhood. Everything in here was mud brown, except the pink and gray tables and chairs. Even the floor was brown. He *liked* brown, but he could see where the joint could use a little updating.

"I don't want to have to wash walls every night," he told his audience, although he directed the protest at Jo.

"Stainless steel equipment, pewter paneling, and eggplant walls," she threw back.

"Eggplant?" he asked in outrage. "What kind of color is that? And pewter paneling? That's just plain crazy. Did you grow up in a circus?"

"Pretty much," she agreed brightly. "And they have pewter-colored paneling down at the supply house. It's supposed to go in kitchens with stainless steel."

"Eggplant's too dark," a woman argued. "Use the turquoise from the Fiestaware. That will fit in with your fifties pink."

"I can't afford stainless steel appliances!" Flint objected.

"Not yet," Jo agreed, "but when we start bringing in more money, you'll be all fixed up and ready for them."

Now he knew how a snowball felt rolling down a mountainside in a blizzard.

"If you're a member of the Chamber, you

can get a discount at the supply store on the paneling," someone called.

Suggestions flew after that, but Flint had pretty much tired of decorating. He glared at Jo. He just about believed her claim to have grown up in a circus. She was a performer par none, and she belonged on the stage. She flirted him another mind-melting grin that made him want to back her up against the stove and kiss the smirk off her face.

But he was already picturing stainless steel in here. A dishwasher that didn't maim his feet. A place his boys could be proud of. One that would make money—

"New paneling, and blue paint," he agreed with a feeling that he'd just been manipulated. "And you'll call the rock-climber teacher?"

"You got it, boss man." Returning to impale an order on the spike by the grill, Jo stood on the toes of her athletic shoes and pressed a kiss to his cheek. Her lips seared a brand he'd carry all day. He nearly passed out from the testosterone overload from her magnolia scent. "Are you calling that lawyer of yours on Monday, partner?" she purred.

"First thing," he agreed grimly. He could

survive one more lawyer. He wasn't certain he could survive another of Jo's steamy kisses. His jeans had grown too tight to walk in. How in *hell* could he work beside this country Madonna for the rest of his life without wanting to get into her pants?

Monday afternoon, Jo pulled the blind down on the door and set the CLOSED sign in the window with a sigh of relief. The weekend had been more hectic than usual. She'd like to believe it was the *Observer* article on the pigs, but school was out.

"I think every kid in town came by to pat Myrtle." She shoved a loose strand of hair behind her ear and began to stack the chairs on the tables.

Standing at the register counting out the deposit, Flint looked gloomy. "Yeah, and to fill up chairs at a buck apiece for soft drinks. I'm working my ass off for dollar bills."

"Hate to tell you this, honey, but next weekend you really will be working your ass off. I worked this weekend because the shop was closed Monday and Tuesday. But there are laws against me working eight hours a day, seven days a week, without overtime. So I hope you weren't planning on rock climbing with the kids."

Alarm replaced the gloom as Flint glanced up. "I was. And to church. That's the whole point of having them here."

"You didn't plan this out real well, did you? I can take off tomorrow and Wednesday and come in this weekend, if you want, but I usually take the nursery at church on Sundays. Charlie liked working weekends."

He shoved the cash in the bank bag and came over to help her swing chairs onto tables. "I'm not Charlie. I'm gonna have to hire help."

"You can't afford help at a dollar a seat." She was good at grasping what was eating at people. "Charlie had this place paid for, but you've got to make payments. What happens to you if I sue Randy?"

"I'll call my lawyer and sound him out when we're done here, but I think you have to sue me, too," he said in resignation.

"Well, that ought to make things real pleasant." She strode back to the closet to get out the mop and bucket. "Why don't you go call him now while I clean up? Let's find out how much shit we're in before we start cutting each other's throats."

"We?" he asked with a lift of his eyebrow. "Looks to me like I'm the one wading deep and getting deeper."

"There's a silver lining in every cloud and a rainbow after every storm," she sang as she filled the bucket with soapy water.

Giving her a look of disgruntlement, Flint stalked off to his office. Jo crossed her fingers behind her back.

She wanted to admire her boss's honesty in admitting that she'd been done wrong and helping her to correct it, but if she had to admire Flint's character as well as his bootie—she'd have to think twice about suing him.

She hadn't seen many silver linings in her twenty-eight years. With her luck, she'd lose her job, earn Flint's animosity, and have to go bankrupt paying legal fees after Randy won the lawsuit.

But damned if she would let Randy get away with theft, if she had to personally carve out his tonsils and sell them on eBay.

❧❦TEN❦❧

"Yeah, yeah, I got that. If one of your clients wants to sue another of your clients, he needs a different lawyer. My friend can handle that," Flint said as heartily as he could. He hadn't wanted to play his hand out until he had the facts. No point in warning RJ what was coming down—as soon as Flint found a new lawyer.

He really didn't want to go down the lawsuit road again. Maybe he ought to let Jo go after RJ with that butcher knife she talked about. Life would be simpler.

But he couldn't live with himself knowing he'd co-wrote songs with a thief who would rob a talented new writer like Jo. He'd earned his money with years of hard work. He wasn't letting a lazy cheat turn the one good thing in his life into a lie while hurting innocents, if one could call a sex goddess innocent.

He'd have to start calling old friends to find another lawyer.

He could hear Jo singing "Amazing Grace" in the other room as she knocked tables around with her mop. Damn, but she was good. She could bring an audience to tears with her voice. Her soaring notes gave him goose bumps all up and down his arms.

She could have a huge career ahead of her if he could clear up RJ's theft. Maybe if he did the right thing, Jo would forgive him enough not to wipe out everything he owned.

He flipped through his address book and found another number to call. His long-distance bills would exceed his income at this rate.

He was still on the phone when Jo appeared in his doorway, her hair tumbling to her shoulders and her cheeks pink with the heat of exertion. She pointed upstairs to her apartment and left before he got his eyeballs back in his head.

Once he had all the information he could obtain over the phone, Flint delayed taking it upstairs to Joella. He'd spilled his guts to her up there, and he wasn't eager to return to the scene of the crime. She had a way of listening that made a man much too comfortable.

He locked up and took the deposit to the bank and debated calling Jo from home so he didn't have to look into her big green eyes and watch her flap those flirty lashes. But that was the coward's way out.

Greeting a few of his regular customers on the street, Flint strode back to the shop. He knew he'd done the right thing to return to Northfork for his sons. He liked the small-town atmosphere. He just needed to get the two-ton weight of RJ's perfidy off his back so he could enjoy life again.

The purple pig with the upturned snout grinned at him as he passed by. In his free-wheelin' days, he would have set the pig on its haunches and put a guitar between its hooves so it would look just like some of the hogs he knew back in Nashville. But he was making an effort to be a sensible business-man these days.

Jo opened the screen door for him before he reached the top of the stairs. Flint could see the anxiousness in her eyes that her smile couldn't conceal.

"Mary Jean can't work yet because of the baby," she told him without preliminaries. "Her sister Peggy can come in some, but she's not real reliable," Jo warned. "You saw her at the gig on Friday night. I have a couple more calls out. People need jobs around here, so it's just a matter of finding someone you can count on to hold down the fort on weekends."

Unable to halt her torrent of information, Flint stepped inside at her gesture and fell into a different world than he'd expected.

She had converted the upper story of his rotten old building into a spacious loft apartment with light pouring in a two-story, double row of windows that exposed a view of the mountain. Sunbeams danced off spirals of color hanging from the rafters in the slanted ceiling. In the breeze from her open door, whirligigs spun, butterflies soared, and crystal prisms caught the sun and reflected bouncing rainbows.

"Did you get the fire department out here to hang them?" he asked in disbelief, risking a crick in his neck to gaze upward.

"Scaffolding," she said. "Slim's an electrician with a construction company. Have a

seat and tell me what you found out. Would
you like anything to drink?"

"No, I'm fine." Bringing his gaze down to
earth, he studied the explosion of color that
was her living space. The wine-purple sofa
didn't surprise him any. He winced at the
orange-brown side chair, but it seemed to
work okay with the loosely woven rug that
could have been made of the plates she'd
broken the other day, the colors were so nu-
merous. Even the walls seemed to glow
with warm gold.

Accustomed to his sterile modern home
in Nashville or the run-down apartment he'd
retreated to after the separation, Flint felt as
if he'd just walked into Disney World. He
took the orange chair gingerly, fearing the
winged arms would fall off. The chair had to
be a thousand years old, but she must have
had the cushions restrung. It sat fine. He
sprawled his legs across the waxed floor
and watched as Jo poured herself some tea
from the galley kitchen on the far side of the
open space.

His gaze found the half wall that probably
hid her bath. A ladder led to a loft above it,
but he couldn't see if it contained her bed.

Everywhere he looked he saw sheet music, amplifiers, and music stands. A rugged-looking guitar and piano occupied one corner. He'd run away from music only to land in a nest of musicians. Figured, that was the way his life worked.

"You hold auditions up here?" he asked as Joella curled up on the couch with her iced tea, tucking those long, tanned legs beneath her. He sucked in a deep breath as his wicked mind took a journey down the road where those legs led.

She'd apparently taken time to clean up a little. Her hair was back in its pins and pony-tail, and without the bib apron, her golf shirt exposed the brown column of her throat. And more. But he was trying not to look there. He was trying to remember she was a talented woman who'd been badly cheated.

She shrugged and looked around. "The guys used to hang out at Randy's place, but since he took off, they've been leaving things here."

"You don't care?" he asked in amazement. "Melinda used to pitch fits when I left my stuff laying around, and we had a lot more space than this."

"Space is for living in. What else would I do with it? Dust?"

He thought of his mother's pristine décor with everything in its place, and the expensive homes he'd been in throughout his life, and decided she was right. They were pretty pictures no one ever lived in.

As a matter of fact, except for all the colors, her place felt like his log cabin, spacious and welcoming. He relaxed his shoulders, and this time the breath he took was one of acceptance. Their goals differed, but they stood on common ground.

"I've called the best lawyers in Nashville," he told her. "You can't use mine because he wrote the contract and has to defend me and RJ. Most I talked to are in bed with the record companies and aren't interested in suing their cash cows."

She sat forward, her eyes shining. Flint really couldn't resist looking down her shirt. He shifted uncomfortably and sought his lost train of thought.

"But you found somebody, didn't you?" she urged him on.

"Yeah, yeah, I did. I found one in Knoxville who specializes in contract law. His name is E. D. DuBois, but I didn't get a chance to talk with him. His assistant seemed to think he'd be interested in visiting Northfork to gather your evidence rather than you going up there, so I made an appointment for him to meet with you on Thursday."

She set her glass on a low table that looked as if it had been made of broken dishes. Except, when he looked, the colors formed a mosaic of a flame azalea.

"Maybe you better tell me what's going to happen," she said quietly.

"Maybe I'd better let the lawyer explain. What I do know is that he'll either ask for a hefty amount of money up front, or if he's confident you have a case, he'll ask for something like half of everything you win. So we're not talking a path to riches here."

"I'd be just as happy slicing Randy into a baloney sandwich," she asserted.

"Well, this is how you do it without getting arrested." Because he couldn't resist following how her mind worked, he asked, "What will you do if you win real money—buy Manolos and Jimmy Choos?"

"Jimmy—to pry open; chew—to masticate . . . Nope, doesn't sound like anything I'd buy." She held up a slender bare foot with hot-pink toenails, showing she knew what he was talking about but was playing ignorant. "I've a hankering for some of those glittery, strapped ankle-breakers if you'll just take out the counter so everyone can admire my toes. Reckon I could win enough to put in a see-through counter?"

Flint couldn't help grinning at the image of Joella tripping around behind a glass counter on high heels. "You'd knock 'em dead, Cinderella, but I don't recommend dancing in them."

"I'm not messing with any more pumpkin coaches," she agreed obscurely, returning her toes to the coffee table. "And someone else can have Prince Charming. Just show me the money."

Flint stood up before he got too comfortable and started enjoying her silliness. Or those long, tanned legs. "Take tomorrow and the next day off, if you can work this weekend. I've gotta go buy some paint."

She ripped a page off a notepad beside the phone and handed it to him. "Here's your rock climber. Jimbo is great with kids. It'll cost you for a private climb, but if you don't mind going with a pack of others, the price isn't bad. Give him a call."

Despite the fact that she'd talked him into changing what he didn't want to change, Flint accepted the number with gratitude.

"Thanks, Cinderella. May the bluebirds of happiness fly up your nose."

Her laughter carried him out the door on lighter feet than he had coming in.

"Are you sure your lawyer is coming? I go up to Mama's and look after the kids on Thursday nights, and I'll need to leave soon." From the top of her stepladder, Jo aimed another nail into the molding she was installing along the café's ceiling.

"Your mother has kids?" Flint asked, pounding the last piece of paneling into the wall beneath the big plate-glass window.

The café had been closed for nearly an hour. Jo sat back to admire the work they'd completed in the afternoons over the last few days. "Amy's kids," she explained. "Mama's sick, and Amy won't leave them alone with her, so I get in my visits with the kids and Mom at the same time. Kind of takes off some of the pressure. Are we putting up shelves for the plates or hanging those ugly photographs again?"

"Will you quit doing that?" He sat back on his heels and glared up at her. "My tired brain can take only one topic at a time. What pressure?"

She replayed her words inside her head and grinned when she reached the offending passage. "I didn't want to be accused of information overload again. My mama nags. Doesn't yours?"

"And then some. Will you stop swinging that hammer before you fall off? You've got paint on your nose. That molding must still be wet."

She laughed. "I bet you sound just like your mother. Will I get to meet her this weekend?"

"Over my dead body. If I fall off the rocks, you can come to the funeral. Get down from there. You're making me nervous."

He didn't look nervous. He looked like six feet of scrumptious irritated male, and she was enjoying irritating him entirely too much.

He was as jumpy about this lawyer as she was and hiding it far worse. "You're covered in sawdust and you've ripped the seam of your shirt," she informed him as she started down the twelve-foot ladder with a can of wood filler in her hand. "Do we assume your lawyer isn't coming and get dirtier, or stop now and clean up?"

Tall, dark, and dirty halted at the foot of

the ladder, and she swung her butt just to give him a good view.

"I told you, he's coming. It's not four yet. I—"

Whatever he was about to say got lost as the café door unexpectedly swung open with a crash. In startlement, Jo lost her balance. The can of filler flew from her hand, and she slipped backward.

With the impetus of her fall, the ladder crashed across the pink and chrome tables, taking the hammer and nails with it. Before she hit the floor, strong arms grabbed her from thin air, then cuddled her against a broad chest that thumped as erratically as hers. Gasping, not wanting to contemplate the unexpected thrill of pressing her nose into the curly thatch of hair above his shirt collar, Jo grabbed his neck and peered around him to the entrance.

A stunning, ebony-haired, model-tall woman in summer white linen stood there, studying them skeptically. "Flynn Clinton and Joella Sanderson, I assume? Or did I walk in on an *I Love Lucy* episode?"

"It was not my fault," Joella hissed as they left the lawyer sipping unsweetened tea and reading Flynn's publishing contract while they cleaned up in the café's only rest-room. "I thought you said she was a he."

"You fell," he growled back. "And I thought E.D. was a man's name."

Jo scrubbed wood filler off her nose with a paper towel while Flint washed his hands. His masculine proximity in the confined space of the restroom certainly didn't settle her already overstimulated nerves. When he stepped back to dry his hands, he brushed against her. And when she took her turn at the basin, his wide shoulders filled the mir-ror. She wasn't wearing heels, and he topped her five foot six by a head, half of it probably that lovely chocolate hair she'd like to dip her hands into.

He had long-fingered, guitar-playing hands. She'd noticed the thin, white scar across the left one from the Harley accident, but it only added to their character. She'd bet his nails used to be manicured, but this past week of scrubbing the grill had tattered the quicks.

Earlier, Flint's arms had held her so se-curely, she'd hated being set down. He'd staggered beneath the suddenness of her fall, but he hadn't dropped her. In fact, he'd

held her a little too long while they both
caught their breath. She ought to blame that
on surprise, but she needed the ego boost
of thinking maybe he hadn't wanted to let
her go.

Thinking like that was dangerous, but oh
so tempting. . . .

"I'm hauling that ladder back wherever it
came from and hiring a painter," he muttered, interrupting her fantasy. "I don't think
workmen's comp covers a waitress on lad-
ders."

"Where did you find her?" she whispered,
letting his grumpiness return her to the real
world. "She looks like Diana Rigg without
the jumpsuit."

"Who's Diana Rigg?"

"Never mind. I get my role models from
old TV shows. Is she for real?"

"She'd damned well better be if I'm hiring
a woman. E. D. DuBois, my ass. I'll slam the
sucker who gave me that name. Leave your
hair alone and hurry up. It looks fine."

"You like the Dolly Parton look?" she
asked derisively, hunting for the pins.

"I like Dolly real fine. Now c'mon. Out of
here." Flint put a hand on the small of her
back and pushed her toward the door.

As fine as that hand felt, she wasn't being pushed anywhere. "You know Dolly?" she asked, stalling. He ignored the question and shut the door after them. "What if she laughs? Will she charge us for coming here and laughing?"

"She doesn't get paid if she doesn't take the case. Move it."

She scampered out of his way before he could smack her rear, and she would be compelled to take him out. RJ used to do that. She wasn't going anywhere she didn't want to go these days. Fortunately for Flint, she wanted to return to the dining room.

"Ms. DuBois, forgive the delay," she said, entering the café. "We lost track of time."

The movie-star lawyer rose gracefully from the counter stool and held out her hand to shake Jo's. "Ms. Sanderson. Mr. Clinton said some fine things about your work. It's a pleasure to meet you."

Jo bit back a surprised *He did?* and backed up against the counter so Flint could step forward. E. D. DuBois was tall and carried off her height with impeccable elegance. Jo hadn't run across too many sophisticated women, and she was a little giddy at being addressed like someone of importance by one.

She fought the urge to put on her apron and take the lawyer's order. She was a *client* now, not a waitress. "You come highly recommended, Ms. DuBois," Flint said smoothly, as if he hadn't been knocked reeling at realizing he'd hired a woman. "Would you rather take a booth? As you can see, the place is under renovation and my office won't hold us."

"I'm fine right here." She settled at the counter where she'd spread out the contract and a legal pad. "My mother was arrested at a sit-in at a counter like this back in the sixties. I like making myself at home where her clients weren't wanted."

Joella laughed and refilled the lawyer's glass of unsweetened tea. "I like you already, Ms. DuBois. I get that feeling every time I step into one of those expensive boutiques in the city. I can't afford them any more than my mama could, but I like making them think I can."

"Please, call me Elise. Are you by any chance any relation to Carl Sanderson, the singer? I understand he's from North Carolina."

"My daddy's name is Carl. He sings over in Europe, but I can't imagine anyone our age has heard of him." Jo had never really known her dad as more than a story her mother used to tell. Seventies rock singers led wild lives, and she was the product of one of them. "Why do you ask?"

"Because my mother is a fan of classic rock, and your father rivaled Eric Clapton in his day. If you're his daughter, you come by your talent naturally."

That wasn't anything her mother hadn't already said, in the same breath that she dismissed the music business as a pipe dream and scorned Jo for following it instead of getting an education. Knowing that the lawyer recognized the name of the man who'd abandoned his family stirred no interest. Jo had more immediate concerns. "Tell me I can cut Randy's throat, and I'm listening."

Elise tapped the contract against the table and looked her in the eye. "Since RJ and Flint filed the copyright on these songs, you do realize that it's not a matter of them proving their innocence, but of you proving they lied about ownership?"

Jo hadn't realized any such thing. Flint

had told her she needed proof the songs were hers, but proving Randy lied? Another hurdle she couldn't jump. She nodded anyway.

"Well, if I understand what you have here, Ms. Sanderson"—Elise waved the contract—"with that proof, you'll be able to *buy* one of those expensive boutiques when we're done."

The lawyer turned on the stool and looked at Flint. "And since you share the copyright, you'd better have a good lawyer to save your ass."

❧ELEVEN❧

As his father's white Expedition rolled up the gravel drive to his cabin on Saturday morning, Flint tried to swallow the lump of fear in his throat. Although the terror of still another lawsuit haunted his nightmares, his heart was elsewhere right now. Money was nothing if he couldn't have his kids. Melinda had ruled their lives when he'd been on the road trying to earn a living. And she'd resented any interference in their upbringing when he was at home. For the sake of peace, he'd neglected them most of their lives.

That had to change.

The SUV parked next to his Chevy extended cab. Flint's sports cars had gone at auction. He'd bought the used Chevy with his advance on RJ's contract, thinking he needed something sturdy for the mountains and something safe for his boys.

Although looking at them standing beside his parents' vehicle, Flint couldn't believe they'd fit the truck in another year. How had they grown from cheerful toddlers willing to tumble around the living room with him to these tall, sullen preteens who wouldn't come near him unless they had their grandparents in tow?

He walked out on the porch to greet them. He'd wanted to look respectable, but if he was taking them rock climbing, he couldn't drag out the designer duds. He'd changed more often than a nervous girl on her first date, only to settle on his usual jeans. Nothing would impress his sons if this adventure included ropes he couldn't grip.

"Hey, Adam, John, how'dya like that highway coming up?" he called.

"They played Nintendo all the way up and didn't see a damned thing." Clint's father stepped up first, holding out his hand. "How are you, Son?"

Floyd Clinton had aged considerably since the mild heart attack he'd suffered last winter. His father had never been as tall as his sons, but he seemed to have shrunk even more lately. Flint crushed his hand and noticed the lack of strength in his father's grip. Flint feared his problems had added to his parent's anxieties, and guilt gnawed at him.

"Doin' good, Dad. Coming with us this afternoon?"

Floyd chuckled. "Not likely. Got a beer and a TV? There's a tournament today."

"Now, Floyd." Garbed in an impeccable watermelon-colored pants suit with matching sandals and scarf on her straw hat, Martha Clinton traversed the flagstone walk carrying a straw bag overflowing with refrigerator containers. "You know you need exercise. We'll stroll around town and catch up with old times this afternoon."

Flint tried to keep his attention on his parents, but he could scarcely tear his gaze from his sons. They were growing tall and weedy the way he had at that age. Adam was getting acne. Flint remembered the painful shyness he'd suffered learning a new school and a new body at the same time. His heart ached in sympathy.

And then there was Johnnie. The boy took after Melinda's family, plump and on the short side. He'd just started wearing glasses and resented them. The friendly little puppy had turned into a taciturn Goth since Melinda's death.

"New earring, John?" Flint asked as his mother's nattering retreated to a low hum. He stepped down to clap both boys on the shoulders and urge them toward the house.

"Yeah." John almost brightened at his noticing, then remembered his cool and shrugged. "Took yours out," he commented flatly, glancing at Flint's ear.

"It was a diamond. I sold it." Cheerfully, he ushered his family into the big open front room. "Come in, wind down, I'll show you your rooms."

"Oh, we can't stay the night," his mother hastily corrected. "We have church tomorrow, and I promised to fix a casserole for the church supper."

"We have churches up here," Flint said, gritting his teeth to stay smiling. "Looks as if you have enough casseroles in that bag to feed an army. Let's play it by ear, shall we?"

Watching the slumped shoulders of his sons as they trailed upstairs to the bedroom he'd prepared for them, Flint fought stage fright and wished today could be as easy as walking into a spotlight with his guitar.

He fully intended to expend as much energy on his kids as he once had on his career. He may have given up on Melinda, music, and the band, but he wouldn't give up on his sons.

Joella looked up the instant Flint walked through the Stardust's door. She could feel the vibrations of a storm rumbling in advance of his entrance.

She'd come to know him so well this past week and a half that she could even hear the thunder behind the glint in his eyes as he introduced his family. He was on the verge of explosion. Or implosion. Her boss tended to keep things all bottled up.

Like the other night, after the lawyer had left. She'd thought the walls would disintegrate from the force of his fury. But Flint had kept it so controlled she'd been afraid to laugh and tell him she couldn't produce the kind of evidence lawyers needed.

His money was safe from her, although it sure was fun taking a ride on the fast-talking lady's dream train. Just taking Randy down would be worth every penny of the lawyer's fee. Jo had spent the night chewing on ways to produce evidence and still hadn't a clue. Scribbled envelopes weren't proof.

"My heavens," she exclaimed, reaching to shake Flint's parents' hands. But her gaze went past the adults to the boys. "You guys are the spittin' image of your dad. I better keep you away from the girls at church. We won't get any prayin' done."

They shuffled their feet, reddened, and sent her surreptitious looks. She remembered that awkward age—not hers, but the boys in her class who hadn't matured as quickly as she had. She shot Flint a laughing glance, but he was too wired to notice. The man needed someone to run a little interference for him.

"Why don't y'all find a table, and I'll serve up some of this fine soup Flint is thinking about adding to the menu."

Actually, she'd thrown it together this morning in anticipation of a moment like this. Their usual lunch fare was hamburgers and grilled cheese. From the way Flint had described his yuppie parents, she didn't think they'd appreciate grease.

"Oh, I brought my vegetable soup and

broccoli casserole for lunch," Martha Clinton said. "We just wanted to see where Flint works."

Flint's mother wasn't admiring the newly painted blue-green walls or gray paneling as she said it. She was studying Joella with undisguised suspicion.

"Well, I can't give y'all doughnuts until you've eaten. So sit right down and have a bite." Jo pointed out a booth she'd saved with a *Reserved* sign just like in a fancy restaurant.

"Johnnie is on a diet and can't have doughnuts," Mrs. Clinton was saying as Jo led them to the table, while the plump kid whined, "Aw, Nana, I can, too."

All right, she saw how this family worked. Jo winked at Flint. "Why don't you show your boys the back room while I take care of things out here?"

A slow grin creased the sides of his angular face as he glanced over their lunchtime audience to his kids, who were looking around with curiosity instead of following their grandparents.

The Buzzards had played last night. Flint had told them to leave the equipment as long as the tables got moved back. If his sons were like the teenagers she knew, Jo figured they'd be far more interested in drums than grandparents.

"I owe you one," he murmured, grabbing the opportunity to steer his sons from the room like a proper dad.

Jo juggled Mrs. Clinton's protests, the grill, and the lunch crowd's curiosity as if she were hostessing a backyard barbecue. After she whispered the identity of Flint's parents to several regulars, recognition set in, and a steady line of locals stopped to reintroduce themselves. Flint's parents didn't have time to worry about the boys after that.

"Hey, Jo." Dave from the Chamber came in to pick up his lunch and waved her over. "The headliner for the festival just quit on us. We're in deep shit unless we can get someone fast. You think Flint could give us some suggestions?"

Oh, crap. The festival was less than two months off. Even Flint couldn't work miracles.

"It's kind of late for him to help," she said slowly, thinking faster.

"Yeah, I know," Dave said in resignation. "Just our luck that the only group we could line up called it quits. If we don't make money, *we* may have to call it quits." He handed her a ten and picked up his order. "We'll just have to put you out there on that stage, Jo."

"Like hell," she said without animosity. "I'll stick to singing from the pews." It was an old argument, and Dave didn't hang around to pursue it.

The memory of her humiliating experience in Atlanta had burned away any lingering urge to show off her voice. She'd hoped songwriting would be an alternative, but Randy had cured her of that foolishness, too. Men were more interested in her looks than her brains, it seemed, probably because her brains didn't add up to a pair of double D's.

She wouldn't touch the MusicFest, but she was letting Flint and his talk of lawsuits raise her hopes—again. Someone ought to just shoot her.

The sums the lawyer had talked about would more than make up for her mother's expiring unemployment, and pay for insurance as well, if and when Joella found any evidence.

She knew Flint was worried he'd lose the

café. It kind of made working around him like walking on thin ice over hot coals. She hated to quit her job now though, just when things were getting interesting.

The noisy clang of cymbals and drums rang out from the back room. Flint kept a guitar in his office, but Jo had never seen him play it. She waited to hear the famous bass riff she'd studied on the Barn Boys CD, but the clamor continued without it.

Seeing Flint's parents glance at their watches, Jo hurried over with some of Amy's muffins and coffee. "Here you are. The muffins are fresh from my sister's oven. Flint ordered this coffee special from Hawaii. You'll have to tell us how you like it."

"We really must be going, dear—"

"It's not yet one," Floyd interrupted his wife. "The soup was excellent, Miss Sanderson."

She was starting to see where Flint had learned his charm. She'd dismissed Floyd as a nonentity lurking in his demanding wife's shadow, but apparently he was wise enough to choose his fights. He didn't look like a strong man. His thinning hair had faded to a mouse brown. But he wasn't bad looking, and his smile and the glint in his eye flashed some of Flint's appeal.

"I thank you, sir. Flint hasn't been here two weeks yet, and he's already started to turn the place around. You must be proud of him."

Martha maintained a stony silence. Floyd cleared his throat and sought a reply that wouldn't offend either of them. "Flint has always got what he wanted."

"But maybe he hasn't always got what he *needs*." Hearing the shouts of the boys returning, Jo slipped away, leaving the parental figures to work that one out.

She ought to be ashamed of herself, interfering in the life of a man far more experienced than she, but she smiled to herself as Flint emerged from the back looking a little less grim. Beside him, his young Goth chattered excitedly about drums, and his older boy aimed straight for the doughnut case as if he were at home.

When Flint glanced her way, Jo winked. His sexy smile of appreciation would have to be her reward for suffering the torments of the damned ever since that dance the night they'd met. She'd been sleeping with the windows open to cool off her dreams.

Flynn Clinton had everything she'd ever wanted and would never have, including two parents who loved him, his own business, and a career in music. It was cold comfort watching the black sheep return to the family fold.

Aching in every muscle, clenching and unclenching his hand to keep it from seizing up, Flint walked up Main Street from the lower parking lot feeling as old as his sons thought him. He'd thought he was in pretty good shape, but after spending an afternoon climbing mountains so his kids could rappel off a cliff, he might never walk straight again.

The church bench hadn't helped. He didn't know how long it had been since he'd graced the insides of a church, but he hadn't remembered the pews as that *hard.*

At least he'd introduced his mother to a woman of whom she'd approved. She'd extolled the virtues of churchgoing women like Sally for so long that Flint had developed a distinct distaste for the poor girl. He hadn't bothered mentioning that the only reason Joella hadn't been in church was that she was covering his ass at the café. He had the feeling the icy absence of Jo's name meant disapproval.

Jo might be another glamour girl like Melinda, but that didn't prevent him from looking forward to her outrageous attire and tart tongue. As much as he'd like to be immune to her looks, she added a little extra spice to his newly staid life. He was pretty damned sure he couldn't run the place without her, not for a long while.

His step halted as he passed the hardware store and spotted Myrtle. The pig was sporting a yellow straw bonnet on her purple head, neatly secured with a red bow, with her purple ears sticking through slits in the brim.

Despite his objection to silly purple swine blocking the sidewalk, Flint grinned. The pig hat had all the earmarks of a Joella tale. Through the heavy draperies on the front window, he could tell the lights were on inside the café, so she must be here ahead of him.

Eager to hear the hat story, he shoved open the door. Overall, it had been a decent weekend. The boys had relaxed around him out on the rocks. He'd taught them a thing or two about their video game. He'd promised them white-water rafting next time they came, and they'd seemed interested. He needed to find some way to thank Jo for—

"I can't do this anymore!" a soaring soprano screamed as only a soprano can. *"I never want to see you again!"*

Flint winced, held the door to his shoulder like a shield, and waited for glass to shatter. When it didn't, he peered around the edge. The chorus of a seventies disco song broke out instead of flying plates, and he nearly collapsed in relief. She was extrapolating again. He'd have to warn her about stealing other people's music.

He recognized the irony.

His heartbeat returned to normal, forcing him to realize that the thought of Jo's quitting had paralyzed him. He didn't want to envision days on end in this place without Jo's laughter to brighten the mood and her creative impulses and quick wit to lighten the day—even if she was turning the place into a tea shop.

He really needed to sit down and examine his head after that insight.

He flipped on the overhead light switch and studied the effects of the new paint and paneling. The half-century-old chrome dinette tables and pink vinyl chairs looked exotic against the turquoise and pewter. Even the tin cans looked as if they belonged. He probably needed recessed lights, but the sun would provide extra illumination if he took down the curtains. Jo was right. They had to go. Shutters would look cool.

"I take it the weekend was rough?" he called as he examined the still bare walls.

"*I will survive!*" she sang, strolling out from the restroom with mop and bucket in hand. At the sight of him, she grinned and did a disco dance step that involved a back bend with the mop and splashing water from the bucket.

"I don't think John Travolta used buckets," Flint informed her, fighting the happy surge of music she inspired. He really shouldn't encourage her dramatics. He couldn't afford to lose more plates.

"But I'm prettier." She emptied the water into the sink and got out the ammonia. "The place was too busy to clean up. Sorry."

"Sorry? *Busy* sounds good. Or was it all dollar-bill receipts again?" He checked the cash register. It was nicely full compared to a weekday.

Jo smelled of roses this morning. His head spun from just walking past her. That was the one drawback of having a brilliant waitress—a permanent hard-on.

"We had a few good tables. I marked up muffin prices for the tourists." She flashed him a wicked grin. "I want that espresso machine, so I figured I'd earn it for you."

Hell, for the thrill of that grin, he'd buy the machine, if he could only afford it. "Do you think your sister can make muffins more often?" He counted the cash, with the back of his brain buzzing with contradictory thoughts.

With her amazing talent, Jo belonged in Nashville. He could help her escape this hole into the big world. His insides cramped at the thought, which proved it was a good idea. She needed to be out of his life before their physical attraction burned through all his good intentions. But where in hell would his business be without her?

"Or should I reimburse her more to encourage her?" he continued, trying not to think too hard without caffeine.

"You're asking me? She's my sister. I'll tell you to pay her more."

"But you want an espresso machine," he reminded her.

"There is that." She pulled off her rubber gloves and studied him.

Flint pretended he didn't notice. She really wasn't beautiful in a perfect beauty-queen sort of way. Her eyes were too far apart, her nose took a wrong turn at the end, and her mouth spread across half her face when she smiled. But her cheerful disposition radiated beauty, and her figure could launch a thousand ships.

Even though she wore her rumpled hair in two ponytails this morning—one over top of the other—she still looked as if she'd just climbed out of bed. A curl beside her ear swayed tauntingly when she leaned against the sink. Unless he found a way of sending her to Nashville, he really was going to have to look for a new apron for her. He was trying not to imagine what she was wearing—or not wearing—beneath that bulky bib. He saw only bare brown throat, turquoise earrings, and collarbones.

"I'll talk to Amy," she was saying intelligently while he salivated. "Maybe you can get a good discount on flour and sugar if you buy by quantity, so she can make a better profit. But the kids keep her pretty busy, and muffins won't buy appliances."

"Yeah, I know." Flint gave up counting money and leaned against the counter, wondering if he'd get her out of his system if he kissed her. "I'm thinking of buying an oven on credit and opening for dinner to pay for it. But I need to find more help if I do."

As he'd hoped, Jo's expressive face lit as if illuminated by fireworks. Her lush lips sprawled, revealing a slightly crooked tooth in otherwise pearly-white perfection. He was so focused on kissing those rose lips that he hardly heard her words.

"You are pure genius! I know a cook I can steal from Mack's Steakhouse, and teen-agers can work evenings. Just weekends to start?"

Flint reluctantly shook off his fantasy of Jo's tongue down his throat. Or in his ear. Or anywhere else on him. Apparently he hadn't outgrown his adolescent fixation on wild women. "Yeah. I can't imagine too many locals stopping by during the week for dinner."

"But during the festival—maybe by August we could stay open every night? There are tourists up here all week when the festival is open." She watched him eagerly with those big green eyes that made a man feel as if he were seven feet tall.

"The festival?" he asked stupidly, apparently still under her spell.

"The MusicFest," she explained with an excited gesture that nearly knocked a sugar bowl flying. "We have local and out-of-town musicians playing every day and in the evenings on the weekend. It's like a big carnival. We hold it at the school because they have parking. We hire a huge tent, but if the weather turns ugly, we can usually squeeze into the cafeteria. It's not as big as the ones in Asheville or anything. We don't have enough room and we can't afford big names. But if we can get enough regional groups, we can draw their fans from as far away as Charlotte and Knoxville."

She'd mentioned the festival before. Flint didn't think he'd comprehended that it was a music festival. He supposed if it was just local groups, it wouldn't be a problem. He could stay here, sell coffee to the tourists, and resist temptation. His hand ached like hell after the beating it had taken scrambling around on rocks this weekend. He didn't need any more reminders of why he'd given up music.

Before he could formulate any reply, Jo bulldozed right on.

"If we could get a real name group," she said with such excitement that she was practically dancing, "we could pack the house. The extra crowd would pay for your oven, and the town might start making money so we could have an even bigger event next year."

Alarm flickered through him. Flint wanted to hold his hand up and stop her before she went any further, but he was frozen to the floor.

"You could help us," she crowed, just as he'd feared.

"Uh-uh. I'm not doing the music scene anymore. Go find another sucker for this scheme." With an arrow straight through his heart, he stalked away.

Now he remembered why he didn't want wild women—they were never satisfied.

❦TWELVE❧

Stunned by Flint's abrupt refusal when she'd thought they were finally understanding each other, Jo didn't immediately charge after him and demand explanations. Maybe she should have waited until he'd had his coffee before hitting him up with new ideas.

The morning rush started after that, and by then, it was too late to divert whatever was eating at him. Flint didn't emerge from his office.

What was this deal with pretending he was a decent human being one minute and then acting as if she'd shot him in the pants the next?

As the morning wore on and she fielded inquiries in his absence about Flint's parents and his kids and his plans for the café, Jo built up a slow head of steam.

"Do you think Flint's boys will start school here come fall?" Sally asked over her morning cup of decaf.

"I don't know," Jo answered curtly. "Why don't you go ask him?"

"I only asked because Mrs. Clinton was so nice in church yesterday," Sally said, looking a little hurt at Jo's tone. "I thought maybe I could help them out some."

"Well, you just go back there and tell Mr. High-and-Mighty Clinton that. I'm sure he'll be properly appreciative."

By the end of morning rush, Jo'd heard all about how Flint had sat with Sally in church and his parents had invited her over for Sunday brunch. Well, that was just fine. Sally had a good job at the school. If Sally married, she could support a family if her husband's job went belly-up because there was no damned business in this damned town because certain people wouldn't get off their royal asses to—

The front door slammed open in a flash of sunlight. "Hey, Jo!" Slim entered with a thump of boot heels across the wooden floor. He wore a dinged-up cowboy hat over his lank brown hair, even though he was an electrician who had never sat on a horse. "I heard the committee's talking about getting Randy down here as a headliner at the festival!"

"Well, then, you better get the hanging tree ready because after I deball him, I'm carving him up for Halloween." That was all she needed. *RJ* Ratfink Plagiarist back here because a certain no-account guitar picker couldn't get off his duff to help. She threw a bagel into the toaster and turned around to see everyone staring at her.

"What? Didn't you ever want to cut a fathead down to size?" She adjusted her original *dickhead* down so as not to burn Sally's ears any more this morning.

"Don't be such a girl," Slim said in disgust. "Randy knows people in Nashville. He could bring us lots of publicity. Just because the two of you had a little spat—"

"There's nothing *little* about this spat. If you don't mind getting screwed by the pissant, then you go ahead and say howdy if he shows up." Jo pulled the butcher knife out of a drawer and rummaged for the sharpening file. "But I'd advise you to keep him out of my line of sight."

It had occurred to her late one night that if she'd had her fair share of Randy's advance, her mama wouldn't be cutting back on medicine and worrying about insurance. She didn't want to carve his ass as much as she'd like to carve out his bank account.

"Hey, Jo, you could write a song about him," Hoss called from his seat at the counter. "Call it 'You're So Lame.'"

Laughter erupted at this attempt to defuse her fury, and several of the wits attempted to top Hoss's title with their own versions.

She ought to tell the whole town what Randy—RJ—Peters had done to her, but Elise had said to lie low until they had a case. She wanted to gather evidence before the record company got wind of it. Jo preferred openness, but if keeping quiet meant she had a chance of getting paid, she'd chew her tongue.

"All right, you clowns. You're all so funny, we ought to have us a songwriting competition," she yelled into a lull in the hullabaloo. "The best song calling Randy an asshole gets to play onstage at the MusicFest."

They voted down calling Randy names— that would be rude to an invited guest. But the idea of a songwriting contest took wing.

Before Jo knew it, her temper had settled, and she was in the midst of the discussion.

Apparently coming out of his little snit—or snagged by curiosity at their laughter—Flint strolled out of his office looking like six feet of bad and dangerous in his tight jeans and navy, tailored shirt. The back of his dark hair brushed his collar, and he hadn't shaved this morning. If he'd smile, Jo figured she would suffer a meltdown, but she could be in-your-face with the best of him if he snarled.

"Hey, Flint, I heard tell you're a songwriter. You want to judge in our songwriting contest?" Slim yelled, apparently still high on the idea of Nashville record producers showing up at their crummy little music show.

Jo crossed her arms noncommittally when Flint turned to her for explanation.

"You got a contest for who can write the worst song?" he asked, pouring the dregs of the coffeepot into a mug and taking a swig.

"That would about sum it up," George Bob said. "These clowns couldn't write a song if their lives depended on it. Jo would win, hands down."

"Why, I do thank you, Georgie," Jo purred. "It's nice to get a little appreciation around here occasionally."

"Uh-oh, men, I know that tone." Hoss stood up and laid his money on the counter. "Better clear out before hell opens its gates."

"That's cause you're pussy-whipped, Hoss," Dave told him.

But Jo noticed Dave got up and laid his money out as well. "Have a nice day, boys," she called sweetly.

Flint just stood there, arms folded, sipping his coffee, watching his customers scatter.

"You think about that contest, man," Slim called, pulling his long hair from his face with a rubber band and heading out. "Maybe get Jo some competition up here."

"Your boys were so sweet, Mr. Clinton," Sally said shyly, coming to the counter to pay her bill. "I hope to see them in church next Sunday."

"So do I," Flint said without inflection, letting Jo handle the register.

Jo wanted to elbow him. How was she supposed to concentrate with all that masculine muscle blocking the narrow aisle? Maybe if she took a bite out of him . . .

"Heard you used to play a little," Herb from the antique store said, handing over his money as Sally slipped out. "Any chance we'll hear you at the MusicFest?"

"Not a chance," Flint replied.

Jo noticed his knuckles whiten on the handle of the mug as he said it. Sometimes, she needed a baseball bat taken to her head to wake her up.

She waited until the last customer trailed out, and she had the dishwasher operating, before turning back to him. Flint had finished his coffee and was measuring the front window, finally removing his sexy carcass from underfoot.

"Shutters," she said. "Gray ones."

"Not hot pink?" He snapped his measuring tape back in its case, then moved on to the bare wall to examine it.

"Baby pink, to go with the tables, but I figured you'd veto that. Rose, to go with the plates, maybe, but that's kind of girly."

Jo waited until Flint turned his steely eyes her way before hitting him up with her theory. "You've got one major chip on your shoulder, Mr. Flint. Want to talk about it or let me guess?"

"Guess, by all means." He returned to measuring the turquoise wall.

"You won't help with the festival or the contest. You won't play for an audience. You act like a surly bear anytime anyone mentions music. Gee, you'd think you'd given up the one thing you love most because your hand hurts."

"You know, you're free to look for a job elsewhere anytime," he suggested, sticking the tape case in his back pocket and stalking toward her.

"You're damned right I am." She started counting out the bank deposit.

She tried not to look at him, tried not to see the pain behind his tough attitude, but she came from a family of pain. She knew hurt way down deep inside her, and it resonated with the anger and hurt in him. "Look, I'm sorry if I'm buttin' in where I don't belong—"

"Then don't," he snapped from closer than she'd realized.

She glanced up in time to note the hot flare in his eyes and to catch her breath before his mouth came down on hers. Hard.

His kiss was every bit as hot as she remembered. And there wasn't anything
wrong with his hands when they clasped
her bare waist and dragged her up against
his hard body. She nearly swallowed her
tongue and his in surprise, but she got into
his face-sucking real fast. She grabbed his
shirt and yanked until the kiss turned into a
nuclear meltdown.

That's when he dropped her like a hot potato and stepped away. "Don't interfere,
Joella," he warned. "I'm walking on the
edge already. Give me the deposit. I'll head
on down to the supply store."

·Flint stoically endured Jo's hundred-watt
glare. He deserved her anger, but he hadn't
been able to resist shutting her mouth the
way he'd been wanting to since the first
time. Blond tendrils curled around her face
from the steam of the dishwasher. She
seemed so very young without her face
paint. And off-limits. He really had to get his
head straight.

He grabbed the deposit bag before he
grabbed what he shouldn't. "I'm doing as
much as I can, Joella. You'll just have to run
the rest of the town without me."

She didn't throw anything at his head as

he left, so he hoped he stood a chance of still having a waitress by the time he got back. He wouldn't blame her for walking.

He was deathly afraid that Joella was the reason the café was still in operation. It sure wasn't Charlie's lackadaisical efforts. Jo was the one who added the banter and laughter and encouraged the small-town discussion that led to ideas and progress.

He'd heard everything they'd said in there this morning. Not being part of the discussion had given him new perspective. Jo ought to be mayor, if she didn't say every damned thing that came into her wicked head. He'd kissed her for the laughter as much as to get his need for her out of his system. His lips still smoldered, so he didn't think that idea had worked out real well.

He snorted as he remembered her attack on RJ. Maybe he ought to be a part of the festival if only to be on the front lines when she lit into him.

But he just couldn't afford to let the music into his life again. Or Joella. His sons came first, over anything else. He had to push all temptation aside.

But if he helped Jo find her place in the musical world, she'd leave him and his coffee shop to run straight to hell without her. Rock-and-hard-place time.

"Flint bought the stove, Ames!" Jo crowed over the phone on Wednesday afternoon. "They're delivering it Friday. It has a grill and two ovens and it's the most gorgeous piece of equipment in the world."

Amy glanced at her own mirrored black oven that was currently blinking midnight. If she checked her reflection, she knew she'd see tearstains. "That's nice, Jo," she murmured, crumpling the stationery in her hand.

"Did I catch you at a bad time?" Jo asked through the receiver. "I thought the kids would be in for their naps. I can talk later."

"No, no, this is fine. I'm glad Flint is sprucing the place up. We'll have to come in and see the new stove." Desperately, she steered the conversation in a different direction. "How did you like that big-city lawyer he hired? Is she really going to work for you or just snow you in favor of Flint?"

"Elise DuBois," Jo said. "She is one fine lady, I'm here to tell you. I can't hardly believe it, but she's been all over Slim and the gang, collecting *evidence*. She really thinks

I might have a case. Her mama used to be
a lawyer when women just didn't do that.
They've marched in protests together. She's
not snowing anyone."

"Is that all she does, fight record companies? That can't be much of a business."
Amy smoothed the letter on the kitchen
desk where she kept her recipe books. She
could hear Louisa singing to herself in the
bedroom. The kids would want to get up
soon.

"No, Elise is a contract lawyer, but from
the way she talks, I think she likes taking
cases that work men over. You know Hank
Barlow, the singer who divorced his wife of
fifteen years and brought in some hot babe
when his album went gold?" Jo didn't wait
for Amy to answer. "Well, Elise is the attorney for his wife. She sued him for breach of
contract on some real estate. Mrs. Barlow
now owns the mansion and the Ferrari. Elise
is one badass attorney."

"That's nice," Amy murmured as Josh
started hollering "Mommy!" at the top of his
lungs. "I'd like to meet her. Listen, I gotta
go. See you tomorrow, then?"

Hanging up after Joella's farewells, Amy
neatly folded the stationery from the legal

firm of Fritz and Fitzpatrick and tucked it into her *Southern Living* cookbook.

She should never have opened Evan's mail. That was wrong of her.

But she'd thought it was a bill, she reminded herself as she took the stairs up to her children. Evan's children. The beautiful toddlers who doted on the dad who was never home.

The dad who had just received a letter from an attorney that started out, *As we discussed earlier, the following are our standard recommended procedures for clients preparing for a divorce . . .*

A lightbulb in the staircase chandelier popped as she walked under it.

The heavy rain of the last two days reduced tourist traffic to a trickle. Flint had used the time to work around the shop—avoiding Jo behind the counter—but he was praying the rain let up for the weekend for his kids' sake. It was Friday and the rain still came down.

"You have to see this, Mama." Jo ushered her mother out of the downpour. "Amy, leave the muffins on the counter and come look."

He watched as Jo mother-henned her entire family, including the kids, into the closed
café. He wished she'd warned him that they
were coming. He hadn't met her mother before. He was still greasy from ripping out the
old grill. He wiped off his filthy hands with a
towel and tried not to admire his hired help
too blatantly.

Despite the bad weather, the back-room
show was still on, and Jo had apparently
fixed up for it. She'd wrapped her gold hair
into some kind of twist that dangled little
curls to the high neck of her formfitting top.
The midnight blue knit had no shoulders to
speak of, so he could see she had no
bathing-suit-strap marks marring that gorgeous tan. Her blue denim miniskirt possessed a modest flare, but there was nothing modest about those shapely tanned
legs and flirty heeled shoes. He really
needed to open a liquor bar and put Jo behind it. He wouldn't even have to fill the
glasses. Men would pay to stand and stare.

And he'd have to live in a cold shower.
His hand itched to catch her elbow and
draw her close so he could kiss that sweet-
smelling spot behind her ear.

"Mama, this here is Flynn Clinton." She

gestured at Flint as if he were part of the equipment and helped her mother onto a stool. "Flint, this is my mama, Marie Sanderson. You've met Amy and the kids. We've come to admire the new stove."

Apparently, the stove had evened out that angry kiss. She hadn't said one word about it since, although he'd caught her speculative glances a couple of times. A man could grow to appreciate a woman who kept her mouth shut after he'd made an ass of himself.

Her enthusiasm was catching. You'd think she'd never seen a new stove before. She'd polished the stainless steel until he was afraid to cook anything on it. "Welcome, ma'am. Pleased to meet you," he responded according to the etiquette of his youth. "Jo's been helping me update the place a little. She's good at it."

Marie Sanderson was the type he called a lean, mean fighting machine, with a lined, weathered face that spoke of years of cigarettes and hard living. But she'd raised two strong daughters by herself, so he had to give her respect.

He suspected Jo had inherited her yellow hair from her mother, but Marie's was crew-cut short. He could get an entire song of worry and woe out of the tired lines in her high-boned face. If he was writing songs anymore, which he wasn't.

Marie spun the stool to scan the shelves of plates adorning the newly turquoise wall. "Charlie would just die if he could see this now. He hated change."

Flint winced before Jo could elbow him. A lot of people resisted change, including him. But he was learning. Of course, if Jo won the lawsuit, she could own all this. No wonder she was excited. It was kind of convenient knowing just where he stood in her eyes. Experience sure wiped the romance out of him.

"Everybody seems to like the change real fine," Jo admonished. "Dave even brought his wife over to buy some of the plates. I didn't know she collected them."

"That's because Dave is a snob but Jane is down-to-earth," Amy concluded, pulling a muffin in half and handing the pieces to the kids.

With the children settled, Amy came around to inspect the stove Flint had spent the day ripping out cabinets to install. "I could bake three batches of muffins at a time in this." She sighed with admiration and smoothed the top with her fingers, just as Jo had.

Outnumbered by women and children, Flint started feeling a little uncomfortable. He wondered if he ought to just bow out and let them chat while he returned to his office and the bills he hadn't yet paid. But Jo was wearing some mouthwatering scent that urged him to lick her all over, and he couldn't quite tear away.

She knew damned well that she fueled his flames, but she didn't seem to acknowledge the term *personal space*. She leaned against the counter beside him, her elbow poking him every so often to make a point.

He liked her proximity too well. He liked the way she included him in her family. He liked the way she thought. And he sure enough loved the way she kissed.

Flint worked his sore hand and contemplated kicking something just to show them he wasn't the teddy bear they apparently thought he was.

He didn't need a counselor to tell him that he was trying to hide from the heart-racing, gut-churning uncertainty that women called feelings.

"If we stay open in the evenings, maybe you could bring the kids in and mix up muffins for mornings," Jo suggested. "It might get crowded behind the counter, but maybe Flint could move it again." Her eyes danced with laughter as she slanted them his way.

The look clamped around his heart, and Flint had only to see the excitement in Amy's expression to know it was a done deal. Hurricane Joella had struck again.

"Would you let me bake cupcakes?" Amy asked shyly. "I mean, if you're going to have dinner customers and all, they might like dessert."

"The ones with the fudge goo inside!" Jo demanded, looking up to Flint for agreement. "You have to taste them to believe them."

"They have to make money," he reminded her. "I'm not a charity."

To his amazement, the sisters immediately began adding up costs of ingredients, dividing them up into cupcake quantities, and performing the kind of higher math that had even his business head spinning.

"We're used to counting pennies," Marie said from the counter where she was minding the kids and apparently reading his mind. "It comes of growing up poor."

"It comes of growing up smart and taking advantage of what you have." He'd grown up rebellious and disdaining everything he had. Like his kids, now that he thought about it. The more he was around them, the more he understood them.

"Well, some of us have to learn the hard way," she agreed. "I was lucky and had two good-spirited girls. If I'd had a boy, he'd probably have turned out like you."

Flint had to laugh. "Mean and ugly?" he suggested.

"No child of mine would be ugly," Marie said with a smile of irony. "And we all can be mean when we want. But men have this one-track mind that leads them down all the wrong paths before they find the right one. Their daddy was like that."

He didn't have time to ask if their father had ever found the right path. Jo grabbed his arm and pulled him around to look at a dark booth in the back corner next to the counter that she thought they could take out.

He was dissolving beneath the pressure of her breasts against his arm, and she was

chattering so fast that he didn't even attempt to follow. The one-track-mind theory
worked real well under the circumstances.

"Don't you think?" she ended the excited
stream of chatter, looking up at him with an
expression in her wide green eyes that
meant he'd just been snowed under.

"Does it matter what I think?" he asked,
just because.

"Of course it matters! You don't see me
dragging you back to where the guys are
setting up, do you? You told me you didn't
want to go, and I left it at that." She looked
at him indignantly. "I am not a bossy woman
who won't take no for an answer."

"Yeah, you are." He grinned at her, feeling
more sure of himself than he had all week.
"But it's okay because I'm a bossy man who
will keep telling you no."

"Yeah, masterful," she breathed, the
same way she had the night they'd met.

For a brief moment, it was just the two of
them again, the stars were twinkling overhead, and he had images of her in his arms
again, hot and lush and eager.

"Hey, Flint, is it okay if we start moving
the tables?" Coming in from the back room,
Slim intruded on their silent communication.

Well, hell.

"Looks like we might have to add tables for Friday evenings if you want to do dinner," Jo whispered, pulling away and leaving an empty space where she'd been.

More money he didn't have. But he had this terrifying notion that if he could have Jo, he wouldn't need money.

How in hell did he know if he'd found the right path until he took it? Jo sure looked like a one-way path to heaven, but so had Melinda.

If his instincts demanded unmaternal glamour girls who sought fame and fortune, did that mean he really was a lousy father?

⚒THIRTEEN⚒

Flint tried to shut out the bass beat of the band as he entered another number into the minus side of his calculations. He'd saved his laptop from the auction, but the keyboard was too cramped for his hand, and he couldn't enter numbers easily. He'd have to buy a bigger keyboard. For now, he could calculate the old-fashioned way—by pencil and Charlie's adding machine.

He stopped at the sound of Jo's clear soprano ringing over the rumble of the crowd in the next room. His toe tapped to the rhythm of her song. It must be somebody's birthday. He'd learned Jo never appeared onstage as she had for him. She usually sat at the table of the friend she was targeting with her song.

He'd give hard money to wander in there and listen, but he didn't think he could settle at just watching her this time. With his eyes shut he could see her wiggling her fanny in that fringed leather. He'd woken up this morning dreaming of her in bed beside him with her golden curls draped across his pillows.

The heat-seeking missile in his pants had found its target and needed only the right excuse to take aim and fire, without considering the consequences.

And in this case, the consequences could be very ugly. Jo wanted what he'd given up. He knew too much to be seduced back into that life again, no matter how hot her kisses. He didn't want to lead her into thinking differently, but Jo was used to manipulating men, and she'd think she could change him.

He tried to concentrate on numbers as Jo's song ended, but every column showed him coming up so far in the red that he didn't want to think about it. Between the mortgage and the credit line at the supply store, he owed more than he was worth. If business slowed down for any reason, he'd have to give up the house and sleep in the back room.

Or in Jo's apartment, but that was back to

mixing business with pleasure and would be disastrous for his relationship with the boys.

He had safely turned his thoughts to entertaining John and Adam tomorrow when his office door crashed open, slamming into the cracked chair behind it.

With backlighting from a lamp in the hall, Joella appeared to hover inside a golden halo, but no angel ever looked like Jo. She had *hot sex* stamped from the supple curves of long legs and arms, to the outline of her full breasts behind the blue knit.

"Mama's took sick, and I need to get her down to the hospital in Asheville. Can you look after the kids so Amy can go with me? We need her SUV."

Flint responded to her panic and not the song his body was singing. "I'm better at driving than taking care of kids. If Amy will let us have the SUV, I'll drive, and Amy can use my truck to take the kids home. Where's your mother?"

Flint was at the door, catching Jo's elbow and turning her around, before she could protest his orders.

She swiftly fell into stride with him. "In the restroom. Everything she ate came up, and now she's shivering and hardly conscious.

She has hepatitis and cirrhosis and takes a lot of medicine. I think it's a reaction to a new one."

Flint had only just met Marie, but he hated to think of that feisty woman hurting.

They found Sally reassuring Josh and Louisa outside the restroom. "If you could drive us to my parents' house, I'd be happy to look after them," she offered. "I can't drive."

"And Evan is out of town—again," Jo said. Her sarcastic tone morphed into cheerfulness as she shoved open the restroom door. "How are you doing in here?"

The question sounded so upbeat that Flint would have mistaken the seriousness of the situation if he hadn't learned Jo's body language well. She was stiff as a board and would have started throwing things if anyone set her off.

"Just take me home," he heard Marie say. "The hospital costs too much. I'll be fine."

"You are not fine," Joella argued. "You have insurance. That's what it's for."

Relieved that Jo's mother wouldn't have to come up with emergency-room costs, Flint turned back to Sally. "I'll take Jo and her mom down," he said, commanding the situation, acting in the only way he knew how. "The kids would be better off in their own beds."

His instinct was apparently correct. Sally looked relieved, and just inside the door, Amy stepped out to gather up her worried children and give him a grateful smile. "You're a saint, Flint. Jo would have driven us off the mountain in this rain, she's that frantic."

He nodded and prayed that he didn't do the same. Jo had the ability to spin his head off his shoulders on a good day. This wasn't turning out to be a real good day.

"She's resting, Miss Sanderson. You can't do anything more. Why don't you go home and get some sleep?" The nurse nudged Jo to the door.

Jo glanced past the nurse, hoping for one more glimpse of her mother, but the aide had pulled the curtains around the bed and turned off the lights. Frightened, Jo didn't want to leave. "I could just sleep in that chair over there," she suggested.

"The room's much too small, Miss Sanderson. I'm sorry. We have to think of

our other patients. Visiting hours start at
nine."

Ushered down the hall to the waiting
room, blinking back tears, Jo had Flint's
arms around her before she remembered
walking into them.

"How is she?" he murmured, cuddling her
as if she were a small child.

He did that so well. His arms were big and
strong, and his wide shoulders shielded her
from a world of woe. She wanted to curl up
against him and weep, but she'd done that
before and didn't want to wear out her welcome. He was being amazingly kind for
someone who had every right to distrust
her.

He'd taken over and returned order to her
chaos. For that alone, she was grateful.

"She's sleeping. They're giving her fluids
and antibiotics. They think it's just a bug."
She prayed it was just a bug. Watching her
mother pass out like that had scared her
straight through. "She's going to kill me
though. The mill's HMO won't cover the
emergency room because we didn't call her
doctor first."

She rested against Flint, absorbing his
strength and life force. He simmered with

passion and energy, and she marveled that he didn't explode from holding it all in. His arms tightened around her, and she didn't fight his embrace, even knowing she should. He'd already showed her plainly that the heat between them had no future. Not in his head, anyway. Hers was ready to accept anything in exchange for more of his kisses. Guess that made him smarter than she was.

"Do you have some way of paying the bill for her?" he asked.

"Amy, except Evan is getting nasty about money. We always figure it out." She dismissed the problem with a shrug, although the constant worry about money was as debilitating as her mother's disease.

"Do you want to get a room here so you can be back first thing in the morning?"

This was a tourist town in summer. Rooms on a Friday night didn't come cheap if they could be found at all. She could stay with Rita, but she wasn't up to her friend's questions. "Amy can drive down. Tomorrow's your time with the boys. Peggy can't handle the café alone."

"We'll worry about that in the morning. Let's get you home."

Jo didn't want to leave Flint's arms. She was a strong woman. Life had taught her to stand on her own. But every once in a while, it was nice to have someone to lean on.

She'd relied on men before and look where that had got her. Jo straightened and stepped back from the security of Flint's ironclad hold. She couldn't meet his eyes. She'd fall apart if she saw the least bit of sympathy there.

"I appreciate this, boss man," she said, putting a distance between them to cool off the sparks they were striking. "You went above and beyond the call of duty."

If he was ticked at her cool response, she couldn't tell. They took the elevator and walked out of the hospital in silence, not touching. The rain hadn't let up while they were inside. Hoping the downpour would cool off any simmering embers, Jo dashed across the blacktop rather than have Flint pull around for her.

She wasn't used to handling SUVs so Flint drove while she turned on a blast of heat in hopes of drying off. They exchanged cursory directions but avoided the personal. The atmosphere was so thick with awareness, she figured they could ignite any moment.

As the big vehicle rolled silently up the mountain, the dark and the rain apparently loosened his tongue—or the silence was too fraught with tension, and he sought to break it. "I talked to Elise DuBois today."

"I wondered when she would call." Jo appreciated the distraction. "Slim says she's been all over him, tracking down the evidence I didn't think existed."

Jo didn't take her scraps of paper very seriously. She was still grappling with the notion that her words were worth selling. She wanted to believe she could earn enough money to help her mother, but after years of disappointment, she'd learned it wasn't that easy. Flint must have done some fancy rewriting of her rhymes, and he was telling her now that she didn't have a case. She wasn't sure she wanted to hear it.

Their conversation sounded normal and harmless, like that of an old married couple and not the minefield that it was.

"The evidence exists," he assured her. "She's in possession of the original lyrics in your handwriting, which constitutes copyright under the law."

"Which is worth the price of a hill of beans if I didn't register them with that publisher Elise talked about." Jo shrugged. She knew nothing about copyrights. She'd just had fun writing rhymes while the guys played. Her payment had been the band's gratitude, audience appreciation, and three years of Randy's promises to take her out of here. She really was old enough to know better. She might crave fame and fortune like a child begs for candy. That didn't mean she deserved it.

"You wrote a couple of the songs on the back of Charlie's invoices."

"Yeah, well, I don't always have notepads laying around and Charlie never filed anything." She'd noticed that Flint had flung out all the yellowing files and trash that had accumulated over the decades in Charlie's office. He'd even bought some fresh file folders in different colors, and she'd actually seen him put things in them. She was impressed.

"The invoices were dated. Elise says that doesn't mean a judge will believe the date on the invoice corresponds to the date of the lyrics, but it's a better indication than anything RJ is likely to produce. She's also

obtained a copy of the CD from the Charlotte studio you told me about. The studio
has good records and can date when it was
done, although both you and RJ sang on it,
so it's also of dubious evidence."

"Well, I never expected manna from
heaven anyway." She had hoped though.
There for a little while—after she'd got past
her fury—Flint had got her excited about
maybe making enough money to help a little. What good was insurance that didn't
cover the emergency room anyway? She'd
have to think about getting a second job.

She turned on the radio, but all she found
was static. The mountains blocked clear
signals. From experience, she knew Amy's
choice of CDs included things like *The
Froggie Went A'Courtin'*.

"I didn't mean that wasn't enough," Flint
said over the static. "I mean that gives Elise
physical evidence to back up the statements the band made saying you wrote all
the lyrics, and they composed the tunes.
Since we didn't use the Buzzards' music,
they don't have a case, but yours still
holds."

Jo switched off the radio and stared at
Flint's profile in the glow of the dashboard.

He handled the clumsy SUV on the mountain curves with the expertise of a race-car driver and the ease of a man not aware of his own strength. He wasn't speeding, just maneuvering the big vehicle on the unlit two-lane as if it were broad daylight, even though the downpour nearly obliterated the view of the road despite the frantic efforts of the wipers.

She hated driving this road with the cliff straight up the right side and straight down on the left. She'd driven it since she was sixteen and had learned to respect the mountain's dangers. But right now, she was stuck on Flint's comments and not his driving.

"We have a case?" she asked in simple terms that she understood.

"*You* do," he corrected. "I don't understand the legal maneuvering, but she's definitely filing the suit if you give her the go-ahead."

"Shouldn't she have told that to me?" she asked, looking for the flaw that would shatter her hopes.

"She still needed to verify a few things with me, but, yeah, she probably should have. It's that good-ol'-boy thing. I'm the one with the name and the contacts, and she wanted to make certain I understood what happens next. You'll probably get a phone call Monday when she has it all together."

She must be more tired than she realized. She didn't go into a rant over good ol' boys, or shout in jubilation over the possibility of little ol' Joella bringing Randy to his knees, although just the prospect gave her a true jolt of glee. She sat there and pondered all the implications, but her brain wasn't too used to that and didn't get far.

Instead, the enormous memory bank of music that apparently took the place of her brain spun old tunes until her toe tapped to a tune no one but she could hear.

With the windshield wipers clapping time, she hummed a gospel song about *the walls came tumbling down*. Her sense of humor kicked in, and the gospel turned to Dixieland. "When the clowns come tumbling down, you'd better be there, in a hurry, when the clowns come tumbling down," emerged from her mouth.

Switching from Dixieland to country, Flint picked up the refrain, adding in a gravelly voice, "'Cause the sight isn't pretty, when the clowns come tumbling down."

She chuckled and sought a rhyme for *pretty,* but a thundering boom rattled the car, interrupting. A frightening clatter on the roof and hood drove all thought out the window. Flint eased up on the gas and strained to see out the rain-soaked windshield. "I didn't see any lightning, did you?"

Now that she was watching, Jo could see a hail of rocks bouncing off the hood. She screamed as they maneuvered a hairpin curve and the headlight beams caught a flurry of gravel cascading from the cliff face—illuminating a boulder the size of the SUV in the highway ahead.

Flint slammed the brakes into a terrifying squeal. The SUV's rear end fishtailed in time to his rabid curses.

Jo held her breath as tightly as he held the steering wheel, waiting for the thunderous crash that would either kill them instantly or send them flying off the cliff to an agonizing death. Tires and brakes screamed. Trees growing out of the rock cliff whipped against the side window. Her seat belt jerked tight, smacking her against the back of the seat as the air bags exploded, and the truck finally rocked to a quivering halt.

Shaken, bruised, Jo stared out the rain-swept windshield as the bags deflated. A boulder taller than the SUV loomed over them, not inches from the front bumper. They were still on the road, although tilted at a bad angle with the back end in the gully between the road and the mountain. Jo shuddered.

"For the blessings we have received this day, my Lord, we thank you," she murmured. She didn't know how else to express appreciation for the horror that Flint had just avoided. Her heart pounded hard enough to push through her chest.

"Repeat that again for me," he said grimly, clenching the steering wheel and staring at the mountain's revenge on man. Abruptly, he began rocking the SUV, seeking traction on the road while attempting to avoid the mudslide. "Does your sister keep flares or anything in here? Let me back down the road away from this rock, then we'd better set up warnings. Use my cell and call the police." He unclipped his phone and threw it in her lap.

She was still murmuring prayers, but she

understood his urgency. Anyone could fly around the curve in this pouring rain. If they were speeding just a little too fast, the SUV would be crushed between the rock and someone's bumper. Logic replaced panic.

"Under the floor in back is the emergency kit." Heart beating ninety miles an hour, Jo hit 911 and waited for the dispatcher while Flint maneuvered the SUV to solid ground, then rolled backward to a wide place off the right side of the road, out of range of the boulder. He climbed into the downpour to rummage in the back.

Cell phones didn't often work out here, but for once in her life, something went right, and the call went through. After giving the location as best as she could since she hadn't been watching, Jo hit Amy's number to tell her what had happened and that she wouldn't be back this evening. She had no idea how long it would take to move a boulder. She'd seen the road closed for months after a bad rockfall, but that had been when the mountain had taken the road out. The road appeared intact.

They'd have to drive around to the Knoxville side of the mountain and come down from the west to get home. It would add hours to the drive. The mill was on the other side. It would be cut off from their East Coast suppliers.

A blocked road could destroy tourist traffic for the entire summer.

Trying not to think like that, she put in a call to Peggy. Maybe if Amy went in and helped Peggy out, the café could stay open in the morning.

By the time Jo had told Peggy how to find the keys to the café, Flint had climbed back in, soaked and dripping all over the leather. "Don't know if anyone will pay attention to those markers in this mess, but it's the best I could manage."

The silhouette of his broad shoulders against the gray window was immensely re-assuring, and the low rumble of his voice aroused a desperate need to be held. Jo valiantly resisted. "The sheriff is sending a car down from Northfork and state police are heading up from this side. It's all we can do." She looked at the narrow road on either side of them and tried not to descend into hysterics. "Can we turn this monster around or do we have to back all the way down?"

"If we have to back down, it won't be far. We passed my drive about a mile back."

As if hearing her thoughts, Flint reached across the seats, cupped her head, and dragged her toward him. Jo surrendered eagerly, letting the heat of his kiss remind her that they were alive. Before the windows could steam up, they both pulled apart. This was neither the time nor the place, though Jo's heart pounded in protest at the distance.

Without a word of comment, Flint switched on the ignition and angled backward until the taillights illuminated the cable fence on the sheer cliff side, then steered hard toward the mountain on Jo's side of the road. "Let's see how this baby turns."

She dug her fingers into the edge of the seat while he shifted back and forth, repeating the maneuver until he had the long SUV turned down the mountain.

"You can breathe now," he told her.

She expelled a lungful of air she hadn't realized she was holding, then giggled with relief at the silliness of her response. Her lips stung from the intensity of their kiss, but she could brush it off for now if he could. "All right, Mr. Big Shot, you win this one. I give you a ten in mountain driving."

Flint flexed his wet shoulders against the

seat back to ease a knot, rubbed the back of his neck, shifted the gear, and started down the road.

"My place or Asheville?" was all he asked.

"Let's not go all the way back to town in this," she protested. The wipers barely kept the windshield clear, and the dark mountain road looked more ominous than ever. "I don't know about you, but my nerves are shot for the night."

After that kiss, she knew what she was saying, but she was a big girl. Flint wasn't likely to jump her bones unless she let him. She was the question mark in this car.

"Did you call your sister?" he asked, not giving any evidence that he was surprised or relieved at her decision.

"Yeah, and Peggy. They'll cover for us in the morning. I told Amy to stay away from the new stove until we're there though."

He shot her a questioning glance.

She managed a wobbly grin, although he probably couldn't see it. "Amy has a magnetic personality. Machines go berserk around her."

"Right." He returned his attention to the

road. "Good thing I bought the service plan."

"At least your kids can get up here if you live on this side of the slide," she said, trying to console him.

Instead, it shut them both up as her words sank in. His parents would be arriving with his sons in the morning. Jo had a feeling his parents wouldn't approve of her presence.

"Would you rather take me back to Asheville?" she asked quietly.

"Hell, no," he said so emphatically that she didn't ask again.

❧FOURTEEN❧

Heart still thumping a death knell in his ears, Flint tried to collect his scrambled thoughts to remember what kind of shape he'd left the house in that morning. But the near collision with a boulder had brutally reminded him of his mortality, and Jo's kiss had recalled too well the benefits of living. Remembering whether he'd thrown his Calvin Kleins into the hamper wasn't registering high on his importance scale.

A few miles an hour faster and he might have rated a back-page story in the tabloids—*Country Songwriter Kills Waitress in High-Speed Crash*—with a subheader of *Clinton's Parents Pull Life Support.*

He turned the glorified truck up the muddy ruts of his gravel drive and shook his head at the paths his mind could take to avoid reality.

"Yeah, that's how I feel, too," Jo agreed, though he hadn't said a word.

He liked the way their minds traveled the same path. "Tell me again why I thought it was a good idea to raise my sons out here where mountains can fall on them." The SUV survived the mud, and he spun it into the empty space where his Chevy belonged.

"Because falling rocks are more environmentally correct than speeding semis on city interstates? I'll have to change my lyrics. It was the mountain that came tumbling down, not the clowns."

"Pride goes before a fall. Fit that in while I go look for an umbrella." He opened the door and stepped into the downpour.

"You won't have an umbrella, and I won't melt." She jumped out on her side.

They raced up to the covered front porch. Flint fiddled with his keys while Joella shivered. The cloudburst had dropped the nighttime temperature ten degrees. Flint figured if he had a porch light, he could probably see her nipples through her wet knit. As it was, he was left admiring the lift of her breasts when she wrapped her arms around herself.

"I haven't tested the heating system yet. I'll throw some logs in the fireplace in a minute." He shoved open the door and flipped the switch that lit the lamp by his recliner. Fifties wiring didn't include overheads in living rooms.

"Gee, I love what you've done with the place." Laughter played beneath Jo's praise as she entered his domain. "Early Male, right? Leather, wood, a couch, a recliner, a TV, and a table to set your beer on, the basic necessities of life. No pillows, no plants, no rugs."

"I haven't had time to play decorator." Unoffended, he started for the stairs. "I need to get out of these clothes and find something dry for you. The kitchen is straight back if you want coffee, or if you want to crash, I can show you the guest room."

Flint had never run away from a woman, but having Joella standing in his favorite room wearing a wet knit top that revealed every voluptuous curve did things to his libido that he shouldn't act on. And after this past half hour, his resistance was at an all-time low.

"My nerves are wired. I don't think I'll be

sleeping anytime soon," she admitted. "If you have a shirt I can put on, I'll fix coffee. You want some?"

"Yeah, same goes for me. I'll get you one of Johnnie's shirts."

He grabbed one of his son's Sunday shirts and dropped it over the stair rail to her before returning to his own room to change. He kicked clothes under the bed and threw the sheets into some kind of order—just in case. He knew the twin beds in the boys' room had clean sheets because he'd prepared the room for their visit.

By the time he hurried back down with his blood racing so fast it overheated his brain, Jo had coffee ready and a fire started.

"No fair. I was supposed to play Mountain Man and impress you with my ability to make fire." Flint took the coffee mug and joined her on the expansive stone hearth. The house was large and echoing around them, and his skin hummed with awareness of the stunning woman warming his lonely space better than any fire.

She'd removed the rest of her hairpins and let the whole golden mass down to dry. It tumbled over Johnnie's plain, blue dress shirt, but on Jo, nothing could look plain.

The shirt fit better than his would have, but she'd left the top buttons open, and the soft cotton molded to high, firm curves untouched by any suggestion of support.

So shoot him. He was a breast man.

Silence fell between them as they sipped their coffee and let the fire warm the chill from their bones. Sparks jumped through the logs in accompaniment with the electric ones leaping between the two of them. He'd pulled on the first T-shirt out of the drawer, but Flint had to wonder if his subconscious wasn't working overtime. The shirt was an old one that clung like GLAD wrap. He didn't think he was a vain man, but Joella wasn't a shy woman. They were both standing there admiring the goods.

"I like my job," she said abruptly.

But not irrelevantly. He understood, because his thoughts had gone there already. They'd nearly combusted the first night they'd met. After weeks of working together, kissing wasn't enough. The coals of desire had blown red-hot. "I don't want to lose you as a waitress," he replied.

She nodded as if that answered her question. "It would never work out anyway. You

want a mom for your kids, someone educated like Sally."

Now that she'd agreed with him, Flint per-
versely wanted to argue. Sally sure the hell
wasn't whom he wanted right now. "Education has nothing to do with what I want."

"Maybe not, but keeping my job after-
ward has a lot to do with what I want."

"We're rational adults," he claimed, arguing even though she was right. They'd burn
the Stardust down if they had sex now and
tried to forget it later.

"No, we're not." Her eyes crinkled in the
corner with laughter. "We're horny dogs and
not thinking at all."

"There's something to be said about not
thinking," he mused. "After that boulder, I'm
ready to adopt a live-for-today policy." Hell,
his blood was boiling, and he was ready to
throw out every vow he'd made, if Jo would
only be kind—or cruel—enough to agree.

"Adrenaline high," she scoffed. "You'll recover and be sorry in the morning. Teach
me to play that guitar over there. I always
wanted to learn."

He could seduce her. Flint knew with
confident male instinct that all he had to do
was drag her into his arms, and she

wouldn't push away. Her kiss earlier had told him that. But since it was only sex and nothing more, she was offering him an alternative—music. Talk about being caught between hell and damnation . . .

Shadows flickered in the far reaches of the vaulted ceiling. Firelight glimmered in the black panes of the windows. Rain pounded against the roof. It was a night for making love. His big black leather couch beckoned. Plush cushions, a willing woman, and he hadn't had sex in so long he'd forgotten what it was like. And Jo was just the kind of woman he liked to have it with.

Even the siren call of music rushing through his veins couldn't compete with the willful, wonderful woman waiting for his decision. He knew she could light his night. And maybe more than a night. Offered the choice between sex and the addiction that haunted his soul and had ruined his life, he'd choose sex every time.

But the music addiction only affected him, and sex affected both of them. He was trying to follow the mature path and think of others. Besides, as she was showing him, lust wasn't a replacement for a full life, a real relationship, and the future of his sons. He couldn't have any of those with a woman who would sue him for all he was worth and take off to Nashville as soon as the opportunity offered.

So he might as well help her along the road and remove her from temptation. He wouldn't repeat the mistake he'd made with Melinda. Jo had the talent his ex never had.

For Jo's sake, Flint grit his teeth and grabbed the guitar from the dark corner where he'd thrown it the day he'd moved in. It was acoustic, the first guitar he'd ever owned. He'd written his first hit song on it.

He shoved it at her. "The strings are old, and I don't have replacements. If they snap, we're out of luck."

She took the instrument without comment, settling cross-legged in the middle of the couch and holding his baby with the care and respect it deserved. He nearly groaned aloud when she stroked the guitar's neck with loving fingers and cradled the pearl-inlaid body beneath her breasts.

She played the scale on untuned strings and glanced mischievously at him. "Doe, a deer, that ate my ear."

He did groan then and dropped into his

recliner, where he wouldn't have to drink in her soft scent or look at her making love to his guitar instead of him. "You can play," he said with disgust at being tricked.

"The scale. I don't know all the finger thingies. Randy was more singer than player and wouldn't teach me."

"Couldn't," Flint said with a grunt, wishing he had a beer instead of coffee. "He just gets up there and whales the tar out of the strings. Can you read music?"

"Nope. Give me a note, and I can probably figure it out. Do you sing?"

"Nope. Give me a note, and I'll probably kill it."

"You were singing in the car."

"That wasn't singing. That was mouthing words in time to a beat. You're the one with a voice that can make grown men weep."

Ignoring his praise, she fingered the strings and sang the scale. Her vocals were a perfect pitch. The guitar far less so. With a growl, Flint swung out of his recliner and took the instrument away from her. Sitting on the sofa, he settled Pearl in his lap like an old friend and began tuning her strings. His left hand curled naturally around the guitar's neck, but every finger movement as he adjusted the knobs shot waves of pain up his arm.

He was ready to fling the instrument to the floor when Jo began to sing softly, "And the walls, the walls come tumbling down."

Her voice seeped straight through him and into his fingers. Flint had to pour it out again or do something rash. He settled for picking the notes she sang, staying with a single chord, adding a backbeat, ignoring the warning twinges as the muscles of his hand tried to seize up. "And the clowns come tumbling with them," he sang on a wry note.

"The mountains, the mountains come tumbling down," she sang in a triumphant voice that echoed from her diaphragm to the rafters.

"That changes the meter. You need a new note." He handed the guitar back to her. "Here, put your fingers on these spots." He settled the guitar in her lap. It was a temptation to put his arm around her shoulders to show her the best position, but he settled for covering her fingers with his, adjusting them along the fret. He didn't have to bend his fingers as much if they wrapped over hers, and the pain lessened.

Except the sensation of covering her slender hands with his jarred him into stupidity. The sight of the full curves of her breasts beneath the opened buttons of his son's shirt held him riveted.

"I think you better play and let me sing," she suggested so softly that he almost didn't hear her through the fog filling his head.

"Yeah, right." He took the guitar and backed off to the far corner of the large couch, working his fingers open and shut to unclench them.

She eased toward the other corner. Flint did his best not to look at her as he returned to strumming the strings, letting his pain flow into the music. The gospel beat easily transformed into a joyous protest to match her earlier transcendent cry.

His fingers wanted to curl up and weep, but the muse that had run off with the accident now found her way back through the glory of Jo's voice and wicked imagination.

As Jo turned the old song into a battle cry of bringing down all that was wrong in the world, Flint let the music soar, and for the first time since he'd worked on RJ's album, he felt better than alive. Renewed. Reborn.

Miraculously ready to take the world by storm.

Jo closed her eyes and let pure joy pour from her throat. In Flint's cozy cabin, with the rain pounding the roof, she felt safe and didn't hesitate to release all the emotion inside her until shivers of excitement ran up and down her arms.

Sometimes, if she couldn't sing, she felt as if she would burst at the seams. Song would seep from her like steam from an untended iron.

But tonight, she didn't have to hold back. Flint didn't fiddle and carp and backtrack and tell her to hush. He kept up with her, note for note, improvising when she changed the meter far better than the Buzzards had ever done, catching up with her and improving as he learned her habits.

As if he already knew and appreciated her habits.

Which he did, if he'd turned her old rhymes into real music. She hadn't fully comprehended what that meant until now. She stopped abruptly and faced him. "Sing one of my songs," she demanded.

A thick strand of chestnut had fallen

across Flint's brow. The hair brushing his nape had dried but curled from the dampness. Whiskers shadowed his hollowed cheeks. But it was the burning light shining from beneath his dark lashes that held her transfixed. She felt that light clear to her bones, and deeper. The ferocity stirred everything feminine in her, but she resisted reacting to the urge.

At her request, he seemed to make a mental adjustment. Tilting his head, he studied the guitar strings. Tapping his fingers again, he grimaced with pain, but he picked a few strong notes. A minute later, his gravelly voice was singing the song of a wicked woman who shaved her drunken husband's head while he was sleeping, then marched off to the city to sell his long, wavy hair and buy a ticket home to mother.

Flint made it sound like real music instead of a silly ditty she'd written after Atlanta when she'd wanted revenge for her shame. His composition of sad and defiant chords reflected the song that had been in her heart when she'd written the words.

Stunned, Jo just sat there when he finished. *She really was a songwriter.*

She knew she could sing. She'd given up

hope of ever doing anything with her singing since vocalists required far more stage presence and training than she could emulate. But if she could *write . . .* If Randy could make money off her words . . .

They'd really used her words. Not just a line or a chorus, but her *whole song.*

Dazed, she let Flint go on to the next tune.

"Do the first one again," she begged when he finished. "I want to learn the melody."

He obliged without protest. He pointed out her flaws when she went the wrong way, started the chord over, and let her try again. By the time she had it all down, he was grinning as widely as she was.

"I think I must have written that music for you," he said. "RJ will sound mighty silly after anyone hears you singing it."

Loving the thought of singing Flint's music, Jo bounced up and down, unable to sit still as the beat strummed through her. "When is his album coming out? If he's coming down here in August for the MusicFest, maybe I could . . ." She stopped. No she couldn't.

"It should hit the air sometime in August."

He watched her with curiosity. "If you sang before he did, you'd steal his thunder, for sure."

"I couldn't, but it's fun to think about." She squirmed beneath Flint's gaze and hugged herself, which tugged the shirt tighter. Her nipples rose hard and aching against the cotton, and she couldn't look at him.

"Why can't you?" he demanded. "Is the lineup full?"

She felt like a fool saying it aloud. "Stage fright," she said with what she hoped was a laugh. "I throw up when the lights come on."

He stared at her in disbelief. "You perform in front of our customers. You sang for me in a room full of people. Don't let fear stop you from having the life you deserve."

The life she deserved. She shivered a little in expectation and stared longingly at the guitar. "I've always dreamed of someday meeting my daddy up onstage, showing him what he threw away." She'd never stated the dream aloud, knowing she'd be laughed at.

The guitar landed in her lap. "Your turn. My hand won't take more. You've got more natural talent in your little finger than I have in my whole body."

Talent? This was coming from a man who'd made millions as a musician. She needed time to absorb his wild claim and decide whether it was just another lie to get what he wanted. She'd thought Flint had been pretty straight with her so far.

She watched his hand as he tried to straighten it. The scar cut a thin white line across dark hair and bronze skin, akin to a rubber band pulling his fingers into awkward shape. Instinctively, she set the guitar on the floor and reached for his hand.

"Have you seen a therapist?" She hadn't noticed the room's chill until she held the heat of his hand between hers. She rubbed her thumb along the line, feeling him flinch from the pressure.

"Yeah, until the insurance ran out. She said it would take more surgery, and even then, she wasn't certain how much function I'd regain. I haven't got the time or the money right now. There are more important things in the world than strumming a guitar."

"Not for you," she said without giving her words much thought. "That guitar riff of yours really makes the Barn Boys' sound."

She had never known it was him until she'd compared the songs done with and without him. Their new bass player lacked Flint's flair.

He tried to pull his hand away, but she wouldn't let him. She circled her thumb over the taut tendons, using the massaging pressure she'd learned to help her mother's circulation.

"My sons are more important than music." He tried to jerk away again.

This time, she made the mistake of meeting Flint's eyes. They burned with the heat of desire, even as he fought to obey her wishes by staying away.

The same hunger yearned in her, and she'd forgotten why she was supposed to deny it. "Your sons need a whole man for a father, not half of one." She'd said a lot of crazy things in her life, spouting off at society and the world in general. This time, she thought maybe she'd made sense.

"You don't know what you're talking about," he said angrily, shaking her off.

"I think maybe I do. You're another man when you're into the music. You're not as angry. You listen."

"I listen all the time." He grabbed the guitar she'd set on the floor.

"With your ears, maybe, but not your heart." She took the guitar away and laid it back on the floor, nudging it away with her foot as she leaned toward him. She tapped his chest and almost went up in flame at the contact with firm muscle. "When you're not roiling with anger, you can hear better."

Flint grabbed her arms and dragged her toward him until his whiskers scratched her chin and his mouth was a hair's breadth from hers. "I'm not angry. I'm being sensible and providing a home for my kids," he told her firmly.

She grinned from ear to ear, unsurprised by his action. With their lips only inches apart, she met his gaze again, loving the way he focused on her to the exclusion of all else. "There are two ways to let all that testosterone loose before it fries your brains."

She didn't give him the opportunity to ask what they were, as if he needed to be told. Twisting her arms so she grasped his biceps, she tilted forward and applied her mouth to his.

≪FIFTEEN≫

Jo's passionate kiss stoked the embers of desire that had smoldered between them for weeks. The caress of her hands along Flint's bare arms ignited him like a torch.

Freed by her first move from any obligation to hold back, he hauled her into his lap and crushed her against him as he'd dreamed about for weeks. Her warmth seeped through his body into all the cold places of his soul. Hungrily plundering her mouth, he held her tightly to prevent losing her in the next breeze of fate. Jo obliged by wrapping her arms around his neck and hanging on like a tenacious vine. He didn't know why people talked about clinging vines as if they were weak. Good kudzu could bring down a tree.

And he was falling rapidly.

With Jo's curves pressed all up and down

him at last, Flint leaned back against the
cushions and thrust his hands into her silken
mass of curls, tilting her head to better ac-
commodate his kiss. She matched him eagerly with parted lips and a heated tongue
that reached straight to his groin. And then
she matched his maneuver by sliding her
hands into his hair and pulling him closer.

Thrilled to the marrow that he needn't
tease and beg, Flint slid his crippled hand
between them to finally knead and shape
the full firmness of breasts.

Despite her tough attitude, she moaned
with vulnerability at his caress. She didn't
pull away but pushed into his palm with a
demand equal to his own.

After that, there wasn't a chance in hell of
turning back. She was right. They were no
better than mating dogs. And that was just
fine with him. He didn't want to be rational
anymore. He wanted every bit of Jo that he
could see, touch, hear, and taste. He was a
starving man who'd been offered a feast.

Flint ripped Jo's buttons in his eagerness
to reach more warm flesh. She slid her palms
beneath his shirt and tweaked his nipples
until he groaned and jerked the cotton over
his head, flinging it across the room.

He swung full length onto the leather cushions, bringing her with him so she lay sprawled on top, her legs between his. The leather was like a second skin against his bare back. He slid her shirt off so he could admire all that lush flesh in the flickering firelight.

"A golden goddess," he murmured senselessly, nudging her sparkling earrings out of his way so he could kiss his way around her earlobe.

"Eve," she muttered in reply.

He laughed and denied her accuracy. "My muse," he countered. He could swear the heat from her skin eased the pain of his hand.

Using his abs so he didn't disturb her position, Flint curled up enough to taste the ripe buds of her breasts. Her moan of pleasure was sweet music to his ears, a soothing balm to his angry soul. How could he have forgotten the soaring joy of pleasuring a woman?

Not that Joella was one to lie still and let him do all the work. Flint laughed again when she shoved him back down, her slender hands only half-covering his chest. He shifted to his side, trapping her against the couch back so he could plunder at will.

She went for his belt buckle.

He located her skirt zipper first.

She stilled when he ran his hands beneath her waistband and cupped the delicious curve of her buttocks in their silky covering.

He stroked, and she melted into him as if they were two parts of the same whole— flesh against flesh, heads touching, hands rubbing, absorbing the heated sensations of each other's body. Their kisses deepened and consumed, communicating the desire they had yet to fulfill.

As Jo tried to shove Flint's jeans over his hips, a brief flash of rationality hit him. "Condom," he whispered. "Upstairs."

"Pill," she murmured back, nipping at his collarbone and tugging at his waistband. "Clean. You?"

"Yep." And that was the end of rationality for the evening.

When Flint rolled off the couch to kick off his jeans, Jo lay back against the butter-soft cushions and let admiration pump hormones directly into her blood. Flynn Clinton hadn't let his physique go to pot as so many men over thirty did.

The fire played along his naturally bronze skin. Broader in chest than hip, tautly muscled in all the right places, he could have modeled as a Greek god as far as she was concerned. Except she didn't think he could hide all that masculinity beneath a fig leaf.

Before she realized what she meant to do, she leaned on one elbow and kissed the tip of his erection before he had time to return to the couch.

He froze where he stood, with a question behind the burning desire in his eyes.

In answer, she licked the salty taste of him.

She smiled as his fists clenched, and he admirably restrained himself until she'd tested and tasted enough to satisfy her curiosity. A man with that much restraint in the midst of passion was a man who could tumble walls with his bare hands.

That she trusted him enough to do this dissolved all barriers.

When she'd tortured him sufficiently, she wriggled out of her skirt. He was on the couch beside her and had his fingers in her panties before the skirt was past her ankles.

"Let me." He kissed her navel and proceeded downward while his big hands swept the scrap of silk away.

She'd spent weeks imagining this man's hands on her. She wouldn't argue now.

Flint played her with the same finesse as he played his guitar. His talented fingers plucked and strummed and tuned until she reached perfect pitch. Jo screamed her release the instant he applied his tongue.

When he was satisfied she was satisfied, he raised up, parted her knees with his, and shoved deep inside her without missing a beat. It was a coming home and a joyous reunion and a hallelujah chorus all rolled into one.

Jo arched upward until she was full to bursting, savoring the moment as Flint rested his forehead against hers and didn't move. He was seated so deep that he tickled her heartstrings and nearly robbed her of breath. They stole that moment of togetherness, blocking out past hurts and future problems to claim the physical connection of the present.

When fear and regret threatened to raise their ugly heads, Flint shattered them by lifting her hips and thrusting deeper, over and over until the music of their bodies built to a crescendo and crashed with ringing cymbals and a drumroll that refused to end until they dripped with sweat and fell together, satiated and beyond thought.

"Umm, yum," Jo hummed as a warm, rough hand closed over her bare breast.

"My thoughts precisely," a deep voice murmured near her ear.

The hard male body behind her moved closer, curving around her back. A stiff poke against her rump informed her of masculine intentions. She'd better rouse from her pleasant stupor if she wanted to participate. Or stop things now.

She opened one eye and peered over an acre of navy satin sheets. She didn't remember this. "Umm, how did I get here?"

"You demanded all the couch, and I refused to sleep on the floor." The voice was low and silky, and the hand was even better.

"I sleepwalked up here?" She wasn't precisely thinking clearly with lust clouding her brain. She pressed backward, letting him slide between her thighs.

"Something like that." Flint leaned over and nibbled her ear. "Good morning, Starshine."

Then he slid his hand between her legs from the front, and it was a good long time before she cared whether she thought about anything ever again. Flynn Clinton had a way of making a girl feel weightless, timeless, and in a special universe all her own.

Next time Jo opened her eyes, sunlight poured through the picture window that was his bedroom wall. Her stomach rumbled. The Lance crackers from the hospital vending machine weren't designed to last until dawn, much less halfway to noon.

She heard Flint's stomach growl in accompaniment to her own and glanced across the sea of satin to the man who had ravished her more thoroughly than she'd ever been ravished, while playing sweet love songs with her body. She still tingled all over and felt as if she belonged in a harem, taking a wanton bubble bath after a night with the sultan.

Flint lounged with his arm under his head, his splendidly nude body sprawled on top of the sheets, his gaze turned hungrily in her direction.

She wanted more. From his state of semi-erection, she gathered he wanted the same.

And they were both out of their ever-loving minds.

Obviously, she was no longer immune to men, or at least to this one man who hid as much pain or more inside him than she did, a man sensitive enough to notice the people around him, even if he didn't know how to act on what he saw.

She might start thinking she could change a man again if she wasn't careful.

Tearing her gaze away, Jo sat up and looked around for direction. Her clothes hadn't sleepwalked up the stairs with her.

She wasn't shy about her body, but she still felt the sensation of Flint inside her, and her hormones whirled like a tornado centered between her legs, knowing he was watching her every move. She had really done it this time. He was her *boss.*

"Bathroom?" she asked without turning around.

"Across the hall. I'm roughing it out here."

"That's the only way I know to live." Standing, she could see his driveway through the trees. The rain had washed away the summer dust and left the world sparkling with diamond droplets. "There's a fancy white SUV crawling up the drive."

He uttered an expletive and hit the floor running. "I'll bring your clothes up."

She left him dancing into a pair of jeans while she darted across the hall to the shower. It was Saturday. Flint's parents and sons were arriving.

She showered hurriedly, using his smelly shampoo. She had to leave her hair wet after she climbed out because she couldn't find a dryer and didn't have her brush. Flint had dropped her clothes on the bathroom rug and run, but her panties were missing. Wearing this skirt without underwear was almost the most scandalous thing she had ever done. Air tickled where Flint's fingers had been not half an hour ago.

She could hear him down below talking to a shrill female voice.

This was beyond humiliating. She could crawl out a window, except she had nowhere to go. She didn't even have her car.

The knit top and denim miniskirt were meant for the show last night. She couldn't wear them in front of his parents. She wondered what had happened to the dress shirt Flint had provided, but he'd ripped the buttons off it, so it wouldn't be of much use.

She slipped from the bathroom and across the hall to Flint's bedroom. She rummaged until she found a heavy, blue denim work shirt to pull over her sleeveless high-necked shell. The work shirt was loose enough to conceal the fact that her only bra was in the knit top.

She would roast as the day warmed up, but the shirt had a long tail that hung past her hem like a big jacket and held Flint's piney scent, so she felt secure, except for the draft where her panties ought to be.

She checked Flint's underwear drawer and decided his Calvin Klein's might be a trifle noticeable under her skirt, even if she could keep them up, which she probably couldn't.

She turned her mind to other things, determined not to let this faze her. She needed a telephone to check on her mama. She couldn't hide up here forever. At the sound of rising voices below, she decided now might be an excellent time to make her entrance. They couldn't get much angrier.

Jo stalked out in her high-heeled slides, prepared to take on the world, and almost fell over the young Goth sitting at the top of the stairs, tapping away on a laptop. He didn't even glance up at her as she approached.

At the sound of musical notes emerging from the box, Jo lowered herself to the top step with him. She'd never owned a computer. Curiosity was her besetting sin, and she was equally curious about the machine and the kid. No Fear was her new motto. Besides, the kid looked too unhappy to fear him. "It plays music?" she asked, studying the screen.

The notes from the computer were erratic and not high-fidelity. She watched in amazement as he punched some buttons to change them.

"Of course it plays music," he answered with the arrogance of the young. "Do you think he has DSL?"

"DSL? Daily Silly Lines? Yeah, a lot." She really wasn't that dumb, but the kid was way too serious.

He shot her a scornful look that was pure Flint. "For the Internet. Or cable, maybe. I didn't ask when we were here last week."

"Sorry. Cable hasn't reached this far into the hills. We have to use the phone lines. What's that making the music?"

"A program." He hurriedly shut it down, turning off the noise. "I need to plug it in. My battery is low."

"Right. Well, I'm sure there are electric outlets. We got electricity a few years ago." She was pulling his leg, but he seemed to take her seriously.

"Why would anyone live in a hole like this? It's the pits." He got up and walked away, apparently in search of electricity.

Interesting. But she didn't have time for child psychology. She liked kids well enough, but her grand plans for fame and fortune had never included them. Ending up broke and supporting two kids like her mother wasn't on her agenda.

With no other diversion to prevent her from entering the lion's den, Jo headed down the stairs where the argument had escalated to sullen silence.

Flint had to bite back a grin of pride as Joella sashayed down the stairs as if she were wearing a ball gown and glass slippers. Her crowning glory of golden curls were no more than lank, damp tendrils dripping over his shirt, and she was still the most glorious sight he'd ever seen.

And he had to quit thinking of her right now. Despite her declaration of stage fright, she had a promising future outside these hills. His kids deserved better than another traveling musician in their lives.

"Good morning, Mr. and Mrs. Clinton," she called brightly, as if his parents weren't staring at her as if she were Eve and the serpent all in one. Jo switched her gaze to him. "Where's your phone? I need to call and check on Mama. Amy might know if they're fixing the rock slide. If Mama is ready to go home, I'll have to find someone to take us around to the other side of the mountain."

All this flowed like musical notes as Jo nonchalantly strolled past him, his parents, and back to the kitchen. Flint followed as if she were the Pied Piper. He noticed his parents did the same.

"How about some eggs this morning?" she chirruped when she found Adam gazing into the refrigerator. "I'd fix you the best pancakes this side of the Pacific if I thought Flint had the ingredients in there."

She picked up his cordless and hit numbers while she gazed over Adam's shoulder into the refrigerator. "You did good. Eggs and milk and maple syrup. A little flour and baking soda somewhere maybe?"

Flint opened the cabinet with the dry goods. He hadn't a clue what baking soda was, but he had pancake mix and figured that was better.

Propping the telephone against her ear to ask for her mother's room, Jo handed ingredients to a startled Adam. She located the bacon and pulled that out.

It wasn't until she started chatting with Marie and mixing pancakes at the same time that Flint recognized what Jo had done. She had thrown a verbal shield around both of them. Unable to get a word in edgewise, his mother grabbed the bacon and huffily prepared it for microwave cooking. His father took his newspaper and wandered back to the front room. Adam had been handed a fork and the bowl Jo had poured ingredients into, and he mixed the batter, unable to utter a word of protest.

"That's good, Mama. I'll find someone to take me down to get you. Are you sure you'll feel well enough to go all the way around the mountain? I could get you a room in Asheville . . ."

Flint suspected she'd twist arms until she found one, too, then would scrub floors to pay for it. He was calculating how much more his credit card could hold when Marie apparently decided she wanted to go home.

"Let me talk to Amy if she's at the café," he managed to squeeze in when Jo clicked the phone off on one call and began punching in numbers for another.

He tried to keep enough distance between them so he didn't smell his shampoo in her hair or accidentally set his chimes to ringing by touching her. Adam watched them with enough suspicion as it was.

Listening for the phone to ring, she nodded while Flint produced a frying pan from beneath the stove. He'd lived on his own before. He knew the essentials.

"Honestly, Flint," his mother whispered, flinging the platter into the microwave, "you expect your sons to live like this?"

"Hey, Amy, stay away from our new stove," Jo called into the receiver with laughter in her voice, drowning out anything else his mother could say.

The kitchen wasn't big enough for two women, Flint decided. He really ought to escape before the next world war broke out, but he couldn't desert Jo like that. Besides, Adam was turning to him with the bowl of pancake batter as if he expected him to do something with it. Might as well show the kid how it was done.

Just as Jo was showing him how handling family was done. Flint admired her style and resolved to learn it. It wasn't as if he'd paid a lot of attention over the traveling years, but the opportunity beckoned.

In a blinding moment of revelation, he realized he didn't *want* a maternal woman like his mother for a wife. He loved and respected his mother. He'd let her take his kids, after all. But a *maternal* woman tended to nest and peck like a hen if a man got too close to her chicks. A woman like his mother would make life hell. *Damn,* now what would he do? Raise the kids on his own?

Shit, he should have known life never provided an easy road.

After Jo had reported on their mother to Amy and discussed alternative transportation, she handed the receiver to Flint and took over pancake flipping.

Rather than examine his latest brainstorm, Flint checked on business. "All right, why don't you close up around two?" he told Amy on the other end of the line. "That will give everyone time to come in and gossip and get a hot meal if they need it. I sure appreciate this. If Sally babysits the kids, I'll pay for it."

Reassured that his customers were taking the roadblock in stride, even if the tourist business was cut off and his profits wiped out for the weekend, Flint hung up to dump coffee into the machine. Unlike Jo, he couldn't do two things at once.

"Adam helped, so he gets first serving." Jo reached for a plate in the dish cabinet she'd located. "Mrs. Clinton, how many can you and Mr. Clinton eat? I'll remind Flint to stock some frozen strawberries next time so he can make strawberry compote for you."

"We've already eaten," his mother replied frostily.

"Oh, then you won't mind if I give this next batch to Flint. He had a long night last night." She said it with a naughty wink in his direction before ruining the effect by adding, "He was a lifesaver helping me get my mama to the hospital. And you should have seen how he stopped that car when the boulder came down! He ought to be in NASCAR."

"We heard about that on the news. We had to go around a roadblock to get here. It's unsafe living in mountains." His mother checked the bacon, then slammed the microwave door. "You really can't expect your sons to live like this."

Flint grabbed Jo and clapped his hand over her mouth before she launched any more verbal volleys. At the breakfast table, Adam snorted and hastily shoved an enormous forkful of pancake into his mouth.

To get even, Jo nibbled on Flint's fingers and ground her lush tush near his groin, but Flint figured it was time he took control. He didn't need a woman fighting his battles, although he sure appreciated her efforts.

"It's unsafe living anywhere, Mom, and you know it. The boys are mine. Don't push me too far, okay? All I want is what's best for them."

It was a pretty good speech and would have worked, too, if Johnnie hadn't walked in right then with what would have been complete innocence, except Flint knew his clever younger son far better than that.

Johnnie held up his Sunday shirt and the thin strip of silk that Flint hadn't been able to locate in his hurry this morning. "Why were these shoved behind the couch cushions?" he asked.

≈SIXTEEN≫

With the *brazen* knocked right out of her, Jo gave up the fight and waited for the humiliating scene to sink her through the floor. Flint's arm had left a permanent impression on her midriff. She was amazed she could still stand upright when he released her.

She mentally cheered as Flint took his son's defiance in stride. Before Mrs. Clinton could open her mouth, he pointed Johnnie toward the door at the end of the kitchen. "Put those in the laundry and sit down at the table if you want to eat."

Shoulders slumped, the kid dragged himself across the tiled floor to do as told. Not as easily defeated, Mrs. Clinton found the outlet she needed for her rage.

"I cannot let children be raised in a house with these kinds of lewd goings-on. This is *exactly* the reason we took the boys in. They need a stable home environment. You have to learn to live the kind of life—"

"Can it, Mom. If we can't provide a solid front for them instead of this constant carping, then it's no better than before."

Jo watched Flint's noncompromising sternness with admiration. She might not know much about raising kids, but he did. And he wasn't afraid to stand up and show it. Any idea she had harbored that he'd abandoned his kids—as her father had—got up and walked out the door.

His mother shut up and poured coffee for herself and her husband, who'd followed Johnnie in. With relief, Jo returned to flipping pancakes and stayed out of the family squabble—even if those were her panties, and she was standing here with nothing on under her skirt, and Flint had to know it.

A night of sex hadn't reduced the steam between them any. It only took one of his smoldering gazes to imagine him lifting her onto that table and having his way with her.

Hands shaking, she set a plate of pancakes on the large pine trestle table just as Johnnie returned to sit beside his brother. She'd like to collapse in a chair until her knees stopped trembling, but Flint blocked her way. He slapped a jar of sugar-free jam on the table beside the maple syrup without a word of comment. Johnnie took one look at his father's face and reached for the jam.

Jo was impressed. Apparently, if he was watching his kid's weight problem, Flint took his responsibility seriously. He'd even bought *sugar-free* ahead of time. Maybe if she dwelled on his superior character, she'd quit thinking about his bod.

"Can your computer at the café play music?" she asked Flint out of curiosity as well as interest in breaking the awkward silence. She began mixing another batch of pancakes before the first ones disappeared.

"Probably, but I don't have cable to download it."

Jo waited for Johnnie to explain about his program, but the kid sat in sullen silence.

"You could get a satellite dish," Mr. Clinton suggested in an apparent attempt to placate the angry cloud drifting about the room.

"I have a radio if I want music." Flint offered more pancakes to his sons, and when they were refused, dumped them on his plate with the last of the bacon.

Jo caught the exchange of looks between

the two boys. Kids wouldn't be kids unless
they were hiding something. She slid the
platter on the table and reached for the coffeepot to freshen everyone's cup. "Johnnie
has a computer program that plays music."

"Stealing songs off the Internet is robbing
the poor," Flint said bluntly. "Ninety-nine
percent of the musicians who get paid by
record sales are struggling to stay alive."

"We know that," Adam said with disgust.
"We don't steal music."

Jo slid in beside Flint, enjoying their proximity on the bench. Her hip rubbed his as
she leaned over to help herself to some of
the pancakes. His hand slid over her thigh
when she settled back on the bench again.

"Johnnie's program *makes* music," she
said brightly, trying not to show the effect he
had on her. "Maybe he could write a song
for the MusicFest contest."

All eyes turned to Johnnie, who turned a
nice shade of maroon.

"We bought that computer so you could
do your homework, young man," Mrs. Clinton said with disapproval. "There is no future in music, as your father has proved."

Deciding this argument came under the
Life's Too Short category, Jo warbled the

first lines of the soft drink commercial about the world being a better place if everyone could sing in harmony.

Adam choked on the bacon he was inhaling. Johnnie stared in disbelief. And Flint removed his hand from her thigh to hide a grin behind his coffee cup. Watching her speculatively, Mr. Clinton reached for a pancake. Mama Clinton shut up.

Letting Flint discuss the foreign territory of computers and software programs with his sons, Jo ate her breakfast in blissful peace.

Tuesday evening, waiting at her mother's for Amy and the kids to show up, Jo watched Marie wince and rub her back as she bent to sit in her ragged recliner.

"Mom?" She held out her hand to help, not that her mother would accept it. The drive around the mountain on Saturday had been interminable, but her mother shouldn't still be aching. She wasn't taking her medicine again.

"It's just a twinge." Marie shrugged her off.

It had been more than a twinge, but her mother had never been one to complain. It

might have been less distressing to watch if
she had. Jo bit her lip, wondering what
would happen when the insurance ran out
and they couldn't buy pain pills. She
opened up a pill bottle and set it on the tray
of food she'd prepared.

"Those make me sleepy. I'll take them before I go to bed." Marie pushed them away.

"Mama, we paid good money for these
pills, and the directions say to take them
twice a day with meals. Unless you're planning on eating before you go to bed, you
need to take one now." Jo knew perfectly
well her mother avoided taking medication
so the pills didn't get used up too quickly,
but she couldn't bear watching her suffer.
Besides the ones for pain, there were pills
for the hepatitis and pills for the cirrhosis
and pills for a little bit of everything. She had
no idea what happened if they weren't
taken regularly, but it scared her half to
death thinking about it.

Dragging the rolling invalid tray over her
lap, Marie stuck a pill in her mashed potatoes, spooned it up, and swallowed. She
glared at Jo and reached for her iced tea to
wash it down. Her fingers were cigarette-
stained, and even though she wasn't sup-

posed to smoke, her clothes reeked of tobacco. Jo didn't have the heart to call her on it.

"I'm not a child," Marie informed her brusquely after she set down the glass.

Jo didn't remind her of the cost of the pills and the hospital if she didn't take them all as ordered. Amy had to pay for both again this time. Evan would blow a gasket. Risking another expensive hospital visit sounded childish to her.

"You ought to have your own children so you're not mothering me," Marie grumbled.

Accustomed to her mother's demand that her daughters marry and produce grandchildren, Jo laughed. "I can just see me at the PTA meeting wearing sequins and heels. Nope, I'll just have to boss you around instead."

"Joella, whether you believe it or not, I'm a grown woman and don't need your nagging. It looks like Amy isn't coming, so why don't you go home and let me rest in peace? You're pacing like a caged cat tonight."

Jo couldn't help pacing. She hadn't seen Flint since Saturday, after she'd taken Amy's SUV to the hospital to pick up her

mother. Under the watchful eyes of his family, she hadn't dared kiss him good-bye.

On Sunday, Flint had someone pick up
his truck at the café and take it around the
mountain to him, but he'd stayed home with
his sons. The road was still blocked, and he
hadn't come back to work even after the
boys had left. Here it was Tuesday, and the
only time he'd called had been at the café to
talk about the bank deposit and ordering
supplies.

So much for harboring fantasies of romance. She'd known better, after all. Sex
was just sex, even if it had been mind-blow-
ing.

Instead of dwelling on the hurt caused by
Flint's silence, she'd spent these last days
dreaming about his claim that she had real
talent. He'd heard her sing. He hadn't
laughed or brushed her dream aside. True,
they'd ended up in bed, but that had been
her decision and not because of any promise Flint made.

Elise had called yesterday. Despite Jo's
lack of confidence, the lawyer had declared
she had all the evidence she needed, and
she would be sending the lawsuit papers for
Jo's signature by the end of the week. The

thought of suing Flint stuck like a bone in her craw, but the hope that she might be recognized as a real songwriter was finally taking root. She'd like to pick Flint's brains and find out more about her new career, but if he wouldn't talk to her, she would drive up to the Knoxville library. She could learn this on her own.

She just hated thinking of Flint selling the café to pay his lawyers. Maybe that was what he was doing right now. Maybe that was why he wasn't talking to her. She'd put him in a pretty bad position, after all.

"I'm hoping Amy will know when the road will be cleared." Preferring to think about the practical and not the impossible, Jo stopped at the window, but Amy's SUV wasn't in sight. "Business is way off. I'm hardly making pocket change."

Jo really hoped Flint wasn't avoiding her. She'd already called herself every sort of fool for falling into bed with him. But she'd do it again in a heartbeat.

"I'm sure Amy could get you a job at the mill if the café closes," Marie said, switching on the television with the remote.

Jo didn't want to work at the mill, running a loom in a dreary barn of a room where she couldn't see outside. Besides, the mill wasn't hiring.

She didn't know what she wanted. She opened the front door on a muggy June evening and watched in relief as a whirlwind of dust approached up the gravel road.

"Here they are," she called over her shoulder.

Her restlessness wasn't entirely about herself. She'd seen Amy only briefly since she'd brought their mother home. It was almost as if her sister were avoiding her. She strolled down the drive while Amy parked the car and got out to unfasten the kids.

"Hey, munchkin." Jo lifted Louisa when the two-year-old tumbled out of her car seat. "Josh, if you get any bigger, you'll have to carry your sister."

Amy climbed back into the car and looked as if she was about to drive off without saying hello. Jo told the kids where to find the brownies, then, opening the passenger door, leaned inside. Key in the ignition, Amy waited without speaking.

"What's wrong?" Jo demanded.

"Nothing. Not a thing. I'm just late."

"Your eyes are red and your mascara is smeared and you're a lousy liar. Besides, you're already late. Come in and have tea and spit it out. I can take it."

"I can't." Amy stared out the windshield. "Not now. Not yet. Let me go."

"Is it the mill?" Jo asked in alarm. "Is Evan closing the mill?"

Amy looked shocked. "Have you heard something?"

"Rumors have been flying since Christmas. If it's not the mill, what is it?"

"Just give me some time to work this out. I'm late. Let me go."

As Jo reluctantly closed the door, Amy shot her a look of gratitude. "Thanks, Jo. You're a brick."

Stepping back from the drive, Jo *felt* like a brick. Thick and heavy and a useless lump of clay. She *hated* being useless. Or helpless.

She hadn't felt useless Friday night. With Flint, she'd felt whole, as if he was the missing piece that rang her previously silent chimes. Making music with Flint was almost as good as making love with him.

But he was making it clear it wasn't likely to happen again.

She understood. She really did. His mother was a dragon. His kids were difficult. She wasn't sweet little Sally. And she was suing him.

Life was shit sometimes.

"I cinched it," Dave declared triumphantly, striding into the café with a folded newspaper under his arm on Thursday morning. "Randy's album is out in August and he's agreed to come to the MusicFest as a headliner."

"Am I supposed to cheer?" Jo asked, pouring coffee for a customer. It was nearly ten, so the café had almost cleared out.

"No, you're supposed to ask the Buzzards to play backup for him." Dave took a stool at the counter. "He'll be in next week with the music."

"He's too cheap to hire his own backup?"

"It's a charity event, Jo. Ease up, all right?" Disgruntled, he shook out his newspaper. "Flint still hasn't found his way around the mountain?"

"He calls to see how things are going, but he hasn't come in." She'd suggested he could stay at her place to avoid the long commute, but he'd declined. Peggy had been helping out through lunch hours. "Did you tell Randy that Flint was down here?" she asked, struck by a sudden thought.

"Nope. Any reason I should?" Absorbed in his newspaper, Dave wasn't paying attention.

"No, none at all." Not any of her business, either. But a wicked imp in the back of her mind giggled. Maybe she wouldn't have to cut Randy down to size. Flint was likely to do it for her. That would almost be as much fun.

The bell she'd installed over the door yesterday tinkled.

"Road won't be open until next week," a familiar masculine voice rumbled.

With her heart leaping foolishly, Jo set down the coffeepot to admire the man framed in the doorway. Wearing scuffed cowboy boots, black Wrangler's, and a black T-shirt that emphasized bronzed, muscular arms, Flint only needed a guitar slung over his shoulder to look as if he'd just stepped off the stage.

Beneath the wayward lock of hair adorning his high brow, he shot a silver-bullet glance straight at her leaping heart—then up to the bell tinkling over his head as he let the door close. "What the hell is that?"

"Early-warning system," Hoss called from his place at the counter. "Jo got ticked when the Yancy kid stole a doughnut while she was in the restroom."

"How did you know it was the Yancy kid?" Striding in with the confidence of a man who owned the world, Flint nonchalantly threw a wrapped package in Jo's direction as he crossed the floor toward his office.

"He stole the chocolate one with sprinkles I was saving for my break," Jo said with the outrage of the innocent as she examined the package wrapping.

"You tracked him down from the smell of chocolate?" Flint crossed his arms and rested his shoulder against the wall while he waited for her to open his surprise.

All those male pheromones blew her circuits. The package gave her a shield to hide behind while she tamped down raging desire and let the discussion swirl over her head.

"Nah. She ran out the back and caught him in the alley. Grabbed him by the ear and duckwalked him back inside to wash dishes. Heard him wailing as if he was being murdered," Dave claimed. "Jo don't take no nonsense from kids. They learn to respect her for it. Eventually."

"He got a decent lunch out of it." Recovering from the shock of her weak-minded reaction to Flint's arrival, Jo tore the paper from his package with a grand gesture designed for the audience watching her every move. She just had to look down instead of at Flint so she didn't get ideas of falling into his arms.

As the paper fell aside, her eyes widened. Gold- and silver-sequined stars sparkled against a midnight-blue background inside folds of tissue. She shook out the soft blue cloth to reveal a bib apron with *Joella, Star of Stardust Café* embroidered in gold lettering over her heart. Sequins and glitter formed a crystalline high-heeled shoe across the front.

It was the most gorgeous, incredible apron she'd ever seen. *"Star?"* she asked. Her voice cracked, so she finally looked at Flint, probably with foolish stars in her eyes.

He stared back without expression in front of their audience. Still, the intensity of his gaze burned a hole straight into her heart. "I didn't think *queen* worked. Try it on."

All this time he'd been gone, had he been thinking of her like she thought of him? Is that what his gift meant?

Her hands shook as she unfastened the ugly apron she'd washed out every night for a year. She let it fall to the floor, then pulled the new one on over her head and tied the strings in back. The hem was well above her knee, and the cut was far more flattering than the old one. She wanted to cry with an inexplicable welling of happiness.

The nearly empty room broke out in applause.

"Hear, hear," Dave hollered. "Let's have a song from our star!"

"I'm not a star," she muttered. "It probably ought to be a pumpkin instead of a glass slipper." She touched the shoe lovingly, then brushed a wayward tear from the corner of her eye. "I'm just a waitress."

"Our *star* waitress," Hoss corrected.

She didn't know how to do brazen when she was all shook up. She wasn't certain what Flint meant by his gift, except that she wasn't fired. She glanced his way again.

He nodded his approval. "Looks better than the feather in Myrtle's hat."

Jo fought back a smile. "I think Myrtle scored last weekend."

Flint flashed a knowing grin—and entered his office.

Throwing things might be an appropriate response to his disappearing act, but not to his thoughtful gesture. She didn't know how to behave. She wasn't certain anyone had ever given her something as tailor-made for her as the apron. It recognized *her* as special. It spelled out in words that she could understand that Flint didn't take her for granted as everyone else did.

Did it also mean he wasn't selling the café?

She gulped back a lump in her throat and passed doughnuts all around. She wasn't a star. But maybe, for a while, she could be Flint's star.

If he would let her.

Jo flipped over the *Closed* sign at three while Flint took a phone call in his office. He'd helped serve lunch as if nothing had happened this past weekend. She could understand that. She hadn't quite figured out how to deal with it considering they'd both turned fumble-fingered every time they got near each other. On her part, she knew it was because she wanted to touch and didn't dare. She kind of thought he had the same problem.

She wondered if she was supposed to take tomorrow off so he could take Saturday to be with his kids, or if his parents were still speaking to him. She wondered where he meant to spend the night. She wondered a thousand things that she had no right to ask.

She'd known going to bed with the boss would make life awkward—especially if he wasn't interested in following through.

She'd just finished sweeping and was carefully folding up her wonderful new apron when the door opened and Amy flew in. Jo hadn't wanted to lock up until Flint was done with his phone call and had taken the deposit out.

"Is the lawyer here? I couldn't get the kids to settle down and Sally wanted to talk and then the car wouldn't start . . ."

The lightbulb over Amy's head shattered. With a sigh, Jo caught her sister's arm and steered her toward a back booth where the bulb was already shot. "Sit. We don't stock

Valium, and I'm not about to give you caffeine. What's wrong?"

Amy's normally neat, professionally highlighted hair was tousled as if she hadn't combed it since morning. Her eyes looked haunted. Her lips trembled as she looked away and clasped her hands on the table. "He's leaving me."

"What?" Jo collapsed on the bench across the table. "Evan? How? Why?"

Amy rubbed the back of her hand against a teardrop threatening to descend. "I don't know. I asked Flint to call that fancy lawyer he found for you. I can't use anyone around here. They all practically bow to Evan."

"You *hired a lawyer*?" Flabbergasted, Jo sat back and tried to take it in. Amy, the sensible, brainy one of the family, had hired a lawyer against her handsome husband? The one who ran the mill? Which was to say, Evan ran the town, since the mill owned almost everything around here except the few acres the town sat on.

"You should see this." Amy pulled a rumpled sheet of letterhead out of her purse and shook it at Jo. "Just look! It's awful. I can't believe he'd do this to me."

Flint emerged from his office as Jo

scanned the letter. "That was Elise on the phone. Traffic is heavy coming down the mountain, but she'll be here shortly." He took one look at the two of them and returned to the counter to fix coffee.

Jo read the letter again. "This is *horrible.* 'Secure your assets.' What the hell does that mean? 'Close all credit accounts.' Did he do that?" She looked at her sister in horror. "Has he closed your checking account?"

Amy's lips tightened and her normally pleasant expression turned grim. "He hasn't seen the letter. I opened it by mistake, thinking it was a bill."

Flint set two mugs of coffee in front of them and appropriated the letter before Jo could crush it into mashed paper. He scanned it and threw it back at Amy. "You should have asked me for a good divorce lawyer. I'd have called the one my wife hired."

Amy burst into tears. "I don't want a *divorce.*"

❧❦SEVENTEEN❧❦

The bell over the door tinkled, and the most glamorous woman Amy had ever seen outside a television show peered through the semidarkness brought on by the shattered lightbulb. "Anyone home?"

"Over here, Elise." With rangy grace, Flint rose from his seat.

Amy figured Flint for a good-looking scoundrel who would break Jo's heart, but Jo was old enough to know what she was doing. Right now, Amy had to look out for herself. And her kids. She wasn't used to that. She'd gone straight from college to marriage. She didn't think she could stand on her own. She didn't *want* to.

Elise DuBois had the glossy, dark hair of a shampoo model, but she wore it all bundled on top of her head with diamond-encrusted combs in it. Amy assumed they were really zirconia, but the effect was dramatic, especially against the fire-engine-red suit and Hawaiian-print, silk blouse. Amy recognized the outfit from the Saks catalog and suspected Elise was slumming by wearing off-the-rack attire for her mountain sojourn.

She didn't care. The lawyer looked like someone who would chew Evan up, spit him out, and smile while doing it. Elise DuBois was everything that Amy wasn't—smart, spirited, and ruthless beyond her wildest dreams. They'd already had a long, informative conversation on the phone.

"Is this the notorious letter?" Elise picked up the epistle from the local legal firm and held it between two manicured, red-lacquered fingernails. She scanned the legalese in a flick of her long eyelashes, then dropped it back to the table. "They stole this from an old book on divorce written by a shark who's been dead for two years. I could notify his estate and have the firm sued for plagiarism."

She took the seat Flint had vacated. "I have a license to practice in North Carolina, Tennessee, and Georgia, but I'm a contract lawyer, not a divorce lawyer, and I can't claim to know the judges in all three states. You may wish to consider my legal advice, then hire someone locally to handle the case."

She turned to Joella without waiting for a reply. "I'm sorry to return for this purpose. I'd hoped only to see you again when I had the lawsuit filed, but I've brought the papers for you to sign." She opened her briefcase and produced a large manila envelope. "I listened to your demo tape. Your talent is quite amazing. Are you writing anything new?"

Stunned by the force of Elise's personality, Amy took a moment to assimilate the various impressions striking her. Flint had sauntered off to fetch another coffee. Jo was gripping the manila envelope and looking as stunned as Amy felt. Although everyone in town knew Jo wrote clever little poems, no one had ever told her she was talented. They all thought of her as a zany waitress. A good-hearted, generous waitress, maybe, but not someone with the brains to write real songs. That this impressive lawyer thought Jo was talented shed new light on her younger sister and gave Amy a respect for Elise's perceptiveness.

As Jo stuttered out an admission that she was playing with something a little different, Amy made up her mind. By the time Elise turned to her, she was ready.

"I don't want a divorce," she said more steadily than she had earlier. "I don't know what's wrong with Evan, but we have two small children who adore their daddy." When Elise merely raised her professionally shaped eyebrows and waited, Amy took courage and hurried on. "I just want to show Evan that I'm not a doormat. I want to be strong. I want to stand up to him and force him to look at what he's doing. He's so used to having everything his way, it's time he got his comeuppance."

Elise broke into applause, and Jo hastily followed. Flint set a mug down in front of the lawyer and backed off with a frown, crossing his arms over his chest in disapproval.

"You'd better go away, Flint," Jo teased. "We're on the warpath and you don't want to get in our way if you're feeling loyal to the male gender."

"I like your sister, and I'm not feeling loyal to any bastard who would desert her or his kids, but I'm feeling like a newt in a witch's cauldron, so I'm outta here. If I'm going to be in at the crack of dawn, I'll need a place to crash tonight. Your offer still stand?"

Amy watched with interest as Jo tried to suppress her surprise and delight, and the big tough man in the cowboy boots wiggled like a fish on a hook. She'd be fascinated by the looks they exchanged if she weren't so terrified.

"Make yourself at home," Jo replied. "Door's not locked."

Flint opened his mouth, apparently to object to that carelessness, took another look at the three of them, and closed it again. With a nod of farewell, he stalked off.

"Jeans look good on tight asses," Elise reflected, watching Flint walk away.

Jo snickered at the double entendre but didn't disagree.

Disregarding her coffee, Elise sat back in the booth and studied Amy until she wanted to squirm. Suddenly aware of her disheveled hair and lack of makeup in the face of Elise's perfection, she wanted to crawl under the table and disappear.

"If you're willing to play hardball, I'm the one to teach you, but it won't be pleasant. There will be a lot of shouting when he learns what you've done. Are you prepared for that?"

No, of course not. She loved Evan. She'd first learned to make muffins to give him something to nibble while he studied for finals his senior year. She'd worked bakery jobs to keep them in food while he got his MBA. They'd lived over his parents' garage while he trained at the textile mills in South Carolina and she'd been pregnant with Josh. They'd both worked hard to get where they were today. She had a degree in textile design that she'd used to help Evan with new ideas for the mills where he worked. They'd been partners. Their tenth anniversary was in December.

"I don't want it to be like this," she whispered, staring at the horrible letter that had ruined her life.

"Is there another woman?" Jo demanded.

Amy flinched. "Maybe. I've been trying to find out. The mill is in some financial trouble and the board of directors has been down here a lot."

"Lurid Linda!" Jo exclaimed without need of further explanation. "I've heard all about her. She's the treasurer, isn't she? Owns a mess of stock?"

Amy ducked her head in agreement.

"Your husband's place of employment is in trouble?" Elise asked, focusing on the matter of importance to her. "Could he lose his job?"

"He'll just take one in another mill if they close this one. He gets offers all the time. I think some members of the board own stock in lots of mills. Maybe he's trying to stay on their good side so they'll hire him elsewhere."

"Well, your case is a lot more clean-cut and simple than suing record companies, and it sounds as if we better act quickly," Elise declared. "First, you have to transfer all your cash into your name only. Can you do that?"

Amy blinked in surprise. "Evan will be furious if he finds out."

"How soon is he likely to find out?"

She thought about it. "I pay the bills, so as long as he can use his debit card, he wouldn't. But if I change the accounts, the card will fail."

"Keep enough in the account so his card isn't likely to fail. If his paycheck is deposited in that account, you'll have to keep it open anyway. Just make certain you reg-

ularly transfer all you need into your account. Do you own stocks? CDs? Cash
them in." Elise started ticking off commands
on her fingers. "Take your name off all the
credit cards. Have him sign the back of the
car title. Tell him you're getting a new license plate or whatever. Busy men don't
care how these things work."

Amy rummaged in her purse for notebook
and pen. Her hand was shaking, but she
could handle practical things like this if it
would get her husband back.

"Run a credit check. See if your husband
has opened any accounts or bought anything that you don't know about."

She started to protest that he wouldn't do
anything like that without consulting her, but
then she remembered he'd consulted a
lawyer about a divorce without mentioning it
to her. She'd seen Fritz in church on Sunday, and the lawyer had looked her in the
face, knowing Evan was thinking of leaving
her. She wished she could take Fritz down,
too. The plagiarist.

"Send me copies of your house deed,
mortgage papers, and tax returns for the
last three years, along with a copy of the
credit report."

Amy carefully wrote each instruction on a separate line so she could check them off as she accomplished them. Why had she never realized that she'd let Evan control her life because he earned a paycheck and she didn't? He only had that job because she was there to help him every step of the way. They were supposed to be partners, equals, but he'd always been the one to tell her what to do and when and how to do it. That could change.

"And I'd suggest you hire someone to document how your husband spends his time. Should it come to a showdown, a paper trail is much stronger than accusations."

The pen fell out of Amy's hand and bounced under the table.

Hire someone to find out how Evan spent all those hours in "meetings"? Did she really want to know for certain that he was *sleeping* with Lurid Linda?

With a cry of pain and grief, Amy leaped from the booth and ran for the restroom before anyone could see her break down and weep like a baby.

"Well, that went well. Not."

Flint looked up from the cookbook he'd

bought in Asheville as Jo stormed in, slamming the door behind her. He couldn't concentrate on the damned book when his mind kept drifting to Jo and that bed hidden up in the loft and what they could do there.

He'd spent these last days trying to get her out of his system. Instead, he'd ended up in Asheville ordering that apron, buying cookbooks to please her, and wondering if he needed to hire a new shrink. She was *suing* him for christsake. If that didn't call for getting his head examined, he didn't know what did.

But watching her now, he saw all the kazillion reasons why she'd infiltrated his brain and seeped into his blood. Jo was not only talented and sexy, but passionate and determined and concerned about others far more than herself. And damned independent, he had to remind himself, before he got any other ideas.

"Divorce is a nasty business," he agreed mildly, although he felt anything but mild watching Jo pace the loft with electricity all but arcing from every hair tip.

She held the papers suing him for everything he owned. His badass side longed to kiss her into insensibility before she threw the papers at him. But he admired Jo too damned much to hurt her. Hands-off was the best policy, even if he had to tie his wrists behind his back.

"Your shark of a lawyer is making it nastier," she declared, throwing the envelope on the chair. "Did you know Elise has a daughter? That she's divorced from the man who was once her partner and had all his custodial rights terminated? I've never seen a woman so stone-cold. How can anyone like that marry and produce offspring?"

Flint would laugh at her naïve outrage, but he figured the subject was volatile and he ought to tread softly. "Life happens. You either learn to roll with the punches or end up battered and broken."

All the spark seeped right out of her. Her shoulders slumped, and she shoved wisps of curls from her forehead. He had the urge to get up and hug her, but she didn't look at him. He figured that was a bad sign.

"You're right. Amy has to learn to roll. I don't want her battered. But those poor kids—" She shook her head and proceeded to the galley kitchen. "Want anything to drink?"

He remembered what she'd said about

wanting to show her daddy how well she'd turned out and figured she was dealing with some issues here. He sure understood the pain of divorce anyway.

Flint swung his legs off her couch. "I'm fine, thanks. Are you sure you're okay with me staying here? I can probably set something up in the office if I need to."

Jo spun around and finally looked at him. In the afternoon light from the high loft windows, she gleamed like a crystal lamp. Her hair tumbled over her long gold earrings to her nearly bare brown shoulders. She wore some kind of sparkly gold off-the-shoulder shirt over pleated, white linen shorts, and Flint would almost bet she had shimmery gold heels to match when she went anywhere but work. She'd kicked off her Nikes when she'd come in and stood there now barefoot, looking rumpled and more desirable than riches.

"You're fine. The couch is more comfortable than a sleeping bag."

Well, so much for hoping they'd share a bed. He knew she had the right of it. That didn't mean logic applied to lust.

Quelling a clamor of testosterone, Flint rose and threw the cookbook on the counter beside her. "I have to pay for that fancy stove somehow. I think we better open for dinner once the road is cleared."

She glanced at the book's title. "You bought a stove to sell fancy hamburgers?"

"It's what I can cook," he said defensively. "I make a mean meat loaf."

"Because it's easier than pressing out hamburgers. Got it."

Flint knew she was being sarcastic, but he wasn't listening. His brain had switched off the instant he'd stepped in reach of all those supple curves he'd only begun to explore. He studied the way naturally rose lips parted to reveal that cute overlapping tooth. If he thought about what she had done with that mouth, he'd spontaneously combust.

"Dave hired Randy as the headliner for the MusicFest," those plush lips were saying.

Flint jerked back from his little head trip. "RJ? Here? Is he crazy?"

Jo stepped out of his reach and leaned against her miniature stove. Apparently gathering the path of his straying thoughts, she crossed her arms to hide her splendid assets. "Randy is an arrogant ass, always has been. He thinks everyone will forgive him because he's so charming and good-looking."

"He knows better than to think I'll do anything but smash his pretty nose," Flint growled.

"I doubt he knows about the lawsuit yet. Does he know you're living here?"

That stopped him in his tracks. "He knows I'm from here, but I haven't spoken to him since he and Melinda . . ." He winced. He hadn't meant to say that. Telling a woman that her boyfriend slept around was asking for dish hurling.

Jo shrugged. "Randy was never celibate. I assume you were divorced at the time?"

Flint nodded, oddly relieved that she harbored no jealous feelings for the bastard. "I didn't buy the café until after she died, so he probably has no idea where I'm at."

"You and Elise would make a good pair."

He heard her sarcasm but didn't grasp its origin. Instantly on the defensive after all the years of fighting with Melinda, he asked, "You think I'm cold?"

"You were married to Melinda for what—ten years? And all you can say about her is that she fell in bed with Randy?" She reached for a tumbler in the cabinet and slammed it onto the tiny counter. "Marriage sure is a piece of shit, isn't it?"

"Where in hell did this come from?" he demanded angrily, caught off guard by her unexpected attack. "You think because I asked to sleep on your couch that I'm a fair target? Or do women just figure they get to cut a man's balls off and use them as keepsakes once they've slept together?"

To his astonishment, a big smile crossed Jo's expressive features, turning her cat eyes up in the corners. "That's a good one. You could put it to music and make another fortune." She tilted her head, narrowed her eyes, then warbled to no tune at all—"I'm ruined for all time, because she kept what was mine, and all we did was roll in the hay."

Flint cracked up. Leaning against the counter, he hooted with laughter, then held his sides and laughed harder when she joined in and the dam of tension broke. Maybe it was relief that he didn't have to fight with Jo that let him breathe easy enough to laugh. It had been a damned long time since he'd been able to let go and be himself.

"You're not doing this to me again,

Joella," he gasped between waning chuckles. "Your singing is inspirational in more ways than one, and I'm under the impression you're not willing to go there anymore."

She heaved a sigh that lifted her gold-draped breasts and inspired him even more than her voice. Flint trained his gaze on the glittering reflection balls dangling over his head rather than admire the more enticing view down here.

"I don't need my heart broke anymore, don't want to end up like Amy, and there isn't much future with a man who has more troubles than I have. So, yeah, I guess we'd better not make beautiful music together." Jo poked him in the chest so he had to look at her. "Besides, I have to go to Mama's tonight. Friends, okay?"

He sucked in a deep breath of her powdery scent and realized right then and there that it wasn't okay. Jo wasn't Melinda. She might be an emotional roller coaster, but she didn't rocket senseless arguments into knock-down-drag-outs. She laughed at herself and calmed stormy waters.

It was all wrong that he had to give up this perfect woman because the world was ass-backward. So, maybe he had to figure out how to set his small corner of the world spinning in the right direction again.

He had to be Atlas instead of Job. Yeah, he could see that happening in the next millennium or two.

≪EIGHTEEN≫

Like the chicken she was, Jo waited for Flint to leave the apartment the next morning before she stirred from her pillows. He'd been sound asleep on the couch when she'd come home last night.

It had been a long, long time since she'd had a man in her house. He'd looked scrumptious stretched out there with only one of her old sheets pulled over his hips. She'd just stood there for a bit admiring his muscular, brown chest decorated with dark curls, and the nut-brown hair falling over a wide forehead hiding way too many brains. In sleep, his mouth softened to almost approachable, and she'd debated shucking her clothes and doing what came naturally. She didn't think he'd fight her off.

She'd resisted and hadn't slept a wink as a result. Still, she figured she'd done him a favor. If he was running the café on his own today, he'd needed his rest.

And she needed to think about those papers Elise had brought. She had to sign them if it meant money for her mother and a shot at a career. She couldn't sign them if it meant Flint would lose his café.

If she were a hard-hearted sort like Elise, she'd worry that Flint had seduced her so she wouldn't sue. But she'd been the one doing the seducing. He was being a perfect gentleman. Well, as much as a guy like Flint could be gentlemanly.

She lay there admiring the red and yellow log-cabin quilt hanging over the rafter above the foot of the bed. The sounds of the town waking up were nearly drowned under the hum of the window air conditioner she'd turned on for Flint's benefit.

She'd had a hard time at Mama's last night keeping quiet about Amy and Evan, or the lawsuit papers. She desperately needed to talk to her mother the way daughters did on TV, but she'd known from an early age that her mama didn't handle disaster well, and now that she was sick, it was unfair to burden her with their problems.

Mama would be hysterical if she knew

what Amy was up to. Marie had never even divorced their runaway father, although during her occasional binges, she would flay his name with acid scorn and tears of regret.

Nope, Mama would tell Jo she had no business suing a man who was only trying to make a living. And she'd pitch a fit if Jo told her that Flint was staying in her apartment. Well, most mothers would do that. If Jo heard one more time that old saw about why should a man buy a cow if he can have the milk for free, she'd kick the next cow she saw.

Still, for the sake of her own soft heart, she would have to figure out how to keep her relationship with her boss professional. She'd brought back a bunch of her mother's recipe cards. Once upon a time her mother had been a good cook. Jo couldn't remember those days, but Amy sort of did. Their parents' separation had shattered their world early.

As it would for Amy's kids. Louisa and Josh loved their daddy, even if Evan was an arrogant prick.

Not wanting to consider that ugly thought this early on a sunny morning, Jo flung back

her sheet and got up. In the cool breeze off
the mountain, she didn't think the air conditioner was necessary. She switched it off
and opened the loft window. She hadn't
been comfortable wearing nothing to bed
with Flint sleeping below, so she'd dragged
out the long jersey knit nightgown her
mother had given her for Christmas. A large
T-shirt would have covered more, but she
had wanted to look as if she owned a nightgown.

She was balancing on one foot, scratching it with the other, and contemplating the
wardrobe she used as a closet when she
heard the first frightening squeal of brakes,
and her heart gripped.

The flashing memory of last weekend's
boulder incident sent her dashing to the
dormer window overlooking the street below.

She was just climbing on the window seat
when she heard the crash. Wincing, she
pried open the screen to lean out. The noise
had sounded as if it was directly below.

She located the Krispy Kreme delivery
truck that had foolishly been backing out of
the alley onto the narrow road. The semi
from the mill had apparently clipped its rear

bumper. Both trucks partially blocked the curve in the mountain highway.

Satisfied the noise was no more than a fender bender, she was about to retreat from the window when she heard the rumble of a dump truck from the rock slide coming down the hill into the hollow that formed the town. And coming around the curve from the opposite direction was a pickup stacked with poultry crates. Neither vehicle was slowing down.

"Move them!" she screamed to the truck drivers climbing out of their cabs.

But she was two and a half stories up, and they were already pulling out their cell phones and couldn't hear her over their angry shouts at each other.

At the squeal of brakes outside the café, half of Flint's customers rose from their seats to check out the action. Since the doughnut truck had a new driver and had been late this morning, Flint didn't have to look. The driver had pulled into the alley instead of backing in.

Arms full of doughnut boxes, Flint couldn't drop everything at the crash. He cursed himself for not having gone out and directed the truck onto the narrow highway, but without Jo here, he'd had a hectic morning and a shop full of customers and his mind hadn't been focused on the driver's ineptitude. He hadn't been thinking about his customers either. He'd been imagining Jo walking in the door and singing her song about survival. She'd royally screwed his head around.

Flint lowered the boxes to the counter and started toward the door.

"Damn, that's the semi from the mill," George Bob shouted, already at the entrance. "I've told Evan they drive too fast through town—"

Massive brakes rumbled with a more protracted roar than the semi's quick squeal. Something with a heavy load was trying to miss the accident in the middle of the highway.

The resulting collision shook the entire building with the force of a bomb.

Flint dived to keep the dish cabinet from falling onto Sally and Dave at the counter.

An ominous creak followed the crash, and in seconds the big picture window with its shelf of rainbow plates imploded in splintering shards and a cloud of dirt.

With the cabinet steadied, Flint vaulted over the counter at the explosion of glass, throwing himself between the window and a couple of Sally's church ladies. Flying debris hit his back as he shoved his coughing customers beneath a table.

While he waited for the roof to fall and kill them all, the air—and his shop—filled with dust and rubble spilling from the overturned dump truck. From somewhere above, like a choir of angels over the steady patter of debris, Jo's soprano screamed curses and worried questions.

Propped up on an elbow to keep from crushing the old lady half under him, Flint rubbed his brow and tried to reorient himself. Jo. Upstairs. He cast a glance to the stamped-tin ceiling. A corner had peeled away at the front where the wall sagged, but Jo's apartment hadn't fallen on their heads. Yet.

"Flint! Are you in there? Is everyone all right?" The cackle of frightened chickens followed Jo's frantic cries.

Okay. He could do this. He was still alive. He was about to be sued for the rest of his life, but he had to make certain everyone was okay first so they could make it to their lawyers.

Apologizing to the old lady who looked more dazed than crushed, he crawled out from under the table to survey the damage.

"George Bob needs help," Sally told him, dusting off her skirt and reaching down to help the women he'd knocked down.

Dave was leaning over the insurance agent, pressing a handful of paper napkins to George's forehead. Flint reached over the counter for some clean towels, handed them to another of the church ladies to press against the wound, then made the rounds of the room, righting chairs and tables and customers, mouthing reassuring phrases while he tried to figure out what the hell had just happened.

The frame of his front window was filled with a mountain of rock and dirt. The lively Fiestaware was crushed into dust. His door was lying on the floor. More gravel and dirt blocked the entrance.

Several of his customers were shouting back at Jo on the outside. Even he couldn't imagine how Jo might have instigated this disaster.

He was in too much shock to do more

than operate on automatic. Jo was okay. His sons were safely back in Charlotte with his parents. That's all he needed to keep going. He righted another chair and helped a frail old man he thought might be the county judge into it. Great. A judge as witness that his shop was unsafe and had caused grave injury and shock to the town's leading citizens.

Flint wanted to get down on his knees and give thanks that no one had been seriously injured, but he wasn't as comfortable as Jo in talking with the Man Upstairs. He let Sally and the church ladies take care of that for him. He wished Jo were in here to sing a hymn. That's what he needed right now. Jo's voice.

As if she'd read his mind, she called, "Coming through!" over the rising murmur of frightened customers. Every shell-shocked and dirty inhabitant of the café turned to gape as pink, high-heeled mules and long, brown legs dangled from the top of the dirt mound in the doorway. The door-frame cut off the top half of her, until she slid down the pile in what appeared to be a long, rose-pink T-shirt that revealed every enticing curve.

A white hen slipped down the mound with her, squawking all the way.

"Hey, y'all," she cried, scanning the room with the efficiency of a kindergarten teacher on the first day of school. Relief rose in her eyes as even George Bob sat up to show all was well. When her gaze met Flint's, his world shifted back in place. Everything would be fine if Jo was smiling. The realization ought to shock him, but he was too busy fighting his urge to hug her.

"It's high time we planted our summer annuals anyway," she announced, to Flint's bafflement. But his customers laughed, obviously understanding her joke.

"What is this, Joella and Chickenwoman come to the rescue?" Dave asked, catching the cackling, frightened hen.

"Oh, y'all are missing the show!" she cried happily, gesturing at the street. "Go on out the back and down the alley. Anybody got a video camera? We could sell this to the news."

She made the disaster sound like a circus produced for their entertainment. Flint was torn between yelling at her for her absurdity and kissing her for it. People were already heading for the rear exit instead of sitting dazed and weeping.

"It's just a scratch, Georgie," she crooned, kneeling beside her childhood nemesis and examining the bloody towel George held to his head.

Flint figured it was more than a scratch to make that much blood, but the skinny insurance agent bravely climbed to his feet under her assurances.

"If you get out there in time, you can have all the doughnuts you can eat," she chattered happily to her remaining audience. "And a chicken in every pot, too. I hope you're not McIlvey's insurance agent, Georgie. It's his pickup that sideswiped the Krispy Kreme. I think he had every hen he owns in there."

From George's curses and the way he hurried for the exit, Flint assumed the unfortunate McIlvey was indeed insured. Shifting booths into place as the last of his customers departed, Flint pretended he wasn't working his way across the room to Jo.

He knew better the instant he reached her. She looked up at him, and her smiling mask crumpled—just before she flung herself into his arms.

He needed all those supple curves pressed against him to remind him that life was good and not the disaster it seemed at this minute. He wanted to shake in his boots and swear from fear, but insane as it sounded—with Jo in his arms, all was well in the world.

He held her tightly, murmuring, "It's okay," over and over, while stroking her slender back. The jersey knit nightgown was no better protection than air against her nakedness. He could feel her warmth, feel the bones of her spine, feel her heaving sobs as she cried into his shirt. He could easily distract himself with thoughts of sex.

But that's what had got him here in the first place—running away from reality. Concentrating on reassuring Jo to keep from joining her sobs, he cradled her against him, kissing her hair, making wild promises to shore up their mutual morale.

"Is everyone outside all right?" he asked as her sobs slowed to hiccups.

She nodded against his shoulder. "Not sure about the chickens, but there wasn't anyone on the sidewalk. I left the drivers screaming at each other."

"Then everything is all right." He rubbed

her spine some more, hoping to reinforce his platitudes. "People are more important than things."

She nodded, but it was a halfhearted effort. "It will be weeks before you can open again. All your pretty dishes—"

She threatened to descend into sobs again. Taking her shoulders, Flint propped her at arm's length and waited until she raised teary eyes. Even covered in dirt, with her golden hair disheveled, she was gorgeous beyond words. Even his muse couldn't create a poem as beautiful as Jo. He was a goner, for sure, thinking like that, but she wasn't looking for flattery and he wasn't looking for sex while knee-deep in catastrophe.

"I'm insured, I promise," he told her. "The policy covers loss of income, not that we can show much of that. I needed a new front door anyway. I'm sorry about the dishes you liked, though. They're kind of busted."

Jeez, he sounded just like her being Little Miss Optimistic. But he was relieved when she wiped away her tears.

She glanced at the shelves now bereft of their colorful array of pottery. "They were ugly anyway." She hiccuped. "I just thought they livened the place up a little."

"Liar. Where are your Nikes? You can't walk in this rubble in those things."

Jo glanced down at her pink mules and managed a smile. "I think these are a stylish way to face disaster. But I'd better find real clothes before I go out again. Let me run upstairs while you take a look at the fun. You might as well enjoy the circus."

Flint accompanied Jo outside and watched her safely traverse the stairs, then strolled out to face the disaster that would probably wipe his livelihood off the face of the map, despite all his brave words.

"I left the kids with Mama and came as soon as I could," Amy said breathlessly after running down the street from the upper parking lot.

Standing on the covered front porch of the hardware store, watching Flint and a half dozen other men shoveling rock and debris out of the café and away from the sidewalk so a bulldozer could scoop them up, Jo shrugged her acknowledgment. Her insides were too twisted to do more.

The café was ruined.

"Oh, no," Amy groaned, registering the scope of the disaster. "That's the mill's load of new designs! Evan was counting on increasing orders with those tapestries."

Jo surveyed the bolts of upholstery fabric scattered across sidewalks and buried under a few tons of rubble. Chickens scratched at brocade tapestries and silk jacquards. Myrtle—feathered sun hat still in place—now sported a purple plaid cloak. The mill had switched the looms to expensive decorator fabrics only recently. A fortune in material adorned Main Street more colorfully than Christmas decorations.

Remembering Flint's assurances, Jo tried to make the best of it. "I imagine they're all insured."

"They're insured at cost, but their profit is wiped out," Amy said gloomily. "And the designer expo is next month. They'll lose next year's sales if the samples aren't in it."

Uneasiness gnawed at Jo's gut, but she had her own problems to solve. Evan would have to solve his. She couldn't just stand here and do nothing any longer.

The boxes of doughnuts had disappeared in a twinkling. Farmer McIlvey was still chasing chickens. The bulldozer could handle dirt. Jo took a deep breath. "Let's rescue fabric then." She marched into the street to grab a bronze jacquard bolt from beneath the dented Krispy Kreme van that had started all this.

A plate-sized oil spot saturated the center of the bolt.

She set it neatly in the alley, anyway, out of the path of tow trucks and bulldozers.

Following Jo's example, Amy grabbed bolts of contrasting gold and yellow from beneath a flock of chickens and set them next to the jacquard.

Stepping from the sidelines where she'd been watching with half the town, Sally joined them, rescuing a bolt from beneath the overturned semi's tire and grabbing the pretty purple plaid from Myrtle on her way to add it to the stack.

Jo knew the cloth was ruined. Oil and dirt and chicken droppings mixed with tire tracks and glass. She couldn't simply stand there and do nothing, and the fabric was too lovely to throw out. Maybe their mama could sew new curtains or covers for her old couch from the salvage.

Reluctant to wash down the street until the bulldozer had removed as much of the dirt as possible and tow trucks had righted the dump truck, the town's volunteer fire department set down their hoses and joined the women in hauling fabric. A line of people formed from the back of the mangled trailer and up the street, passing the bolts to every available doorway once the cloth filled the alley.

Jo's muttered "Yo ho, heave ho" soon took an upbeat turn to Disney's "Whistle While You Work."

When enough dirt on the sidewalk in front of the café was cleared for her to traverse, she carried a spectacular bolt of plum and turquoise through the smashed door-frame and draped the cloth across the counter. On her way out, she passed Flint, who had stripped off his sweaty T-shirt in the increasingly warm June sun.

"I like a man who can use his hands," she murmured, brushing a kiss against his bronzed biceps, thrilling at the sexy smell of musky sweat and heated skin. She had to back off to keep from wrapping her arms around his naked waist.

Flint had his hands full of shovel and dirt and couldn't grab her as she sashayed past. But knowing she left him grinning instead of growling made her lighthearted.

Chickens scattered across the two-lane as a silver Mercedes sedan rolled down the street, not stopping at the parking lot but driving up next to the water truck. As a tall, well-dressed pair emerged to survey the damage, Amy stood beside Jo.

"Lurid Linda," Amy said, naming the female driver while brushing chicken feathers off her filthy jeans.

With her shining auburn hair captured in a chignon, wearing an immaculate gray designer suit and white silk blouse, the board treasurer stepped out.

"And Evan, come to survey the disaster," Jo surmised, recognizing her elegant brother-in-law climbing from the passenger seat. His dark blond hair was so neat, she had to assume he used hair spray. In contrast to the jeans everyone else was wearing, Evan looked untouched and professional in his blue pin-striped suit, despite the rising June heat.

Jo had to admit, Evan and Linda made a spectacular couple.

✖NINETEEN✖

Sensing work halting all around him, Flint flung another shovelful of dirt off his front step into the street, then turned to see what disaster loomed next on his horizon.

His upper arm still burned where Jo had seared it with her kiss. She was an unabashed mix of optimism, passion, and talent, and he felt the tug of her presence no matter where her busyness carried her. He'd heard her singing the "Volga Boatmen's Song," smiled when it changed to a country version of the Disney dwarfs' "Heigh-ho, heigh-ho," and eagerly awaited her next choice of music.

With a jolt of fear, he realized that it was her silence that had warned him.

He had to climb up the mound of dirt and stone to see the Mercedes parked in the middle of chaos. A handsome couple stood beside the car, consulting with heads bent, ignoring the frozen townspeople watching them with varying expressions of hope, wariness, and cynicism. Flint ground his molars, wondering if the sharks had smelled blood and arrived already.

To his amazement, quiet little Amy was the one who stepped forward, carrying a bolt of the fabric Jo had been squirreling away to safety. Neither of the pair in suits offered to take the heavy bolt from her, although both were taller and probably stronger. They examined the damage, glanced around at the remaining fabric buried under dirt, and shook their heads.

Flint suffered the horrible notion that they'd just condemned the town to death.

He started down the dirt pile to join Jo and find out what was really happening when he noticed a tanker truck heading a little too fast around the bend toward them. Due to the rock slide, truck traffic on the highway had practically halted except for local deliveries. The town had no gas stations. He couldn't imagine why the tanker was out here—or how it would get out now that it had reached a dead end. The road wasn't wide enough for turning around.

Apparently not noticing the obstruction until he drove past the post office on the curve, the driver slammed his brakes into a grinding squeal. A flock of escaped chickens flew up from the roadway, hitting his windshield and bouncing off.

Distracted by the chickens, the truck driver veered to his right—in the opposite direction of the café for a change. The semi cab's forward motion slowed, but on the hill, the tank behind it had a momentum of its own.

Flint had seen trucks jackknife before, and his heart lodged in his throat. He dived down the mound, caught Jo's arm, and all but threw her toward the café on his way out to the street. Oblivious to anything but her confrontation with the Mercedes couple, Amy remained where she was, arguing heatedly. Flint dashed into the street as the semi's brakes ground to a halt. He grabbed Amy, hauling her backward to the sidewalk. With Flint's actions as warning, everyone in the street scattered.

The steel tank continued its slow slide at an angle to the stopped cab. Flint flattened Amy and Jo against the building as the trailer's wheels hit an obstacle—not inches from the fire truck and the Mercedes.

The heavy load of liquid sloshing inside the tank didn't stop as neatly.

The trailer tilted. Screams of warning split the air. The driver jumped from the cab just as the tank tore loose and toppled—straight onto the Mercedes and the fire truck.

Unlike in the movies, flames didn't soar dramatically into the air. Instead, in an anticlimactic hiss, brown liquid dribbled from the busted seams of the tank where it had dented upon impact. The drips increased to a steady flow as the tank settled into the fire truck ladder. Within moments, the brown goo reached the roof of the Mercedes, trickled down its windshield, and created a river over its hood to the street.

A white hen squawked, flew up to the Mercedes hood, and was quickly coated in sticky brown. Her cackles drew more of her feathery friends.

Shaken, Flint wiped his brow. Jo stood beside him, and he wrapped his arm around her without thinking. She'd donned a halter top that didn't cover her much better than the nightgown, but he was grateful for the warm flesh he grasped. His imagination had envisioned explosions and rolling balls of flame, and terror had struck down deep in his soul.

"Adrenaline rush," she murmured, recalling the night of the boulder when she'd said the same, and they'd ended up in bed. Flint wished he'd gone up in her loft last night and shared that bed. He was starting to think that life in this damned town was too short to deny themselves pleasure. He'd carry her upstairs right now except he feared the building would collapse before they reached the top.

"What is that slime?" he asked, seeking a more suitable direction for his straying thoughts and lighting on the Perfect Couple. They hovered on the sidelines, staring in dismay at their shiny car disappearing under a river of brown syrup and a flock of feathers.

"Molasses," Amy gasped from Jo's other side, holding her hand over her mouth.

Flint couldn't decide whether she was holding back laughter or tears.

"For the cookie plant down by the mill," Jo explained.

Molasses? Tacky brown hens strutted up and down the street, tracking goo and

feathers from the Mercedes to the flying pig
before the full impact of this made-for-TV
drama bypassed his terror and hit his funny
bone.

Molasses! Holy shit. Flint had to chew
back a shout of laughter. Molasses and
doughnuts and chickens and rocks. If the
Man Upstairs was trying to tell him something, he was doing it with a wicked sense
of humor.

A chicken squawked and leaped from the
Mercedes to Evan's head as he inspected
the damage.

Jo giggled. Amy chuckled. And before
Flint could warn them about inappropriate
behavior, they fell into each other's arms
and roared until tears ran down their
cheeks.

Flint bit his cheek and kept a straight face
as the tall blond guy wiped the hen off his
hair, then came toward them looking as if
he'd chewed sour grapes for breakfast.
Sour grapes with molasses dressing. A
rumble of laughter started inside Flint's
belly, even though he had to agree with the
guy stalking toward them.

"This isn't funny, Amaranth," Evan said
furiously, wiping at his face and hair with his

handkerchief, while the sisters broke up and laughed louder. "Without the profit from that shipment, we won't be able to make next month's payroll."

Amaranth? Flint tried to concentrate on the ludicrous, but Amy's laughter suddenly dried up and Jo's grip transferred to his bare arm, warning of worse to come.

"Work some overtime and put out a new shipment," Amy suggested. "Call in some of the people you laid off. They're all good workers. They can do it. One truckload shouldn't shut down the mill."

Shut down the mill.

Trying to ignore the growing pain in his gut, Flint glanced around. He wasn't the only one who had heard Evan. Others had eased closer. Lips tightened. Women wept. Work-worn hands balled into fists.

"Those were our samples." Evan flung his arms wide to encompass the stacks of bravely rescued fabric. "Next year's orders are based on them."

The rich colors suddenly looked soiled and sad beneath his disparaging gesture.

"We can't sell what we can't show." Without a word of comfort to his distraught wife, Evan stalked up the sidewalk, past his stunned audience, in the direction of the parking lot. The woman he'd arrived with fell into step with him.

"He's taking your car," Jo muttered. "I hope you got that title signed."

"Josh spilled juice in the front seat this morning." Wiping her eyes, Amy hiccuped and put on a brave face to match Jo's. "Lurid Linda will have to sit on the wet spot."

Flint decided then and there that he didn't want to get on the wrong side of the Sanderson sisters and their subversive attitude. Using Jo's method of rationalization, Flint figured that not only came under the heading of Life's Too Short, but started a whole new column of Dare at Your Own Risk.

Joella slipped into Flint's office, out of the cacophony in the dining room. The café had always been the town gathering place. Despite the lack of window and door, things hadn't changed.

"You have company," she said softly to the man slumped in Charlie's battered chair.

Flint had washed up in her apartment and donned clothes from his duffel bag after the bulldozer and tow trucks had finished their work. He looked reasonably clean, although tired and dejected as he jotted a note on the pad he kept by the telephone. She wanted to rub his neck and whisper sweet nothings in his ear and make the world go away, but the world was pounding on their door.

It looked as if he'd been making telephone calls rather than just sulking as she'd feared. Every time she wanted to nail him as a typical male, the kind to whom she was immune, he caught her by surprise and impressed her.

He barely glanced up while he flipped the cards in his Rolodex. "It sounds like the whole town is out there already. Which part is company?"

"The family part?" She hugged her elbows, uncertain of his reaction. It was late in the day, but it would have taken his family hours to drive all the way up from Charlotte to Knoxville and down again.

Flint laid down his pen and rubbed his wrinkled brow, not looking at her. "Do you think it's too late to go back to being a badass guitar picker?"

That had been her question from the first, and she didn't think either of them had the answer. "Your decision, boss, but your kids are looking pretty worried."

That got him out of his chair. "They brought the boys? Why the hell did they do that?"

"Because they were anxious about you?" She didn't think Flint heard as he pasted on a facsimile of a happy face and raced past her.

"Did you see the pictures in the news?" he was asking jovially as Jo trailed out behind him. "I think we even made CNN."

He grabbed Johnnie by the shoulder for a hug and tousled Adam's wavy chestnut hair. His customers were trying to keep a polite distance, but Jo knew they could hear everything that was said. Unlike Evan with his cowardly retreat, Flint stood tall and strong in the face of disaster, and his hearty response relieved worried frowns around the room, including Jo's—even though she knew his casual assurance was a fraud. She recognized brazen when she saw it. Tears of deep down understanding welled in her eyes.

"The boys insisted that we come," Martha Clinton was saying. Her tone held its usual disapproval, but this time, Jo could tell it also hid a well of concern. "I told them we'd just be in the way."

"No, of course not. I'm glad you're here." Flint ushered them toward a vacant booth. "The electric company turned off the utilities until we could get the building inspected, but Dave loaned us a generator so we can make coffee and keep the refrigerator running. I'm afraid the doughnuts are gone."

"We saw them all over the road on TV," Johnnie said with more excitement than Jo had ever seen him display. "And you were digging up a mountain of dirt." A note of pride crept into his pre-adolescent voice.

"Hoss had his video camera in his trunk." Jo set fresh coffee on the table for his parents and milk for the boys. They made faces, but she noticed they drank it. "And then the local newspeople sent up a helicopter. It's been a real circus." None of the news stations had mentioned the town's predicament, though. The official announcement of the mill's closing hadn't been made yet.

"It looks like the structure is still sound," Floyd Clinton said, studying the gaping holes in the front wall.

"It's not safe," Martha said firmly. "Flint

needs to come home with us. That road out there is a death trap. It's just a matter of time before one of those monster trucks plows—"

"The town has been here over a hundred years, Martha," Floyd interrupted. "The building has withstood flood and blizzards. It can tolerate a little molasses and rock."

The boys snickered. "Did you see that Mercedes?" Adam asked of no one in particular. "With the chicken stuck on top of it?"

Jo patted Flint's arm and left him to reassure his family. She'd hoped he would be spending the night with her, but it looked as if he'd be leaving. It was a good thing they hadn't got involved. He deserved better than a town on the verge of bankruptcy and a business that couldn't survive.

That relieved her guilt over suing him. Flint didn't have anything left to lose. Randy would have to cough up his cash instead. With wicked triumph, she decided to sign the papers and take the envelope to the post office first chance she got.

"Hey, Jo." A table of customers waved her over. "Is Flint keeping the place open?"

Jo glanced at the bare wall the pretty

plates had once adorned, and an aching sadness crept over her. They'd worked so hard to build up the café. She hated to see it go. At least the pewter paneling had stayed up. "I don't know. Guess it depends."

On the insurance. The mill. His kids. She wouldn't be a factor in the decision. It was time she started looking for a better-paying job anyway. It wasn't as if she expected the lawsuit to produce results anytime soon, if at all.

Dave from the hardware joined them. "I can get more plate glass up here tomorrow. The supply store has some real fancy doors that would look good."

"Flint would have to borrow the money," she reminded him gently.

Everyone knew what that meant. If the mill closed, Flint would have no customers and no way to pay his debts.

"I've got an old door out in my barn," George Bob offered. "He can have it for nothing. When the insurance check comes in, he can use the money on something else."

"If we build a frame, I've got some old sashes that might fit," someone else of-

fered. "It would look purty with them win-
dowpanes up there instead of all that bare
glass."

Jo's naturally ebullient spirits began to lift
as she pictured a cottage look for the front.
"We could paint the outside a pretty salmon
and put in a window box with geraniums!"

She felt Flint's muscular build behind her
before he dropped a big hand on her shoulder. She caught her breath as desire rock-
eted through her. How could she think
about sex when the world had just turned
upside down?

Flint's confident voice calmed her flutters
into a different kind of longing.

"No salmon. No geraniums. No ferns," he
said firmly. "I'm sending my family up to
Knoxville for the night. I'm gonna have to
board up the place, folks. Hate to break up
a party—"

She didn't want him to go. Anxiously, Jo
cut him off. "Amy has tons of room. Let me
give her a call. Company will keep her from
killing Evan."

Heart pounding with foolish hope, she retreated to his office, leaving Flint to discuss
plywood with the men. By the time she'd
confirmed the invitation and returned to the

dining room, Flint had his family on their feet, prepared to leave. He wore a mask of resolve that Jo feared was death to her pitiful hopes.

"We want to stay, Dad," Adam was protesting. "There's nothing to do at home."

Jo lifted her eyebrows in surprise and kept her mouth shut at this turnabout.

"It's going to be hard work, guys," Flint warned. "I'll be roughing it up here."

He was staying? He was staying! Jo almost did a jig of delight. "Amy said you're all welcome to stay with her," she intruded quickly before his parents could argue. "Evan had to go down to Charlotte, and she'd love the company." She crossed her fingers and prayed. If Flint's family would help instead of carping . . .

Floyd overrode his wife's objections. "If you don't mind, Joella, we'd like to accept that invitation. It was a long drive up here. Flint, if you'll show us the way—"

"I'll let Jo do that." With a smoldering glance that nearly incinerated Jo and left her in ashes, Flint took his mother's arm and started the procession out the door. "I'll be staying here tonight."

He was staying here tonight? Did that

mean he wanted to pound her into the ground for her interference or . . . Jo didn't dare let her hopes ride too high. A man who could turn her to ashes in a single look was explosive property.

"We can stay, too," Johnnie said eagerly. "There are still news trucks out there. We can show them—"

Flint chuckled and gently clipped him on the ear. "They'll all be going home to supper shortly, and you'll be complaining the rest of the night about sleeping on hard floors. Get all the sleep you can. I'm putting you to work first thing in the morning."

Jo sucked down a lump in her throat at the sight of Flint's affection for his sons. She'd never known a father, but she was certain he was an example of a good one, if he could hold a job that kept him home. All this time, she'd been looking at Flint as a piece of sugar pie, yummy to look at but not good for the health. Watching him with his kids produced unsettling perspectives that she wasn't prepared to entertain. Sex, she understood. Anything more . . . Maybe she ought to push him at Sally. Sally would love to have kids.

"Will you come up after us later?" Adam asked.

Jo was already out the door, car keys in hand, when she stopped with his family and waited for his reply.

Catching Jo's eye, Flint shook his head regretfully at his son's question. "Sorry. Maybe I'll run up for a bit to see you settled in when I'm done here, but with all that molasses on the street, I have to stay here tonight and keep the bears out."

"Bears? You have bears up here?" Adam asked in a tone that showed more excitement than fear.

The boys' excited clamor drowned out Martha's protests, and a warm heat stole around Jo's foolish heart. Bears were a Bunyan-sized excuse.

He was staying here. For her.

❧TWENTY❧

Jo had her hair scrubbed, blow-dried, up-swept, and dangling in perfect little curls on her neck while waiting for Flint to return from supper at Amy's. When she'd come back from showing his family to her sister's earlier, he'd already had the front of the café boarded up and had washed and dressed.

His crisp appearance and eagerness to see his sons had made her feel like dirt. Now that she saw him as a family man and not just her boss or a famous guitar player who could leave here anytime, she felt guilty as hell about what she'd done.

She'd stopped at the post office and mailed the papers to Elise. She'd had to do it. The café was gone. Her job was gone. The mill would soon be gone. If Randy was making money off her words, then her family deserved a share. She hated that she had to take Flint down with him, but he couldn't keep a business going without the mill anyway. Maybe she was doing him a favor by pushing him out.

Guilt didn't keep her from spiffing up. Foolish optimism would be her downfall. Maybe she and Flint didn't have a future, but they had tonight. At least she was being practical about this affair, unlike the last two.

She took one last glance in the mirror to make certain she hadn't smeared her mascara or forgotten her earrings. She wore what would have been a prim, long-sleeved, white blouse except the first button didn't fasten until the silk exposed her cleavage. She'd debated linen slacks so she could look at least moderately sophisticated, but she'd given in to the urge to wear a white leather miniskirt. She was hoping she wouldn't be wearing it very long.

So much for her decision to keep things professional. She might be immune to most men these days, but Flynn Clinton had crept under her defenses in so many ways that there was no point pretending any longer. Besides, if the café closed, they weren't working together.

Hearing her apartment door open, she squirted a dash of cologne between her breasts and emerged from her tiny bathroom into the main living area, heart pounding in anticipation.

"Hey, Joey!" the man picking up sheet music from one of the racks called. "How are folks supposed to get in down there with the front all boarded up?"

"Slim!" Jo sighed in disgust at the sight of the Buzzard's lead singer dressed in what passed for his stage clothes—jeans and a clean shirt. He'd apparently had his hair trimmed, and for the moment it looked reasonably neat. "The café is closed. We have no electricity. Didn't you hear? I thought the whole world saw us on TV."

"The back room's on a different switch box, like this place up here. You got lights, right? Didn't you hear us warming up? Folks are wandering around out there, not sure they can get in. Open it up for them, honey."

Jo blinked and looked around. Sure enough, she had lights. And she'd used her blow-dryer and microwave. Duh moment. Her head had really been in the clouds.

So much for her long evening with Flint, not that he'd showed up yet anyway. Maybe he'd changed his mind. Maybe he was making calls, looking for a new job, or already heading out to Nashville. If she'd learned nothing else from experience, she'd learned she couldn't rely on a man's choices to make her own.

Faced with choosing between her selfish needs, and her loyalty to her friends and the town, Jo caved. Just as her mother had said, friends and family came first.

"We'll have to direct them down the alley," she told Slim. "The front might not be safe. Maybe we could give Myrtle a flashlight."

"Got one in the truck. You stand out there on the porch in that white thing you got on, and they'll see you fine."

Musicians had a one-track mind, Jo reminded herself. That was not a compliment from Slim. It was his way of saying white stood out in the dark, and she was better than a flashlight.

She obediently stood on the porch leading into the back room and waved at people as they came down the alley. Everyone greeted her with a relief that proved she was doing the right thing. People needed a little normality in their lives after a day like this one. Maybe they needed a little music to help forget their troubles, too.

The band had struck up their first tune, and she was just about to go inside, when Flint strode down the alley in the dying beam of Myrtle's flashlight. The white pearl buttons of his black shirt reflected the light of the room behind her as he climbed the steps, and her heart did a wicked two-step of excitement.

He looked her up and down with those smoldering silver eyes until her toes curled.

"We have electricity?" was all he asked.

Hoo, boy, did they have electricity. Jo thought the hair on both their heads ought to be standing on end. Flint's mouth tilted slightly at one corner, so she figured he was reading her mind as well. But she could play it as cool as he did.

"Apparently the back room was a new addition on a separate circuit box. Maybe we can move the kitchen."

"Maybe," he answered noncommittally, eyeing the back room with its pounding rhythms as if making some decision. "Why the hell not," he concluded, catching her elbow and drawing her inside.

Jo had a feeling his decision had nothing

to do with the kitchen and everything to do with the smoky light in his eyes as he steered her toward the dance floor left by the lack of tables.

"Did Amy feed you okay?" Jo asked, trying to be sensible even after Flint transferred his hand to the small of her back. The vibrations of the amplifiers and the sensation of his hand combined like a caffeine jolt to her weary nervous system.

"Just fine." He leaned down to talk over the crash of drums, and his breath tingled her ear. "Amy and my mother were talking kitchen appliances when I left."

Unable to bear Flint's hand at her back and his chest just inches from her own without acting on her urges, Jo swayed in time to the music. "Amy kills appliances. She shouldn't be allowed near a kitchen when she's upset."

"Well, she's mightily upset tonight. The stove caught fire."

Jo glanced at him in alarm, but Flint suddenly clasped her waist with both hands and moved with her, his eyes sparkling. The dour Flint was gone, replaced by the laughing cowboy she remembered from their first night. She didn't know how catastrophe had caused the change, but she gladly swung with him. "Before or after dinner?" she asked, moving in close.

"After. She was scooping ice cream when the stove started sparking. I think we were talking about the mill, so maybe she was a little more than upset. Interesting trait, killing appliances." He swung her in a circle, their hips brushing, setting off sparks of their own. His rough hand clasping hers was strong and sure.

"Appliances, lightbulbs, computers, anything electrical or electronic." Jo lifted her arms over her head and clapped in time to the music. Flint ran his hands up and down her sides, and she thought she could fry a few lightbulbs of her own.

His thumbs brushed beneath her breasts, and she got his message loud and clear. Heart pounding, she knew they were right back where they'd started. Only this time, the stakes were higher. This time, her heart was in serious danger. Wordlessly, she placed her hands on his shoulders and moved in closer.

"You should be up there. Your voice was made for that stage," he murmured as the band hit the last note of the song.

Jo assumed that was a genuine compliment and not a come-on, but she needed to quench any notion he might be entertaining of taking her down that road with him. "There are church choirs all over the country filled with fine singers," she replied without resentment. "It takes more than I've got to make the audience sit up and take notice."

"You have the pluck and presence and more. You'd knock them out," he argued with a determined set to his square chin.

Jo shook her head. "Nope. I've got all the attention I want. I sure the heck don't need more."

He shook his head in disagreement, but the band struck another tune, and he didn't argue more. His fingers kept time on her waist. Jo tapped her toe. The beat changed, and she swung her hips. His hand helped her sway. She wanted to sing. She figured he wanted to play. They couldn't do either, and frustration built.

The band took a break, and the lights went up. Flint signaled Peggy for drinks.

"I'm so glad you stayed open," Peggy shouted over the noise of the crowd. "We're gonna need this money extra bad if the mill closes."

Flint handed Peggy the few bills he had left in his wallet. Discovering he had just enough to cover drinks and a tip jolted him back from fantasyland. There hadn't been a bank deposit today.

He didn't know what the Man Upstairs was trying to tell him, but apparently settling down to the staid life of a responsible businessman wasn't part of His plan. He was more in a hole now than he'd been when he was a party animal. If he couldn't provide a home for his kids either way, he'd just as soon party.

Except now he had new responsibilities. He hadn't paid Jo today.

She was worth way beyond what he could afford, but she didn't seem to know that, not any more than she realized she had more stage presence than any other singer he knew. He wanted to take her upstairs and accept the promises shining in her eyes, but acting on urges was the specialty of the old badass Flint. The new one had to think things through.

"I'll write out your check in the morning," he told her.

She shrugged, apparently not concerned with the mundane. "Mama's insurance isn't due until next week." She suddenly looked stricken. "If Amy gets a divorce, she won't be able to help pay Mama's bills."

"Don't go borrowing trouble. Evan will see reason." Flint tried to relax while the out-of-town singer set up onstage. He itched to take Jo upstairs, just as he itched for his guitar. He had to learn that scratching his itches often had results other than pleasure.

She looked at him in disbelief. "Northfork isn't Wonderland. We're no different here than in the city. Amy's worth five Lurid Lindas, but did you see Evan today? He's not looking at anything but that Mercedes and plastic boobs."

Flint coughed on his drink, sputtered, and couldn't formulate a sensible reply.

"Evan's a prick, and I'd say she was better off without him, except for the kids and the money," she continued.

"If it comes to divorce, he'll have to pay support and alimony," he reminded her. Been there, done that. At least the huge payoff Melinda had demanded had gone to his kids when she'd died, so they had their education funds. He was a mean bastard to think that way though. Melinda hadn't deserved to die that young.

His sons hadn't deserved to lose their mama so soon. He was beginning to see a pattern here, once he got past his own problems. The kids weren't just rejecting him, they were grieving for their mother. Just because he'd adjusted to Melinda's loss long before she'd died didn't mean they'd had time to accept it.

"Amy can't afford that house even with alimony," Jo continued. "She'll have to move back home to Mama. Maybe we can all find jobs in Asheville."

That was an ugly thought, shocking him into realizing he'd had enough change. He wanted to put down roots. Jo and her family were part of those roots. And he'd better quit thinking like that. Jo belonged in Nashville. "How's your mama doing?"

"She's keeping her food down, but she won't take her medication like she should, says it's too expensive. Let's not talk about it. Let's take tonight for fun."

Flint agreed wholeheartedly with that sentiment. If he didn't find an outlet for his frustration soon, his brain would explode like an overripe melon from thinking too much.

The lights dimmed, and the out-of-town singer stepped onstage with his high-crowned Stetson and big guitar. The crowd hooted and whistled, and the performer tipped his hat before belting into his first song.

The unexpectedly harmonious composition jolted Flint like an electric shock.

Standing here in anonymity, arm wrapped around Jo's swaying hips, he could acknowledge that he didn't need to be up there on that stage. He'd never craved adulation. He simply lived for music. He wanted to work again. His head was full of tunes reflecting the flood of feelings he'd been dealing with since moving back here. Jo had turned him on in more ways than he cared to admit.

He hadn't earned enough to have his hand operated on. He couldn't play again.

This evening, Adam and Johnnie had sounded more excited than he'd heard them in years. They'd actually talked to him. Adolescents were weird. Seeing him on national television must have given them ideas of some sort. He sure the hell hoped they didn't want him to go back to the Barn Boys so they could bask in his reflected fame.

He'd have to be closer to them to understand how their minds worked.

If he didn't have an income, he couldn't be closer to them.

"Let's get out of here." Not even considering how Jo would take his demand, just knowing he had to escape, Flint tugged her toward the exit.

She glanced from him to the singer, and he suffered a moment of despair, until she shrugged and followed. With impatience, he led her through the crowd. He didn't know if it was the music, sex, or his own thoughts fermenting and exploding inside him.

Outside, people milled in the alley, smoking, drinking from flasks, and laughing. Flint came to an abrupt standstill. He hadn't counted on an audience when he took Jo upstairs.

"Hey, Flint, we're holding an emergency Chamber meeting Monday. You be there?" someone called out of the darkness.

"If I can get away." Hell, he didn't want to embarrass Jo. She'd suffered enough of that in her life. He was practically foaming at the bit and couldn't move.

"Aren't you staying tonight, Joella?" a female voice called.

"I'm wiped. You comin' in for our dirt-and-doughnut sale in the morning?"

"Dirt-and-doughnut?" several voices inquired.

"Yeah, for every cup of dirt you clean off the floor, you get a doughnut."

Jo's laughter threaded with that of the others. Without a second look back, she took Flint's hand and tugged him up the stairs.

"People will get the wrong idea," he protested as she opened her door. Despite her lead, he still felt responsible for protecting her from herself.

"Most likely they'll get the right idea." She entered the wide-open space of her apartment and started pulling pins from her hair.

Pure gold silk tumbled around her shoulders, and Flint had to clench his fingers into fists to prevent them from sliding through all that temptation. "You don't mind what all those jokers down there are thinking?" he asked, letting the door slam behind him. The band's bass vibrated her floor.

"I'm a waitress. I'm built like a two-bit whore. I sang in a *strip* club." She looked at him as if he'd just stepped from a Victorian painting. "Every man jack of them has hit on me at one time or another."

"Why the hell do you dress like that if you don't want men hitting on you?"

She ran her hands through her hair to shake it free, apparently unconscious of the sexiness of her gesture. "Why should I change the way I dress because men are idiots? I wear what's comfortable and makes me feel good. I don't have much except looks, so why should I hide them?"

Flint wanted to pound a little sense into that warped mind of hers, but he wanted her in bed even more, so he tried not to be too blunt. "You have a damned sight more going for you than looks. You could wear gunnysacks to your ankles and people would listen."

Her eyes crinkled with laughter. "Uh-huh. Tell me another one, big boy. Let's get back to the real question here—your mama is gonna hear about this. Do you care what your family thinks about you being up here?"

"Never paid them no never mind before," he admitted. He couldn't straighten out Jo's perception of herself while his mind was on her body—just as she figured. He could scarcely follow her conversation while her perfume filled his head, and his clenched hand ached for reasons besides torn tendons. "I'm trying to learn, but there are limits."

She aimed for the kitchen. "Okay, I can understand that. I didn't tell my mama that you're here. We all have our hang-ups. Want some coffee?"

Hell, no. But figuring she was telling him he couldn't have what he really wanted, Flint tried to be rational about it. They both had good reasons for resisting the electric rhythm pumping between them. They'd fallen in bed the first time in a burst of white-hot flame and no thought, and he'd embarrassed the hell out of her when his parents had shown up. So maybe her invitation to stay the night was just that.

Or maybe she wanted romance this time around. That scared the shit out of him. He couldn't make commitments, which left him wondering how he went about seducing a woman who knew his every move and would laugh at him if he tried romancing her. He settled on accepting the offer of coffee. "Sure."

She cast him a knowing glance but continued measuring beans.

Trying not to think of hauling Jo straight to bed, Flint stewed over what she'd said about herself and men hitting on her. His natural inclination was to punch out anyone who insulted her. Since there weren't any men present, and it was Jo doing the insulting, he was up a creek. He cleverly kept his trap shut. Maybe that's what romancing women was about—just listening.

He sat on the couch and removed his boots while Jo efficiently worked her way around the kitchen. "I like what you've done to the place," he finally took a chance on saying. What he really wanted to say was that he wanted to take her home with him, to his house. He liked her colorful nest, but it was small and airy and not quite real. He wanted her somewhere solid and permanent, like his cabin.

Jo laughed and threw him a naughty look that took in his flashy shirt and made his tight jeans tighter. "Yeah, the scenery is improving."

Well, that showed him the pointlessness of flattery. They'd both liked what they saw from day one. Sex wasn't their problem. It was all the other complications that had them tied in knots.

Unable to watch Jo and not touch, Flint got up to examine her music CDs. "I don't think we can open in the morning," he said without inflection. He hadn't wanted to correct her in front of others. The business was shot, any way he looked at it. He wasn't certain there was any purpose in borrowing to fix it up.

"Sure we can." She poured the coffee as fast as it brewed into the pot. "No air-conditioning, maybe." She shrugged. "But we're tough. We'll provide flyswatters until you get the windows in. How good are you at construction?"

"Not very, even when my hand was reliable. I'm real good at supervising," he added drily, putting a CD into the player. She came over to hand him a mug of whiskey-scented brew.

Women didn't normally make him nervous. Jo had him so spun around that he couldn't carry on an intelligent conversation. He was actually listening to her foolish optimism when he ought to be planning another means of supporting his kids.

Sipping her coffee, she lingered close enough for him to notice that she smelled of cologne and makeup and woman. Male in-

stinct demanded that he take what he
wanted, and the mature adult thing he was
trying to learn abruptly took a leave of absence.

The music roared to life, but nothing
could deflect his awareness of the woman
temptingly within reach, studying her CD ti-
tles. It was a lot simpler thinking of Jo than
the disaster that was his life.

"I know it's the end of the month and bills
will be coming in," she continued the conversation that he wasn't following, "but if
you hand out free food and coffee, everyone
will pitch in to fix things up. Slim's an electrician. He can look at the wiring. He owes
you. You can pay the bills when the insurance check comes."

He didn't want to think about bills and insurance. His fingers itched to play with the
wild disarray of curls brushing the silk of her
collar. He wanted to murmur sweet nothings
in her ear and feel her arms circling his
neck. He watched her slender throat and
grew hard just watching her swallow. He'd
promise her anything about now. "We can
try," he agreed, not totally certain what he
was committing himself to.

"Trying is what we do best down here."

She set her coffee on the CD stand and flipped through the selection with a smile playing on her lips.

Flint couldn't tear his gaze from the curves of Jo's waist and backside in that formfitting leather as she bent over the shelf. She could wear a sack, and he would see through it. "This better be decaf if we're getting any sleep," he warned.

"Yeah, that's what I thought." She slid in a different CD.

She turned around, and a thrill shot straight to Flint's groin as her wise green cat eyes challenged his. One of his songs pounded from the speaker. To his amazement, he understood—she was showing him how she wanted to be romanced. His heart kicked a fast lick.

"No one's going to believe we just sat here all night and talked," he predicted, thankful Jo didn't need a lot of chatting.

"I agree with you on that point, too," she said with a grin. "Does this mean we're in agreement on more than we thought?"

"Doubt it." Flint set his cup next to hers. His appreciation for Jo's understanding ways went bone deep, but they still had mountainous issues between them. He wrapped his arm around her waist and pulled her into the music with him. "I think it's just this one topic that we can count on, and that probably only lasts until the luster wears off."

Running his hand from her waist downward, he pulled her close, until their hips circled together. He could dance with an erection—for a while.

"If wearing off the luster will make it easier to work with you without wanting to jump your bones, let's polish the tar out of it," she agreed, following his lead without hesitation.

She wanted to jump his bones? Damn, but he'd known he liked the way she thought. Flint grinned down at her and whirled her across the floor.

He'd spent a lifetime confusing music and sex, but what Jo did to him was deeper, more intense, and far scarier—and he'd never wanted anyone or anything more in all his life.

He suspected polishing their luster would only deepen the beauty of their attraction, but he'd always been a risk taker.

≪TWENTY-ONE≫

"You live in an eagle's nest," Flint said with what Jo interpreted as wonder layered over male satisfaction.

The pounding beat of the band had died some time ago, but the lingering chatter of voices still drifted through the open windows from the street below.

They lay in her bed, with all her familiar possessions around her, and she still felt as if the world were new again. The heat of raw male warmed her. She touched her toes to his, and Flint scraped his muscled leg over hers to trap her ankle. She shivered in anticipation with merely that minor touch. Even in the aftermath of sex, her hormones skittered and collided and sang just lying there with their naked hips touching.

Or maybe it was her soft heart leaping with foolish joy.

"I like listening to the trees rustle at night," she murmured. "The owls hoot over the river. I always thought of the loft as a tree house, but an eagle's nest works."

"They logged the trees out by my cabin. It's sitting there on bare hillside. I'll have to tell my landlord to plant more trees. I like it up here."

Flint's voice rumbled over her as sensuously as his hand stroked up and down her arm. It would take one hell of a lot of polishing to wear off this luster if she could be aroused just by the sound of his voice—after they'd already had sex once. She turned on her side and ran her fingers down his hard chest, tickling his nipples the way she wanted him to touch hers.

"You won't stay there long enough to see the trees grow," she said, reminding herself as much as him that there wasn't any future in what they were doing.

"One day at a time," he agreed. Neither of them were talking about trees.

A shaft of moonlight spilled over the sharp angles of Flint's face, and Jo stroked his bristly jaw. She was experienced enough to read masculine desire in his eyes, understood when his gaze dropped to her breasts, and recognized the response between her legs. And still she couldn't resist believing she answered a yearning in him that was more than sex.

She threw her leg over his groin and settled where he wanted her—where she needed him.

Flint grabbed her hips and surged strong and deep inside her, and for this one night, neither of them worried about tomorrow.

"I don't remember the pig's hat having turkey feathers in it," Amy said, balancing boxes of muffins and studying Myrtle's chapeau on Saturday morning. "Chicken feathers, I could understand. But wild turkey? There must have been some partying here last night."

Helping carry boxes from Amy's car, Jo stopped to admire the selection of hard-to-find striped feathers. Three. She hadn't put them there. Flint must have had a busy morning. A warm spot settled in her midsection at knowing he'd guessed who had placed the first feather and that he'd appreciated the symbolism enough to copy it. In her experience, men didn't usually grasp her weird notions. "Guess someone couldn't find crow feathers," she answered enigmatically, heading for the café door.

Flint had pulled the plywood off the doors and windows before breakfast after Dave and George Bob had arrived with an old wooden door and a truckful of window sashes. Neither man had commented when Flint had run down the back stairs, tucking in his shirt, with Jo following behind him to start the coffee.

Putting Amy's muffins into the doughnut case, working behind the counter, Jo wanted to crow her joy. She settled for watching Flint as often as she dared without giving her foolishness away. She was a grown woman, not an infatuated schoolgirl. She didn't need to sigh over the studly way he lifted that heavy door without help, swinging it into place so the other men could mark the hinges. And she fought the urge to giggle when he glanced her way for approval as he did it. His knowing look burned all the way to her middle.

Silly, silly, silly, she scolded herself. But nature sure had its hooks in her. She didn't even question the wisdom of rebuilding the café if it wouldn't have any business soon.

Flint exuded a confidence that rubbed off on everyone.

The arrival of his family distracted her. The boys begged to be given something important to do and kept sneaking peeks at Main Street, probably hoping for more news trucks. Jo grinned at the predictability of teenagers. She enjoyed teasing them, and they responded with grins so much like Flint's that she could easily fall in love all over again.

While Flint assigned tasks, Jo handed out coffee and muffins to anyone who showed up to help. She sent the boys upstairs to choose music to keep everyone entertained. They came back down making fun of her oldies, but she noticed Hank Williams and Patsy Cline erupted from the back room not much later.

The phone in Flint's office started ringing around nine. It could have been ringing all night for all she knew. With the band playing, no one would have noticed. And Flint wouldn't have been home to take his personal calls. With Flint's name attached, the news clip of the Mercedes, molasses, and chickens had rated national TV coverage.

By the third call, Jo sent Johnnie upstairs

to retrieve her cordless phone and plug it into Flint's wiring so they could carry the receiver outside.

"Yeah, Travis, thanks. It looks worse than it is. Did you see those chickens?" Flint roared with laughter as he talked to still another of his Nashville friends.

Everyone continued working around him, but like Jo, they all knew *Travis* was the lead singer for the Barn Boys. Johnnie and Adam were the only ones who ignored the conversation. They'd grown up with famous people in their living room.

Martha Clinton frowned in disapproval and returned to scrubbing at the muddy floor. Jo pretended to stay busy washing down their new paneling. If Nashville had already come knocking, how soon would it be before Flint felt the call to return there? He was an extraordinarily talented musician who didn't belong behind a coffee shop counter.

Maybe the disaster was a good thing, saving her from heartbreak and providing Flint with an excuse to go back where he belonged. Maybe the band would give him enough money to have his hand fixed so he could play with them again. He could give her the café as his share of the lawsuit, and they'd both be happy.

She didn't feel real happy thinking about it.

"Sure, come on down. I can still tell you when your song sucks." Flint carried the receiver through the dining room and back to his office, oblivious of all the gazes following him. "I'll mark my calendar and hang around that day. Sure, sure. No problem."

The CD player blasted out a Barn Boys song and drowned the rest of the conversation.

"'Hey, hey, hey,'" Jo sang along, swinging with the rhythm as she climbed a ladder to clean the top walls. Rather than accentuate the negative, she let new ideas spin madly in her mind. She had to take out her energy somewhere. "'Don't go breaking my heart . . .'"

"Because like a worm, it will make two and multiply?" Flint's warm voice asked from the foot of the ladder.

She dropped her sponge on him. He wiped dirty water out of his eyes and still didn't quit laughing at her.

"Come down here and try that," he dared her.

Her libido did a happy jig in the sunshine of his eyes, but she remained where she was. "Give me the phone. I want to call Dot. I bet she knows half a dozen artists who wouldn't mind hanging their work on these walls. That will be even better than plates. You're not the only one who knows famous people around here."

He quirked his eyebrows and handed her the receiver. "Eavesdropper."

"Name-dropper," she retaliated. "Are you sure I won't tie up the line in case Dolly or Shania wants to call?"

His grin grew wider. "Jealous?"

"Hey, Dad!" Adam called from the counter. "Reckon Travis would bring the band down to play for the festival?"

If silence could drop like a wet blanket, Jo reckoned that's what it did now. Every ear in the place strained to hear Flint's reply. Even the hammering on the windows halted.

Stepping back from the ladder to gaze around at his audience, Flint threw up his hands in surrender. "Y'all know I can't promise nothin'," he warned them. "But I've already asked, all right? They're checking their calendars."

Jo started the cheer, and the little café

soon rang with applause and rebel yells. Disaster couldn't keep them down if they had something to hope for. The Barn Boys playing in their dinky festival would give the town something to talk about for years.

And Flint was the hero willing to set aside his pride and bring them here.

"Son, we have to be going. That's a long drive around the mountain," Floyd Clinton said, drying his hands on a towel in the café on Sunday afternoon.

"Come along, boys," Martha called. "You need to wash up before we leave."

"Ah, Nana, we want to stay," Johnnie called. "Hoss said he'd take us rafting, and Jo said she could show us a good place for fishing out back of here."

Stunned by his sons' willingness to stay, Flint waited for his mother's reaction. She shot a dirty look in Joella's direction. The two of them had been rubbing each other wrong all weekend. Or rather, his mother got wrapped around an axle every time Jo opened her mouth, and Jo blithely ignored her. He wasn't certain ignoring his mother was the proper way to win her favor, but he sure as hell couldn't blame Jo for steering clear.

Since he wasn't helping any by sleeping with Jo, he figured he'd keep his mouth shut on that subject as well. The two of them showing up at church together this morning hadn't eased the tension. Sally had treated him like a leper.

Given that he'd recklessly invited his dangerous old life into his new sedate one, maybe maturity was beyond him, but he still wanted his boys to stay.

"They're welcome to stay with me," Amy said cheerfully from in front of the oven Slim had wired to the rear circuit. "The boys are great with Josh and Louisa."

"We've signed them up for swimming and tennis at the Y," Martha replied stiffly.

Not budging from the floor where he was showing five-year-old Josh how to play his Game Boy, Johnnie whined, "I don't wanna play tennis."

"You need the exercise, and you don't eat right unless I watch you. You ate nothing but muffins and junk all day yesterday."

Amy slammed a pan on top of the stove. "I made raisin bran muffins with Splenda just for him. Do they make something more nutritional down in the city?"

Everyone in the dining room turned to stare. Quiet Amy never spoke out. She blushed at their stares and turned her back on the room.

Evan hadn't been home all weekend.

"Your baking is a lifesaver, Amy," Flint intervened. He wanted to say he'd pay her when he could, but he wasn't letting his parents know his financial situation. "And I appreciate you taking in my family. I don't want to ask you to do more."

"I like having them," she muttered, turning on the water in the sink to clean out her bowls. "They're perfectly welcome to stay."

"We don't want to sound ungrateful," Martha said firmly, "but it's too dangerous up here. If anything should happen to either of them, with that road blocked, the nearest hospital is all the way up in Knoxville."

Flint watched Jo arranging pictures on the wall with the help of her artist friend. He figured she was listening to every word but wisely staying out of the argument. He wanted to stay here again tonight with her, but her apartment was no place for his boys.

He had reverted to his badass ways all weekend, ticking off his parents, falling in lust with a glamour girl working her way up the music ladder, pushing away the maternal woman who would make a good mother to his kids. He needed to get his head straight again.

He had to get back to putting his sons first. If they actually wanted to stay with him in this tiny town, he'd set up a tent on the highway to live in if he had to. For the first time in a long time, he let hope peer out of the box he'd locked it in.

"The county says the road down the mountain will open on Tuesday," he argued. "If Amy doesn't mind putting up with us another couple of nights, I see no reason why the boys can't stay. I can use the extra hands around here." He appreciated his parents' willingness to help, but he couldn't let that be compensation for their guilt at stealing his kids.

Johnnie and Adam cheered. Josh and Louisa joined them, even though they had no idea why. Amy sent him a shy smile. Behind his mother's back, Jo gave him a thumbs-up.

Nearly falling over in relief and pride that

he'd finally brought his boys around to for-
giving him, Flint listened to his mother's arguments with half an ear as he finished
screwing together a chair that had lost a
leg. He had the courage of conviction on his
side.

"Mom, I appreciate what you and Dad
have done for us," he said as she wound
down. Setting the chair on the floor, he
rocked it to see if it would wobble. It stood
firm. "But school is out, and now is the time
for me to take them off your hands. Let's
just see how it works, okay?"

Flint hugged his mother as he said it. She
stiffened, but shut up. He glanced at his
dad, who looked thoughtful but didn't disagree. "The two of you deserve awards for
bringing up the three of us. You don't need
to be raising my two as well. Why don't we
just play it by ear for a while?"

His mother glanced over his shoulder at
Jo. "They need your undivided attention,"
she said for his ears only. "You can't be
staying here and sending them home with
Amy. I won't have it, Flynn. I'll go to court to
get them if I have to."

That's all he needed—his parents suing
him as well as Joella. Why not? Maybe he

should go back to school and get a law degree so he could defend himself. Rather
than argue, he patted her on the shoulder.
"We'll be just fine, Mom. You and Dad have
a safe trip home and give us a call when you
get there."

He shut all his fear and doubt inside as he
and the boys said their farewells and ushered his parents out the newly rebuilt front
door. When his parents were gone and out
of sight, Flint grabbed both boys and
hugged them. "Now, let's party!"

The kids whooped, and the women
looked at him as if he'd gone insane. Maybe
he had. His life was in shambles, but he had
his kids back, and he couldn't wipe off his
silly grin. Reality could hit later.

"Put that big old smiley-face sun in the
middle," he ordered Jo and Dot. "That's the
best one of them all."

"It's an imitation Mexican decoration,"
Dot protested. Short and skinny, with a purple braid hanging down her embroidered
smock, she stood back to check the
arrangement of artwork. "The metalwork is
nice, but it's hardly worth the center position."

Jo took the smiling sculpture in question,

found a nail, and pounded it right smack in the middle of the turquoise wall where Flint wanted it. The cheerful copper sun caught the light from the newly installed window-panes and sparkled merrily.

"O sole mio," she warbled, "it's now or never . . ."

Grinning, Flint grabbed a paint can to start on the window sashes. Her Italian might need a little work if she thought *sole* referred to the sun, but Jo's heart was in the right place.

He was afraid his heart had been kick-started and returned to action, and he couldn't do a blamed thing about it but let it pound in his chest and suffer. The gap between where he was and what he wanted had never looked so large as now, but he was confident he'd set his foot down the path in the right direction.

⫷TWENTY-TWO⫸

Jo patted the dirt around the red geranium she'd planted in one of the flowerpots Dot had created out of Fiestaware shards. She studied Myrtle and decided to tuck the flower beneath the little evergreen like a bright red Christmas present. Satisfied, she dusted off her hands, straightened, and gazed up and down Main Street in the June dawn.

Over the weekend, pink and red geraniums had sprouted in whiskey barrels and galvanized tubs in front of stores and along the sidewalks. Bright pink, purple, and red impatiens glowed in the shade of overhangs. The dirt from the dump-truck disaster had been turned to good use, a fine example of positive thinking.

She proudly inspected the gleaming window panes in the café storefront. Flint had painted the entire front of the café in a silvery blue that sort of went with the pewter and blue-green on the inside. It wasn't as bright as she'd like it, but it was a nice, welcoming color with the geranium set against it. And he'd painted the new door a bright red.

She was head over heels over that man, and she knew full well the pain of that kind of tumble. She just didn't seem able to stop her stupid heart from opening up to any man who treated her nice. And Flint had been nicer than any other man she'd known.

Not that he let on that a big heart beat beneath the macho attitude. She smiled as she watched him walking down the road from the parking lot with his kids in tow. He was practically strutting like a rooster, and still his gaze fastened on her as if he were starving and she were the biggest piece of apple pie he'd ever seen.

Her head would grow to twice its size under his regard, except the boys arguing over a handful of CDs reminded her of all that she was not, and her sister trailing behind them with her two kids reminded her of all that she must be.

The sight of Marie bringing up the rear of the parade jolted Joella to a momentary standstill, until her head kicked into gear, and she hurried to take her mother's arm.

Marie waved her away. "I can walk. I don't need a nurse."

Flint handed his keys to Adam and strolled back to join them. "Your mom wanted to see how we fixed up the place. I offered to drive her to the door, but she said—"

"She didn't need babying," Jo finished for him, relieving him of any responsibility for her mother's orders. "Mama, you're *supposed* to let us help. It makes us feel better."

"Oh, stuff it, Joella." Marie gazed around at the newly tidied street. She'd quit dying her fading hair, but the crew cut said she hadn't lost her rebelliousness. "They did good. Did someone catch all the chickens?"

"I had one roosting on my porch rail this morning," Jo admitted, "but she flew off when I came out."

"Well, it's too warm for chicken soup anyway." Taking Flint's arm, Marie ambled painfully toward the café.

Jo could only watch in astonishment as

the big music man treated her obstreperous mother as if she were a piece of crystal, opening the door for her, helping her into a seat in the most comfortable booth in the house. What the devil was going on here? Her mother could peel shellac off a pulpit with her acidity. What was with the sugar and spice?

Amy already had the mixing bowls out and was beating batter behind the counter while all four of the kids disappeared into the back room. Jo had left her CD player down here last night, and she could hear a Barn Boys song blasting out.

"Is this what happens when I let y'all get together behind my back?" Jo asked, reaching for the big ketchup bottle so she could fill containers while Flint made the coffee. "Did you have a big old family fest last night while I sat here by my lonesome?"

Flint had spent the night with his boys at Amy's. If she hadn't known how faithful Amy was to Evan, Jo would have been jealous— except, Amy had every right to cheat if Evan was doing the same.

As if she'd heard Jo's thoughts, Marie spoke up. "I asked how come Flint was staying, but Evan wasn't. Where'd you stick them dry goods the TV showed you hoarding?"

Amy wouldn't look in Jo's direction, but Flint raised his eyebrows and tried to send her a telepathic warning. It didn't work real well, but Jo proceeded cautiously while gathering ketchup containers off the tables. "We needed the back room for Friday night, so Dave stored some of the bolts, and George Bob took a pickup load to his barn. They're here and about."

"The mill makes damn fine material. If Evan can't do anything with it, I know people who can," Marie declared. "It's a waste to throw out all that hard work."

Jo couldn't disagree with that, but her talent wasn't in homemaking. "Evan doesn't want any of it back?"

"He'll just call the insurance company and write it off as a loss," Amy said with what for her passed as disgruntlement.

Marie beckoned Jo closer. "I think they've had a spat," she whispered.

Oh, she'd definitely tread cautiously with that one. Their mother thought Evan walked on water. No one dared tell her that Amy had hired a lawyer. Jo nodded knowingly and joined her in the booth to start filling containers. "So if Evan doesn't want all those scrumptious materials, what will we do with them?" she asked.

"Make pillows," Marie announced with satisfaction.

"Upholster chairs," Flint said gravely, carrying mugs of coffee over.

His gravelly voice raised goose bumps up and down Jo's arms. She needed to touch him, to reassure herself that this weekend hadn't been a figment of her imagination, but his kids could run in here any minute, and her mother was sitting across from her, obstinacy etched in every line of her sun-wrinkled face.

"Upholster chairs?" Jo repeated in disbelief. "What chairs? How?"

"You could start with these ugly things in here," Marie pointed out. "I remembered they was bad, but I hadn't realized how bad."

Jo gazed around at the pink and gray vinyl on the booth benches and chrome chairs. Charlie had replaced the old covers back when she was still in high school, but he'd kept the original fifties colors. Friday's debacle had cracked the vinyl and ground dirt into every crevice. "You want to put that expensive upholstery on dinette chairs?"

Flint slid in beside Jo, touching his thigh to hers under the table. "Yup," he answered noncommittally, sipping his coffee.

Jo choked. She knew he liked the café just the way it was. She'd been overwhelmed that he'd actually worked to restore it yesterday instead of giving up. But upholstering plastic benches was way beyond being a good sport and into the realm of dangerously stupid. How did one clean french-fry grease from upholstery?

But it was gorgeous material, she had to admit, all in richly woven combinations of rusts and wines and dark blues and golds that could all work together—not completely unlike a fabric form of Fiestaware.

"I can make seats for the chairs," Marie declared with satisfaction. "And Ina and Flo can upholster those cushions. Their unemployment checks are running out next month, too. Maybe Flint's insurance will pay some toward the booth damage."

Oh, wow. Oh, double wow. Rock-and-hard-place time. Jo squeezed Flint's thigh beneath the table, and he covered her hand with his to reassure her. So, this was what it was like to work in partnership with a man. She'd always kind of wondered.

"I'm going to come in and cook dinners when Flint starts opening in the evening this weekend," Amy declared from behind the counter.

Grasping this reprieve from the upholstery dilemma, Jo dared a look at Flint. "You really think we can pull this off?"

"Have to," he said without rancor, meeting her gaze with one that reflected concern and warmth at the same time. "It's almost the end of the month and I'm broker than I was when I started. I'm hoping maybe all that publicity will draw a few tourists."

A thrill coursed through her. He was staying! Knowing how much he was risking for the town and his sons shook her like an earthquake.

Jo released his thigh before she went up in flames. "Okay. I could let Peggy handle tables in the morning, and I could come in Friday night. I'm in the back room most Fridays anyway."

Flint captured her hand and squeezed it on top of the table where everyone could see. "Thank you. You make customers feel at home."

"Guess that settles it," Jo declared, trying not to distill any meaning out of his gesture or words. "You're going to have yourself a restaurant instead of a café."

"Upscale coffee shop," Flint said solemnly, lifting his cup to his lips, his eyes dancing over the brim as they met hers.

Damn, the man had a way of making the impossible seem possible. She had to keep her foolish heart from believing the promises in his eyes.

"Hey, Dad." The boys came running out of the back. "Can we plug the laptop in your office?" Johnnie asked.

"Not until the electrician hooks us up. Isn't there a socket in the back?"

"We need a desk, and Louisa has to go potty," Adam announced matter-of-factly, reminding them that the boys weren't quite old enough to babysit a toddler.

"I'll look after them young 'uns." Marie slid from the booth. "Y'all got your hands full out here."

She sent Flint's and Jo's joined hands a pointed look that made Jo giggle.

Flint leaped up to help Marie out of the booth, and Jo slid out to flip the *Closed* sign to *Open,* and to join Amy behind the counter.

"You want to cook dinner for these slobs?" Jo murmured to her sister.

"What's my alternative?" Amy whispered back. "Go to Taiwan for a job?"

"You and Evan will work things out." They had to. Her sister's marriage was the only one Jo had ever seen work, and she longed to believe that happy-ever-after was possible. "You have a college degree. You don't belong here flipping hamburgers."

"You can flip hamburgers," Amy said, pouring flour for a new batch of muffins. "I'll just cook the meals I usually cook for dinner. The menu selection will be limited." She glanced around, saw that their mother had hobbled her way to the back room where Josh and Louisa were chattering, and continued, "Flint said he'd call Elise and ask her to hire someone to see what Evan is up to. He only called once all weekend."

Oh, filthy bad word. Jo slammed a pot on the burner. "I vote we get Evan and Randy together in one room, lock them up, and throw away the key."

"And pour in molasses and chickens?" Amy asked with interest.

"While your muffins bake and smell delicious on the other side!" Jo added, her mouth watering as the first batch filled the air with the aroma of baking blueberries.

"And you sing Randy's stolen songs?" Amy managed a weak grin.

"Yeah, we can rock-'n'-roll!" Jo pumped her fist in the air and swayed to her own music as the first of their morning customers entered.

"Not this early in the morning, Jo," Dave groaned, flopping down on a seat at the counter. "Remind Flint of the Chamber meeting, willya?"

"Consider him reminded." Flint strode back into the room.

"You really think you can bring in the Barn Boys?" Dave asked what was on everyone's minds.

"If their schedule permits." Flint slid a doughnut down to him as Jo poured his coffee. "How big is this place you use for the festival? It has to handle a good-sized crowd or it's not worth their setting up."

Flint watched as faces fell all around. Damn. He'd spent the night thinking about how to make this festival work—so he didn't have to think about how he missed having Jo naked by his side, buoying his spirits in the dark hours before dawn.

When silence reigned in response to Flint's question, Amy turned two shades of red, bit her lip, and twisted her hands. The lightbulb over the stove blew out.

Everyone turned to regard her with interest.

"Spit it out, Amy," Flint said gently. He was learning a little about Jo's older sister. Amy wasn't exactly shy, so much as intimidated by speaking her thoughts aloud.

"I'm not supposed to tell," she whispered. "Evan swore me to secrecy."

Jo snorted and shoved a mug of coffee at her sister. "Evan is a rat's ass right now. It's time we yanked his tail. Spill."

Amy clutched the mug between both hands. "The board is closing the mill. The only chance of keeping it open was those samples, and they probably would have shipped the business to Mexico if the samples sold well. They think the buildings here are too antiquated to update." While everyone stared in horror, she finished hurriedly, "The festival could use that big building they stripped of machinery this spring. It's just sitting there empty. It could hold a huge crowd."

Stoically, Flint topped off cups all around.

His hand ached like hell from all the hammering and shoveling. He'd have to borrow money to have the tendons operated on in hopes that he could go back on the road once the shop shut down. Joella could sue him for everything he was worth, and all she would get was a building mortgaged to the hilt in a town that would close down by the end of the summer.

The only hope any of them had of survival was a half-assed music festival that was only a month away.

George Bob walked in, followed by a few more of the regulars. "What's going on in here? You holding a funeral?"

That just about summed it up, Flint figured.

Jo flipped the *Closed* sign over at three. "I don't *ever* want to experience another day like this again."

Dave had announced the mill closing at the Chamber meeting, and it had been all over town by noon. If nothing else, the news had been good for café business. Every person in the county had stopped in to confirm the gossip. They'd run out of coffee by one, and Jo had been reduced to beg-

ging a customer to run up to the grocery to
buy Folgers. Even the electrician had come
in early to hear the gossip. At least the air
conditioner was back on.

The news of the mill closing had been
lousy for morale. Half the Chamber was
ready to call off the festival to save money.

"Why don't you go upstairs and relax?"
Flint told Jo. "I can put the boys to slinging
chairs and mopping. You went above and
beyond the call of duty today." He flipped
chairs onto tables on the way to his office
where he'd left Adam and Johnnie. Amy had
taken her kids and Marie home before the
lunch rush. Her muffins had sold like hotcakes all morning—*better* than the hotcakes.

"I've been thinking," Jo replied, starting
on the chairs on the other side.

"Well, hold those thoughts." He opened
his office door and caught his sons leaning
over the laptop they'd set up on his desk. A
pounding beat that he didn't recognize emanated from the machine's speakers. They
threw him such guilty looks and turned off
the music so quickly that he figured they'd
been stealing music again. "Time to earn
your keep," he ordered. "Come on out and
help clean up so Jo can rest."

The protests that had been on the tip of their tongues shut up when he mentioned Jo. She might not be maternal, but she sure the hell knew how to be a boy's best friend. She'd fixed them special snacks all day, talked to them about their taste in music in between, and generally conquered them with her laughter and camaraderie. He was happy to see they were gentlemen enough to return the favor.

"Your head okay?" he asked his youngest before he could escape. Neither he nor Melinda had realized the boy needed glasses until Flint's parents had taken him to a doctor for his chronic headaches.

"Yeah, it's okay," Johnnie answered grudgingly. "Jo gave me aspirin. Do you think Mom would have liked her?"

Ouch. Where had that come from? Flint sent a quick glance across the room, but Jo was chatting with Adam and not paying attention to them. Well, not paying attention for Jo meant she wasn't looking in his direction, but Flint knew she had eyes in the back of her head and picked up signals without his saying a word. He'd been aware of her on so many levels today that it was a wonder he was still coherent.

"Yeah, I think your mom would have liked her." He supposed Jo and his late wife had a lot in common on the surface, and Jo was very likable. It occurred to him that Jo would have seen through Melinda, though. She was sharp like that.

"Mom probably wouldn't have liked it here," Johnnie said tentatively, a deeper question hiding behind his words.

Why the hell did kids pick the worst possible times for these discussions? Flint rubbed his brow and tried to guess what his son was really asking. "No, I'm afraid not, Son. Your mama wanted things I couldn't give her. It's kind of like how some people like Merle Haggard and others like Shania Twain. We had different tastes."

To his surprise, John nodded wisely. "Yeah, that's kinda what I thought. I'm glad you can live here now. Are you gonna stay?"

Oh, hell. That wasn't a decision he was prepared to make right this minute. But the kid wanted reassurance that he had a home with a parent in it, and Flint could offer no other choice. "I'm gonna try."

Johnnie beamed. "That would be cool. Nana wouldn't talk about it."

His son liked it here, without pools and

soccer teams and YMCAs? Flint tried not to show his shock or the burden of decision that had just been laid on him. "Your nana doesn't want you to be hurt if things don't work out, but you're old enough to understand. Go get the broom and start sweeping so Adam can come after you with the mop."

Flint threw the last chair onto the table and straightened to discover Jo beside him. He checked, and Adam had followed his brother to the cleaning closet.

"I think you just passed your first daddy test with flying colors," she murmured, pressing a kiss to his cheek. "You're a good man, Charlie Brown."

She was back behind the counter and reading the instructions on how to set the oven to clean by the time the kids had returned with mop and bucket and broom.

Flint wore Jo's kiss like a Medal of Honor for the rest of the afternoon. Maybe his career and business had gone to hell, but maybe, one of these days, he could be a good dad.

For that kind of reward, he would move mountains.

⊰TWENTY-THREE⊱

Walking across the oil-stained planks of the unused mill building, Flint imagined the echoes of crowd applause, the crunch of peanut shells beneath his feet, and an introductory drumroll.

He couldn't go down this road again.

Rubbing the crease between his eyes, he tried to erase the memories, but they were in his blood, and he'd have to erase himself to be rid of them.

Country music was written for big old barns like this. The soft pine floors and high rafters absorbed and echoed the music at the same time. The bass would rattle the tempo right through a man's boot soles and into a woman's heart.

The mill was an ideal venue for any country musician worth his salt.

And he couldn't do it. He couldn't go

back to those days of drinking, flirting, and playing. The music created an artificial high that made him believe he was superman, that he could do it all, have it all—and he couldn't. He just wasn't made that way. He could have fortune and fame, or family and love. He'd suffered the torments of the damned learning which he wanted.

"Hey, Dad, look at this!" Adam called from the back end of the enormous building. "There's a loft up there for the light system."

And rafters for speakers and video screens. And room enough for a high stage and a thousand people. This temptation was precisely why he'd left Nashville.

Flint dragged his boot heels toward his sons, who were practically bouncing in excitement. He'd never taken them on tour. They'd never understand how precarious music was to their existence.

"The offices would make great dressing rooms," Jo sang out as she emerged from a door in the rear. "There are big restrooms on the other end for the audience."

She was glowing and bouncing even more than the boys. Flint bit back a sarcastic reply, unwilling to pop their balloons. They had little enough to be happy about.

The mill had officially filed for bankruptcy yesterday, sent the employees home, and locked the doors.

They weren't supposed to be here now, but Amy had known a maintenance man with keys.

"The players would have to stay in Asheville," Jo continued worriedly, apparently reading his face. "But we could rent a bus to transport them, couldn't we?"

"*Everyone* would have to stay in Asheville, including the tourists," he said. "You have only one motel up here."

"Can you imagine how that would change if we can make a success of this? We could have music shows out here every weekend." Jo swung in circles, obviously hearing the music in her head already.

In his head, too. He could hear an entire symphony dragging him into the whirlpool, sucking him under.

"What happened to RJ?" he asked. "I thought he was coming in this week."

"Randy never did anything he said he would in his entire life," Jo said as she climbed into the loft. "I think Slim talked to him. He probably figures he can wing it, and people here will still swarm all over him."

"Arrogant asshole," Flint muttered, although no one could hear. The kids had turned an old wooden crate into a drum and had their own jam session going.

That was another fear ripping at his gut. He didn't want his sons caught up in the undertow of excitement and carried out to the sea of unkept promises that was the entertainment world. He hadn't taught them how to survive yet.

"We could invite some of our friends down for the festival, couldn't we, Dad?" Johnnie shouted across the barn, bright with eagerness instead of sulking in gloom. "There's enough room at our house for them to stay. They could bring sleeping bags."

Our house. They were thinking of his cabin as home. Guilt hammered him. They didn't have friends here yet. They missed the big house they'd grown up in. He'd torn their lives apart. He had to help put them back together again.

"Yeah, we could do that," he agreed. Of course, if it was only RJ playing at a dinky concert at the school, their friends wouldn't have any reason to travel here.

Torn so many ways he couldn't think straight, Flint watched the sway of Jo's rounded backside as she climbed down the ladder. Her show made him feel infinitely better, if only for the moment.

The highway had opened Tuesday, so he had no good excuse for staying at her place. And with the boys around, he'd had no opportunity. But Jo hadn't condemned him for his choices. She'd cheerfully taken the boys fishing when he'd had to go down to Asheville for supplies and cooked dinner for all of them when he got back. He'd even caught her a time or two squirreled away with the boys and their laptop, singing at songs they guiltily shut down at his appearance. He pretended not to notice.

When she came to stand beside him, she was humming the song they'd created the night they'd first had sex. Flint couldn't use terms like *make love* yet. That implied a commitment he wasn't in any position to ask for, although just standing next to Jo made him want to grab her waist and beg her never to leave. He figured that was just his old impulsive ways creeping up on him, and he crushed the urge.

"I want to hear my songs up on that stage," she whispered, revealing her longing. "Isn't that silly? I hate RJ. I want to rip out his innards and feed them to the chickens. But I want to see how the audience reacts when he sings my words to your music."

Damn, and double damn. Heart cracking, Flint stonily stared toward the invisible stage where John and Adam drummed rhythms out of a crate. A maelstrom of music whirled through his head, and he was going under for the third time.

"I know," she said with disappointment at his silence. "They're crap and the audience will laugh him off the stage, which will serve him right. But that song we worked out together—wouldn't it sound grand in here?"

Heart thoroughly broken by her soft wishes, wishing he could offer her the world, Flint dug his hands into the silk of her upswept hair. He tugged her close to plant a hasty kiss on her brow. "Your songs aren't crap, Joella Sanderson," he said with a fervency he felt clear through him. "And if you want, we can nail that tune, and I'll get it registered so the band can play it."

She stared up at him with eyes starry with wonder. "You'd do that? *Can* we do that? You'd let the Buzzards *sing* our song?"

Flint cupped her ears and gently shook

her head back and forth. "Get it through that pretty head of yours, Jo. You are a brilliant songwriter. Your songs touch the heart. People will love them. The *Barn Boys* will sing your song. Once we get your material in the right hands, you can write your own check. Just be certain you're ready for success when it comes. There are two sides to everything," he warned.

Just saying it tore the last shreds of his heart out. He would be opening the road for her to leave. At the beginning, he'd wanted that, encouraged it, needing this last temptation out of his life. But he so hated the thought of losing her that he'd let things slide since then. He was a termite. She had a family who needed her income, and he ought to be offering her all the help he could summon.

Jo hooted her disbelief. "Ain't gonna happen, but it sure does sound pretty. Mama can't make a living selling pillows."

"I wish I could pay her and her friends more," he said with regret, accepting her digression rather than dwell on his pain. "They're working like demons."

"They're working like demons on chair covers you don't even want," she scoffed.

"You're just a big old softy. We'll probably have to replace them in a month."

They both fell silent. Unless business turned around, the café wouldn't be there in a month. He was spending his ticket out by promising his insurance money to the women.

"We'd better get back and start cranking up for your grand opening," she said with forced cheerfulness. "Now that the road is clear, the tourists will find us again. Maybe we ought to provide entertainment and let a few chickens loose."

"And molasses. We could make cleaning the streets an annual event." He had to grin at the image, even if his insides churned in anxiety. "C'mon, guys, we have to get going," he shouted over the clamor.

"I think a chicken is nesting in Myrtle's hat. We need to check it for eggs." Jo snickered, squeezed his arm, and sauntered off as if she hadn't a care in the world.

She had an immense career ahead of her, and she dismissed the possibility as if he'd told her the sun would come up blue tomorrow.

Someone—or maybe life in general—had

sapped her confidence. She didn't believe his promises, or in herself.

Flint thought he ought to kick himself three ways from Sunday. He'd just accepted her talent as part of the wonderful world that was Jo. Instead of helping her, he'd wallowed in selfishness, not giving half a thought to Jo's future.

He could fix that.

Maybe if he had a reason to build this show that had nothing to do with himself, he could survive. Let Jo be the music.

It would eventually mean severing her from his life, but that's what he wanted, wasn't it? Remove temptation and go back to looking for a mother for his sons, one who wouldn't take the music train out of here. Besides, he owed Jo and her family.

With a different purpose to his tread, Flint noted all the barn's features as he walked through it. If the Chamber could get permission to use this place, he could sell it as a music venue with one hand behind his back.

All he had to do was give up his soul. No big loss.

*   *   *

Wearing her *Star of the Stardust Café* apron over a green, floor-length gown, Jo thought she'd achieved a funky respectability for the café's dinner opening. Admittedly, the skirt had a slit up to her thigh, and beneath the apron, the halter top had a big heart cutout over her cleavage, but, hell, she was wearing an *apron.* She had to get her kicks somehow.

She needed to ground herself solidly in the here and now so Flint's tempting devil words didn't slurp her brains out.

He'd said the Barn Boys might play their song. Sing *her* words.

That had her giddy enough to swing on rafters without listening to his other promises. She'd heard them all before. It was easy to promise fame and fortune, far less easy to accomplish it. She knew better than to crave stardom, but she still desperately longed for recognition.

Elise had called to say she'd filed the lawsuit. Suing Randy's pants off was Jo's best chance of earning some respect.

Whistling to clear her head of impossible dreams, she hurried downstairs to the café—the *restaurant.* Flint would have to

change the name if the dining room caught
on.

"It's about time you got here," Amy said
nervously when Jo hurried in. "I need more
potatoes." She gestured at an unpeeled
stack on the counter.

"Amaranth Jane, I am not peeling potatoes and waitressing, too. Are you out of
your *mind*? You can't fix mashed potatoes.
It's too much work."

"Flint said he could make meat loaf, and
you can't have meat loaf without mashed
potatoes," Amy insisted. "We won't open
for another half hour. I have the first pot
cooking. Oh, and we need more pots. I had
to bring my own pans for the lasagna. This
place doesn't have enough."

"Of course we don't have enough. We
don't *cook*." In exasperation, Jo took a seat
at the counter, accepted the knife Amy
handed her, and started peeling. "Where is
the great man? Shouldn't he be fixing his famous meat loaf?"

"They're in the oven. He's gone home to
change. The boys wanted to go to the show
tonight, and he wouldn't let them. He's being mighty grouchy for some reason."

"He's nervous. He keeps things all bottled

up, and it seeps out like steam. So, what did y'all do with the kids?"

"They're at Mama's, with Ina and Flo." At Jo's questioning look, Amy hastily added, "Mama's doing fine. And Ina and Flo are there to call if she gets sickly."

"Okay, I know. I just worry. You know her joints are hurting." Jo dropped a spiral of peel in the empty ice cream bucket Amy handed her.

"If only this pillow-making would work out . . ."

Even in her optimism, Jo couldn't see how it would, but she wasn't one to say a discouraging word.

Flint came in spiffed-out in a tan suede blazer and black slacks that draped on his muscular thighs like thin silk. Instead of his usual black, he wore a tan-and-black-striped shirt with a stiff collar and cuff links. With his dark hair trimmed and slicked back, he was too pretty for words, so Jo whistled.

He grinned at her and held up a tie. "You think I should put this thing on?"

"You want to drive away the audience?" Jo nodded in the direction of the back room. "The womenfolk would swoon and the men would hate your guts. Leave it off."

"That's what I like, a woman who knows all the answers." He shoved the tie in his pocket and leaned over to kiss her hair. "Umm, you smell good."

"Yeah, but I think I've just been disrespected, so you better watch out, handsome, or you'll be peeling potatoes instead of me."

"Disrespected?" Flint asked in incredulity, disregarding her double entendre. He traveled around the counter to check the meat loaf in his new oven. "How's that?"

"Men don't like women who have all the answers," Amy answered for her. "Mama taught us that, but Jo never believes a word she's told."

"I don't want a man who's afraid of a woman who speaks for herself," Jo said, refraining from reminding Amy that Evan did what he liked because Amy never objected.

"There's speaking up, and then there's flaunting it." Flint removed the meat from the oven, and the redolent aroma of beef and spices wafted around them. But the heat of the admiring glance he sent Jo had nothing to do with meat loaf.

The beef bubbled in hot juice, and Jo felt a kinship for it. Flint's gaze had her stewing in her own juices. She jumped up from her seat and hastily wiped the potatoes off her hands. "I better set a few places. It's a shame we lost so much of that Fiestaware. It would look perfect with those colors in the new upholstery."

Amy looked from one to the other of them, laughed, and returned to icing her cupcakes. "Jo flaunts her opinions," she informed the world at large. "That's why the whole town listens to her, and she hasn't got a man. They're all afraid of her."

"They're all girlie men," Jo said with disdain. "Why would I want a man who's afraid of my opinions?" But Flint wasn't afraid, a little voice whispered in her ear. Flint had listened. And acted. And that was why she was madly in lust with him.

"Why would you want a man at all?" Flint asked, coming up behind her with a stack of cloth napkins that hadn't been aired since the Second World War. "You can be rich and famous all on your own."

"No, I can't. Randy used to tell me that, and here I am, still wearing an apron." Jo smoothed the sparkly stars. "At least it's prettier than the old one."

Leaving the napkins on the table, Flint fiddled with the knot at Jo's waist. Jo tried not to squirm while she wondered what he was up to.

"So, don't wear the apron," he said. "Show me what you're wearing under it."

From the sexy rumble of his voice, he wasn't wondering what was under the *apron.* How could she resist his invitation? Jo pulled the apron over her head, then stepped back and faced him, daring him to look and not touch.

It was Flint's turn to whistle. He checked her out from her green, spiked heels and slit skirt to the revealing cutout over cleavage obviously not contained in a bra.

"You may have to put that back on, Jo," he said with regret. "I don't want the men so busy looking at those opinions you're flaunting that they forget to order."

Amy's crystalline laughter broke the tension. Flinging the apron at Flint, Jo strode off to flaunt her assets elsewhere, sizzling from the heat of Flint's regard.

She knew men liked to look at her. She'd

taunted, teased, and tamed with her looks for as long as she could remember.

She wanted it to be different with Flint, but damn if she could tell if he was flattering her brains so he could get at her boobs.

And as usual, she wasn't certain whether she cared what he thought as long as she knew he'd be back in her bed sooner or later.

There was just a little too much of her rebellious mama in her.

≪TWENTY-FOUR≫

Amy bit her bottom lip as Elise entered the nearly full café.

The tourists paid no attention. Caught up in their own family dramas, they ate home-cooked corn and green beans, sucked down gallons of iced tea, and chattered, oblivious to the emotional storm approaching.

The few locals with enough cash to eat out turned to stare at the elegantly dressed stranger.

Taller than Jo, draped in a lavender silk pants suit that would have done justice to a Manhattan restaurant, Elise wore her ebony hair coiffed and held with diamond combs. The lawyer's dramatic appearance eclipsed even Jo's earthy looks, Amy had to admit.

Mouths gaped as Jo ran up to welcome the new arrival with a huge smile, ushering her to a small chrome table with a *Reserved* sign. Amy clenched her teeth and returned to mashing the new batch of potatoes with the antiquated mixer.

It was almost eight and Flint and his sons were in the back room helping the band set up chairs. The show wouldn't have tables for drinks tonight. Fortunately for everyone, all the dinner tables still held paying customers.

"Who's the babe?" George Bob whispered from his seat at the counter where the single diners had gathered. "Jo must know her."

Amy glanced over her shoulder. Jo and Elise were in deep conversation. This must be about the lawsuit, not Evan. Amy tried not to look too relieved. "That's Jo's lawyer," she murmured back, adding another cup of cream to the potatoes. "You'll have to ask her what it's about."

George snorted and cleaned his plate with his fork. "Maybe Jo's suing the mill for closing. Or she wants to buy it, paint it pink, and start a chicken farm."

Amy reached over to pat his hand. "You're better off without her, Georgie. Why don't you go over and say hi to Sally? She's looking lonely."

Amy checked on Jo again. Instead of looking excited and triumphant, her sister looked pale and worried. Amy did her best not to shake in her shoes, but the mixer in her hand spluttered and died. She wanted to heave it across the room but didn't dare. "Blasted ancient equipment anyway," she said in reply to George Bob's knowing look. Jo had half the town believing her superstition about Amy's ability to kill machinery.

Removing the beaters from the bowl, Amy found a whisk and splattered potatoes over half the sink with her efforts.

Their mother's health could depend on Jo's winning that lawsuit. Amy had to set every penny aside for the day Evan walked out. She couldn't pay her mother's bills anymore. She was reduced to hoping Flint made money so he might offer her a job.

She was wiping up splashed potatoes when Jo slipped behind the counter and whispered, "Elise wants to speak with you."

"About what?" Nervously, Amy reached for a towel. "What did she say to you? You look like a ghost."

Jo forced a smile. "The record publisher

called her. She thinks Randy may have caved under our evidence, but they're not admitting it yet. They've talked to the lawyer who drew up Flint and Randy's contract, and they're threatening a countersuit unless we settle out of court."

The newly replaced lightbulb over the stove shattered. "You've got faulty wiring," Amy complained, picking up the shards. "What does a countersuit mean?"

Jo shrugged as if her whole future didn't matter. "That Flint has to hire a lawyer to defend his rights against me, Randy, his publisher, and everyone else."

"Then why does Elise want to talk to me instead of Flint?"

"I think it's about Evan. Are you okay? Want me to go with you?"

Amy shook her head, handed Jo her towel, and, chin up, marched over to Elise's table and sat down.

"I wish this place served alcohol," Elise said sympathetically. "I never wanted to be a divorce lawyer for just this reason."

Amy closed her eyes and pretended she didn't see the sympathy in Elise's eyes. "I moved out of his bed and upstairs with the kids last week, and I'm not sure he even noticed. You're not telling me anything I don't already suspect."

"I brought you a list of the best divorce lawyers in the state. I advise you to hire one immediately. Your husband's already talking to the top firm in Charlotte," Elise said softly.

Amy swallowed hard and fought back tears. No matter how softly Elise spoke, it didn't alter the fact that ten years of marriage were sliding down the drain, and for no good reason that she could see. The kids would be devastated.

She'd wanted to be brave like Jo and stand up and fight for her marriage, and this is what it had come to. A whimper. "He's seeing her?" she whispered.

Elise nodded and reached across the table to squeeze her hand. "I'm sorry. I wish I was trained in mending marriages, but that's not how the law works."

"It's okay," Amy murmured, trying to reassure Elise. That had always been her place in life—taking care of others. What would she do now? "I think I knew it was over anyway. I just hoped—"

But she couldn't hope anymore. Evan had

a *lover.* With a cry of defeat, she pushed back her chair and ran for the restroom.

The restroom was already occupied.

Sobbing, she turned and fled through the back, past Flint, past the ticket taker, and out the door. The alley was already filling with people who'd come to hear the band. She had nowhere to run, nowhere to hide.

With a wail of misery, she fled up the stairs to Jo's place.

Jo had already deserted the counter and was racing after Amy when Flint intercepted her in the hallway between the café and back room.

"What's wrong with Amy?" he demanded, catching her arms. "Did one of my customers insult her?"

His fingers dug into her arms and concern lined his forehead. Jo wanted to kiss him for worrying about her sister, but she didn't have time. "No, she was talking to Elise. I'm sorry, I have to go." She ran off, leaving him to deal with the café.

Standing worriedly at the entrance, Peggy pointed her toward the stairs.

"Find someone else to take tickets," Jo yelled as she ran past. "Help Flint out front."

She didn't wait to see if the teenager obeyed.

Rushing in, Jo found Amy sprawled across the couch, weeping her heart out. Not knowing whether to cry or curse, she wet a washcloth with cold water and took a seat on the sofa cushion at Amy's head.

"We'll work it out" was all she knew to say, wiping at her sister's tears.

They'd climbed mountains and scaled obstacles all their lives. They could do it again. But when would they ever be allowed a little happiness?

When Amy gave a helpless cry and struggled to sit up, Jo hauled her into her arms and offered her shoulder. She didn't have a word of comfort left in her.

Jo's heart ached for her sister. She knew all about the devastation of heartbreak, that's why she had to think for Amy right now. She had to be the glue that held the family together until Amy realized she was too good for a jerk like Evan. Amy had been their caretaker for years. It was Jo's turn.

And for a change, she might even be in a position to help. If Evan was leaving, Amy would need a job. The children would need babysitters. Her mother would have no one to fall back on for emergency expenses.

From what Elise had told her tonight, Jo could provide it all—if she dropped her claim to Randy's songs and accepted a lump-sum cash settlement for more money than she'd ever be worth in this lifetime.

All she had to do was forget her dream of a career that would give her recognition and respect. No big deal.

Watching the last of his dinner customers wander toward the rocking chords of the band in the back room, Flint jiggled his keys in his hands. He was aware of the perfumed lawyer standing shoulder to shoulder with him at the front door as he closed up for the night, but his mind had traveled to the women upstairs. He didn't have room left in his head for the slick city lawyer. He'd had about enough of cities and lawyers anyway.

"I appreciate the offer," Elise was telling him, "but Knoxville isn't that far."

He dragged his attention back to the moment, wishing he had Jo's ability to think three things at once. "My place is just a mile away. You shouldn't be driving that mountain alone at night. I'll be staying here." He didn't know where, but he would feel like an asshole if he packed up his kids and went home, leaving the women crying upstairs. It just didn't feel right.

She shook her head at the keys he offered, but regarded him with interest. "Jo hasn't talked to you yet, has she?"

Flint shrugged, even if he felt like flinching at the impact of her question. "I reckon I know what you told her. It's not as if I didn't expect it."

"You know how the business works. This case could drag on forever with everyone suing everyone else. You'll need a lawyer separate from RJ's to defend your interests."

"I've talked to a few," he admitted. "I'd have to sell this place to pay their fees. I'd rather just give it to Jo." He worked up an imitation of his old smile. "Maybe she'll hire me as short order cook."

"You're an unusual man, Flynn Clinton," Elise said thoughtfully.

He didn't think he saw the usual predatory interest in the way she said that. He really was losing his old charm, and he didn't much care. "And you're an unusual lawyer," he retaliated, figuring he had nothing to lose. "Not many would come all this way to talk to a couple of backwoods clients."

He thought he saw something raw disappear behind the smile she carefully arranged on her lips. "I have my reasons. Call it God or fate or the stars, but sometimes I really believe Someone is pulling our strings. Good night."

She brushed past in an airy flutter of silk and scent that had no effect on him. The music in the back didn't call to him either, not while his heart was this heavy.

Staring thoughtfully at his keys, Flint debated his next move.

With a will of their own, his boots carried him out the front door.

He didn't know if he believed in God or fate or astrology, but some things were purely inevitable.

Jo looked up the instant Flint walked in. Amy had dried her tears and washed her face and was making noises about going home. Jo couldn't let her go alone. The look on Flint's craggy face said he understood without being told.

"Why don't I pick up the kids and take

them to my place?" he suggested. "You two stay here and take a girls' night."

Jo didn't know whether to laugh or cry at the stiff way he made his magnanimous offer. For a man who doubted his parenting abilities, he'd just slit his wrist and let it bleed by offering to look after two little ones. How could she not love a man willing to make that sacrifice? Louisa still wore diapers at night.

"That's generous of you, Flint, thank you, but I can make it home all right. Did we have enough food for everybody?" Hastily wiping the last tear from her eye, Amy rose with a briskness of purpose.

"I made 'em hamburgers when we ran out of meat loaf. There's only a bit of lasagna left. We did okay. Y'know, you're the second woman who's turned me down tonight. I'm thinking I'm losing my touch."

He didn't look too sorry about it. He lounged there with his shoulder against the doorframe, looking at home in his boots. A good thing he hadn't worn his expensive tie and had discarded his fancy jacket. He had grease stains on his shirt from the folding chairs.

"You offered to take Elise home with you,

too?" Jo teased in an effort to match his attempt at lightening the black cloud in here.

"I offered her the house anyway. Think she'd have stayed if I offered more?" Despite his self-mockery, he asked Jo silent questions over Amy's head.

She handed him the final piece of her heart right then. Any man who could worry over her sister *and* the lawyer who was suing him had to possess the Right Stuff.

"Elise figured I'd come after her with a butcher knife if you did that," Jo said carelessly, as if she wasn't admitting that she wouldn't share him. "She's not dumb."

A slow smile creased the corners of Flint's mouth, and he studied her with appreciation. "Yeah, my luck doesn't run to dumb women these days."

He took the car keys from Amy's hand when she tried to pass him. "And smart women don't drive mountains at night after tippling Jo's beer. You've taken care of my kids and me this week. It's my turn."

Jo's jealousy kicked in as Flint took Amy's elbow the way he always took hers. Maybe her sister and Flint were made for each other, two lonely souls seeking help with their kids, but she wasn't feeling that generous right now. "Can I go, too?" she asked, trying not to sound needy.

The heated look Flint sent her told her all she needed to know.

"You don't want to raise a little hell downstairs?" he asked, raising his eyebrows to show he understood what Elise had told her.

He knew. He knew he was losing it all, and despite that, he was giving her room to celebrate the riches Elise had told her about.

Celebrating the ability to buy all the Jimmy Choos her closet could hold just didn't hold the appeal it should. "I think hell has been sufficiently raised for one evening. I'd rather make it go away."

She grabbed her purse and, following Amy's muttered protests, turned out her lights and shut the door.

❖TWENTY-FIVE❖

Sitting in a row of folding chairs in the back of the café while the town council discussed the concert that was only two weeks away, Flint thought he understood how Amy blew out lightbulbs. If something didn't explode soon, he might.

"Muffins," Jo hissed from his right, leaning around him to talk to Amy on his left. Her breast brushed his arm, and blood rushed straight to his groin in response. He tried adding up the long empty nights since they'd had sex.

Not since the arrival of his sons. Too many things were happening at once, and he couldn't dump Adam and Johnnie on strangers so he could scratch his itch. Not that he ought to be thinking about itches with a woman who was suing him for what little he was worth, much less one who

made him think of a lifetime of morning coffee over sunny breakfast tables.

"Not enough ovens for baking," Amy
murmured back, leaning around him. "We
could sell chair covers," she suggested.

Flint hadn't a clue what they were discussing. He was desperately attempting to
focus on the stage. It looked like the whole
damned town had turned out. And all he
could think of was the sexy scent emanat-
ing from the woman wiggling restlessly at
his side. Jo had been jumpier than a hoppy
toad ever since she'd told him about her
meeting with Elise.

He couldn't say he was resigned to losing
his restaurant to pay lawyers. The future
looked damned black if he had time to think
about it.

Fortunately, he hadn't had two minutes to
call his own since the Barn Boys had decided to make Northfork their charity of the
year. Announcing they'd organize a "Mill-
Aid" concert had turned the town on its
head. And shook out all their brains, from
the looks of it, Flint concluded.

The future of Northfork's inhabitants
looked bleaker than Flint's unless the concert generated a whopping lot of cash. And

cash didn't guarantee the court would let the town buy the bankrupt mill. Losing his café lost its importance in the sum of the economic catastrophe facing all the unemployed mill families. And still they all enthusiastically turned out to help with the concert.

"Booths along the drive," Jo whispered across him, while up in front the mayor described the events leading up to this town meeting.

"We can use the outside electric lines from the Christmas light display!" Amy cried excitedly, causing a few warning frowns and hushes around them.

To Flint's immense relief, the sisters straightened up and faced forward at whatever decision they'd reached. He was swimming in perfume and frustration and couldn't be responsible for his actions much longer.

He scanned the room to locate his boys in a corner with a group of other kids their age, passing headphones back and forth. He tried not to imagine how many royalties they'd stolen from other musicians with their music habit. One of these days he'd

have lots of spare time to investigate their
disk and make a list of people he owed.

Not that he could pay anyone back in the
foreseeable future.

"The bankruptcy court has agreed to
withhold disposition of assets until we have
time to gather our resources," the mayor
was saying.

Flint knew all this. He'd attended all the
Chamber meetings, heard all the arguments. He was more than willing to do his
part to help out.

He just didn't see how the town buying
the mill would save him or his future.

"With the aid of government grants and
loans, the proceeds from the Mill-Aid concert, and a lot of hard work from everyone
present, we have a chance to bid on the mill
and save our jobs."

A cheer rocked the roof. Everyone in here
had heard all of this in one form or another
over the past weeks. Flint figured this was
more pep rally than town meeting.

"Mama needs to borrow Adam and Johnnie," Jo whispered in his ear.

Her breath against his skin tingled his
spine, and he lost what concentration he
possessed. "Why?" he growled back.

"Clear out the barn on her place so Ina and the others can set up more cutting tables." She snaked her arm around his and trailed a pink-painted fingernail up the inside of his bare forearm, sizzling his skin. "And to help move all those heavy bolts of fabric."

He hoped she wasn't asking more than her touch was telling him. The kids needed to learn to help others. The exercise would be good for them. But his mind swept straight past those practicalities to other consequences of loaning out his kids. "When does she need them and what will you be doing then?"

Jo's sultry smile warmed all the cold places in Flint's soul, and his inner Neanderthal roared in triumph. He craved Jo more than music.

That thought didn't rock his socks as it ought. He couldn't even blame Jo for wanting a future for herself outside of this town, so he knew he was a desperate man.

"I'd rather be anywhere than at Mama's with all her cackling cronies," she murmured, ignoring the applause around them as the mayor increased the level of his rah-rah speech. "Tonight?"

"Tonight," he agreed without hesitation. He had a list of phone calls to make for the music committee, the lawsuit his lawyer had sent to read through, and bills to pay, but they could all wait. "You'll be at your mother's when I drop off the boys?"

It was almost five now. Flint figured he could feed them and have them delivered by six if necessary. His pulse was tripping so erratically he'd have a heart attack if getting Jo into bed took any longer.

"I'll be upstairs," she purred, "working on that welcome song for the boys."

She didn't mean his boys. She meant for the Buzzards. Flint scowled at this hitch in his plans. "I don't have time to help you write a song."

It was bad enough suffering through the ignominy of calling up all his old friends and begging them to participate in the concert. It was hell telling everyone he wasn't available for backup. It would be pure damned torture to help Jo write her ticket out of here. He'd been avoiding her place for more reasons than his kids.

"I only need a little inspiration," she murmured. Releasing his arm, she stroked his thigh just as the rest of the crowd stood up and cheered.

A part of Flint stood up and cheered with them, and it had nothing to do with the mayor's call to arms.

As Joella disappeared into the talking, excited crush of people exiting his back room, Flint focused on getting his kids out of here and up the road.

He didn't have music or business on his mind as he rushed them out the door.

Nervously, Jo tucked a stray curl behind her ear and returned to tuning her guitar. Flint had provided her with the sheet music he'd composed for her lyrics. She'd been practicing every chance she had—which was a lot more empty time than she wanted.

He had been so stone-faced and inaccessible these past weeks that she'd backed off to regroup. Everyone was caught up in the excitement of the concert, and multitasking had become a way of life. So it wasn't as if Flint were avoiding her. Or vice versa. They were just overwhelmed and avoiding potential pain.

She understood that. She was as guilty as he was of looking for excuses to steer

clear of confrontation. She hadn't agreed to
the record company's cash settlement yet.
Her family had another few weeks before
money ran out. Elise said it was good to
make the record executives sweat. If Jo decided to sue instead of settle, the bad publicity might sink the album, so it was better
to wait for the album's release to bring in
money first.

She simply couldn't stand the frustration
any longer. Working side by side with Flint
five, sometimes six, days a week, finishing
each other's sentences, handing each other
the needed tool without asking, laughing
and joking together, was just too damned
intimate. She was a horny nest of nerves,
lust, and uncertainty. She despised uncertainty. She couldn't see love and marriage in
their future, so what in heck did they have?

They could at least work out the sex part
before they set the café on fire. Or the
church. Or any other place they came in
contact, which was just about the whole
town. She'd even run into Flint at the supply
store, and it was a wonder they hadn't
found a cleaning closet and just had at it
that day. Who knew that nails were such a
turn-on?

The phone rang, but she continued practicing a chord Flint had written for one of her funnier lines. She loved what he had done with her lyrics. She could actually think of them that way now, as *lyrics.* Not ditties or silly poems, but real songs. She owed him for that. It was because of him that she was brave enough to consider holding out for copyright and not just cash.

The band hit a practice note in the room below. They didn't usually start until seven, but they were scared stiff about playing backup for some of the biggest groups in the country. Even Flint had been infected by the Buzzards' fear and had helped them out a bit. She hoped he wasn't down there now, ignoring her invitation.

The answering machine kicked in and Amy left a message about selling pillows at the concert and another about Friday night's menu. The dinner meals on weekends had been working out well. Flint had paid off part of the new oven, but he still wouldn't order an espresso machine. Jo couldn't blame him. It was far better that he was paying Amy for her efforts.

She heard the tread of heavy boots on her stairs and hastily checked her breath and smoothed her hair. Bare feet tucked under her, she called a cheery greeting at the knock on her door. She prayed she didn't look as nervous as she felt. She wasn't used to being nervous around men.

Flynn Clinton was more man than she'd ever known, in more ways than just the physical. But it was the physical setting her heart racing now.

He entered looking all Johnny Cash broody in his black T-shirt and jeans, with a hank of hair falling in his face. He carried a pint canning jar containing roses he'd stolen from someone's garden. He didn't smile when he saw her, just closed the door behind him and approached the couch with a look that boiled the July-steamy air.

"No songwriting," he insisted, taking the cushion next to her and replacing the guitar on her coffee table with the bouquet.

Jo swallowed at the sight of the gorgeous colors of the roses—yellow and orange and pink and even a lovely silver-purple. Just the rich perfume made her stomach go all weak. He was courting her, in his own inimitable way. Not with fancy jewelry or expensive florist bouquets, but with flowers he'd handpicked with her love of color in mind.

"I've been practicing your songs," she said breathlessly, eyeing the flowers but focusing on her words. "I have a lot to learn, but the way you put together notes that fit right in with what I was trying to say—" She halted for breath at the lift of Flint's dark eyebrows but managed to continue. "You can't give up music!" she cried.

There, she'd said it. The words had been bubbling in her for so long that she couldn't contain them any longer. If he could keep writing songs, playing . . . Maybe they could form some future together. There, she'd let that hope out of the bag.

"I can and I have," he said, firmly dismissing her hopes. "My kids come first."

She had to give him credit for not offering to ride out of here on her dreams. He could be wooing her into dropping the lawsuit, and she'd probably be dumb enough to cave. Instead, he was helping her fight Randy and ruining his own future.

Without further discussion, Flint wrapped an arm around her shoulders and dragged her toward him, showing her exactly why he had come here.

Hot, deep, and hungry, Flint's kiss scorched clear to Jo's toes. She forgot all

her carefully prepared speeches, all her brilliant insights, all her impassioned pleas. She
forgot everything except the way Flint's
mouth belonged on hers, her hands belonged in his hair, and their tongues were
meant to stroke.

He had her sprawled against the sofa
cushions under him before she could remember if this was even what she wanted.

"You smell better than Amy's muffins," he
declared, taking time from her bruised lips
to sip at her earlobe and nibble her neck.
"I've been wanting to take a bite out of you
for hours. Days."

He had his hand up her shirt and cupping
her breast as he said it, and Jo took his flattery for the sweetest love song she'd ever
heard. "You smell like fried onions and mint
Listerine." She laughed as he nuzzled the
base of her throat. "Mama must have fed
you."

"I'm trying to seduce you, if you don't
mind," he growled, unhooking her bra front.
"No kids or parents are allowed in our heads
right now."

"Can't be avoided," she murmured, tugging his shirt loose of his jeans and rubbing
her palms up his hard abdomen, thrilling at

the rough texture of hair over hard, hot flesh. "Life is about family. Sex is about family."

Flint halted his depredations to rise up on one arm and stare down at her with a concerned expression. "Are you trying to tell me you're pregnant?"

The anxiety reflected on his strong, masculine features caused Jo to chuckle and smooth his forehead. "Hardly. I'm not that kind of girl," she teased.

Instead of looking relieved, he frowned. "It would be simpler if you were."

Before she could question, Flint lifted her from the sofa pillow and drew her tank top over her head, flinging it toward the guitar. When he fastened his mouth on her breast and sucked, Jo forgot what she wanted to ask. All confusion fled beneath a wave of desire.

He rearranged their positions so her backside was against the sofa and he was on his side facing her. He used both hands to push her breasts together and lap at them alternately. "You're so real," he said between strokes. "I need you to keep me grounded."

She'd heard better praise, but Flint's

words were far more honest than the fancy lies others had told her. *Grounded* spoke of connections and commitments and all those things she craved and never had. She feared she couldn't have them now, but that fear was lost in the power of the moment.

"Ground me then," she muttered, fumbling for his belt buckle. "Ground me before I explode like one of Amy's lightbulbs."

Flint laughed and kissed her hard, sliding his hand inside the waistband he'd loosened. "My thought exactly. Plug me in before we both burn up."

He tugged off her shorts and panties, pushing them down to her knees so she could kick them off while he unzipped. When they were both naked, he stopped, propping himself on tendoned forearms above her, his eyes glowing with appreciation while he studied her supine position.

Jo had to remember to breathe beneath that heated gaze.

"We haven't got all night, but I want to make this last," Flint said, catching her by surprise. "No matter what we do or where we are in the future, I want this to be something we can remember in our old age."

As if she could ever forget the rugged

shoulders and chest swelling over her. A band of hair nearly hid the tattoo of a guitar on his pecs. The same band of hair ran down the flat line of his abdomen to the nest of curls at the juncture of his thighs. Jo swallowed hard as she contemplated the full length of Flint in all his male glory. *That* was a picture she would remember for the rest of her days.

"Dance with me," she said, utterly astonished as the words fell off her tongue. She'd been thinking of Flint and music and sex so hard, they'd all run together.

He looked startled, then glee lit the darkness that had shadowed his eyes earlier. "That'll work."

In one athletic movement he was on his feet and padding across the floor to her stereo. Without checking the contents of the CD player, he hit the power button, and a Barn Boys tune roared from the speakers.

"Your favorite song," he remembered.

Jo scrambled up from the couch before he could touch the switch. "You wrote it," she said. "I checked the label." She stepped in front of him, not shy of her nakedness, despite the spotlight of his appreciative gaze.

"I had too many words in my head and no other way to say them," he admitted. "Let's dance." He pulled her into his arms rather than say more.

It was the most erotic dance of Jo's life, and she figured she'd remember it to the grave and beyond. Flint wasn't afraid to use his body to woo and seduce. He swung her to the beat of the song, then pulled her back against his chest, rubbing his muscled arm across her breasts while he pushed his arousal against her backside. He made her feel as if the body she'd been given was a gift made just for him, and not an asset to be exploited.

He swung her away on the next verse, and Jo raised her hands to display all her assets the way he liked. She loved the way his delight lifted every crease in his face and sparkled his eyes with pure male pleasure. He caught her shoulders and moved her across the floor in time to the music, swaying hip and waist in a seductive call more potent than foreplay.

By the time the song ended and the next began, Flint had literally danced her into a corner. Jo bumped into the piano keys, and bass notes rang in tune to their bare-assed dance. She held his neck tighter to keep from imprinting the G chord on her backside, and he leaned into her in a tongue-taming kiss that melted all her synapses.

Flint lowered his head to lap at her breasts, and Jo propped her hands behind her to keep from tumbling over. The keys crashed in discordant counterpoint to her ecstasy.

Between them, they played a tune that old piano had never known.

Flint lifted her to snap the lid closed over the keys. Jo jumped, then squealed when he raised her from the floor. He slid the cushion from the piano bench beneath her and set her on it in a single movement.

"Perfect," he murmured, returning to their kiss now that she was seated at a height equal to his.

The ancient upright piano was perfect in other ways, Jo soon discovered when Flint stepped between her legs.

"Flint, you can't—"

But he could. Holding her by the waist so she couldn't fall off, spreading her thighs with his hips, watching her expression as he did so, he slowly slid inside her.

Jo couldn't tear her gaze from Flint as he

claimed her. Dark fires burned behind his eyes, and his skin stretched taut with self-control while she adjusted to his intrusion.

The cushion shielded her bottom and thighs. The hard edges of the upright branded her spine. And Flint burned a passage straight to her core. The pressure that had been building for weeks reached the point of explosion and strained for release. Whimpering, Jo pushed for more.

"Now," he murmured, thumbing her breast in time to the thundering rhythm of the CD player. Lifting her, he brought her down on him, until she clung to his shoulders and wrapped her legs around his back and his front was plastered to hers.

He pumped inside her once, twice, hitting sensitive nerve endings in a grinding rhythm until the heat and pressure exploded in a tumult of song and waves of release. She screamed into his ear and dug her fingers into his skin and fell apart in his arms.

"My turn," he whispered relentlessly.

Throwing the cushion to the floor, he lifted her from the piano and laid her down, propped up her hips, and kneeled over her. Jo clung to his arms as he gave in to the bass beat, thrusting and pounding until she climaxed again. Shedding his control, Flint threw back his head and roared his release.

She wanted to say *Wow,* but her tongue wasn't connected to her head. The only connection she recognized was the one between them, and not just the hot and heavy one between her legs. A fine bond wrapped around them, invisible and unbreakable, a thread of bone-deep understanding that they'd forged together in this moment, more durable than any the mill had ever produced.

Still holding his weight off her so he didn't crush her into the floor, Flint pressed his forehead to hers. He didn't say a word. Jo heard him anyway. This had to be love. She'd had sex with other men, and they'd used her and walked away. Flint asked for nothing except what she wanted to give. Whatever had happened here was large and scary, and she didn't know how to handle it.

He wasn't any more certain than she was. They danced some more after they recovered. They shared drinks. They talked of the mill and the concert and his sons. Flint even helped her write down the notes to the song they'd created together.

They didn't talk of the insurmountable objects between them or make love again. The aura of their connection held them in its glow, and Jo feared tarnishing its shine.

Tomorrow, she would return to the real world, the one where Flint was losing everything he owned, and she had the power to build her future on the ruin of his.

A tear slid down Jo's cheek as he dressed, and she wrapped in a robe to say good-bye. Flint pressed a kiss to her brow and ignored the moisture in her eye.

"One day at a time," he murmured. "That's all there is."

She nodded and watched him go. Holding the terry cloth around her, she broke into a torrent of tears when she heard him talking below to one of the guys in the band.

She knew better than to love another music man. She really did. But her soul cried out for the rhythm of Flint's, and she couldn't stop herself. Even though he made no promises, he carried what little remained of her heart.

❦TWENTY-SIX❧

"I'm storing the pillows in the family room for now." Amy led Jo and Flint through her house to the slate-floored room currently buried in stacks of mill products. "I've wrapped them with tarps to keep the kids from bouncing on them. I don't know how we'll get all of them down to the tent at the mill."

"There are enough pickup trucks around here to haul them if you've got tarps," Flint suggested. "What are those things?" He nodded at a stack of colorful fabrics covering the early-American settle she'd refinished in its original maple color.

"Ina is trying her hand at making slipcovers," Jo replied for her. "The elastic is kind of expensive though." Jo opened one up for Flint to see, draping it provocatively over her shoulder as if it were a lacy gown.

Anyone with half a mind could see that Jo had fallen for her charismatic boss. And Amy suspected behind the neutral mask he wore so well that Flint was having a tough time dealing with his place in Jo's life. But she wasn't taking care of her baby sister anymore. She had her own life to hold together.

"I think the quilts will sell better, but they take forever to make. We just don't have enough time between now and next week." Amy lifted a blue plastic tarp to distract Flint from Jo's performance and show him the items the former millworkers were frantically putting together as their contribution to the town's coffers. She was proud of the miracles wreaked from the damaged fabrics, but the future still looked bleak from her perspective. Her rose-colored glasses had been smashed and ground into dirt.

Flint whistled in appreciation, and Amy smiled politely for the benefit of her guests. Before either of them could comment, the front door slammed open.

"Uh-oh, I didn't lock it behind me." Amy clenched the tarp until she feared her fingernails would shred it. She'd had the locks changed after her last meeting with

Elise so Evan couldn't walk in on her anytime he liked. She'd never seen him pitch
such a fit as he had the day he'd discovered
the locks and had to come looking for her
when he'd thought he'd sneak in and pack
his suitcase. She had wanted to feel triumphant at winning a battle, but she hadn't.
Since then, he'd only communicated with
her through his lawyer.

She knew what this invasion was about
though. The bank had called yesterday to
tell her the account didn't have funds to
cover a large check Evan had written.

"Amaranth!" he roared furiously from the
foyer. "Where are you?"

Flint stepped protectively in front of her.
Jo caught her arm and tried to get her to
leave through the back. Amy dug in her
heels. "No, I have to talk to him. Both of
you, go outside and help Mama keep the
kids from coming in."

Flint looked reluctant. Evan's footsteps
over the hall's wood floor echoed with
anger. Amy prayed she knew her husband
better than anyone else. She pointed at the
kitchen and set her mouth as firmly as she
could to hide the way it trembled.

Giving Amy a hug, Jo dragged Flint out the back.

"I'm in here," Amy called. "You could have phoned, you know." She was trying to be more assertive, but that sounded just plain whiny.

Evan burst in looking one volt short of blowing a fuse. Amy wondered if she could pop his circuits the way Jo accused her of doing to the café's. He still looked gorgeous, even if his blond hair needed a trim, and he was wearing a golf shirt instead of a suit. Since when did Evan play golf?

"What is the meaning of this, Amaranth Jane?" He shook his checkbook at her.

"Let me guess." She tapped her finger against her lips. "Leather, brown, rectangular—a cow died to protect your checks?" Once upon a time she used to tease him like this when he asked obvious questions. He didn't laugh now.

"It's *empty,* Amaranth. I deposited my paycheck in there Friday, and it's *empty.*" He flung the checkbook at the table and drove his fingers into his hair. "I put a deposit on an apartment, and they called me this morning to say it *bounced.* How is that possible? We have a money market to back up the checking."

"An apartment?" she asked as pleasantly as she was able. She was wilting inside, but she refused to show her spinelessness. "Does this mean you're no longer living with Linda?"

"That's irrelevant! Where is my money?" He paced up and down as if he didn't know what to do any more than she did. For ten years, he'd told her what to do and how to do it. And now he'd lost that right.

His sudden vulnerability raised her foolish hopes. She was almost ready to grant him the right to tell her what to do again—if only the last few weeks would go away.

Just conjuring up the image of Linda kissing that freckle on his neck reduced Amy's shattered heart to dust. She'd honestly thought Evan loved her, that they would get through rough times together. Instead, he was opting for the easy way out. "You really do think that just because I don't argue with you, that I'm dumb, don't you?" she asked, curiosity getting the better of her common sense. For the sake of the kids, she really needed to know that there was no hope left for their marriage.

At her question, he stopped and stared. "Have you been drinking? I know your mother used to tipple . . ."

"Keep my mother out of this." Suddenly furious at this example of how little he knew about her—and how little he cared—she pointed at the front door. "You can just walk yourself back out of here, Evan Warren. What did you think I would do when I found out you were leaving me? Break down and cry myself stupid? That cash belongs to our kids. If you're going to desert them, then you can damned well take money from Linda to set up your love nest."

"Did I ever say I minded supporting the kids? I deposited my paychecks so you could pay the bills." His gaze swept the family room Amy had so lovingly decorated, his glance taking in her mother's hopes for the future and seeing only disarray. "But I see no reason I have to support a house this size. You don't need the place for entertaining."

"My house?" Amy's bravery stumbled into retreat at this unexpected blow. Elise had warned her, but she had honestly believed the man she'd married cared about his children. *This wasn't the man she'd married.*

"You can't take the house," she protested in horror. "This is where your children *live.*" Ice coated her heart at the possibility that he would rob Josh of his beloved play set in the yard, and Louisa of her brightly colored nursery.

"You'll have to move when you get a job anyway," Evan said, shrugging as if he wasn't ripping lives into tatters. "You won't have me to suck dry any longer."

She'd have to move. Away from her mother and Jo and her support system.

Amy shivered and stared incredulously at the man to whom she'd given her heart so many years ago. "Why would you do this to your children? Do you hate me that much?"

Evan looked at her pityingly. "You never had any ambition, Ames. Northfork is a roadblock on the road to success, and you want to stay. I don't. It's that simple."

"You didn't *ask* me to leave with you." She hated that she could even feel hurt after what he'd done, but she needed the pain to cut the ties binding them. "What about all those times you said you couldn't have done it without me? Did you never mean that?"

He glanced impatiently at his Rolex. "Of course I meant it, but you're not the only

person in the world who can be useful. I
have a meeting later today. Give me a check
for half of what you've stolen so I can pay
my rent, and I'm outta here."

"Useful?" Anger began to steal across the
hurt. "That's all I was, *useful*? I put you
through school, helped you get jobs, gave
up my own career to build yours, had your
kids, and that was being *useful*?"

"Look, we can do this the easy way, or I
can call my lawyer, all right? I said I'd pay
support. What in hell more do you want?
Everything I own?"

"Got it in one, big boy." Her heart had just
been hacked out with a hatchet, but for the
first time in a long time, Amy smiled—even
if it was a malevolent smile. "I invested ten
years of my life in you, and that note's come
due, with interest. You owe me what little bit
you're worth and then some. I'm gonna
make sure you pay every dime."

How had she never understood that ambition had turned her husband's soul to
stone over the years? She'd have to learn
that trick to survive.

"What are the two of you doing?" Marie
demanded, joining Jo and Flint at the par-

tially open kitchen door where they'd stationed themselves to make certain Evan didn't hurt Amy.

"Nothing, Mama." Jo hastily closed the latch.

Flint winced at her mother's suspicious regard and got out of her way when she opened the door to hear for herself.

At the sound of Evan's shouts, Marie's eyes narrowed in fury. "I'll be *damned* if I let that turd talk to my daughter like that!" Tilting forward at full throttle as fast as her joints allowed, she slammed inside the house, mother hen going to the rescue of her chick. Although in the case of Jo's mother, it was more like irate eagle after a turkey buzzard.

Jo collapsed into his arms, and Flint protectively tightened his grip, but uneasiness crawled beneath his skin. He remembered all too well those days of screaming matches, before he'd walked out on Melinda just so the kids wouldn't have to watch their world disintegrate. He couldn't do that to his sons again.

"Amy just declared her independence," Jo murmured. "Mama's gonna kill them."

"You don't think Evan will hit her?" he asked, expressing his immediate concern.

"Nah, Evan's not that kind. He'll hide behind lawyers. Mama's likely to rip a piece of hide off him before he escapes. We should go put sugar in his gas tank."

"Not if Amy's changed the car title to her name," Flint said wryly. "I'm almost sorry I introduced you to Elise. You Sanderson women are scary enough without legal aid." It was bad enough watching the lawyer help Jo tear his music apart. What would happen if he and Jo got involved and it ended like this? As it had to. He wasn't returning to the world opening up for Jo.

She broke away to perch on a deck chair and watch his sons teaching Josh to bounce on the trampoline. "Elise has been helping Amy find a good divorce lawyer. We both owe you."

She hesitated, and Flint figured she was trying to find some way of bringing up the subject they'd both been avoiding. They'd all been working 24/7, which had made it simple to avoid confrontation. But the angry shouts inside raised ugly images.

"Elise says the record label won't sue you if I take the cash," she said tentatively.

Flint shrugged and tried not to let his gut grind at the thought. "I'll still pay. The lawyers will negotiate for some of the settlement to come out of our royalties."

A year of hard work, down the drain. His hopes for a future income for his boys, gone. He'd be much safer not calculating the extent of his losses. Anger at the injustice simmered just below his skin, but he had no business taking it out on Jo.

"They never put my name on the album, so I have a bargaining chip or two," he continued, rubbing the bent fingers of his left hand. "Elise explained that you can get more if you continue with the lawsuit instead of settling now, didn't she?"

Might as well dig his own grave while he was at it. A drawn-out lawsuit with a shark like Elise would ruin his reputation and guarantee he wouldn't have an income for the next decade.

Beside him, Jo nodded. "She told me I could get my name recognized and put on those songs, and I'd be paid royalties for the rest of my life, *plus* Randy's advance money. It just might take years. What do you mean, they left your name off the album?"

He couldn't sit still and discuss this. He got up and paced the deck. Accidentally kicking a tennis ball, he leaned over to pick it up, then squeezed it between his fingers as he tried to find words that didn't make him sound like the sorryass he'd become. "Since I dropped out of sight, our business manager has been pushing Randy's career, helping him kiss Martin's butt. That's the head honcho at the record label."

He didn't know why he was helping her tear his heart out. Except for that one spectacular night a week ago, they weren't even sleeping together. "Reckon they figure it'd be better for sales if everyone thinks Randy wrote and sung those songs himself."

Jo's eyes went wide and she jumped up, apparently on the verge of erupting like Mount St. Helens. "*We* wrote those songs, and Randy still gets credit for them, even if I make him pay through the nose?"

"If you take the cash route and don't sue," he agreed. "Look on the bright side, he'll have to pay someone big bucks to write songs for the next album. There's your opening."

His reward for trying to be peaceful was Jo's fist slammed into his biceps. Flint stared at her in disbelief. He knew better than to tell her she was beautiful when she was mad, but she lit up like a July Fourth fireworks display.

That his heart could do backflips in admiration at a time like this told him what he'd been denying for too long—this ache in his middle wasn't going to go away anytime soon. He loved her beyond reason—which was why he was willing to let her go.

"You're building up a caseload of resentment to get rid of me, aren't you?" she demanded. "You're shoving me away just the way you did Melinda and your music and your family. Well, maybe you're right. If we're going to be staring at each other across a courtroom for the next decade, we can't ever be friends, can we?"

Or anything else. Flint's rage at fate found an outlet in this stupid argument. "I've already given you the rope to hang me, what more do you want?" he shouted, flinging the tennis ball at the basketball goal on the drive rather than shove her against the wall and kiss her until she promised him everything he wanted. Only little boys believed they could have everything they wanted.

"A little trust would be good," she

shouted back. "For just once in your life, Flynn Clinton, admit that you can't do it all yourself!"

"Oh, right, this is coming from someone who thinks her brains are in her boobs, and that she'll never be more than a friggin' *waitress*! Grow up, Joella. This is the real world. Every prize has a price. You gotta fight for what you want and not quit just because a couple of dickheads took you for a ride."

Her big eyes stared at him in astonishment. "Look at the pot calling the kettle black." Before she could hit him again, she stalked off, head high, golden curls flying.

Flint figured she'd walk clear back to town that way. What in hell had made him say those things to her?

Maybe she was right, maybe he *was* trying to tell her to get the hell out of his life.

And maybe he was right, and that's what she needed to do.

Or maybe, just maybe, she was right and he was a friggin' shitpot who needed to stand up and fight for what he wanted. Except what he wanted meant messing up her future just as Evan had messed up Amy's.

≪TWENTY-SEVEN≫

Friday afternoon, the day before the Mill-Aid concert set off the MusicFest, eighteen days and fifteen hours after he'd last made love to Jo—not that he was counting—Flint learned about Jo's meeting that morning with the city men in suits. She hadn't called yet to tell him if she'd decided to sue or settle.

At least she'd had the decency not to rub his nose in his fate by bringing the Nashville cats to the café. She'd been all that was polite ever since last week's harsh exchange of words, but the atmosphere in the café wasn't the same. Flint almost wished he could tick her off so she'd throw dishes at him.

"They drove up in a big Rolls-Royce," Hoss was saying, not having any understanding of the spikes he was driving through Flint's soul. "Heard one of them wore a diamond ring bigger than a golf ball."

Not lawyers, then, Flint concluded. Record producers. They must be pushing for the cash settlement.

He would lose regardless of her choice, so there was no point in adding his opinion. She'd practically moved in with Amy to help her sister cope with the divorce, anyway.

This one-day-at-a-time business sure looked bleak without Jo in his tomorrow. Despite her differences with him, she and his sons had become thick as thieves. The way his kids took to her, he'd even caught himself picturing her at his side when he had to deal with their awkward teenage years. Jo could give them the sensible woman's view that he couldn't. She might not be maternal, but she knew how to keep males of any age in line.

Flint had to smile at that knowledge, even if it was a hopeless dream. This must be what was called payback time. Now he had some understanding of how Melinda had felt staying home while he was out on the road, taking the glory.

"Sure it wasn't Randy who picked her up?" he asked, disguising his heartbreak.

"He's supposed to be in town by tomorrow."

"Didn't see them myself, can't say," Hoss replied, unconcerned and clueless. "But I reckon I'd've heard if it was."

That was something anyway. Flint glanced over at his sons. They'd had their heads bent over that computer for weeks, earplugs in place as if they were fooling him about the stolen music. He didn't have wireless Internet in here, so he couldn't imagine what in heck they were doing when their fingers flew over the keyboard.

If he could have kept the café, wireless Internet would be an interesting possibility. Jo wasn't the only one who could be creative.

After Hoss settled his bill, Flint strolled over to his sons' booth. They hastily shut down their program, and he tousled Adam's hair to show he knew what they were up to. Both boys grinned with innocence. "It's almost time for the dinner crowd. Set up the tables before Jo gets here, willya?"

They jumped up eagerly, unlike the sullen kids they'd been in the spring. His heart swelled with pride and love as they chattered about their friends coming tomorrow. He wanted them to always be this happy.

He never wanted to smash their world apart again.

Well, he could always let Jo have the café, and he could move into the loft upstairs and work for her. For his kids, he might just consider crawling that low.

Promptly at five o'clock, Jo swept in on waves of excitement so vibrant that every person in the room turned to stare. Of course, that shimmering red outfit of hers practically screamed *Look at me!* Since that first dinner, she'd dropped the apron in the evenings and gone for the hostess look. She would have graced the finest restaurant in Nashville.

"I talked to the record label," she whispered to him as she grabbed the stack of colorful tablecloths her mother and her cronies had whipped up out of the damaged materials. "They're taking me out to dinner after work."

"You know what they say about sitting down with vipers," he said laconically, drying off a mug and shutting the dishwasher with his hip.

The fire of challenge rose in her eyes, and he figured she was just about to light into him when his cell phone rang. With regret, he answered it rather than enjoy an exchange of barbs with Jo at her best.

She hurried off to spread the cloths while he assured the Barn Boys' manager that hotel rooms were arranged and ready. Whether he liked it or not, he'd become the contact man for half the people coming in. If he were rich, he'd open a damned hotel.

"That upholstery is *purple,*" Amy complained, tying on her apron and joining him behind the counter as he hung up his phone. "I know Jo likes color, but *purple*?"

"All the other fabric was too heavy or too light or something." Flint had let most of the decorating discussion go over his head. At this point, he'd even hang ferns if he thought it would help. The ladies had assured him that covering the pink vinyl would be all he needed. He'd yanked the booth cushions off their frames, and they'd stapled away as if they knew what they were doing.

"Well, it ought to hide stains if you don't cook anything greasy." Amy popped a roast into the oven.

Jo showed Johnnie and Adam how to make little castles out of the white linen napkins, then hurried back to the counter.

"The record company wants me to send them recordings of all my songs," she whispered.

"You don't have any recordings except the one with the Buzzards," Flint pointed out, glad that the glory hadn't gone to her head, and she was still talking to him.

Apparently already apprised of the news, Amy began chopping sweet potatoes for a casserole, ignoring their whispered conversation.

"Elise has been negotiating. The label said they would set me up with musicians in Nashville as part of the settlement," Jo continued hurriedly as more customers entered. "It will just be a studio record, one your publisher can use to sell my songs to other artists."

She rushed off to welcome their guests before Flint could discern the significance of that. He couldn't believe the record company was blind enough to believe that she was anything less than the next star on their horizon. Why in hell weren't they offering her a recording contract? They were about to make lemonade out of the lawsuit lemon and couldn't see the potential of chiffon pie. He'd have to put a flea in his publisher's ear.

A singer made a heck of a lot more than a writer.

"She's going to be famous, isn't she?" Amy murmured.

"She deserves it," he grunted. And she'd been smart enough not to have kids, who would be hurt by her career. Smarter than he had been.

Amy shot him a sympathetic look. He didn't want pity. He just wanted this next week to be over so he could figure out what to do next. Maybe he could write songs for Jo.

He wanted to write songs *with* Jo. That should have shocked him, but he was beyond shock by now. Jo had lit his drab world like fireworks, opened up possibilities. He'd have to return the favor. He'd already sent her new song to the publisher and the Barn Boys as he'd told her he would. Once she made her choice, he would make a few calls to be certain she got noticed. He still had some influence in Nashville.

Friday night before the big concert meant tourists and music groupies were crawling all over town. The gift shops and antique stores had stayed open, and the restaurant boomed. Rational discussion was impossible. Flint made coffee and iced tea and meat loaves, sliced Amy's chickens, and tried not to drop dishes when he served customers. In between, he helped his sons clear tables and fill the dishwasher. His hand ached like hell, but he couldn't help savoring his brief success. He could have made the restaurant work if life hadn't kept whopping him upside the head.

He had taken the new electric beater from Amy to figure out why it wasn't working when shouts of excitement at the door warned him to look up.

RJ sauntered in, his wavy blond hair styled to perfection, his subtly embroidered black silk shirt screaming *designer,* and the bling on his fingers broadcasting wealth. Or debt deeper than he could pay, Flint figured.

"Randy!" some of the locals called in welcome.

Randy brushed them off. Flint watched as his ex-friend scanned the room, not even noticing Flint behind the counter but focusing on Jo. Even though her calf-length silk skirt was modest by Jo's standards, her strapless red top gleamed against the silver-blues and purples of the café. Combined with Jo's shiny gold hair and bright smile, she was impossible to miss.

As was RJ. The two of them stared at each other over a sea of heads. Damn, but they made a beautiful pair. Some PR flack back in Nashville would be drooling gravy.

Flint handed the beater to Amy as RJ headed straight for Joella.

"Lay your hands off me," Jo muttered when Randy caught her arm and tried to steer her away from her customer.

"That's all right, dearie," Ina said cheerfully. "I can pour my own tea. You go talk to your pretty fella."

"You're looking good, Jo," Randy said with the sincere admiration that had turned her head once before. And with the same tenacity that she had once thought manly, he didn't release her arm. Flint had taught her that a real man listened instead of forcing himself on others.

"I have a car outside. Let's go somewhere quiet and talk." Randy tugged at her.

Jo jerked her elbow away and propped her hands on her hips. She could see Flint winding his way through the crowded room in her direction. In her heart of hearts, she was thrilled that he would come to her rescue even after their disagreement, but she was taking Randy down on her own. "I'm working, and there is no such place as quiet around here if you had eyes in your head for anyone but yourself."

"Jo, I know you're mad, but I just talked to Martin at the record label, and he says everything will be fine once we work out our differences. You don't have to sue me to get money, Jo. We'll be rich. You're too good for this two-bit job." Randy flashed his most charming smile, the one that used to make her swoon. Now all she noticed were the cheap silver fillings in his back teeth.

She'd learned her lesson all right. She would never follow another selfish, shallow man down that long lonesome highway. Flint had opened her eyes to a world of possibilities, and instead of tearing her down to build himself up, he'd encouraged her and offered his help, even if it meant her leaving him. She couldn't believe she'd actually valued herself so little that she'd thought a lying Ratfink was her only path out of here.

Flint came up behind Randy, but he didn't do anything except cross his muscled arms and wait for his cue. Jo wanted to kiss him for that, and for a lot of other reasons, but she had to get even with him for the *brains in her boobs* line first.

"I like my two-bit job," she said sweetly, taking one fight at a time. "And I think you're belly-crawling, low-life scum to come back here and try to talk me out of what is mine since you can't get away with outright theft. I don't need you to make my fortune."

"Now, Jo, you know you don't know this business like I do. You need me, girl. The crowd's all down in Asheville. I'll take you clubbing and introduce you to a few people. You'll be a sensation." He snaked an arm around her waist and drew her toward him.

She'd forgotten how much she hated Randy's spicy cologne. If he patted her on the ass, she was taking him down right now. She shoved out of his embrace.

"Need help, Joella?" Flint asked in a disturbingly flat tone.

Randy's head jerked around at the sound of a familiar voice. "Flint?" he asked in disbelief. "What the hell are you doing here?"

"Helping me get back what is mine, *RJ*," Jo said. "It might cost Flint every penny he earned, but he did what was right. Do you get that at all, *RJ*?"

"Now, honey, you know how it is when you get all caught up in the excitement. I meant to do right by you. I'm here now." Randy patted her reassuringly—on her ass.

Without a second thought, Jo plowed her fist into his midsection.

Randy grunted, grabbed his abdomen, and doubled over in pain.

"Are you hearing *no* yet, Randy?" she inquired politely, keeping her bruised and aching fist balled up and in sight. "Or do I need to speak a little louder?"

"I think he got the message. If not, he can sniff around later when we're not so busy." Flint grabbed the collar of Randy's silk shirt and steered him toward the door. Every head in the place turned to stare.

Jo knew she wasn't strong enough to really hurt him. She figured the big oaf was pretending hurt just to keep from facing the stares. Randy sure lacked abs of steel, though.

"How's your hand?" Amy asked, hurrying up to hug her.

"Wishing it could do it again," Jo retorted. "Wishing I had smashed the scum's jaw while I was at it. Now I understand why men have fistfights."

Which woke both of them up. With muttered *uh-oh*s, they raced for the front door.

Hoss jumped up from his place at the counter and placed his brawny arm across the doorway. "Uh-uh, ladies. You go back to making pretty. I don't know what just went on here, but I reckon Flint is taking care of bidness. You don't need to be gettin' involved."

Jo could hear what kind of *business* they were taking care of. Two solid blows and a muffled groan told the whole story. She supposed Flint had as much or more right to lay Randy out as she did, but she didn't want Flint hurting his injured hand.

She darted under Hoss's outstretched arm and into the street where a crowd had already begun to form. Flint was just hauling Randy off the sidewalk, dusting him off in an elaborate charade of gallantry before shoving his ex-partner into Slim's arms. Randy's former band member looked disgruntled but grabbed Randy's shirt to hold him up. Slim and the band had just learned about the plagiarism and had worked up a fine rage for Jo's sake—and maybe a bit of their own—these last few days.

At Jo's arrival, RJ glared, wincing as he

spoke through a cut lip. "Didn't take you long to find another sucker for sleeping your way out of here, did it?" he asked in scorn.

Flexing his injured hand, Flint halted in midflex and balled up his fingers. Jo caught his arm before he could swing again. He had muscles of steel and could easily shake her off, but he obliged her by refraining. "There are better ways of getting even," she reminded him. "Remember tomorrow."

With Flint in charge of the Mill-Aid committee, Randy had been demoted to the bottom of the playlist. He'd be lucky to have a few drunks sleeping it off in the audience by the time he reached the stage.

Flint nodded in recognition of what she was saying. With a flare of fire in his eyes, he captured Jo's elbow and steered her into the café with a proprietary grip.

She liked Flint's hand on her far too well. She loved walking by his side, and having him take her part put her in orbit. And she wished she knew if he felt the same, or if he hated her. She wondered if she punched Flint in the stomach, if he'd spill his guts.

"I'll let Slim introduce him tomorrow," he growled. "I sure the hell won't."

"No one can expect you to emcee all day

and night," she agreed. Nothing like a joint enemy to make allies. But she wanted Flint as more than an ally. She was tired of guessing where they stood. Tonight, she had to make some tough decisions. She wished Flint would help her, but he was making it pretty plain that he was staying out of her business. Fine then. Two could play that game. She just wished she was as good at it as he was.

She glanced around the restaurant and found Adam and Johnnie staring at them with worry and awe. She winked at them, and they grinned in relief.

She hadn't told Flint about their surprise. They'd thought it up all by themselves, and she'd only helped a little. Let Flint think she was the one who had used the songwriting-contest application.

"The record company is taking me to dinner tonight," she murmured. "Elise will be there. Don't pinch me. I don't want to wake up."

Flint's eyes looked powerfully sad as he released her arm. "You're not dreaming, sweetheart. The kingdom is yours for the asking."

She had enough experience to know

kingdoms turned into pumpkins at midnight, but she couldn't help hoping maybe this time the glass slipper wouldn't break if she said the right words.

⫷TWENTY-EIGHT⫸

Holding a crystal glass of champagne, Jo settled back on the tapestried bench seat and gazed around the elegant restaurant to which the record people had brought her. The last time she'd had champagne had been in Atlanta when He-Who had seduced her before putting her out on the strip-club stage. She didn't like the taste of champagne any better now than she had then.

But she'd never been in a restaurant like this, and she was soaking up the ambience. They'd even painted the *ceiling.* She bet Dot could paint something more original than fish swimming in seaweed.

She was perfectly aware that she was hiding behind denial, pretending she hadn't reached a crossroad that would decide the rest of her life. Flint had done everything except kick her out the door to point her in the right direction. She was sure one of these days she would be mature enough to thank him for not making promises he couldn't keep. That time wasn't now, though. She wanted to throttle him for leaving her to sink or swim on her own.

This should be her Cinderella night at the ball. She should be dancing around the ballroom in joy at finally accomplishing her dreams. But damn it, she still needed her prince to make the magic work. Dancing alone sucked. This business nattering sure as hell couldn't rev her engines like the seductive tango she'd performed with Flint.

Champagne and fancy restaurants weren't as magical as a stormy night on a leather sofa making music with Flint.

She had the world at her feet, and she couldn't enjoy it without a man who hadn't said he loved her. Would she ever learn?

Martin, the guy the suits were kissing up to, interrupted her internal squabble. "It's a shame RJ is indisposed this evening. He's been looking forward to seeing you again, Joella. He could tell you all about our plans."

Indisposed. Jo hid her smirk. She was *so* glad Flint had relieved her of the bastard's presence on this, her evening of triumph.

"We can get you out in front of the public this weekend," Martin continued. "You can go on with RJ so we can see if you're as good as we've been told, and the Barn Boys might let you do a little backup with them. If you've got what it takes, we can start the rumor mill rolling so your name is on everyone's tongue. RJ's making a follow-up album. You can do a duet or two with him. By the time you have enough original material ready for your own CD, everyone will know who you are."

Maybe she ought to start listening instead of gliding along on daydreams. Since when had they started talking about her singing in front of an audience? Jo glanced at Elise to see if she had any reaction.

Her lawyer was sipping champagne and watching everyone at the table with a noncommittal expression. Jo would give good money for Elise's style. Even though the lawyer wore a navy designer suit with sequined trim and a black silk shell that displayed her bosom to good effect, she didn't look out of place here as Jo did. Jo wanted to learn how to do that, but she figured it took money to be flashy and not trashy.

Martin was promising to make her

dreams come true. Jo knew better than to trust promises—especially when they saved the promisee a nasty lawsuit. She remained silent, turning to Elise for corroboration.

"We haven't agreed to the terms of the settlement yet, gentlemen," Elise said in her pleasantly modulated lawyer voice. "Let's not get ahead of ourselves."

"It won't hurt to have her out there, just in case," wheedled one of the suits. "If all goes well, we can get her on RJ's tour bus, doing the shows. We can settle the last few terms over lunch when we're back in Nashville."

They weren't waiting for her to speak, so Jo swirled the champagne and listened, her heart pounding erratically in anxiety and expectation. Flint seemed to think she had brains. Maybe she ought to apply them instead of panicking.

With the insight he'd taught her, she understood these city slickers were simply Randy in fancy suits. She might have stars in her eyes, but her family's future as well as her own rode on making the right decision. To sue or not to sue . . .

She prayed she had the strength and wisdom Flint thought she had, because she sure felt dumber than a doorknob and more scared than a wide-eyed babe.

"No, Harry, the boom lights are for the stage!" Flint shouted in the maelstrom that was the mill barn an hour before the first act played.

The Buzzards were taking the warm-up spot, followed by the contest winner singing their song with the Buzzards for backup. The band had practiced the songs from the finalists in the barn all week. At least he'd finally pried them out of his back room.

His cell rang, and Flint clipped it open with his bad hand while carting one of the bass amps to the front of the stage with the other. Fistfighting with RJ hadn't helped the pain much, but it was good to know he could still form a fist if he had to.

He was trying hard not to think about what decision Jo had given the Nashville suits last night. He had no claim on her. She was free to fly where she willed.

"Yeah?" he shouted into the phone. "Hey, Travis. You climbed out of the grotto yet?" Diverted by his friend's laughter and description of the decadent spa in Asheville's finest resort, he grinned. The guys could afford it.

"Yeah, we have bus parking. Get your asses up here and enjoy the music. It's nostalgia time. You won't believe this place." Flint set down the amp to sign a receipt for the drink concession and glanced over the huge mill interior. They'd rented every folding chair in the mountains, it looked like. And every one of them was sold-out.

Johnnie ran up to show him shots he'd taken with his digital camera of the arts and crafts booths lining the field around the parking lot. After assuring Travis all was in place for their arrival, Flint stuck his cell phone back on its clip and admired the photos in the camera's window.

"Man, how many of those pillows do they have?" he asked, studying the shot of Jo's mother and her cronies standing in a tent stacked with colorful pillows and throws.

"About ten million. And they're asking buckets of money for them. Amy says the rich tourists won't think they're any good unless they pay a lot. The parking lot is filling up, and there's people everywhere. Can we go up in the loft to take pictures?"

"Sure 'nuff. But stay out of their way up there. The booms are dangerous."

"Aw, Dad." Johnnie brushed off his warning with a teenager's indifference. "Is Jo here? Mama Sanderson wanted to talk to her." He took the camera back and flipped through the pictures again.

"I thought she was out there somewhere. If you see her, tell her I need to talk with her, too. Run tell Dave that the concessions are here, willya?" Flint waved Johnnie off as his phone rang again.

Hanging up on that call, he hastily punched the programmed number for Jo's apartment. Surely she wasn't sleeping through the big day? She hadn't called him when she'd got in last night, so he figured the record company honchos had kept her out late. He was trying real hard not to fret while he waited to hear what she'd decided, but he itched under his collar something fierce.

He got her answering machine. Jo didn't have any assignment except as gofer, but that was an important task with their limited budget. He didn't understand her refusal to use her glorious voice onstage today, but given what he knew about her past, he wouldn't push her. She had to be here somewhere, or on her way. He hung up his cell. Setting aside the cowboy hat he usually wore onstage, he swung up the ladder to straighten out Harry and the lights.

He had exactly one hour before he had to step in front of the audience and introduce the first act. He didn't have time to think about how it would feel walking out there without his guitar.

He just knew he wouldn't look half as bad as Randy would with a black eye and split lip. He smiled in satisfaction at the memory of Jo's sucker punch. If he had to fall in love at a ripe old age, at least it was with a woman who could stand up for herself.

"You're the man, Flint." Dave smacked him on the back as Flint straightened his tie and arranged his low-crowned Stetson prior to making his stage entrance. "Make us a fortune out there." He jumped down from the narrow piece of makeshift stage behind the curtain, leaving Flint alone with his Nashville cronies.

"Go get 'em, boy," Travis said in his guttural growl. "Make 'em rowdy."

Travis had showed up to check out the stage conditions—and probably to check out Flint's chord hand. Flint didn't begrudge his old friend the curiosity. He did begrudge

him the company he'd brought along
though.

"It's only nine in the morning and the
house is full," RJ murmured in disgust.
"Don't these people ever sleep?"

He'd arrived backstage in full regalia:
skintight leather pants, white silk shirt open
to the navel, and ten-gallon hat. Someone
had applied enough makeup on his black
eye for a busload of church ladies, Flint noticed.

RJ had already thrown ten fits when he'd
discovered his place on the lineup, so he
damned well knew he wasn't on until after
all the big acts played. Flint didn't want to
know why the scoundrel had showed up
early.

If Flint wasn't so worried about Jo's absence, he would have been delighted to an-
ticipate her reaction to her ex's appearance.
If he was really lucky, she'd find a bucket of
pig shit and christen the bastard.

Except for worrying about Jo, Flint was
primed to run out in front of the audience, to
hear the applause and feel the lights one last
time. He'd never needed the glory. It had always been about the music. But a farewell
appearance would ease the parting.

The band out front played the cue for Flint's entrance.

The kind of scream that made a father's blood curdle erupted behind him.

Instead of running onstage, Flint swung toward the backstage area to locate his boys. A creak followed by more screams froze him in his tracks, and he anxiously scanned the makeshift setting, catching the sway of the scaffolding for the backlights just before it collapsed in a cloud of dust and a crash of timber—with Johnnie and Adam in the middle.

Shoving his wireless microphone at Travis, Flint ran down the stage steps in a blur, not distinguishing anything except the crumpled figures of his sons beneath broken two-by-fours and fractured lamps. They'd had cameras. In a blinding flash of hindsight, he knew what they'd done. They'd climbed the scaffolding to catch his stage entrance. He didn't have enough curses in him to cover his stupidity in not predicting this.

Panicked shouts and the press of people didn't register as Flint bullied his way through the crowd to kneel beside Johnnie, whose leg was bent at an angle Flint knew wasn't right. Adam lay unconscious yards away. Using all the prayers he thought he'd forgotten, he cradled his frightened youngest in his arms and shouted for an ambulance.

He was more terrified than Johnnie. Desperately, Flint wished Jo would get here *now.* He needed her to check on Adam. He couldn't be in two places at once.

Sally rushed up to hold Adam's head as he'd wanted Jo to do.

Flint thought his insides would crush with the pain of knowing Jo would never be there when they needed her. Sucking in a deep breath, he nodded curtly at Sally and waited for help to arrive.

Travis came down to lay a heavy hand on Flint's shoulders. "Let the medics handle it, boy. You got a show out there and a lot of people counting on you."

Flint glared at his good buddy. "They're not counting on me. They're counting on you. I'm damned well not leaving my boys."

If he'd learned anything at all in his life, it was that the show would always go on without him.

❰TWENTY-NINE❱

Cursing the late night and the unaccustomed alcohol, cursing the alarm that hadn't gone off on one of the most important days of her life, cursing the button that had fallen off her cuff and the hair that wouldn't stay in its damned clips, Jo parked her aging Fiesta in the far back field of the mill. Still fighting with the clips in her hair, with one sleeve dangling open, she dodged through a sea of parked cars, crossing trampled grass and cow patties toward the pounding rhythm of a band. She was beyond late.

Why was it that everything always went wrong at the worst possible times? She'd planned this outfit for weeks, the silky, cream shirt with the flirty collar, the suede miniskirt to match Flint's suede jacket, the knee-high suede boots with stout heels made for walking because she knew damned well she wouldn't sit for twelve hours. She wanted to make an impression on Flint's Nashville friends. And on Flint, she wasn't too proud to admit. And now the damned cuff wouldn't fasten, and she didn't have time to sew on the missing button. She couldn't even get the safety pin in it with one hand.

She'd tried calling Flint from the apartment to say she was on her way, but she'd only got his voice mail. She'd be there before he bothered checking messages.

Her heart beat frantically. She needed a chance to talk to Flint. By now, he probably thought she'd run off with RJ and the Nashville cats.

Maybe that's what he wanted her to do—get out of his life.

The ghost of an old song whispered—*too late to say you're sorry.*

She didn't intend to be sorry. Through all the drinking and thinking, she'd made up her mind about how she'd handle this sue-or-settle thing. She hadn't told anyone yet. She still had time to change her mind. She didn't know if Flint would appreciate her decision. She was still scared witless that she was doing this wrong, but she knew what she wanted. If she was wrong, well, it wouldn't be the first time.

But right now, she didn't want to miss the boys' big chance. She glanced at her watch. The Buzzards should be starting their set. She'd listened to them play the songs of the finalists all week and had recognized one. Flint would be so proud.

Discovering the ambulance behind the barn set her pulse on fire. *Mama?*

She jerked open the employee entrance to the mill building and almost slammed into a stretcher on its way out. Holding the door, she stepped aside, and her heart stopped beating as she recognized Adam's pale face. His eyes were closed.

She located Flint holding Johnnie's hand as his son was carried out on a second stretcher. The boy was trying hard not to cry but released a pained sound when the cot bumped over the sill.

Flint caught sight of her and relief flooded his face. Jo's heart did an inappropriate dance of joy. She'd never thought to see the day that he needed her.

"Thank God!" he cried. "Get out there and stand in for me. RJ is chomping at the bit for being kicked down the lineup. Keep him the hell away from the mike, or he'll take over the whole CD."

Caught by surprise, Jo blinked. She had no clue what he was talking about. Her only concern was for those two boys and Flint. "Wait a minute, I'm going with you!" she yelled as he hurried past without looking back.

She started to run after them, but then realized from prior experience that there wouldn't be room in the ambulance. She'd left her car out in the back field. She glanced around, hoping to find someone with a car closer. Before she could act, Dave raced up with clipboard in hand.

"Joella, get the hell out there and do something!" he whispered harshly, grabbing her elbow and dragging her inside.

"Do what?" she protested in confusion, fighting him off and trying to escape. "I need to go with Flint. What happened? Will the boys be all right?"

"Broken bones, the medic said. Amy's gone for her car to follow them. We need you here." With panic clearly written in his eyes, Dave tugged with more strength than she'd realized the older man possessed. "It's going to hell out there, Jo. You know these guys. Make them behave before they ruin everything. The whole town is counting on this concert." He shoved her up the stairs toward the break in the curtains at the stage entrance.

The stage entrance. With terror for the boys already shredding her nerves, Jo stared through the gap in the curtains to the bright lights bouncing off the stage. She hastily backed away from the sight of an enormous sea of strangers on the other side. "What the devil are you—?"

Before she finished her question, Randy's singing voice echoed over the top of the Buzzard's raucous music. "Oh my word. What's *he* doing out there?"

"Randy took over the minute Flint turned his back. Why in hell isn't he singing the song the band is playing? The audience will be walking out any minute. He's ruining *everything.*"

Randy, onstage—with the band that had every reason to hate his guts. Had Randy had anything to do with whatever had happened to the kids? Jo couldn't believe that. He was a selfish jerk, but not a monster.

All the scary things that might be happening in that ambulance frightened her more than the bright lights, the audience, and the testosterone overload out there ruining everything. She needed to be with Flint.

Amy was with him. Probably Sally, too. Flint hadn't wanted her with him. She wanted to cry, but she was shaking too badly. If she couldn't have Flint, then she'd made the wrong decision last night, and her future was out there on that stage. The town's future was out there as well. She gagged on a swell of nausea. Had she been taking the easy road?

"You're the only one who can sweet-talk them into behaving. Get out there, Jo." Without giving her further time to question, Dave shoved her past the curtain.

Jo stumbled over a warped board into view of the entire barn filled with a standing-room-only crowd. The lights blinded her, and she froze, trapped in a time warp when hoots and catcalls had shamed her. She wanted to fall down and crawl out of sight before she threw up again.

"It's a tired old love song," Randy crooned into the mike on center stage.

Those were her words. She was hearing her song onstage for the very first time since she'd figured out she'd actually written a song—and Randy and the band were crucifying her baby.

Randy was singing Flint's haunting version of her song, while the band was playing the line *one my mammy used to play,* in time to the original rocking composition the Buzzards had helped create before Randy deserted them.

Flint had given Slim and the band the new music. They knew they were playing the wrong tune. The Buzzards were getting their revenge by screwing with Randy's head. At any other time, Jo would have laughed and enjoyed the joke, just as the local people in the audience who knew her songs were doing. They'd seen her entrance. They thought Randy was part of some prank she was perpetrating on them.

That was her song they were mangling!

Not only her baby, her ticket to fame and fortune, but the future of the town.

They were ruining the festival. She couldn't let Randy's ego bring down her friends and family, not if she had to crawl out there and heave her guts across someone's loafers. Flint had made it clear that she couldn't help Adam and Johnnie, but

Dave was right. She knew how to make Randy and the boys behave.

Flint thought she could do this. He was counting on her. His future was riding on this concert, too. Those spotlights out there weren't on her—they were on Northfork. Hell, looked at in the clear light of nausea, her whole life had been a rehearsal leading up to this. What would Erin Brockovich have done?

Sweat puddled under Jo's arms, but the fury of righteousness shoved terror aside. The image of upchucking on Randy's snakeskin boots carried her forward. With her loosely pinned curls already falling down, she staggered into the lights with Ratfink in her gun sights and the need for justice providing momentum.

She was taking Randy down. Randy was every damned man who'd ever hurt her, starting with her father, right through the ya-hoos in Atlanta, up to and not stopping at the unknown clerk who'd denied her mother disability, and Evan for deserting Amy. She would show them all that they couldn't keep a good Sanderson down.

The band cheerfully switched to Flint's melody as soon as Jo reached center stage.

The familiar tune supplied her with a backbone when the spotlight hit her. Instead of freezing or staggering, she shot the Buzzards a glare that should have mowed them down like an AK-47. Slim waved. She ought to barf on his shoes first. Randy was a closer target.

Turning from the Buzzards to study the audience waiting outside the cone of white light, Jo swallowed the sour taste in her throat, thankful she hadn't had time for breakfast. Randy's singing had finally fallen into rhythm with the band, but Flint was right. He couldn't do justice to her music. And she was standing here like a shaky statue, afraid to grab the moment and run with it.

Her mama had told her she belonged here in Northfork, where people knew her, that she was pretending she was bigger than she was to want more. She'd already made a fool of herself twice trying to prove her mama wrong. She ought to run after Flint, prostrate herself at his feet, and pray he would take a silly waitress who wrote foolish rhymes.

But then she'd never know if she could have been more, a grown woman who could have saved the concert, and made the fortune to help her family.

Frozen in the spotlight, she could hear the audience, hear their rustle of expectation, the nervous coughs, the titters. She could crawl off now. It wasn't as if she could do much when her mouth was so dry she couldn't even speak.

The desperate desire to make the festival work welled up as Randy hit a flat note. They were taping everything sung here today, and he was butchering her claim to fame. Jo forced her fear so far down inside that only her hands trembled as she marched forward to snatch the mike away from Randy, who'd blindly been ignoring her entrance.

Now that she had the mike, she could either hurl or offer the audience her best sugary smile. The smile came first. The band lowered their volume.

"H-h-howdy, everybody!" she shouted, waving into the lights, doing her best to pretend she was in the coffee shop in front of friends while Randy glared. "Welcome to N-N-Northfork, North Carolina," she stammered, before closing her eyes so she couldn't see the stage lights, "where the people are friendly and the music is crazy."

Polite laughter agreed with her assessment. Something tight in her chest loosened, but the leers and heavy breathing still occupied the dark corners of her mind. She had to open her eyes again and do it right this time.

She could feel the sweat stains ruining her good silk shirt, but they wouldn't be visible beneath her suede jacket. Now that she'd got the band and RJ to shut up, she lost the momentum of fury and had to search for words.

"What the hell are you doing out here, Jo?" Randy whispered, trying to recover the mike. "You'll ruin everything."

That was all the inspiration she needed. She held the mike tight and switched the sugary smile to him. The anger in Randy's handsome face held her steady. If anything told her how little he regarded her, it was his inability to accept her out here with him. She'd bet her lawsuit money that with all his masculine self-confidence, Flint would have grinned and played for her without any fear of competition.

"This here's *RJ* Peters, a hometown boy

made good," she simpered into the microphone. "RJ's album will be out this month, but he ain't anything without me."

More laughter. Okay, she'd got this far without hurling. She had friends here. They would laugh with her, not at her. They were depending on her.

Flint was depending on her. If she thought too hard about what was happening with him and his sons, she'd scare herself even sillier, so she wouldn't think.

"Let's show the people how the song was meant to be sung, honey," she oozed into the mike. She knew how to tame all that testosterone threatening to torch the show. She flapped her lashes and turned away from Randy to signal Slim. "Okay, boys, hit it!"

And they did, with Flint's wonderful version of her song. She could sing this one number for him. They could do the contest next. The boys! They were supposed to sing their composition if they won. Punching down her anxiety, she belted out the song the way she had written it—the way Flint had meant it to be sung.

RJ stood there, gaping, as she let her voice soar.

Tickled that she'd stunned Mr. Big Mouth, Jo did a little dance wiggle just for him, adding a big smile so Ratfink knew what he was missing. She recognized the light in his eyes when it flicked on. Randy was a selfish turd, but not stupid. And he was still male. She flashed him a brief glimpse of her cleavage and chortled as his gaze drifted down instead of to the audience.

Satisfied that she'd showed him she was a little more than an insignificant country waitress that he could walk over, she forgot about the strangers in the audience and sang out the joy and love she'd felt when she'd written the lyrics.

Realizing she was stealing his thunder, Randy attempted to reclaim the audience and the song. He strangled the fixed mike, glared at her, and picked up on the refrain.

Jo continued as if he weren't there. Her notes were higher, purer, and Randy didn't have the talent to harmonize. She confused him by adding new words and changing the old. Caught up in her own bubble, she had the *power,* and inspiration flowed. Randy stumbled to keep up, and laughter tittered through the audience.

Confident that she had made the song

hers again, knowing how it felt to be laughed at, Jo finally took pity on him and reined in her voice to complement his limited range. With a look of disgruntlement when he realized that she was singing down to him, Randy set the mike down and walked off.

Jo thought she heard him yell at someone offstage. Her voice was lifting to the rafters again, and she didn't care. Remembering the night she'd sung for Flint in his cabin, how her notes had floated to some transcendental realm she might never conquer again without him, she closed her eyes and let the last bar soar.

The audience erupted in foot-stomping applause before the band played the last note.

"Along with the fractured right tibia, Johnnie has multiple contusions, and Adam has a possible concussion and a sprained wrist. I want to keep both boys in the hospital for observation overnight," the doctor said as Flint paced up and down the narrow floor of the room to which the boys had been brought.

"Dad, no!" Adam shouted. "We've got to

get back there! You promised." He was
struggling with the blankets and the sling for
his arm and trying to stand up, even though
he was whiter than the bandage patching
the back of his head.

At sight of his older brother's struggle,
Johnnie was attempting the same, but he
was looking pretty groggy. Flint thought his
heart would carve its way straight out of his
chest. He squeezed the bridge of his nose
and nodded at the doctor's instructions.
He'd never seen so much blood in his life.
He'd been pleading with God to take him instead of his boys. He wasn't taking a
damned chance of anything happening to
them again now that he knew they would
live.

"You're not going anywhere, either of
you," he said in his best stern-dad voice,
when what he really wanted to do was grab
them and never let go. "There's a whole
week of activities ahead. If you don't stay in
those beds, you won't be able to do any of
them."

"But, Dad," Johnnie argued, "we got to
be there if we win. We're gonna be rich."

Flint ran a litany of every curse he knew
through his head, nodded as the doctor

raised his eyebrows and politely departed, and waited until the door closed before speaking. "What the f—devil are you talking about?"

"The contest," Adam said insistently, sitting on the bed's edge and looking for his bloodied clothes. "We wrote a song for the contest, and Jo said it was the best thing she'd ever heard outside your stuff. We're gonna win."

They might as well have taken a two-by-four and whopped him upside the head. Flint sat down abruptly in the hard hospital chair and pointed his finger at Adam. "Back in bed, right now, I mean it."

He needed time to absorb the news that his sons were writing *music* and that Jo knew about it. And hadn't told him.

He needed time to come to grips with the knowledge that she'd got his sons all excited about a business he'd sworn to give up for them. And that she'd wormed her way into their hearts—just before she'd walked out and left them. As he had. And their mother. They thought Jo was going to be there for them, but after today, she'd be gone with the Nashville suits. How the hell would he deal with that?

"But, Dad," Johnnie whined, "we gotta go."

Flint rubbed his jaw and wished he knew how to hug them and tell them it would be all right. He might lie to himself occasionally, but he wasn't too good at lying to his kids.

"You don't need to be there if you win." Were they good enough to win or had Jo just been feeding them bull? He couldn't believe she'd do anything to hurt them, but she might not understand how easily they could be hurt. "And I'll work something out so you can hear your song up there some evening, okay?"

"But they're recording the songs *today,*" Adam protested. "And Matt and Sean are waiting for us."

Flint had left the boys' friends with Sally. He had to get back and look after them. He couldn't leave his kids here alone. He needed to call his parents. He needed to clone himself. How the hell did single parents do it?

"You just don't want us to have any fun," Adam protested in that high-pitched voice kids used when they were just short of tears. "If we get rich, we could all go back to Nashville with Jo. She's going to go off and leave us and *it will be all your fault!*"

Kids sure knew how to hit the nail on the head and pound it in. He was the one who had encouraged Jo. He was the one who had told her about RJ and sent his publisher her song. He was the one who hadn't told her he loved her and needed her and didn't want her to leave—because he knew he'd ruin her life if he did.

Try explaining that to kids groggy with pain pills. At least the boys were wise enough to understand she wasn't staying. They weren't helpless toddlers anymore. With a sigh, he got up and gently returned Johnnie's broken leg to the bed. Sitting down beside his youngest, Flint wrapped him in his arms, while staring sternly across the space between the beds at his eldest. "It's not your job to make it rich or follow Jo or get us back to Nashville, Son. It's mine. If that's what you want, we'll talk about it when you get out of here. Right now, you just have to get better. Let me be the dad and take care of things, all right?"

Johnnie sagged against him, and Flint's heart cracked when he felt a wet spot form on his best shirt from his trying-to-be-tough youngest's tears.

Adam searched Flint's face. "You mean that? If Jo leaves, you'll go with her?"

He hadn't thought that far ahead, but he'd obviously said something his kids wanted to hear. And if he let himself think about it, he'd said what he wanted to do—he wanted to be with Jo. His hand and the music and the café and the lawsuit were all just excuses. She'd been right. He was still walking away from his life, this time dodging something even bigger and scarier than failure.

He tried to stay honest. "It depends, Son. You're gonna have to trust us."

Flint wished with all his might that Jo was here to help him out, but he'd been the one to cut her free. She deserved sunshine and rainbows, and he wouldn't darken her big day with his woes. But when the day was over . . . What would he do then?

Amy popped her head in as the boys were settling into sleep. She glanced at their closed eyes and whispered, "I talked to the doctor. Do you need anything here? I can't leave Mama with my ruffians much longer."

Flint shook his head. Gently laying John-

nie's head against the pillow, he rose from
the bed and crossed the room so he could
shake Amy's hand. "I don't know what I
would have done without you, thank you."

Amy was polite and quiet and had driven
over here as fast as she could after the ambulance. She'd sat with him in the emergency room and patiently waited as he'd
settled the boys in. She was a soothing
presence, the kind of mother he'd wanted
for his sons.

But he could never want maternal Amy
the way he needed ebullient Jo. He knew
now that he could handle his boys without a
woman's help if he had to, but he didn't
know if he could live with himself without
Jo. Every fiber of his wicked soul cried for
her laughter, her optimism, her hand in his
to keep him happy on his new path in life.

Amy smiled without a trace of any of the
doubts he suffered. "You want to come
back with me? You can't do anything else
here, and they really need you at the mill.
Mama and I can take care of the boys'
friends. Your dad and mom will be here in a
few hours. I just called them."

Flint shook his head. He might have lots
of doubts about the steps that had brought

him here, or his right to claim any happiness after he'd mucked everything up, but he didn't have any doubts about his decision to skip the concert for his boys. "I've seen all those acts before," he said, crooking his mouth up in a half smile so she'd think he was okay.

"You'll have lots of company once I get word around," she assured him.

Not after he'd selfishly let everyone down like this, but he didn't tell her that. He just nodded and let Amy go.

He longed for his guitar and a lonely place where he could put his blues to good use, even if he had to do it without chords. Now that he knew he had the strength to walk away from music for his sons, maybe he could let it back into his life, a little at a time.

Maybe if he learned to do it right this time around, he could teach the boys how to prevent the glitter from going to their heads. Telling them to stay away from music was futile, as he'd already proved. So maybe he could share the music with them. He'd like that. He'd like that a lot.

He'd like it with Jo even better.

≪THIRTY≫

"All right, folks, hold your breaths now," Jo called to the audience.

She'd managed to get reports on the boys from Dave, who'd talked to Amy. They were telling her all would be well. She was praying they weren't lying.

But excitement over the contest had her bouncing up and down, completely in tune with what she was doing and disregarding the bright lights as she waved an envelope around. "The finalists were judged in Nashville by recording-company professionals. You've heard the names of the runners-up. I am holding the envelope with the winner chosen for our First Annual MusicFest songwriting contest. If the winner is in the audience, they or their representative may come up onstage to sing for us and for the CD we're recording live."

Jo had seen Martin and his suits enter and take seats saved for them at the side of the stage, and she waved at them, hoping they couldn't see the sweat on her palms. She'd learned last night that one of the suits was from Flint's publishing company. Flint had apparently told them about her, and they were interested in her songs—once the copyright problem was settled. She'd officially be a *songwriter.* That didn't guarantee fame or fortune, but glee rocked her anyway.

Instead of making promises, Flint had acted on his belief in her. That was the reason she'd made the decision she had last night.

"The monetary prizes are free tickets to next year's MusicFest and free rooms at the Northfork Motel 6 for the week," she called to the audience, "but the real prize is letting promising new artists have their material heard by music-publishing professionals. So all you poets out there, have your pens ready for next year."

Her hands shook as Flint's friend Travis from the Barn Boys came onstage to open the envelope. Now that she had half a minute to think, she wanted to hand him the winning envelope and flee, but she didn't know where to run. With Randy's departure, she was out here all by herself. The only thing holding her in place was her knowledge that the boys' song had to be the winner. They hadn't been one of the four runners-up.

Travis took the envelope and turned to the audience, giving Jo the opportunity to step back toward Slim and the band and out of the spotlight. Clenching her teeth to keep them from chattering, Jo listened as Travis ran through a speech about Mill-Aid and how the profits from the day's ticket sales and the sales of the CD being recorded would go to Northfork toward the purchase of the mill to support the town's economy. Flint was supposed to have given that speech earlier.

She didn't know what she should do next. She wasn't supposed to be out here. She didn't know the lineup like Flint did. He ought to be standing here when the boys' names were called out so they could enjoy his shock and pride. They'd worked hard for this moment, and they weren't here to revel in it.

"And the winner is . . ." Travis ripped

open the letter to the band's dramatic drumroll. "Adam and John Clinton!" he shouted.

At the ecstatic applause and foot stomping from the audience, Travis glanced at the paper again, then back at Jo and the band, who were hooting and clapping. He raised his eyebrows questioningly and stepped back. "Flint's boys?" he inquired softly.

Until she started shivering with joy, she hadn't realized how proud she was of them, how much she wanted to see them out here taking credit for their hard work.

Or how much she'd wanted Flint to see what good kids he had. He worried so much over being a bad father. She wanted him to see he'd done the right thing coming here where his kids could blossom with the attention of the people who loved them.

Travis frowned, and Jo's heart did a nosedive.

"The judges were from Nashville," she explained hastily, fearing Travis thought the contest fixed. "The recording had no name on it. They won it, fair and square."

"Yeah, but they're not here to sing it," Travis explained the obvious.

"You'll have to sing their song, Jo," Slim

said from behind her where he'd been preparing to play the tune. "I can't sing that number right."

Travis caught her elbow before her knees buckled at the idea of going out under those spotlights again. She'd done it once out of anger and a sense of justice. Was her accomplishment a onetime thing or could she do it again for the boys?

"You know the song?" he asked.

"Of course." She glanced toward the exit and escape. She needed to be at the hospital with Flint. Travis could handle the emcee job. But the boys had worked so hard . . .

Travis ignored her hesitation and dragged her toward the fixed microphone.

"Ladies and gentlemen." His voice boomed through the speakers and settled the crowd expectantly. "Flynn Clinton is the man who brought us all together for this momentous event. He's written many of the songs you'll hear today. He lost his wife about a year ago. He's been bringing his sons up here in this town where he grew up, and he's been trying to give back to the community everything he's got from them."

Travis paused dramatically, in a way Jo could never have done. Tears spilled down her cheeks as she recognized the truth in everything he was saying.

"His boys had an accident in back just before this event began."

A chorus of gasps and murmurs rose from the audience.

Travis waved them to silence. "They're a bit battered, but they'll be all right. The point is, Flint had to give up this opportunity to take credit for all his hard work so that he could be with his sons. For those of you who aren't from around here, Adam and John Clinton, the winners of the contest, are Flint's sons."

He paused to let the crowd murmur some more before continuing. "Obviously, they can't be here to sing their song. They're missing their chance to be on our CD with all the biggest names in the business. But we won't let their song go unheard. Your own Miss Joella Sanderson is here today to perform it for you. I want you all to give a big hand to this little lady, and in the years to come, when those boys are writing the songs you'll be hearing on the radio and Miss Jo will be singing them, you'll remember you heard them here first!"

The crowd roared. Jo knew Dave and

George and Hoss and all her friends were leading the stomping, but she managed a watery smile as she wiped her eyes. Down in their corner, Martin and his suits were smiling proudly. Travis worked for them. He was giving her the opportunity to show them what she could do.

But this song was for Flint and his sons, not for her.

Without adding a word to what Travis had said, Jo turned and signaled Slim to begin. Praying with all her might that the boys would hear this someday, she let their words fly with all the power in her.

When the song ended and the audience was still enthusiastically applauding, she murmured into the microphone to be recorded, "That song was for a man who gave up everything because it was right, a man who is a hero to his sons, an inspiration to all, and the writer I hope I can be some-day."

She handed the portable mike to Slim to announce the next act, then rushed off the stage in search of the nearest exit.

She prayed no one knew how scared she'd been, but she'd proved to herself that she could sing onstage if she had to. She was proud that she'd done it, but she didn't need to do it again. Now that it was over, her only thought was to find Flint and the boys.

Even as her family and the men in suits came rushing up to congratulate her, Jo knew the decision she'd made not to go to Nashville was the right one. Singing for friends expressed her love, but applause wasn't sufficient reward for baring her soul to strangers. She never again wanted to feel as if she *had* to sing.

Now, all she had to do was explain to these big men wearing bling and designer suits what she *did* want and try not to get kicked out of their Rolls while she was at it.

Carrying a cardboard cup of the black fuel oil the hospital called coffee, Flint wandered the dark corridors back to his sons. He was lucky that both beds in a semiprivate room had been available so he could stay with them, but he couldn't sleep.

All afternoon visitors had wandered in from Northfork, bearing gifts and concern and news. He knew about as much of what happened at the concert as if he'd been there.

He wished he'd seen Jo wow them with her song. And could have heard her sing his sons' song. He was so damned proud of them that it almost hid his heartache.

A song had been humming in his head ever since the boys had fallen asleep, but he didn't have a guitar to pick out the notes on. He'd got desperate enough at one point to look for a piano but couldn't find one. He'd tried scribbling a few verses, but Jo was better at saying the things he was feeling. He needed the music.

As if thinking of Jo had conjured her into reality, he heard a soft croon drifting down the hall. Foolishly, his heart skipped and his pace quickened.

He knew better. He'd heard all about how Jo had left the concert in triumph in a Rolls with the Nashville suits. After the performance she'd put on, they'd be quick to lock her in tight. He couldn't blame them. He'd like to lock her in as well, but she needed to spread her wings and fly. She'd do it much more sensibly than he had, and she deserved every bit of fame she earned.

He just didn't know how he'd live with the emptiness where her laughter belonged.

He'd avoided thinking about losing her

during the day, but it was tough not to at night in empty hallways with nothing else to occupy his mind. He finally had to admit that his life would be damned lonely without her. He could follow her back to Nashville, he supposed. Maybe if he was just there for her, it would be enough . . .

Hell, no. A piece of her would never be enough. He might as well slit his throat and remove his head. If he'd loved Melinda half as much as he loved Jo . . .

He stopped stock-still in the doorway to his sons' room.

A woman sat on Johnnie's bed, smoothing his forehead with slender fingers. Moonlight filtered through the blinds, haloing golden curls. She sang quietly, as naturally as breathing, settling his son's restless slumber.

Flint would imagine an angel come down from heaven, except she'd doffed her fringed jacket to reveal a purple tank top instead of the shirt she'd worn earlier. Her miniskirt stopped halfway up her thigh. He doubted angels wore miniskirts and cleavage.

"What are you doing here?" he asked

gruffly. Then regretting how he sounded, he offered his coffee in apology.

Jo wisely refused his offer but searched his face as if expecting something he wasn't prepared to give until he knew what the hell was happening. She was supposed to be on her damned way to fame and fortune. What was wrong?

"You should have let me come with you," she reproached him.

"Don't be ridiculous." He slumped in the hard hospital chair that had stamped permanent creases on his ass. "They needed you onstage more than we needed you here." If anything proved he had no way with words, that ought. Even he winced.

She looked at him sadly, then adjusted the sheets over Johnnie's narrow shoulders. "They didn't really need me. Travis could have gone out there and thumped Randy on his fat head. Dave could have told the band where you'd gone and guilted them into behaving. They were just acting like babies and needed slapping."

Flint chortled, comfortable with Jo's familiar outrage. "That's not the version I heard. You rubbed RJ's nose in his own shit. You were so good, he had to pull out someone else's material for his set. Your voice will make that CD."

She shrugged and switched to Adam's bed to brush a rumpled curl off his brow. "How are they? Will they have to stay here long?"

"Just overnight. They were ready to walk up the mountain to hear you sing until the pills kicked in." He struggled with all the things he wanted to say, then settled for saying, "Thanks for making their song famous."

She studied on that a moment, then shook her head. "Fame isn't what the song was about. It was you they wanted to hear it. Males are so predictable. They just can't come out and say what they're feeling."

"Women wouldn't have anything to complain about if we did," he agreed with a smile that came from deep down inside him where their understanding warmed the icicles he'd been hiding behind. He took a chance on telling her some of how he felt. "I've got a song I've been wanting you to help write. I'm not as good with the words as the music. You heading out to Nashville soon?"

She cocked her head and stared through

the darkness at him. A hint of her usual mischief crept into her reply. "And miss the fried
Snickers bars and the rest of the festival?
No way. If Nashville wants me, they know
where to find me."

Nashville didn't work that way, but Flint
couldn't help letting hope lodge in a corner
of his heart. "What about the demos? You
have to have those to sell your songs."

She chuckled. "You don't think Randy's
album is a good enough demo? I need
some new songs first. I can't write music.
What do you say, we help each other?"

He wanted to relax and say he could handle that, but he couldn't, not if she meant to
leave, and she hadn't promised not to. "I'd
like that real fine, but my boys have to come
first. I don't want them counting on having
you around, and then you disappearing
someday, so I'm thinking us spending too
much time together is risky until we know
how things are gonna turn out. I'm not doing risk where my boys are concerned."
There, that was about the most he could
say.

"Risky, hmmm?" she said reflectively.

Jo sounding reflective was a damned

dangerous sign, Flint figured. He waited for the broadside to follow.

She merely rose from the bed and lingered near his chair long enough for him to drown in the sexy scent of her bath powder.

"So, you're planning on being a steady business type, are you?"

He stood up. In his boots, he towered over her enough to intimidate even this steel magnolia. "I've got me an idea or two," he admitted, slipping deeper into his Southern drawl. "The boys like it here, and I've a hankering to stay."

He wanted to kiss her until her head spun, and she was willing to agree to anything he asked, but he wasn't having any of her regrets later. He'd stated his case. It was her turn.

Instead of accepting his meager offer, she ran a hand down his stubbly jaw and stood on tiptoe to press a kiss where her hand had lingered. "In that case, I'll see you tomorrow. Give the boys a hug from me when they wake up."

She left on a cloud of scent, leaving Flint aching with hunger and disappointment.

He wanted to run after her, pin her to the wall, and demand that she stay with him until they'd wrestled out some way of making this work. But he didn't need the memory of Jo punching Randy for forcing her to know that was a bad idea.

He'd give her time to sleep on it. In the morning, she might come to her senses. Or he might. He still didn't know how big a piece of his future she owned.

"Look, guys, I'm not taking the blame for this, got it?" Sunday morning, still wearing his dress-up Stetson, Flint steered his pickup past the drive to his house. He wanted nothing more than to go home, shower, and shave, but he'd told Amy he'd pick up his sons' friends at the restaurant first. *Restaurant.* Jo even had him thinking of it that way. He was the highfalutin owner of a popular *restaurant.* Until he signed it over to Jo or the lawyers, at least.

"I told you to stay away from the booms," he continued. "You didn't. You missed the show. You've no one to blame but yourselves."

He'd spent the night sleeping on a foldout chair in the pediatrics ward, and they were back to sullen silence again. Some days, being a parent was shit. Of course, a lot of

days were shit and being a parent had nothing to do with it.

He'd called his folks and told them that
he had everything under control, and they
could continue on to their golf tournament.
He'd have his head examined the next time
he had a few minutes.

"Reckon Jo will sing our song on the radio someday?" Johnnie asked, sounding
more like a wistful little boy than a budding
teenager.

"I'm sure she'll be proud to. I wish you'd
let me hear it first, though. I'm probably the
only person in the whole county who hasn't
heard your song. I don't even know how the
hell you wrote it. You don't play any instruments."

"Computer, Dad," Adam said impatiently.
"We made it play the notes we wanted until
we got it right. Can we take guitar lessons?
I hate soccer."

Wham, right upside the head again. This
time, though, Flint grinned proudly. Chips
off the old block. "I'll see what I can do," he
promised.

They seemed to accept his promise without surprise, as if they knew he'd provide

what was important to them. Maybe this parent thing wasn't so hard.

"Jo kinda helped us with the words," Johnnie admitted. "We got stuck a bunch. The Buzzards put it on CD for us."

"We wanted it to be a surprise," Adam grumbled.

"Well, you succeeded. I was surprised as h—heck when they called to say you'd won." The traffic was thick heading into town for the second day of the MusicFest, and Flint concentrated on his driving.

The Nashville stars would have left last night, but the festival had a good regional lineup today. Sunday noon, and the first parking lot was already full. He drove on into town, thinking he'd just park in the alley to pick up Matt and Sean.

A gleaming silver Rolls filled the alley.

The boys whistled and stared as Flint drove past to the upper lot, his heart stuttering and stopping again. Jo had promised to be here today. Had Martin stayed over, ready to whisk Jo off to Nashville once she saw the boys? She'd need to line up a business manager, pick out some costumes, and put in hours of practice with whoever was touring with RJ. There wasn't much time if the tour left in a week.

As they crawled past in the line of traffic, Flint noticed Myrtle was looking pitiful. Her hat had never recovered its jauntiness after the truck crash, and someone had stolen her feathers. He was thinking he'd have to buy the damned pig when they held the auction. Nobody had bid on her all summer. Besides, he'd got kind of attached to her.

"Hey, guys, mind if I borrow that toy guitar Hoss gave you?" Hoss had showed up yesterday carrying a tiny guitar he'd picked up in the hospital gift shop.

"Whatcha want it for?" Johnnie asked.

"I thought Myrtle needed a little music." Pulling the truck into the far lot, Flint caught a space just opening and snagged it. "You gonna be able to walk on that cast or you want me to leave you here?"

"I can walk," Johnnie said with the assurance of the very young. "Maybe Travis is still here and can sign it."

Travis drove a Corvette, not a stuffy Rolls, but Flint didn't destroy his illusion.

Carrying their toy guitar down to the café, the kids watched with interest as Flint tilted Myrtle on her purple haunches so she was sitting upright, her pink polka-dotted snout pointed skyward as if she were about to yodel out a song. He propped the imitation Fender between her front legs, and the boys howled in glee.

"We need a CD player in the guitar playing our song!" Adam shouted, coming out of his sulk.

"That would work," Flint agreed, wrapping his arms around their shoulders and drawing them into the Stardust. He needed a good grip on them to prepare for the sight of the counter without Jo behind it. Maybe he'd get used to her absence in a hundred years or so.

"There you are!" Amy cried as they entered. "Just in time. The microwave is giving off sparks."

The place was packed. They had customers leaning against the wall, chowing down on barbecue. *Barbecue?* He didn't have that on the menu, although it was a damned good idea now that he thought about it.

He couldn't help searching for Jo. He didn't expect her behind the counter, but she'd promised to be here. Jo was hardly someone who disappeared into the woodwork. She wasn't here.

His glance fell on Elise sitting in a purple booth with a couple of lawyer types, and his heart fell to his stomach. Martin had taken Jo and left his lawyers with the Rolls. This was where he signed his life away.

"Don't use the microwave," he told Amy as Johnnie and Adam found their friends in a back booth and rushed over. He noticed they stopped politely to talk with the locals who called out to ask after them. He was proud of their maturity. He needed to give Melinda some credit for their upbringing now that he could think of her without a defensive shield of resentment. Jo had taught him a new perspective—and lightened his burden in so many ways that he couldn't count them all.

He grabbed a heavy tray from Peggy and carried it to the counter so she could help a customer. But he knew he was just delaying the inevitable.

Flint slid into the space across from Elise and a company lawyer, next to a silver-haired gent who didn't look up from his perusal of a sheaf of legal paper. "I thought you'd be on your way back to Nashville with

Martin, dotting your *i*'s and crossing your *t*'s."

Elise offered a pleasant expression that told him nothing. "I like your hat," she said, tilting her head to admire the Stetson as Peggy rushed over with a coffeepot. "We've been waiting for you."

"That's swell of you." He gulped the coffee black, conscious of his grubbiness. So much for Flint the Swinger. He set the hat down on the table between them.

A hint of mischief danced behind Elise's dark eyes, then disappeared before he could be certain he wasn't imagining things. Every now and then, the snooty lawyer showed a spark as wicked as Jo's.

"Jo has a creative mind. She thought you ought to be offered a choice. She can't prevent your publisher from suing you and RJ. That's the way it has to be for the law to straighten out the copyright. All she can do is encourage them to settle swiftly by stating her preferences for payment."

So, she hadn't taken the label's cash and promises and let RJ steal her songs. She'd held out for copyright. Good for her. Flint waited for the ax to fall.

"She's agreed to sign on with your pub-

lisher, so they're willing to listen to her request. RJ's lawyer is trying to save his hide.
He'll probably take whatever Jo demands,
including adding both your names to his album where they belong." Elise tapped one
of the stacks of paper to indicate that was
Jo's agreement with Randy.

"You can take the same arrangement as
RJ, if you prefer, but given the circumstances, she's willing to offer you another
deal. We understand you'll need your lawyer
to go over the terms." Elise took a second
stack of papers from the clerical-looking
guy. She shoved both stacks in Flint's direction.

"These are just drafts of what she has
suggested. This first one, the one RJ is being offered, settles for ten percent of all future income—*all,* royalties, business, everything—"

"Not ownership of the café?" he asked in
surprise. Ten percent of nothing if he had to
sell the place wouldn't earn her anything.
She knew he wouldn't have any future royalties. She'd be better off taking the cash
settlement. She was letting him off lightly—
with no ties binding either of them. His heart
dissolved in a wave of acid.

"The café is the other deal."

Flint's curiosity grew as Elise tapped her finger on the second stack of papers.

"Jo will forgo future income and accept half ownership of the café if she's allowed to keep her job."

"Her *job*? *Here?*" Flint tried to pick his jaw up off the table. He could make no sense whatsoever out of this choice. "Why in hell would Jo want fifty percent of nothing and a waitress job when she can have the bright lights and a fortune out there?" He gestured to the front window and the Rolls.

"I think you'll need to ask Jo about that," the lawyer said with a hint of smugness.

Even as she spoke, the clash of cymbals jarred him into motion. He glanced around. His kids were gone.

Jo was *here,* in the restaurant, just as she'd promised.

Trying not to look too eager, Flint slammed his hat back on his head and shoved out of the booth.

❧ THIRTY-ONE ☙

Jo anxiously watched the back room's entrance while pretending everything was fine. She showed Johnnie how to hold the guitar chord for the opening number of their song and jerked around nervously when Adam hit the cymbals. She had no way of knowing when Elise would be done explaining all the legal papers to Flint, and she was just about to jump out of her skin in nervousness.

It didn't help that all their friends and neighbors had started gathering back here as if they knew something special was going on. She ought to smack Amaranth Jane for whatever she was telling their customers. Or maybe it was Flint's parents who'd started the rumors. After apologizing for missing the opening concert, they had arrived this morning to proudly arrange chairs front and center so they could hear their grandsons' winning song.

Jo had thought Martha Clinton had come to kill her. Instead, she was sitting there like a queen royally acknowledging parliament as everyone came up to speak with her. The woman was having a damned field day, while Jo stood in front of a growing audience, sweating. At least they didn't have spotlights.

Would Flint understand what she was trying to tell him? If he meant to make her beg, she'd walk all over his face. But she suspected he was just being macho and *protecting* her by hiding what he was thinking. Men were goofballs.

He'd asked her to write songs with him. That was the hope she clung to. He had opened opportunities, but he hadn't pushed her at Nashville or grabbed the chance to impress the suits and leave her behind, or any of those things she'd come to expect from the men in her life. He'd left her to make her own choices. She would love him for that if she wasn't so worried that he'd pitch a fit when he realized the choice she'd made.

She didn't want to be an entertainer. Martin had made it clear that's where the money was and what he wanted from her. When she'd been eighteen, her eyes would have lit with stars, and she would have taken that road without a second thought, believing fame and fortune meant success and happiness. She knew better now. Flint had shown her what happiness really was. She wanted—needed—the magic they shared together. Without it, no matter how successful she was, she'd only be a hollow shell painted in glitter.

A murmur rippled over the crowd, and Jo glanced up again.

Flint stood straight and tall in the doorway, his Stetson shielding his eyes. He still wore yesterday's clothes, minus the tie. His suede jacket hung from broad shoulders over a black, high-collared shirt with pearl cuff links and silk-thin slacks that draped his narrow hips with more sophisticated sexiness than anything Randy had ever owned. Her heart stumbled when he located her.

Flint halted in the doorway of the back room and scanned the unexpected crowd.

He found Jo on the stage with his sons, and he went all hot and cold inside at the sight.

She was wearing her Stardust apron with the Cinderella slipper. She wore her long hair in her usual funky ponytails and looked so spectacular that he almost rushed through the crowd to carry her off.

At some signal Flint missed, Adam shouted, "Ready, set, go!"

The drum crashed. The guitar squealed. And Jo greeted him with a smile as wide as a watermelon slice and so intimate that they might as well have been alone. His heart probably stopped right then, but his feet didn't. They carried him down the aisle between the packed chairs to the stage and Jo. He didn't even glance at the audience, although he was vaguely aware half the town occupied the room and more were entering the back door as the Buzzards took over from his sons' awkward introduction. The Sunday after-church crowd was arriving.

Jo stepped up to the mike and, with only a momentary hesitation in front of the audience, announced, "This song is for one of the Good Guys." Not waiting for applause, she held Flint's gaze and swung into a low and seductive croon: "He's all that I can ever be, all that I'll ever want, all that I'll ever need . . ."

Somebody shoved a chair in Flint's direction, but he kept on moving toward the stage and the siren call of Jo—singing as if he were the only person in the room. He wanted her to be singing to him so much that he was sick with the need of it. One of the Good Guys. Not a badass anymore, even after he'd left her and the town stranded yesterday and all but kicked her out of his life. She understood?

It wasn't until she let her voice rise and ring out with "He might not always be my friend, but he'll always be my dad" that Flint nearly sank to his knees in shock.

She was singing his sons' song. She had stayed here so he could hear what they had written. He choked and halted near the stage as he tried to absorb his sons' sentiments from the song. They didn't think he was a full-time jerk, the man who'd driven away their mother and deserted them? His kids were speaking through their song as he once had, showing him that music could be a gift when it was used right.

Johnnie shyly hobbled up to him. Flint

draped his arm over his younger son's shoulder and hugged him. He wasn't a crying man, but his eyes were wet as Jo belted out the chorus one more time. Seeing Adam hovering behind the band's guitar player, Flint beckoned for him to join them. Looking proud and embarrassed at the same time, Adam took his place on Flint's left. Tall, with his dark hair falling in his face, he'd chosen a black sling for his wrist and looked like a pirate.

Flint knew all about meter and rhyme and market niches, but all the prosaics of the business flew out of his head, leaving only the thought that he was hearing the most beautiful, heartrending piece he'd ever heard in his life. He may have done most everything wrong, but his sons were willing to forgive. If he died right this minute, it would be as a proud and happy man.

But he didn't intend to die anytime soon, not when he'd just been offered the chance to have the sun and the moon and the stars. Instead of dodging the difficult and hiding his hurt behind attitude, he had to take the risk of falling flat on his mug in front of friends and family and an entire town.

He sure the hell was man enough to do

what a man ought to do, no matter how high
the danger that Jo would punch him in the
nose and walk away.

This time, he wouldn't give up what he
loved without a fight.

Jo sobbed out the last note. Flint looked
so stricken standing there in his Sunday hat,
with his arms wrapped around his boys,
that she wanted to break down in tears and
turn back the hands of time. The three of
them looked good together, stalwart and
strong, despite the cast and the sling.

She smiled a little at that. Boys would be
boys. She understood that just fine. But
grown men now, that was another kettle of
fish. She was just a wee bit shaky at her
presumption.

She had no idea what was going through
Flint's head. She didn't know if he had any
notion of what she was telling him. So far,
everyone had told her she was crazy.

And she was. She was so crazy in love
that she was willing to risk it all, all over
again. She had grits for brains. And a heart
that desperately needed to love.

The music ended, and she didn't know
what to do. She'd said everything she knew

how to say, in the only way she knew how to say it. She didn't have any more *brazen* left in her. The audience was clapping and laughing and Flint was still standing there, staring at her as if she might disappear at any minute.

Like an ice cream cone. Or a miracle.

She wiped her eyes and smiled big at that, and he covered the last few steps between them in the blink of an eye. Hopping up onstage, he shoved the mike back in its stand without once tearing his gaze from her. Mesmerized, she tried to take him in all at once—the tired lines around his eyes, the bristles on his jaw, the tousled hair falling from beneath his hat, the smile that spread wider than hers as he hauled her into his embrace.

Jo wrapped her arms around Flint's neck and clung, weeping into his broad shoulder as if she were a big baby. She didn't ever want to be parted from him again.

"You're the craziest woman I've ever met," he whispered in her ear, "and I'm never letting you out of my sight. Life would be hell without you, so I guess I'll have to follow wherever you go. Can I be your stagehand?"

She laughed and hiccuped and buried her face against his shirt. "I don't want a stage-hand. It was awful out there without you. Please don't ever leave me alone like that again."

He hugged her tighter, rocking her in front of an audience that had grown unusually quiet. "I don't want to, baby, but that life out there means I can't always follow you. But I love you, and I'll keep at you until you're ready to give up the glitz and settle down and marry a tame respectable businessman like me."

She laughed again, sounding a little stronger this time. Lifting her head from his shoulder, she poured kisses over his face. "You're about as tame as a grizzly after a long winter's sleep. Don't treat me like a dumb waitress, Flynn Clinton. I know a good man when I see one, and I know the difference between glitter and gold. And I'm not saying anything else in front of a whole audience of Nosy Parkers except I want a fern in the front window. I don't know how to turn off a microphone."

Laughter rang out behind them, and there was a hurried scuffling of feet and chairs. Flint turned around and glared, and their audience began to scatter. He glanced down at his sons, who watched him wide-eyed. "Go get some rope. We're hog-tying and keeping her."

The kids and the remains of the crowd whooped in agreement.

"Say yes, Jo," a voice that sounded like Hoss's rang out. "You two would sure look purty up onstage together!"

"You better treat her right, Flint," Dot cried out over the laughter, "or every woman in town will see you tarred and feathered!"

"And every man will be gunnin' for your balls!" George Bob added.

Deciding he wasn't pouring out any more of his guts for their amusement, Flint swung Jo into his arms and marched down the stage steps with her. Slim and the band struck a rowdy rendition of the "Wedding March." The crowd broke into yells and cat-calls. Jo gasped, laughed, and grabbed his neck.

To Flint's embarrassment, his parents stood beside the exit. His father gave him a thumbs-up. His mother looked concerned, but he understood where she was coming from now. Love and fear made a cranky combination sometimes. He'd have to hug her for her understanding some other time when he didn't have an armful of hot woman in his arms.

With a weepy smile, his mother ushered the boys and their friends away.

Undeterred, Jo leaned back in Flint's arms as he carried her up the stairs to her place. "I'm glad I don't have an audience the first time I tell you I love you, but I expect they'll hear it often enough after this. I love you, Flynn Clinton. What are you gonna do about it?"

"Marry you tomorrow," he said promptly. "I can't go shacking up with my kids around. I'm trying to atone for my mistakes, you know."

He grew serious then, and Jo knew what was coming. She pressed her fingers over his lips before he could say it. "I'm being totally selfish. I figure I might or might not find fame and fortune in the big world. But I'm a grown-up, and I understand that even if I find it, fame and fortune can't keep me from being lonely and heartbroken. I'm a girl who needs her family. So I guess I'll just have to find some other way of helping Mama and

Amy because I want to stay here with you and your boys, if that's okay with you."

Flint crushed her in his arms and shoved open her unlocked door with his shoulder. "I'll be there to help you take care of them. We'll make beautiful music together. And you'll still be rich and famous. You have the talent, and I'll see that you get the recognition you deserve, if I have to build a studio in the back room to do it."

Catching his face in her hands, Jo sealed their promises with a kiss.

❧❧EPILOGUE❧❧

"Will I have to find scaffolding to hang your glittery things from the rafters?" Flint asked, gazing up at the roof of his cabin from the pillow-strewn wooden floor, feeling a contentment he'd never experienced in his fast-lane life.

It was the last day of their honeymoon, and his sons were still with his parents. He and Jo had accepted a wedding gift of a weekend at Asheville's famed Grove Park Inn and Spa, but Jo had been more than happy to slip back to his place for the rest of the week. They'd turned off the telephones and hidden the vehicles and pretended they were in the mountains of Colorado.

"I like sparkle," she admitted in reply to his question, then held up the tiny diamond on her ring finger so it caught the light from the front windows.

Flint had caught her playing with the sparkles off the tiny chip a dozen times this past week, and he'd had to grin at the deep down warmth her joy brought him. He could have given her a great big piece of glass that shimmered the same way, and Jo would have been equally happy. But he wanted that ring on her finger to be as real as his feelings for her.

"You didn't have to buy this, you know," she told him earnestly. "You had me hooked without bling."

"I used to wear a diamond bigger than that in my ear. It's worth a little debt to give you glitter. Maybe I'll buy you a bigger one each year—especially if I don't have to climb on scaffolding to hang Christmas balls."

She laughed, and the happiness of that sound tingled right down to the place he thought he'd just exhausted. His new wife was as creative in her lovemaking as she was in her songwriting. He'd need to build a separate wing on the cabin if he bought it—just so they'd have some privacy. She inspired him in more ways than one.

"You bought Myrtle, so I don't need orna-
ments, and I'll hold you to that big diamond
when we're rich," she agreed with a husky
chuckle that said she didn't believe or care
if that day came. "For now, we'll just call our
company Diamond Records and each song
we write will be our sparkle." With the grace
of a woman well-pleasured, Jo used her
bare foot to nudge the guitar they'd been
playing out of harm's way and drew her
fingers along a sensitive area of his chest.

Sprawled on the pillows Jo had brought
from her place, Flint just grinned at the high
beams above him, content to have the
woman he loved in his arms, more than
content to have her naked. "I like this business of being your manager. If I'm not touring, I can devote a lot more time to the
money end than I could before."

Jo snuggled into his arms and did stimu-
lating things to a part of him that would
make a good flagpole about now.

"I like it even better that writing music
means we can be here for the boys instead
of traveling," she added. "I can't wait until
you propose the idea of a Music Barn to the
Chamber. Just imagine us up on that stage,
singing our songs together. With your con-

nections, we can call in the best talent around."

Flint finally lowered his gaze to Jo. Her assets were definitely in that active brain of hers. "If the world wants to hear you sing, they'll have to come here. I like that just fine."

"And hear you play," she reminded him, her eyes smoking with the same lust filling his. "We'll get your hand fixed. The restaurant could—"

"Don't get too carried away," he warned. "If the town can't buy the mill . . ."

The sound of a car pulling up in the drive ended that negative thought. Jo shot straight out of his arms and toward the stairs. "That has to be your parents! They're a day early. I can't let them see me . . ."

Flint doubted his parents would let the kids out of their sight a day early, but she was gone before he could argue. Tugging jeans over his not-yet-flagging pole, he peered through the big front window to check his driveway and snorted.

Jo's sister and lawyer were out there. Amy had produced the most spectacular wedding cake a reception could ever need, so he couldn't yell at her. Not too loudly,

anyway, or she'd bring down his ceiling fan.
She was still a mite nervous around him.

Elise, on the other hand, was smiling like
a malicious madonna, knowing damned
well she was interrupting their last precious
moments of privacy, and anticipating vol-
canic reactions. He'd have to be extrasweet
just to throw her off-balance.

He buttoned his jeans and shrugged into
his T-shirt before they reached the porch.

Pulling her hair back in a clip, Jo ran
down the stairs in time to catch Flint opening the front door. She'd pulled on shorts
and one of Flint's shirts so she'd at least be
covered, but the sight of Amy and Elise
made her want to throw things. She loved
them both, but they brought the world into
their idyll before she was ready.

"This had better be good!" she shouted at
them from the stairs. She was still tingling in
anticipation of their interrupted lovemaking.
She'd never get enough of Flint's kisses. To
her good fortune, he was generous with
them. And with compliments. She'd never
heard a man invent so many flattering
phrases—all of which would eventually be
included in her lyrics because they played

like music in her head. For once in her life, she had a real man, and she meant to take care of him.

Elise waved legal file folders, and Amy held up a box of muffins.

"We come bearing gifts of peace," Amy said as Jo landed in front of her. "We need signatures before Elise takes the papers back tonight."

"Which papers?" Realizing she was starved, thinking she couldn't take real good care of a man if she never fed him, Jo grabbed a muffin and handed the box to Flint. "We have to rely on Amy for food, so I guess we'd better play nice."

He winked. "You can feed my hunger anytime. Amy's baking is just dessert."

Jo wiggled under the intensity of his gaze, tingling in places that said the honeymoon wasn't over. "I do whip cream real well," she murmured suggestively.

"We'll let the two of you get back to your games in a minute. But if you want money to play them with, you need to sign the papers settling the suit with Randy." Elise handed her the top folder. "The record company has agreed to advance Jo the same amount Flint received as payment out of the album's future earnings, so you'll have a nice fat check coming."

Jo shrieked and hugged Elise's neck. The elegant lawyer bore her embrace with fortitude and waited until Jo moved on to hug Amy before handing Flint the next folder.

"These papers transfer the Stardust into a company owned equally by the two of you. They include the bylaws and so forth if you intend to expand the business into songwriting and music management. You need to talk to a tax lawyer about copyrights."

"I wish you would set up an office down here," Flint said, flipping through the file. "We'll be needing someone like you around."

Elise shrugged. "I've been spending so much time here, I might make it my second home. Think the town could use a new lawyer?"

Amy nodded decisively. "A woman lawyer, yes. But you'll have to do more than contract law. The women here need a lawyer who will respect them."

Ashamed of her happiness in the face of her sister's heartache, Jo hugged her sister harder. "Evan might come around, honey.

Just let him see what a cold, hard world it is without the ones who love you."

A stubborn look that Jo had never seen before set Amy's lips in a straight line. "I'm saying Mama needs a lawyer who can take her disability case to court. I've got my own lawyer already. Evan wants me to sell the roof over the kids' heads! I wouldn't take that sucker back now if you *gift wrapped* him."

Flint squeezed Jo's waist, easing the emotional outburst. "I'll steer both of you and your mama away from wrapping paper," he drawled, "so you're not too busy tying up Evan to hold down the restaurant. Are you ladies planning on helping out for a while?"

"They're my posse," Jo declared, escaping his hold to grab Amy and Elise by the elbows. "You sure you're ready to take on a woman with a posse?" She tossed her head and met his gaze with laughter and defiance.

Flint grinned and kissed her forehead. "Baby, I know what I like."

Whistling "Chantilly Lace," he grabbed her waist again and danced her away from the others and into the kitchen, where they could spread out the papers that would seal their future for the next thousand years or so.

Jo scrawled her signature binding her financially to Flint with the same kind of joy and satisfaction that she'd felt on their wedding day—the satisfaction of trust.

She'd found a man who was far better than fame and riches—a man so cocksure of himself that she couldn't shake him if she tried. She probably wouldn't give up trying, just to watch Flint come after her with that arrogant grin of his, but she figured their badass days were over. Respectable business owners were supposed to act like pillars of the community—in public, at least.

Jo glanced up the stairway leading to the bedroom she now shared with Flint. In private, they could be anyone they wanted. She had lots of creative plans for the future. One of them was to hang guitars on that big blank wall so they could make music and love together whenever the spirit took them.

She planned on making that happen real often.